"You're the stormbird!" he exclaimed in awe. "I saw you flying through the clouds the night before you saved me from the yevi!"

Duranix cocked his huge head. "Stormbird, eh?" he said. "I like that. Much more elegant than 'dragon.'"

Duranix's chest heaved. He thrust his serpentine neck forward until his massive head was less than an arm's length from Amero's wide eyes. The effect was so terrifying Amero's knees failed and he sat down hard.

The dragon opened his mouth, revealing wickedly curved fangs. It took Amero a heart-pounding moment to realize that Duranix was actually grinning at him.

"What do you think of me now?" the creature asked. The voice was still recognizably his, but the sheer power of it, even at a whisper, rattled Amero's teeth.

The boy opened his mouth but no sound came out, so he swallowed and began again. "I hope we shall always be friends."

For more about the world of Krynn . . .

### *Dragons of a Fallen Sun*
Margaret Weis and Tracy Hickman

### *Downfall*
Jean Rabe

### *Brother of the Dragon*
*The Barbarians* • *Volume Two*
Paul B. Thompson and Tonya C. Cook
(August 2001)

## THE BARBARIANS • VOLUME ONE

CHILDREN
of the
PLAINS

Paul B. Thompson
and
Tonya C. Cook

# CHILDREN OF THE PLAINS
## The Barbarians
©2000 Wizards of the Coast, Inc.
All Rights Reserved.

Cover art by Corey Wolfe
First Printing: September 2000
Library of Congress Catalog Card Number: 00-101633

9 8 7 6 5 4 3 2 1

ISBN: 0-7869-1391-6
620-T21391

U.S., CANADA, ASIA,
PACIFIC, & LATIN AMERICA
Wizards of the Coast, Inc.
P.O. Box 707
Renton, WA 98057-0707
+1-800-324-6496

EUROPEAN HEADQUARTERS
Wizards of the Coast, Belgium
P.B. 2031
2600 Berchem
Belgium
+32-70-23-32-77

Visit our web site at **www.wizards.com/dragonlance**

To Our Parents,
who know what it's like to raise barbarians . . .

PRE-CATACLYSM

ANSALON,

AS KNOWN TO

THE BARBARIAN

TRIBES

Thon-Tanjan

SILVANESTI

Silvanost

Thon-Thalas

South Plains River

The Savanna

Kharland

Great Plains River

Lake of
the Falls

Battle
Site

QUALINESTI

Qualinost

Unknown

The Edge
of the World

2000

Miles

0

# Chapter 1

~

The sun was low in the morning sky, yet already the heat was stifling. Denizens of the night had retreated to their dens, burrows, and nests, away from the glaring sun and the promise of even worse heat. Small herds of elk, having grazed when the grass was still shiny with dew, clustered together under widely separated trees, monopolizing the only shade around. Not even a heat-crazed panther could shift them from the meager cover. As the sun climbed higher, only two kinds of creatures were moving in the heat: flies and humans. Neither could afford to remain idle while there was food to find.

Five humans, lean and brown, lightly clad in buckskins, silently crossed the empty savanna in single file. Widely spaced to cover the maximum amount of ground, they swept the grass on either side with their eyes, the butts of their spears, and sticks. Anything that moved was fair game.

Leading the group was Oto, father of the three children. He'd seen thirty-eight seasons on the plain, and his face was seamed with cracks, like a lake bed baked hard by the dry season. Oto's light brown hair had thinned to the point where his scalp showed through and was now burned as brown as the rest of him. Streaks of white stained his beard. Though old for a plainsman, Oto's eyes were still sharp and his hunting sense legendary.

Ten paces behind Oto walked Amero, his eldest son. At thirteen, Amero's chin was beardless, and his voice still had a child's squeak. Not yet a man, custom denied Amero a man's weapon. The boy used a boy's tool, a long springy pole suitable for probing rabbit burrows and gigging fat frogs. Amero was sweating under his buckskins. He would have loved to strip down to his loincloth, but the path was dotted with thorny scrub and knife-grass, either of which could shred flesh to the bone in an hour's forage. Sighing, Amero hung his hands on the pole across his shoulders and concentrated on keeping his father in view.

Eleven steps back, his mother, Kinar, hefted her baby off her aching hip. Menni was almost two, a strapping boy-child. He nodded against his mother's shoulder, his legs dangling and his hands draped around her neck. Kinar longed to put him down, but she knew Menni could never keep up with Oto's swift pace.

Last in line was Nianki, the oldest child and the last surviving daughter. Kinar had borne Oto seven children, but they were a lucky family. She knew other women who'd birthed more babies yet had none left to show for it. That Nianki and Amero had survived to such advanced age was a tribute to Oto's skills as a hunter and her own wisdom in foraging.

Nianki was a strong girl who could run half a day without stopping, climb any tree, and snatch a black viper from its sunning rock faster than it could strike, but she was no help to her mother. There was no point in handing her the baby. Inside ten paces Menni would start to cry, and Nianki's usual solution was to slap him.

Kinar had tried to pass on to her daughter the knowledge she'd acquired in thirty-one summers—when to pick berries so they didn't cause a gut-ache, the way to tell poisonous mushrooms from the delectable kind, how to soothe cuts with the sap of soft-tongue plant, and how to harvest honey from a wild beehive without getting stung. Nianki preferred to run after her father and be a hunter. Oto would not allow a female to carry a spear, so Nianki had made her own weapon, a throwing club with a sharp flint head.

Nianki didn't notice her mother's glances back at her. The girl's eyes were on their surroundings, constantly scanning for danger or prey.

The earth was still dry from winter. Hard red clay showed through the tufts of grass. The last rain had been three days ago, a brief shower accompanied by much lightning. It softened only the surface of the soil, which dried quickly. Here and there Nianki saw random footprints of animals who'd crossed the trail while the clay was wet—a rabbit, an elk, the flat, wide prints of a young bear. A flurry of circular dents in the soil told of the passing of a party of centaurs. Oto got along with centaurs, but he always gave them wide berth. He said you never knew what a centaur might do or say—they were wild creatures, not human at all.

Beside the elk prints she spotted another set of tracks. They were smaller, and of unusual shape. Nianki dropped to one knee to study the unfamiliar spoor.

The prints were long and narrow, with a short pad and strangely long toes. She traced the dried impression with her finger, then sniffed it. A faint odor, pungent like rotten meat. These were the footprints of a predator.

Soundlessly, Oto appeared out of the bush on her right. "Why are you stopped?" he said, resting the butt of his spear on his right foot. It was a lifelong habit that had left a callus on his foot that fit the shaft like a socket.

She pointed to the tracks. "I don't know this animal, Oto."

"What can you tell about it?"

Her brows met over her nose as Nianki frowned. "It smells of dead meat. I think, a hunter."

"Not a scavenger?"

"It followed a live elk." She indicated the other tracks with a sweep of her hand. "A lone bull. I think this beast culled him from the herd."

Oto knelt and studied the tracks with a practiced eye. "Yes. The bull was running, but not hard. A single animal was dogging him, driving him—" He lifted his sun-darkened face to the southern horizon. In the distance was the highest relief on the plain in all directions, a pile of upthrust boulders. A hundred wolves could hide in the rocky crevices.

"Ambush," Oto said.

"A pack?"

Her father nodded.

"Have you seen animals hunt like this before?"

"No. Only men."

Kinar and Amero had noticed something amiss and doubled back to find Oto and Nianki. The baby stirred and began to fuss. Kinar rocked him gently and made soothing noises in her throat.

"What is it?" Amero asked.

"Animals Oto doesn't know. A hunting pack."

Amero scanned the bush nervously. "Are they still around?"

Oto stood. "The elk have bedded for the day. They would not do so if there were a hunting pack near."

Nianki stood. "We should go back," she declared.

Oto folded his arms. "We've left last night's camp. Game has fled, and Kinar has picked the land clean. Going back means going hungry."

"I don't like this," Nianki said.

"Nor do I," added Kinar worriedly.

Mother and daughter seldom agreed, and their sudden cooperation was unnerving. Amero shifted uneasily. "Perhaps we ought to go back?" he ventured.

"You're not the hunter," Oto replied sternly. His dark eyes rebuked all of them. "We go ahead. To go back is to go hungry."

"To go ahead may mean danger!" Nianki insisted, stamping her foot. Kinar hugged the baby closer and backed away from her. Father and daughter had fought before, and over less than this.

Surprisingly, Oto chose to talk rather than use his fists. "No hunting pack would attack a whole family. We are too many and too wise. These beasts, whatever they are, are hunters like us. They like easy prey. They cull slow-witted bulls or weak calves. They don't stalk the strong."

Amero stared. He'd never heard Oto speak so many words at one time. As he looked from his father to his defiant sister, it suddenly occurred to him that Nianki was as tall as their father. Next to her, Oto seemed a gnarled old tree bending to the wind of a fresh storm. Amero wondered if his father's thoughts were the same as his: This time, if he dared strike Nianki, she might strike back, and her blows could cause more hurt to him than his to her.

Menni burped loudly and began to cry. This broke the awkward silence. Oto handed his spear to Nianki and took his son from Kinar's arms. He held Menni at arm's length in scarred, callused hands.

"Last child," he said in an odd, hollow voice. "I give you my protection."

He balanced the boy on his hip and used his free hand to lift a dark, shriveled object that hung around his neck on a thong. It was the dried paw of a panther, black as a moonless sky. Many seasons ago the panther had crept into their camp and killed Oto's firstborn son, Ibani, while the boy slept. Oto had slain the panther after an epic chase of forty days. Since that day, the spirit of the panther had been bound to Oto and done his bidding, warding off evil.

Oto tied a knot in the thong to shorten it and hung the talisman around Menni's neck. Kinar's face glowed with happiness. She took Menni back and held him close, no longer fretted by his size or weight.

Nianki paced past them, resuming the trek to the next night's camp. Amero started after her but stopped when Oto gruffly ordered them to halt.

"Spear."

Nianki hefted the weapon and tossed it sideways to her father. He caught it easily with one hand.

"I'll make the path," Nianki announced. "Come."

Amero watched in silence as she strode away. Oto waited until Nianki was ten paces ahead, as custom prescribed, then resumed the march. Kinar and the baby followed him, leaving Amero to bring up the rear.

Amero looked back at the mysterious footprints. Little was left of them. The clay had cracked under Oto's heel. A fresh breeze stirred the taller grasses, carrying with it the sighs of spirits. Amero blinked. Was the panther ghost passing nearby, seeking its new charge?

He turned and hurried after his family, the end of his long stick trailing in the dust behind him.

\* \* \* \* \*

Precious little game could be found on the high savanna that day. Even rabbits were scarce, as though another hunting party had passed down the trail ahead of them. Kinar found some wild onions and a handful of sticky tuber-roots. The onions were bitter and the tubers too sweet, so their midday meal was both skimpy and unpleasant. Oto finished quickly and resumed the lead position. Nianki fell back again.

When they drew near Mossback Creek, Oto, in the lead, suddenly made the quick, downward, chopping gesture that meant "take cover." All of them dropped to the ground silently. Not even the baby made so much as a whimper.

5

Nianki left her mother and brothers in the cover afforded by the scrubby bushes and crawled up the slight rise to where Oto lay motionless. As she crested the hill on her belly she could finally see what had caused the alert. The savanna was no longer empty. Two people crouched on the bank of Mossback Creek.

They appeared to be excited about something, pointing to the creek. The errant breeze brought only snatches of their voices to Nianki's ears, but she could understand none of their words.

"What is it?"

Nianki flinched as Amero's whisper sounded from below her left shoulder. Instantly she froze as the two strangers rose to their feet and looked in their direction.

Amero gasped at the strangers' appearance, and Nianki's left hand moved over to pinch his arm, signaling silence. The strangers appeared not to see them and went back to their study of the creek. After much talking and gesturing, the pair shook their heads, crossed the creek, and headed away from the hidden plainsmen.

Oto waited until the two were far distant, then got to his feet. Nianki and Amero followed suit.

"Who were they?" Amero asked excitedly as they rejoined Kinar and the baby. "Did you see their faces? They were black! Dark as the night sky!" He touched his own skin, burned brown by the fierce sun, and repeated, "Dark as the night sky!"

"Why did you leave your mother and the baby?" Oto demanded.

Amero's enthusiasm faded in the face of his father's obvious anger. He hung his head, saying nothing, knowing there was no reason he could give that would satisfy Oto.

Nianki shook her head at her brother's foolishness. He had been wrong to leave Kinar. His whispered question had nearly betrayed their presence to the strangers. Amero was always asking questions, wanting to know things. He could not be content to do a thing because he was told it was right, or because it had been done a certain way for as long as anyone remembered. He always wanted to know why. It was not a trait that endeared him to their father.

Oto was still glaring at his eldest son. Nianki spoke, distracting her father. "Have you seen men like that before?"

With a final shake of his head, Oto turned toward the creek.

"No," was his curt response.

"Then why did we hide?" Nianki demanded of his back. "They might've known where we could find game. We could've asked about those strange prints we saw earlier."

Oto said nothing, but just kept on walking. Nianki shook her head in disgust.

"Oto is wise."

Nianki turned to look at her mother.

Kinar added, "He's kept us alive by being cautious."

"There were only two of them."

Kinar clucked her tongue in that annoying way of hers, hefted Menni higher on her hip, and followed after her mate.

Amero had gone to the top of the slight rise and was staring in the direction the two strangers had taken. As she drew near, Nianki cuffed him on the head.

"Stupid," she said, though without malice.

He ignored the blow and continued to gaze into the distance. "Who knew there were people like that?" he said. "Their skin was black as the night sky. It was so strange."

Amero's hair, like Nianki's, was light brown, straight as a spear, and reached to the middle of his back. They wore their hair tied back with a leather thong. The strangers' hair had been close to their heads, and so tightly curled it didn't move when the wind blew.

"I wonder—"

"Enough," Nianki ordered. When Amero began a sentence with those two words, there was no telling where it could lead, nor how long it would take the boy to get there. She gave him a rough shove. "Stop mooning and start walking. I'm thirsty."

Unfortunately, when they joined their parents and Menni, they found the creek had been fouled. Both banks were churned up with many footprints—the same narrow prints they'd encountered that morning.

The torn carcass of a red deer lay in the water, its fleshless face pointed skyward. Clouds of flies rose from the bloated hide when Oto's shadow fell across it. By the smell, it had been dead for some days. Amero recoiled from the rank odor and plucked a green grass stem to hold over his nose. At her request, he pulled one for his mother too.

"I guess this is what the strangers were so excited about. No wonder they didn't drink," Nianki said. "Never saw animals dirty a stream like this. Why would they do it?"

Oto frowned. "Marking territory. This means, 'all others, keep out.' "

"Fair warning. We should listen."

In answer, Oto crossed the water twenty paces upstream from the deer carcass. Reluctantly, the rest of the family followed. The normally cold creek water was tepid from the long day's heat, but it still tasted good.

The east bank proved as empty of game as the west bank. Even birds had abandoned the plain. The poor hunting, prolonged silence, and empty vistas wore on their nerves. Without realizing it, they closed ranks, the gaps between them shrinking.

The sun was halfway to its rest when the smoky blue peaks of the mountains first appeared on the horizon. They resembled thunderclouds piled up in the eastern sky and were much farther away than they looked.

Amero took his turn making the path. Being slower than Nianki and having less stamina than his father, Amero's pace was almost leisurely. He picked his way through the grass, swinging his stick in a wide arc to expose gopher holes and dislodge vipers. His stomach grumbled loudly. To assuage his empty belly, Amero chewed a grass stem. It didn't help much.

*Ye-ye-ye.*

He stopped dead, his stick falling to the ground. It had been quiet so long that the distant call sounded like thunder. Amero knew all the songs, screams, and chatter of the plain. He'd never heard this noise before.

A hand fell on his shoulder. He jumped, alarmed. Oto could move like mist when he chose.

"Hear?" he whispered close to Amero's ear. The boy nodded. "Stay," hissed Oto and made a gesture behind his back. Nianki glided off to the right, into the sun-gilt grass.

Kinar and the baby stood close behind Amero. Menni

Children of the Plains

knew enough to be quiet. He buried his face in his mother's neck and clutched the panther talisman with dirty fingers.

*Ye-ye-ye.*

There was a scattering of dwarf elms about a hundred paces in front of Amero. The strange yelping came from there.

Oto angled off to the left, crouching, with his spear held high. He hadn't gone a dozen steps before the sour smell of meat-eating predators reach his nostrils. Near, maybe fifty paces, and moving—moving to his right. The old hunter glanced in Nianki's direction. She was just visible, walking upright through the dry weeds.

Nianki smelled nothing. The wind was on her right cheek, blowing toward Amero and Oto. She slipped the thong off her wrist so she could hurl her ax if necessary.

Something flickered through the grass ahead, a gray shape against the faded green of the dry foliage. She raised the ax and waited.

*Ye-ye-ye.*

Close—very close! Impatient, she charged forward, axe held high. She reached an area of trampled grass from which a trail led off to the left. Tufts of long gray hair stuck to the sharp grass. Nianki plucked a few and sniffed. Not wolf, not cat. What then?

Oto heard movement as well. He planted his left foot and hurled his spear at a target he sensed rather than saw. The keen flint head hit and buried itself solidly in something. He could see the spear shaft bob in tiny circles—his prey was still breathing.

He rushed forward, drawing his obsidian knife. As he parted the greenery, he saw a shaggy brown coat and a pair of stout yellow tusks. Wild boar? He'd speared a pig?

When he killed the great panther, Oto's limbs had felt labored and slow, as if he were swimming in mud. Kills were like that sometimes. The spirit of a beast sometimes put a spell on the hunter to ward off a death-thrust, to spoil his aim. When Oto recognized the creature he'd killed was only a boar, the same sort of spell of slowness descended on him. Then he saw tooth marks on the snout and throat of the pig.

9

It had been dragged in front of him as a decoy. He'd wasted his cast on bait.

Fiery pain ripped into his leg. Oto's lethargy vanished at the sight of his own blood coursing down his calf. Over his shoulder he could just make out a large gray beast, vaguely wolf-like in form, clamping onto his right leg. Oto roared in outrage and reached for his spear. Before his hand could close on the smooth wooden shaft another gray mass hurtled through the air and seized his wrist. Oto was jerked off his feet, falling facedown in the grass. Sharp fangs closed on his other arm, and he was dragged away, roots and rocks tearing at his face.

Oto's cry spurred Nianki to a run. She tore through the grass toward her father. The hot odor of fresh blood filled the air. So too did the call *ye-ye-ye,* vented from a dozen or more beastly throats. Four-footed forms passed on either side of her. Nianki turned and brought her axe down on the hindquarters of a galloping animal. It shrieked and fell in the grass. She overran it and had to leap to avoid its snapping jaws.

"Yeee! Yeee!" it howled. Opening its long muzzle the wounded beast showed heavy, pointed teeth and a black tongue.

Bite this! she thought, whirling to hurl her ax at the creature's head. There was a crunch of splintering bone, and the thing ceased howling.

There was no time to examine her kill. Nianki ran toward her father's last shout. She found a dead boar with Oto's spear in it. The grass was trampled flat all around and blood stained the leaves. There were signs something heavy had been dragged away.

A new scream—Kinar! The pack had doubled back!

Nianki jerked the spear from the pig's carcass and ran toward her mother. She burst onto a horrible scene—Kinar and Amero back to back, Menni clutched tightly in his mother's arms. Amero's flimsy stick whipped in a desperate arc, holding off five shaggy gray monsters. They resembled wolves, having four legs, long canine snouts, pricked ears, and bushy tails, but there was something alien about their bodies. Their shoulders were massive and muscular, the

forelegs too long, and all four paws gripped u.
hands.

"Nianki! Help!" Amero cried. One of the animals n.
gotten hold of his stick. Two more took it in their teeth, and
it was torn from his grasp.

Nianki speared the nearest beast through the throat. It
screamed like a man, rolling and flailing in the dust. Another of the strange animals tried to seize the spear shaft in its
jaws, but a blow from Nianki's ax discouraged him.

"We've got to get away!" she gasped.

"Where?" her mother shrieked.

The only possible shelter in sight was the elm grove. "The
trees! And pray to all the spirits these beasts can't climb!"

Amero pushed his mother ahead, guarding her back.
Nianki cut a path through the circling pack, jabbing at them
with the bloody spear head. For several terrifying moments
the creatures refused to yield. Then, without warning, they
vanished into the untrampled grass. Panting heavily, Nianki
urged her family on.

"Hurry! They're not leaving—just regrouping!"

"Give me the baby," Amero said to Kinar, pulling Menni
away. The little boy cried furiously. "I can run faster with
him than you can."

Tears streaming down her face, Kinar agreed. The elm
grove was sixty paces away. She forgot her sore feet and
empty belly and ran for all she was worth. Despite his claim,
she soon outstripped Amero. He called to Kinar, warning
her not to get too far ahead. She paused, turned back to
answer him, and was hit at the knees and neck by a pair of
the gray predators. In an instant she was gone, dragged into
the weeds.

"Mama! Mama!" Amero began the cry and Menni took it
up. Raggedly, the older boy jogged to the spot where his
mother had been. Another beast appeared in front of him.
Amero recoiled, turning away to shield Menni. Instead of
sharp fangs, he felt the shaft of his father's spear scrape along
his ribs as Nianki impaled the leaping beast.

"Mama!" he gasped, eyes wide with horror.

"I know," said Nianki grimly. "Get Menni to the trees.
Hurry!"

11

The first elm he reached was nothing more than a sapling, incapable of holding the toddler's weight, much less his own. A larger specimen stood a few yards away. The beasts were yelping behind him, and fear of them gave Amero strength. With Menni in his arms, he leaped up the trunk to the lowest branch. It cracked under the strain. He pushed Menni against the trunk and said, "Hold on there! Hold on hard!"

"Mama! Mama!" the child wailed, but he held on.

The broken branch giving way beneath him, Amero slid to the ground. Rough bark tore at his hands and knees. Menni clung to the trunk above him. Unless the pack could climb or leap, he was safe for now.

Amero spun around and saw Nianki fighting three of the creatures. They had surrounded her and now took turns darting in, trying to get their teeth in her. She crushed one's skull with her axe, but she lost her grip on the weapon in the process. A fourth beast appeared and leaped at her exposed back. Down she went, and Oto's spear flew away.

"Nianki!"

Amero took one step in her direction, but was promptly cut off by two of the animals. Their black lips curled, blood-flecked saliva drooled from their gaping mouths. Defenseless, Amero backed away. The closest empty tree was a good twenty paces behind him. If he turned his back, the beasts would be on him before he could make it that far.

"Ha!" he shouted, stamping his foot. "Go! Go!"

The nearer animal halted its advance and made its *ye-ye* call. Amero had the insane idea the creature was laughing at him! He picked up a stone and hefted it significantly. The pair of predators spread apart. They were making it harder for him to hit them, Amero realized in astonishment. What sort of beasts were these, who showed such careful cunning?

"Ha!" he shouted again, and feigned throwing the stone. The nearer beast sprang aside. Once he was farther away, Amero threw the rock with all his might at the other. It struck the monster on the nose, and Amero took off running.

He tried not to hear the swish of long gray limbs in the grass behind him. He ran faster than he'd ever run in his life, his toes barely touching the ground. His goal was a stout gnarled tree, with a trunk as thick as his waist. A low branch beckoned as a handhold. Only five steps to go. Hot breath on his heels, the fetid smell of the creatures' breath. Four steps. Something touched his buckskin-clad leg, and he put on a burst of speed he didn't know he possessed. Three paces to go. Claws raked down his right leg, ripping his chaps, and grasped at his bare heel. Amero kicked free and coiled his legs to leap. One step. He launched himself at the branch and snagged it with both hands. Paws with sharp, grasping digits grabbed at his dangling legs. Amero swung his feet up and wrapped his legs around the tree. With a supreme heave, he rolled over on a stout branch less than two paces off the ground.

Panting, two of the pack circled beneath him, waiting to see if he would lose his grip and fall. When he didn't, they trotted away, lolling tongues pink with clay dust. Amero heard Menni whimpering from his perch but the intervening trees blocked his view of the child. Once Amero managed to catch his breath, he climbed higher in the elm and searched for his mother, Oto, or Nianki. The air was still, and he could see nothing but grass.

*　*　*　*　*

After being knocked to the ground, Nianki had managed to gather her legs under her. Pain raced through her left forearm as the jaws of one of the creatures snapped shut there. Agony gave way to anger in an instant. Instead of trying to pry the animal's mouth open, she resolved to cause it as much damage as possible. In short order she had gouged its eyes and kicked it repeatedly in the ribs. It slackened its bite, and only then did Nianki go for its jaws. She pried its long yellow fangs apart until its jaw snapped. Yelling at the top of her lungs, she grasped the monster by its hind feet and swung it in a wide circle, releasing the limp body, which tumbled into the tall grass.

Blood seeped steadily from deep wounds in her arm. Nianki held the injured limb tight to her chest and ran into the bush. She knew she had no hope of outrunning the pack, but she had killed several, and others had gone off in pursuit of Amero and the baby. If there were just one or two left, she might be able to turn the tables on them.

13

Her vision blurred. The hammering pain in her arm was spreading. Staggering with effort, Nianki skidded down a slight draw. In the rainy season there was a swift stream at the bottom of this hill. At this time of year it would be a dry wash, but where water passed, there would be rocks, and rocks were the tools Nianki needed.

She slammed into the thin trunk of a weeping willow and clung to it, gasping. She could hear animals crashing through the underbrush on both sides of the ravine. Were there two of them? More?

She slid off the tree trunk and pressed onward. A soft sand bank gave way to a bed of pebbles. Several boulders, washed smooth by the brook, rose from the dry stream bed. Nianki found two fist-sized stones, and with one in each hand, climbed atop the biggest boulder. She had hardly reached its summit before the beasts came yelping through the bush, their strange cry echoing in the still, hot air. There were three.

"Come!" Nianki yelled, forcing deep drafts of air into her aching chest. "I have stones enough for all of you!"

The monster on her left leaped. She brought both hands together and cracked the creature's skull between the rocks. Its blood and saliva sprayed her face. As it fell heavily at her feet, its claws and teeth tore the tough buckskin of her shirt. The beast rolled off the boulder and fell lifeless to the stream bed.

A second animal approached more stealthily and succeeded in biting her on the back of her right thigh. Nianki screamed in pain and pounded her attacker's jaws. Each strike cost it teeth, and the monster let go before she crushed its skull as she had the others. Nianki lost her footing—the boulder was slick with blood—and fell on her back. For a moment, all she saw was bright blue sky. The click of claws on rock followed, and the third animal seized her by the throat.

The beaded collar of her shirt saved her from death. The beast's fangs could not penetrate completely the closely studded bear-tooth beadwork. Nianki pulled a knee up and tried to lever the creature off, but it gripped her shoulders tightly with its fingerlike claws.

She could feel her pulse thundering in her head and knew she was bleeding from the throat. Her left hand opened, releasing a rock. She had no strength left to hold it. With all the life that remained in her body, Nianki brought the stone in her right hand down on her attacker's forehead. The savage creature's response was to tighten the grip on her neck. Fangs penetrated her flesh more deeply. She hit the beast again, and was about to try one last time when she felt the animal stiffen and shudder.

Nianki pried the jaws apart and let the furry gray body fall to the side. She tried to rise, but her strength was spent. The world went dark before her eyes, and she collapsed across the smooth granite in a spreading pool of her own blood.

## Chapter 2

~

For many hours Amero remained in the top of the elm tree, his back braced against the knobby trunk. He'd heard shouts far away, but it had long since grown quiet all around him—quiet as death. Menni had cried weakly for while, and then he too fell silent.

Amero called now and then to his father, his mother, and his sister, but no one answered. He was afraid to call Menni. The little boy might try to get down from the tree and come to him, and he had no doubt the killer pack was still out there in the grass, watching, lurking.

Finally, he had to give up shouting. His throat was too parched to continue. From his uncomfortable perch he took stock of the situation. He feared the worst. There was no escaping the fact that neither Oto nor Kinar would abandon their children if they were alive. They might have found some place to hold off the beasts, but this was the only grove of trees in the vicinity—hilltops or caves were in short supply on the savanna. The realization of their deaths made his eyes sting and his throat tighten. Amero scrubbed his smarting eyes. Not yet, not yet! His first task was to live. There would be time for grief later.

He had no food, no water, no weapons. His hands, knees, and feet were raw from falling and climbing. His right leg burned where the creature had raked it with its claws. His buckskin breeches hung in tatters. He pulled them off and draped them on the branch. It was cooler in his loincloth anyway. His life seemed to depend on how long he could remain in this tree. Without food and water, it wouldn't be long.

The sun dipped below the horizon, and the first stars appeared in a flawless purple sky. Amero gazed at the emerging lights. His mother had told him about the stars—how they were the eyes of great spirits on the shore of heaven and how there were patterns in their arrangement. Her people had named these patterns. There was the Winged Serpent,

symbol of the great spirit Pala, which stretched from one side
of the sky to the other. Facing him across the vault of heaven
was the stormbird, Matat. Kinar always called Matat "she,"
and Pala "he," though she never explained why.

Amero yawned. He had to keep alert. To occupy his mind,
he tried to recall the names of the other constellations, but
none came to him. Failing that, he dredged up more of his
mother's stories. His favorites by far were the tales of far-off
places and things seen by Kinar's father, Jovic. Jovic had witnessed and done amazing things, things the boy Amero
always wished he might do some day.

His eyelids closed, his head slowly coming to rest on the
branch.

"Long before I was born," Kinar always began, "my father
Jovic traveled to the mountains far to the west. There he saw
heaps of stone shaped into blocks with even sides. The blocks
were so big Jovic realized whoever shaped them must have
been giants, at least three times the height of normal men."

Amero smiled sleepily at the memory. The giants grew
with every telling of the story.

"Jovic saw strange markings on one block, pictures carved
and colored," continued Kinar. "The pictures were of faces
like his own, but unlike too. The stone faces were painted
blue, and the hair on the faces' heads was white as snow."

Amero's eyes snapped open. His injured right leg had slid
off the branch, jerking his body sideways. He drew it up
quickly and shuddered. A leaping beast could have dragged
him to the ground by that dangling limb.

Were the animals even still there? He strained his eyes in
the darkness, gazing deep into the shadows for signs of the
pack. The songs of night birds were a good sign the beasts
had departed. Perhaps he could descend, backtrack to the
stream, and fill his belly with cool, fresh water.

The sound of a dry twig snapping rang out. The birds
ceased their rhythmic call.

"Oto?" he said in a loud whisper. "Is that you? Kinar?
Nianki?"

"Oto?" replied a voice in the night. Amero gripped the tree
harder. It was not a voice he knew.

"Who's there?" he said more loudly.

17

"Who's there?"

He'd once heard an echo-spirit in a canyon, but he'd never heard of one living on the plain. "Nianki, don't jest with me," he said uncertainly.

"Don't jest with me."

For a fleeting instant, Amero spotted a pair of glowing white eyes a dozen paces away. They were low to the ground and wide-set, just like the eyes of the killer pack animals.

"Who's there?" he demanded.

"Who's there?" mocked the voice.

"I'll not come down!"

"Come down. Come down." From the shadows all around the tree, the two words were repeated, over and over. More eyes gleamed. Amero counted ten pairs in all.

He sighed and sagged on the branch. Wasn't there easier prey for them to catch? Then his eyes snapped wide open.

They had *talked* to him? What sort of unnatural beasts were these?

Shaking with fear, he climbed to the highest part of the tree that would hold him and wedged himself into a narrow crotch. He picked open the lacings along the sleeve of his buckskin shirt and braided the ends together to double the strength of the binding. He dropped the useless shirt onto a lower branch. Looping the braided lacing around his waist, Amero tied himself to the tree. The hide laces would not support him if he fell, but they would steady him enough to sleep.

One pair at a time, the eyes below vanished. When they were all gone, the only sound was their peculiar yelping cry—slower now, sounding more and more like cruel human laughter.

The night seemed endless. It passed in fits and starts, as every cricket in the grass, every bat flickering through the treetops brought Amero to instant wakefulness. When at last he did sag into deep slumber, a horrible apparition invaded his rest.

Out of the darkness crept one of the beasts, glowing dimly. The creature slunk to the foot of the elm tree and slithered up the trunk without using its paws at all. The combination of snake-like movement and blood-smeared muzzle sent shudders of fear through Amero. He tried to untie the thongs holding him in place, but his arms would not rise. His lips parted to cry for help, but no sound came forth. Closer and closer the faintly luminous creature came, its dark eyes fixed on Amero's face. When its cold, damp nose touched the sole of his dangling foot, he found his voice. He woke screaming.

The sun was well up. He blinked against its bright rays and raised a hand to shield his eyes. Memory of the terrifying immobility that afflicted him in his dream caused him to raise and lower both arms, just to assure himself he could. As the evil image faded from his mind, a lingering impression remained; someone, some *thing* not human was nearby. It was watching him with curious detachment, the way Amero studied anthills or wasp's nests when he was a little boy.

Wind stirred the sparse elm leaves. There were clouds aloft this morning, small puffs of white on a field of hazy blue sky. Amero fervently wished for rain. He'd had no water since yesterday, and the heat and his exertions had left him wrung out and very, very thirsty. He pulled a slender branch close and licked the underside of the leaves. The faintest patina of dew remained, and tasting it only made him feel thirstier.

Amero loosened his lacings and stretched his stiff limbs. He spotted a line of black gardener ants trooping along a lower branch. He swept a dozen or so off into his palm and ate them quickly. They were tart, a little crunchy. He'd eaten ants before when nothing else was available.

Clearing his parched throat, he called to Menni. His brother's tree was only twenty paces away, but he'd heard nothing from the baby for a long time, and he was worried. It was one thing for a thirteen-year-old like Amero to spend the night in a tree, but a toddler less than two? An ache grew in Amero's chest as imagined the worst. He had to check on his brother. He must find out whether the boy was all right.

He plotted his way before leaving the safety of his tree: If he took a roundabout route to Menni's tree, he could move from the safety of one climbable tree to the next. The first tree that could support his weight looked to be eight paces distant; the next one after that, six.

Cautiously, Amero descended. The grove was quiet. Only the hum of locusts broke the silence. He darted from tree to tree, keeping low, with every sense alert for the sound of the returning pack.

By the third climb he had Menni's tree in sight. Amero wanted to call to his brother, but he was terrified the child wouldn't answer. Leaving his last perch, he picked up a fallen limb—a feeble weapon—and advanced slowly on Menni's hiding place.

Something in the tree stirred with every breath of wind. Amero squinted against the glare and tried to make out what it was. It was too small to be Menni.

Within a few steps he realized his brother was no longer there. The object blowing with the breeze was a scrap of cured rabbit pelt. Menni had worn a bonnet lined with rabbit fur.

Mutely, Amero plucked the pathetic scrap from the tree. The slim trunk had lost much bark, the marks fresh and still bright with oozing sap. It was easy to imagine what had happened. The pack had butted and battered the small tree until Menni lost his hold.

Dark bloodstains on the ground lent painful support to this vision. Amero let the tears run down his cheeks for a moment, grieving for his lost brother. He knelt in the dirt and closed his hand around Oto's panther talisman. It had done Menni little good. Perhaps the spirit of the panther owed protection only to its conqueror.

A rustle in the bush brought Amero's mourning to an abrupt end. His heart contracted to a small hard knot when he glimpsed gray forms flitting through the grass. They'd been waiting for him! He threw down the worthless talisman and bolted.

The pack had already maneuvered between him and the center of the grove. He had the impression of six or seven animals in front of him, maybe four or five behind. There were trees all around, but none were much more than saplings. Still, given a choice, Amero preferred to take his chances in the trees rather than on the ground.

He angled for a likely looking elm. The beasts saw his change of direction and closed in rapidly. Up he went, clawing at the rough bark. He heard the snap of empty jaws as he swung his legs up and over a low branch. Having failed to catch him, the beasts immediately fell to slamming their broad, ugly heads against the truck. The blows were powerful. As Amero clung to the tree for his life, he realized little Menni could never have held out against such an onslaught.

There were eleven of the gray beasts below him, circling and yelping. In a strikingly uniform movement, they all dropped on their bellies and lay still, gazing up at him.

Now what? Having failed to catch him on the ground, were they planning to wait until hunger and thirst loosened his grip?

He crept up, a finger at a time, putting the maximum distance between him and the pack. In his mind he named the animals *yevi*, "laughing dogs." All predators were smart, but the yevi exhibited intelligence beyond that of wolves, panthers, or bears. Were they spirits of some kind? They bled and died like other beasts. Were they people—people of a beastly sort? He'd seen centaurs, and he'd heard the story of Grandfather Jovic's meeting the bull-headed men of the east, so it seemed possible the pack were a strange race of people.

The treetop bowed under his weight, and he lost his grip for an instant. Frantically, he hugged the slender trunk as it bobbed from side to side. The tough green elm hadn't cracked yet, but he doubted he could spend the night up here. Other, stouter, trees were too far away.

The springy treetop reminded him of one of his father's old tricks. Oto was widely skilled in trailcraft, and once he had shown Amero and Nianki how to make a snare from a live, bent-over sapling. Game as large as wild pigs could be snared, and the force of the unbending tree was often enough to fling the catch in a complete arc and dash it to death against the ground. If only Amero could use the power of the elm to toss him to another, bigger tree. He tried deliberately bending the treetop down, gauging the force required to hold it in place. However, he had to abandon the notion. There was not enough strength in the tree to throw him to safety, but more than enough to throw him to the waiting yevi pack.

He retied his rawhide lacings around the trunk and settled down to wait out his foes. As the sun mounted higher in the sky, he noted with grim satisfaction the yevi were panting in the heat. He resolved to die in the treetop if need be, but he would not fall. He could not allow the pack to claim his entire family. Better that his dry flesh should feed the crows.

\* \* \* \* \*

At sunset, half the yevi pack rose and departed silently into the bush. Their sudden movement, after so many hours of stillness, roused Amero from his lethargy. His heart leaped at the sight of the departing beasts, but when he recognized only half the pack was leaving, he knew they were simply going for food and water. The remaining yevi stayed behind to keep their eyes on their treebound prey.

He was finished. If they could go for sustenance and he couldn't, Amero was doomed. He couldn't outlast them. As night arrived, Amero sank into despair. He was so weak from hunger and thirst. Even signs of approaching storm clouds didn't bolster his failing spirits. The yevi would never give up. Their single-minded devotion to his destruction went far beyond the normal needs of predators. A herd of elk, passing by in mid-afternoon, garnered no special attention from the pack. Why did they so earnestly seek his life?

Clouds boiled in from the east. Blue-white flashes of lightning illuminated the thunderheads from within, sometimes breaking into the open and crashing to earth. The sound of thunder rolled across the wide savanna, and the elm grove tossed in the wind. The first raindrops to fall were fat, heavy, and startlingly cold. Amero licked his lips gratefully each time he caught one.

The yevi remained in their vigilant positions, never flinching at the thunder or lightning, never seeking shelter. They reminded Amero of the stone fetishes he'd seen in the Khar land, carved by men of the southern plains to appease the spirits of the hunt. Wind and rain came in gusts, enough to appease the worst of Amero's thirst, but still the yevi waited.

A close flash of lightning lit up the entire sky. By the dazzling light Amero glimpsed an extraordinary sight—a vast dark shape high in the sky, silhouetted against the purple clouds. It was long and sinuous, with a pair of immense,

narrow wings flapping slowly. It was certainly the biggest
bird Amero had ever seen, but before another blast of lightning could bring him a clearer glimpse, the thing nosed up
into the clouds and was gone.

"Stormbird," he marveled aloud. Oto had spoken of these.
Like the star-pattern in the sky for which they were named,
stormbirds were enormous, rare creatures.

"They fly in the edge of every storm, carrying lightning in
their claws and thunder in every stroke of their wings," Oto
had said. "They never touch earth and can swallow an entire
flock of geese as one meal."

Amero could hardly believe he was seeing a stormbird
with his own eyes.

Just then, fiery fingers of lightning struck the ground less
than a hundred paces away. The tree trembled, and bits of
scorched wood and dirt pelted him. He ducked his head to
avoid the debris and saw the yevi were on their feet, milling
around and whining. Amero cinched the lacings tighter and
wished for another, closer strike. Perhaps that would send
them away for good.

Thunder boomed in the grove, and still the yevi didn't
leave. They did break their circle around Amero's perch, col-
lecting in a tight knot on one side of the tree. Amero devoutly
wished they would skulk into the bush, driven away by the
crackling lightning and booming thunder. Instead, they
remained, huddled together and evidently quaking with fear.
Common predators would have abandoned Amero to his fate.
Why did the yevi remain?

The storm blew itself out at last, rolling westward across
the plain toward the great forest. Before long Amero saw stars
through rents in the clouds, and the incessant flashes of
lightning galloped away. The night was left dark once again.

Refreshed by the rain, Amero resolved to escape the yevi
on the morrow. He slept a second night in the treetop. One
way or another, it would be his last night there.

\* \* \* \* \*

Dawn arrived, fresh and bright. The short, sharp rain
had brought green shoots out of the ground overnight, and

23

the air was filled with buzzing insects. The abundant bugs attracted swarms of birds, so the morning was astir with noisy, colorful life. Amero stretched his aching arms and legs and wondered if his neck was developing a permanent bend.

Ten members of the yevi pack were still on watch beneath Amero's tree. Drying mud matted their fur, and they looked generally bedraggled, but their menace was unchanged. Amero felt the cold clutch of helplessness again as he tried and failed to come up with a plan to escape.

Four more yevi appeared from the bush, looking quite clean and rested. Without a sound the pack spread out in a circle around Amero's perch. Strangely, the beasts aligned themselves facing outward, not inward, as though they were defending the tree instead of besieging it.

"Get out of here!" Amero shouted in exasperation. "Go! Go now!"

There was no answer from the yevi. Could he have imagined hearing their voices the other day?

A flock of birds whirled in and filled the branches of Amero's elm. There must have been a hundred tiny black-and-tan birds, all chirping at once, making a tremendous din. They were highly agitated—some hopping back and forth from one limb to another, fluffing their wings, some even daring to land on Amero's head or shoulders. The shrill peeping reached a crescendo, then in a body the noisy flock took to the air. They circled the grove once and flew away.

Curiously, the yevi were backing up, slowly contracting their circle. A few on the west side broke ranks and trotted around to the east side, filling the gaps between the beasts already there. Whatever was coming, whatever had startled the birds and worried the yevi pack, was coming from the east. From the mountains.

Straining to see in that direction, Amero was surprised to feel a sudden chill run down his back. He was even more astonished to look up and see a man come striding toward the grove. He was too far away for Amero to make out his face clearly, but the boy could tell by the stranger's shock of red-gold hair that he wasn't Oto. Amero had never seen anyone with hair that color before.

"Stop!" he shouted. His voice was a weak croak after his prolonged ordeal. "Beware! The pack—the yevi!"

The animals were rooted to the spot. On came the stranger through the widely spaced trees. He carried no spear nor club Amero could see. The boy was horrified. The yevi would tear the man to pieces.

"Go back! Danger!" Amero cried.

At last the man seemed to hear him. He halted twenty paces away and looked up at him. Though the sun was bright and the glare terrific, the stranger didn't shade his eyes.

Two yevi crept forward a few steps, lips curled, snarling ferociously. The stiff gray fur on their humped backs rose, flaring like lion's manes.

Surely the man could see them! Amero thought. Why did he approach so casually?

The stranger resumed his easy pace toward Amero. Two yevi detached from the circle and charged, their claws tearing up clots of muddied soil. Amero closed his eyes and turned away. He'd seen enough of what the yevi could do.

The air quivered, as if from thunder, but there was no sound. The hair on Amero's arms stood up. Instead of the man's screams, he heard a concerted yelping from the pack. He opened his eyes cautiously and saw the two attacking yevi had been thrown back. Their bodies lay unmoving, limbs jutting out at twisted angles.

What had happened?

Three more beasts broke ranks and attacked. The fiery-haired man extended his left hand, the fingers spread. When the yevi were within leaping distance, he waved his hand, as if shooing a fly. The air before him blurred—once more Amero felt the hair on his arms stand on end—and the three attackers seemed to be grabbed by invisible hands in mid-flight. They were hurled backward with great speed, landing in a heap near the foot of Amero's tree. From the way they bounced, they must have broken every bone in their bodies.

The pack exploded. The gray killers flung themselves at the stranger, who repeated his gesture with both hands. Not only the air but the earth trembled, and the yevi scattered like leaves in last night's storm.

25

Once the grove was clear of the pack, the man stood in the shadow of Amero's elm and looked up. He was tall and well-made, though not unusually big or brawny. His skin was lighter than Amero's, lightly tanned by the sun, and it was smooth and free of scars and marks. He was barefoot and wore a simple loincloth of buckskin, inlaid with strips of some shiny green hide—tortoise shell, or snakeskin of some kind. It was the stranger's hair that intrigued Amero most. Not only was the color unique, it was short and shaped to his head like that of the black men Amero had seen just days ago. While theirs had been tightly curled, this man's hair was as straight as Amero's.

"You can come down now," said the stranger in a low, musical voice. "They will not bother you again."

"Who are you?" asked Amero, trying to maintain a firm grip on the tree.

The stranger did not respond, but merely stared up at him with a mildly interested expression. In spite of his innate wariness, Amero found his fingers slipping. He was so weak, so tired from his long captivity in the tree that it was hard to hold on another moment.

Helplessly, Amero asked, "You'll not . . . hurt me?"

The stranger sighed. "What I did to those creatures I could do to you whether you are in the tree or out. Remain there, if you wish."

His words sounded logical, and Amero was simply too exhausted to resist further. He loosened the laces that held him to the tree. Soon his feet were on firm ground, but his legs wouldn't support him. His knees folded, and he found himself sitting down hard on the ground.

"My family, out there," he murmured. "Have you seen anyone else?"

"No." The stranger's eyes—a light blue color, like the sky—betrayed no hint of emotion. "I saw only you."

Amero pulled himself upright. "Are you a spirit? Do you command the wind—is that how you defeated the yevi?"

" 'Yevi?' Ah, you have named them already."

Amero was about to repeat his question when a single animal reappeared from the tall grass. The boy pressed his weakened body against the tree, unable to haul himself up. However, flight was unnecessary.

The stranger frowned at the yevi. "Begone," he said simply.

*You thwart our hunt.* Amero heard the words distinctly, though the beast's jaws never moved. *Why do you protect our prey? What is he to you?*

"This is my land," the man replied, smiling. "I do as I will. You don't belong here. Tell your master to send no more hunting packs into my domain. I won't tolerate poaching."

*You dare challenge Sthenn?*

The stranger shrugged. "I know your master well. He can seek me any time he chooses, but he won't. He's a coward. He prefers to use vermin like you, you 'yevi'—" he nodded at Amero in acknowledgment for the name—"to accomplish what he wants."

The gray beast let loose a guttural yelp. *And what will you do, mighty one? Take up humans as your favored pets?*

"They're too frail and stupid to make good pets, but I won't have you randomly butchering creatures on my land, either. Go and tell your master what I've said."

He turned his back on the yevi and started to walk away. Amero pulled himself to his feet, intending to follow the man, but the yevi sprang for the boy's throat. It never made it. There was a brilliant flash, the smell of singed flesh, and the yevi was blasted to scorched bits.

Amero rubbed his eyes, and his vision quickly returned. "You destroyed it!" he said, agog.

"I should have known a creature like that could not be trusted. Well, when none of the pack returns, my message will be just as clear."

He walked carelessly away, Amero limping at his heels. "You never told me your name," the boy said. There was no response, so Amero added, "I have no family, no one. Can I go with you? I can . . . I can serve you."

The boy limped faster, hissing in pain each time his injured leg touched the ground. Desperate, he began listing his accomplishments. "I can fish, gather berries and roots, make snares, skin rabbits, knap flint, and . . . and if this Sthenn comes looking for you, I can guard your back."

At the mention of the name, the stranger whirled and seized the boy with both hands. An image flickered through Amero's mind, an impression of vast size and enormous power. A light seemed to glow from within the man's oddly colored eyes, and Amero feared he was about to be roasted like the last yevi.

"Where did you hear that name?" the man demanded.

"The beast spoke it," Amero replied in a strangled voice. The man's grip was painful.

His blue eyes narrowed. "You understood what the beasts said?"

"Yes. They spoke to me yesterday, trying to lure me out of my tree—"

"Tell me what else it said!"

The boy hastily recounted the exchange he'd just heard between the yevi and the stranger. When he was done, the man released him. Fear and exhaustion robbed Amero completely of strength. He sank to the grass.

"Now that's . . . interesting," was all the stranger said.

"What will you do with me, spirit-man?" he said weakly.

His rescuer seemed lost in thought, but finally said, "Duranix."

"What?" asked Amero.

"My name is Duranix, and no, I won't kill you. In fact, you may follow me." It didn't sound like a request. Duranix strode away, due east toward the distant mountains. A little stunned, Amero hobbled after him.

"Where are you going, Duranix?"

"Home."

"What's home?"

Duranix glanced back. "A place to live. Where one sleeps at night. Where is your home, Amero?"

"I have no home." Amero swallowed a lump in his throat and looked down at his scraped, dirty feet. He would not cry. He was a man, and men did not cry. Oto never did. "We make a new camp every night. If you stay in one place too long, you go hungry. All the food gets eaten or runs away."

"I see what you mean. I too travel a lot, but I always return to my home."

28

In spite of his grief, Amero felt a stirring of curiosity. Lifting his tear-stained face, he said, "Where's home?"

"Where the mountains meet the plain and a river breaks on a high cliff, that is home."

"Oh, a waterfall. How large is it? What is it called?"

Duranix smiled. "Just 'home.' What would you call it, Amero?"

"I don't know. I'd have to see it—but I could make up a name for it, if you want."

"No doubt you would. Humans name things the way bees work a field of cornflowers. Here's one, here's another, here's ten more."

Heart singing with hope, Amero pushed himself to his feet. He took a step, then the sky seemed to spin around his head. The ground rushed up to meet him and he knew no more.

Duranix looked down at the unconscious boy for a moment, then effortlessly plucked him off the ground with one hand and tucked him under his arm.

"How can you understand the beasts?" Duranix said to the unconscious boy. "Why did I hear your thoughts of pain?" He answered himself. "Time will tell. Sleep now, boy. When you wake, we shall be home."

# Chapter 3

~

Nianki awoke in stifling darkness. Memory of the previous day's terror returned. After slaying the last of the beasts stalking her, she'd crawled to the foot of the boulder and burrowed into the loose sand of the dry creek bed. Handful by handful she'd hollowed out a hiding place, and while the red moon still blazed like an ember in the sky, she crawled into her makeshift cave and slept like a dead person. The overhanging bulk of the boulder had warmed her during the night, but it must be daylight now—the sun-baked stone made the hole unbearable. Breaking through the thin wall of gravel and sand she'd erected to hide the opening, Nianki crawled into fresh air.

The gully was empty. The bodies of the beasts she'd slain were gone. Nianki tried to stand, but her wounds flamed with pain. Bracing herself against the boulder, she forced herself erect. This last movement drew her mouth open in a silent howl, but she did not allow herself to give voice to her torment. Even if the killer pack was no longer around, there were plenty of other scavengers who would find the injured Nianki a tasty morsel.

She found a length of dried vine to use as a crutch. It was as thick as her wrist and curled along its entire length, but it was stout. With its help she limped down the creek bed. A fallen tree blocked the way a few paces on. Nianki dragged herself over the obstruction and moved on, leaning heavily on her stick.

She knew her family was dead. If Oto were alive, he would have found her by now, and if he wasn't, none of the others could be. Kinar, Amero, and Menni were not strong enough or swift enough to escape the deadly gray marauders.

So be it.

With each agonizing step, Nianki swore a private oath to Chisa, the great spirit of nature, that none of those creatures would be spared from her wrath—not male, female, or pup.

She would slay them all without mercy, until there were no more left to kill. It was an ugly, black vow, but it filled her with purpose and kept her moving forward.

Flies followed her, drawn by the smell of her wounds. Her tongue ached for water. The gully slanted down at a shallow angle, so she kept to the dry ravine in hopes of finding water.

Near midday the smell of water teased her nostrils. Nianki quickened her step, dragging her mangled leg through the loose gravel. Ahead, the gully was closed by a hedge of ferns and dense creeping vines. Now, she could hear the water as well. She tore through the greenery with stiff, bloody fingers and found a spring bubbling out of a split boulder. It collected in a moss-rimmed pool a hand's reach below. Nianki wept at the sight of it.

She lowered herself on her belly beside the pool. Cupping her hands, she raised them brimming to her parched lips. Her first swallow tasted like blood, but she bolted it down nonetheless. Two more handfuls followed, the fourth she threw on her face. The clear pool grew murky. Exhausted, she let her face rest against the soft moss.

Kinar had tried to teach her which leaves and roots were soothing to wounds. Nianki had always been too impatient to heed her mother's words. Only clumsy hunters allowed themselves to get wounded, she had thought. In fifteen years she'd suffered nothing worse than a few cuts and scratches. Now she worked her memory hard, trying to pry out the information Kinar had labored to impart.

*Sumac soothes, larchit heals.* The phrase surfaced in her fevered mind. Sumac was a woody shrub with pointed, shiny leaves, four leaves per stem. Larchit, also called soft-tongue, grew in dry places. Its leaves were like dark green, fleshy fingers. When cut, the leaves exuded a clear sap.

Nianki opened her eyes. Kinar's words, Kinar's voice, resounded in her head as clear as sunlight.

*Silver algae from a fast-flowing stream is good for burns,* she'd said. *The meat of acorns, dried and ground to dust, will stop bleeding.*

"Mother—"

*Be still, Nianki, and listen. This is slippery gum, and this is koti weed.*

31

Nianki pushed herself up on her hands, half-expecting to see Kinar standing over her, but she was alone by the pool.

Gingerly, she peeled off her dirty, blood-soaked buckskins and slowly bathed her wounds. Those on her leg and neck were the most severe. She dipped a scrap of hide in the water and squeezed out the excess, using the soft nap of the buckskin to scrub away the dried blood and encrusted dirt. It was agonizing. Nianki banished the urge to weep by concentrating on her task.

She shivered. It was natural enough, sitting there half-naked, washing in cold spring water, but the strange heat in her face told her this was more than a normal chill. She'd seen bull elks survive a panther's mauling, only to succumb a few days later to wound fever. Oto's own father died after being gored by a wild pig, though his wounds had not seemed severe.

Nianki knew there were herbs for fever, but she found it increasingly hard to remember what they were. Sumac and larchit were fixed in her mind like trail signs. Lose them, and she would be lost indeed.

When her cuts and bites were clean, she dressed in her damp skins. Though it was another hot day, Nianki trembled as she threaded the lacing of her kilt and tunic. She put a smooth pebble from the pool in her mouth. Sucking on it would slake her thirst. Leaning heavily on her vine staff, she climbed out of the gully and surveyed her surroundings.

Their scattered, frantic flight from the pack had taken Nianki's family far off their usual track. She could see the eastern mountains clearly enough, but the peaks presented an unfamiliar pattern. To the north and south lay trackless plain, as far as the eye could behold and well beyond. Back to the west lay several days' worth of grassland, and after that, the great forest.

Huge clouds filled the sky north and west, the flat undersides growing darker and darker as more clouds piled up. Having no desire to limp through the rain, she decided to head south, away from the coming storm.

More than dislike of rain turned her feet south. Kinar came from there. Her people followed herds of wild oxen as they grazed northward in winter and south in summer. They lived in bands of twelve or more, often unrelated by blood. If anyone would be disposed to tolerate a lone hunter like Nianki, it would be the ox herders.

\* \* \* \* \*

With her back to it, Nianki felt the storm coming before she heard the first thunderclap. The air was oppressive, and the dry heat of a typical late spring day was replaced by sullen humidity. Limping along with her arms full of sumac and larchit leaves, she took shelter under an aged cedar. After wedging herself into a crevice in the split trunk, she began to treat her wounds. Sumac had to be pulped before it was applied, so as the storm overtook her she methodically chewed sumac leaves, pressing the resulting spicy-smelling paste to her torn flesh. Chewing also kept her teeth from chattering. Fever burned deep within her breast. It was a cold fire, like Soli, the white moon.

When her neck was covered in sumac paste, Nianki broke a larchit stem and smeared the clear sap on her leg wound. It stung, but not as badly as washing it had.

In the distance, she saw the rain begin as a wall of mist sweeping across the savanna. Lightning crackled in the clouds, sometimes breaking out and striking the parched earth. Deer and birds fled before the storm. The sight of so much game made Nianki's empty stomach growl. She chewed more sumac, which was oily and pungent; it dampened her desire for food.

The sighing wind rose to a drone as the storm came closer. Whirlwinds of dust danced by, chased by an army of errant leaves. Nianki flinched as a bolt of blue-white lightning stabbed the ground a few hundred paces away. Dry grass flashed into fire, only to be doused by the ensuing downpour.

The rain finally reached her, and she huddled deeper into the cleft of the tree. Rain raked over her, the cold droplets feeling like a lash of thorns. Nianki threw her good arm across her face to shield it from the driving spray. As she peered over her own elbow at the storm, she heard the drumming of massed hooves above the gusting wind. A herd of elk was stampeding. Her hunting instincts aroused, Nianki pushed herself up for a better view.

Elk were accustomed to thunderstorms—thunder alone wasn't enough to send them trampling over the plain. Something else must have frightened them.

She saw no smoke. No grass fire could survive in the downpour anyway. Nianki braced herself against the tree and stared through the rain at the oncoming herd.

There! Topping a slight rise, a huge, winged shape came swooping after the terrified elk. Nianki gaped in wonder. Tapered, leathery wings rose in a high arc, the tips almost touching, and swept down again to brush the storm-tossed grass. The monster had a thick, streamlined body and a serpentine neck and tail. Its scaly hide had a shiny reddish-gold cast.

All she could think of was her father's tales about "stormbirds," huge flying creatures who lived in the sky and brought violent tempests in their wake. Nianki never imagined a monster like this could actually exist, much less fly with such speed and precision.

So rapt was her attention on the stormbird that she forgot the elk herd was bearing down on her. All of a sudden, a wall of brown bodies, antlers, and churning hooves came over the low hill just two hundred paces away—aiming straight at Nianki. There was no way she could outrun them, so she ducked behind the old cedar and fervently hoped the herd would split around this slight obstacle.

The stormbird opened is massive jaws, revealing fangs as long as Nianki's forearm. Its snake-like eyes rolled back in its head.

A bolt of lightning erupted from its throat.

Stones and dirt flew, and the blast flung Nianki to the ground. She rolled over, expecting at any moment to be trampled by elk or seared by lightning. The ground heaved and shuddered for some moments, gradually settling down. Nianki raised her head.

The herd had split around the cedar tree and was rushing madly for the horizon. Charred carcasses littered the plain, and a smoking rent in the earth thirty paces long lay within spitting distance of Nianki's tree.

Shaken, she hauled herself to her feet as the stormbird swept overhead. The air from its beating wings washed cold over her.

The monstrous snake-head darted down and snatched up one burned elk after another. It gulped the carcasses down amid a loud snapping of bones. Flapping its wings hard, the stormbird circled and gained height. Rain streamed down Nianki's face as she watched it climb.

The monster glided in a wide half-circle, and for the first time noticed Nianki. Eyes the size of sunflowers peered down at her. She thought it would strike her with its lightning, but the monster held its turn and flapped away after the quickly disappearing herd. It looked back once, dropping its long neck in order to peer under its own wing.

Soaked to the skin and shivering, Nianki stood there long after the monster had vanished. The past few days had been a revelation. She who thought she knew so much about nature, about the world of the plains, had suffered two rude shocks. First, the pack of misshapen predators that had killed her family—now this! Had the world turned inside out? Were there spirits and monsters behind every tree, beyond every hill?

The smell of burned meat penetrated her reverie. She wandered among the charred remains of eight large animals, a head here, a haunch there. Hungry as she was, she couldn't bring herself to take any of the stormbird's leavings. She'd heard of people who burned their meat with fire, but the idea disgusted her. Meat should be eaten fresh or dried, not burned. Only scavengers ate charred food.

Yet, Nianki's stomach writhed with hunger, sending shooting pains through her gut. Weak and injured as she was, she couldn't hunt her own game. She needed food to regain her strength—and there was food all around her, though blackened and smelling of fire. Swallowing hard, she slid to her knees beside a still smoking haunch.

Life's a struggle, Oto always said. If you knock down an anthill every morning, the ants will build it back by evening. The ants had no choice, if they wanted to live, and neither did Nianki. She wrenched off the elk's leg, hoping the flesh closer to bone might be less burned.

No luck. The lightning had blackened the poor beast right through to the marrow. Nianki sighed and chewed in silence as the rain continued to drench her and the dark, empty savanna.

\* \* \* \* \*

She wandered south. Her fever got worse, and she lost track of the passage of time as she slept more by day and walked by night. Perhaps four days after seeing the storm-bird—she couldn't remember exactly how long it had been—Nianki found the cold remains of a hunter's camp. They ate well, these hunters. She found the bones of a slaughtered pig, a pile of wild grape stems, and a broken birch-bark box that once held salmon jerky. She licked the grease from the bark box and gnawed the cast-off pig bones. It was her first food since the burned elk.

Barks and thin howls announced the arrival of a pack of wild dogs. Nianki feared the dogs more than she would a bear or big cat. Bigger predators were wary of humans and their cunning ways, but dogs were stupid and fearless.

She rooted in the debris left behind by the other hunters, thinking to find the boar's leg bone or some other suitable club. She had better luck than she dared hope.

Tossed in the grass with the offal was a stone-headed spear. The shaft was broken midway, but the careless owner had thrown it away, flint head and all. Nianki held up the shortened spear and examined it by the failing light. The milky gray flint was finely knapped and quite sharp.

Just holding a spear, even a broken one, filled Nianki with new strength. When the dog pack's scouts yelped close by, she howled back at them, daring them to attack. There followed only the sound of crickets, singing in the twilight. When she next heard the dogs they were farther away. For the first time in many days, Nianki smiled.

Moving on, she found a swampy water hole. With her new spear she gigged a few fat frogs, then dug some tender cane shoots out of the malodorous black mud. She crouched on a stone by the water hole, washing the shoots and gnawing on them.

The food and her weapon gave her new confidence. She walked all night, and just before dawn she smelled smoke. A thin smudge rose from a pine copse ahead.

Hunters in these parts often slept with a slow fire going, feeding it with resinous green pine. The resulting smoke kept mosquitoes away and usually warned off prowling scavengers.

Still limping on her mangled leg, Nianki crept up on the strangers' camp. She saw two man-sized lumps on the ground, a smoldering heap of pine boughs between them. A hide bag hung from a tree branch, out of reach of badgers and rats. On the other side of the camp a tripod of sticks stood with a bark box balanced carefully on top. Soundlessly, Nianki entered the camp and sat down on the upwind side of the fire.

One of the men, a tall fellow with bare brown shoulders, rolled over on his back. He began to snore loudly. His companion stirred.

"Shh!" the sleepy man hissed, throwing a convenient pine cone at his snoring friend. It landed nowhere near him.

The snorer rasped on. The one who'd thrown the pine cone gave a disgusted sigh and rolled to his feet. He had a cape wrapped around himself—soft elk hide studded with a crow-feather collar—and he hitched this up around his shoulders. He shuffled toward his friend, unaware of Nianki.

"Pakito, turn over!" he said fiercely. The snoring man remained heedless. His snores were so loud Nianki thought he'd scare away all the game within a day's walk.

"Pakito! You worthless pile of ox dung!" The caped man aimed a kick at the snorer's hip. No gentle nudge, it rolled the clueless offender over on his face.

"Ow!" he yelped, sitting up and blowing brown pine needles out of his mouth. "Pa'alu! Did you kick me?"

"I did! You were snoring again."

"Is that any way to treat your brother?"

"You're lucky I didn't use an axe."

Nianki let out a brief, sharp laugh. Both men started and stared, noticing her for the first time.

"If I were a panther," she said, "you'd both be feeding my kits by now."

"Who are you?" demanded Pa'alu, the caped one. Nianki ignored the question. Pakito, taller by a head than his brother and broader in the chest, tucked his feet under him and faced Nianki. He had a round face and dark brown eyes.

"You look like you've been fighting a panther," he observed pleasantly. "Since you're here, you must have won."

Pa'alu was staring at the short spear in her hand. "Your weapon—may I see it?" he asked. She held it out for his inspection, but did not relinquish it. Pa'alu's eyes widened and he said, "Pakito! You said you lost your spear when the boar's mate ran off with it. How did this—this scarred one get it?"

"My name's Nianki. I found this a night's walk from here."

Pa'alu rounded on his brother. "You threw away your spear!"

"It was broken," the big man said sullenly.

"It has a good head of gray mountain flint! The shaft could have been replaced!"

Pakito gave an exaggerated shrug, saying nothing. Nianki decided the strapping fellow was actually the younger of the two, no more than seventeen or eighteen seasons old. Pa'alu seemed a few years older.

"It was a bad luck spear anyway," Pakito finally said. "It never hit anything."

With a shake of her head at such thinking, Nianki reversed her grip and hurled the shortened weapon at Pakito's feet. It struck at his toes. He yelped and fell over backward. Pa'alu snatched up his own spear and held it high, ready to impale Nianki. She sat quietly, hugging her knees.

Pakito got up, visibly shaken, but exclaimed triumphantly, "You see! He missed me, as close as he was!"

Pa'alu snorted, but his eyes never left Nianki.

She slowly stood, saying, "I'm a she, giant. And you have a cut between the first two toes of your right foot."

Pakito lifted his foot, grabbed it in both hands and spread his toes apart. A crimson bead oozed from the tiny cut.

"I'm bleeding!" Pakito sat down heavily and blew on his toes. His brown eyes looked accusingly at Nianki.

Pa'alu grinned. "You have a plainsman's eye," he said approvingly. "Where'd you learn to throw a spear like that?"

"From my father. He is—was—a great hunter."

Pa'alu yanked the spear from the ground and handed it back to Nianki. "Keep it. It doesn't seem to bring bad luck to you." He eyed her many injuries. "Or perhaps bad luck is finished with you already."

Nianki sat down cross-legged, laying the short spear across her lap. Pa'alu offered her a hollow gourd with a long thong tied around its neck. She shook it, heard sloshing, and sniffed the open neck. Water.

She drank deeply, gulping rapidly to prevent any spillage. When she was done she handed the empty gourd back to Pa'alu.

"A handy thing," she said.

"I made it," he replied. "Haven't you seen a water-gourd before?"

"I'm not from these parts."

Little by little Nianki relaxed. Pakito was good-natured and devoted to his brother. Pa'alu was a bit harder to fathom. He had the quick reflexes and keen eyes of a hunter, but he also seemed clever in the way her brother Amero had been—always making things and thinking of new ways to do things. Cleverness like that made her uncomfortable.

They shared their breakfast with her—raisins, salmon jerky, and soft white mush Pakito called "cheese." It smelled spoiled to Nianki, and she declined to eat it.

"What happened to you?" Pa'alu asked. "Who attacked you?"

"Animals. A hunting pack. Never seen their like before."

"Wolves?" mumbled Pakito through a mouthful of raisins.

"No." With painful economy, she described the beasts who had destroyed her family. "I alone survived," she said. She bit off a piece of jerky and chewed in silence.

"What will you do now?" said Pa'alu.

She shrugged. "I'll live the best I can."

"You can come with us," Pakito said, looking to his brother for confirmation.

Pa'alu's expression was unreadable. "You are welcome," was all he said.

Nianki stood up. "I will go where the wind takes me." She lifted her head, watching the clouds stream to the southern horizon. "Alone."

Pakito was crestfallen, but Pa'alu nodded solemnly. He placed a few pieces of salmon in a bark box, tossed in some raisins, and handed it to Nianki, saying, "May the spirits of the sky and plain favor you."

"They haven't yet," she replied.

\* \* \* \* \*

The brothers departed westward, laden with their food and implements. Nianki couldn't understand why two hunters would burden themselves in such a way. Why carry so much food when it was all around, waiting to be picked or caught? Still, she couldn't fault the brothers' generosity. On the strength of their food and water she felt reborn.

That evening she reached a broad river and found it teeming with birds—ducks, geese, cranes, herons. Raiding a few nests, she added four eggs to her provisions. Afterward, she bathed her wounds by swimming out to midstream and floating on her back for a while, letting the current carry her downstream. Curious minnows followed her, nibbling at her fingers and toes. It was an odd, teasing sensation that she half enjoyed, half ignored until it called up memories of the storm-bird gobbling down whole elk. Everything in the world fed on something else. The mouse ate the grub, the fox ate the mouse, the vulture ate the fox—humans ate nearly everything and were eaten by still larger predators. Even the mighty elk were just morsels for the stormbird.

And who ate him? What did the stormbird, he who breathed lightning and flew on the crest of a tempest—what did he fear?

Her eyes closed. She lay, bobbing gently, until an errant wave sent water into her nose and she jerked upright, coughing and spitting. The minnows vanished into the depths.

The broad red orb of the sun was setting, so she swam to the south shore. The other side of the river was a cacophony of birds quacking and trumpeting as they came to roost for the night.

Nianki climbed a sandy hill overlooking the river and bedded down for the night, her back against a sturdy vallenwood tree. It was just a sapling by vallenwood standards, yet still bigger around than she could reach. She laid Pakito's broken spear against her chest and slept deeply. Only once did a noise in the night alarm her—a panther prowling nearby let out a scream. The high, almost-human sound brought Nianki rolling to her feet, spear ready. When next it screamed, the panther was farther away, so Nianki resumed her place under the tree and slept undisturbed.

# Chapter 4

~

For Amero, the trip to Duranix's home passed in a dream, one he would recall often in later years. He was flying through the air. There was wind in his face, pulling at his hair. Stars raced by through gaps in the clouds. Amero had dreamed of flying before, but never so vividly. Once he struggled to awaken so that he could see where he truly was, but sleep, like a blanket of fog, enclosed him again.

His first impression after the odd dream was of noise—a low rumble, loud, yet not painful to the ear. The cool air was heavy with the smell of water. Amero opened his eyes.

High above him was an arching expanse of rock streaked with red and black minerals. A pulsing, bluish light filled the air. Amero sat up. He was in a shallow, scooped-out hollow in the floor. The depression was full of fir boughs and freshly torn-up grass; some clumps still had dirt clinging to them.

Around him was an enormous cave, a hundred paces along each of its three walls. The curved ceiling must have been sixty paces high. Light entered the cavern from three points. The first was a hole in the ceiling below the apex and facing outward, not straight up. The second was a large circular opening in the outside wall on the extreme left; it was well off the floor, and anyone entering there would have to do considerable climbing just to get down to the cave floor. The last was a small opening on the far right, at floor level, just the right size for a grown man to use. A wall of plunging water screened the view. A waterfall. That accounted for the persistent rumble.

Amero climbed out of the bough-filled pit. His right leg where the yevi had clawed him was still painful, but much less so than before. He forgot his injury as he examined his new surroundings.

The cave walls were unnaturally smooth, without stalactites or stalagmites. The floor in the wide part of the cave—

the waterfall side—sloped gradually upward. In the rear, a level platform at least eighty paces wide filled the corner. The only other noteworthy feature was the smell. The cave smelled vaguely sour, like overripe fruit.

Not seeing anyone, Amero limped to the lower, smaller opening and looked out. A column of foaming water thundered down the mountainside, concealing both entrances to the cave. To his astonishment, he found the cave was hundreds of paces above the ground, set in the side of a vertical cliff face. His head swam, and he lurched back from the precipice.

How did I get up here? he wondered. Where was Duranix? There had to be a trail, a passage ascending from the river basin below.

Recovering his nerve, Amero mounted the slope to the rock platform. The face of the platform was curiously notched with long, parallel scratches that served as handy footholds. After scrambling up, he found the upper floor was also hollowed out in the center. And there he found Duranix, lying in this upper-level bowl.

His strange benefactor was curled up in a strange position, his knees bent backward in a way Amero had never seen a human's legs bend before. Even odder, the floor was littered with peculiar objects, like large tree leaves, only these were stiff and shiny. Amero picked one up. A little bigger than the palm of his hand, it was oval-shaped, heavy, hard, and the red-gold color of autumn leaves. What could it be?

"Rubbish."

Amero flinched and dropped the object. It rang loudly when it hit the floor. Duranix had rolled over and was watching him, his head propped up on one hand.

"Wh-what?"

"I answered your question," Duranix said, eyes narrowing. "Those things—they're rubbish."

"My question?" Amero's confusion cleared when he realized the man had overheard his thoughts. Well, he decided, nothing such a powerful spirit-being did should surprise him. "I didn't mean to disturb you," he said awkwardly.

"Then don't think so loudly. I'm bound to hear." Duranix sat up with a quick, fluid movement Amero found hard to follow.

The strangeness of his host, the unfamiliarity of his surroundings, began to overwhelm him. Backing to the edge of the platform, Amero asked, "How did you get me into this place? We must be a whole day's climb from the bottom."

"Three hundred sixty-two paces, as you would measure it," said Duranix as he rose and stretched. Amero saw there were several of those shiny leaves where Duranix had lain.

Duranix straightened his loincloth and walked down the notched platform ledge. Amero hobbled along at the taller man's heels, trying to keep up.

"How long have I been here?" Amero asked.

"Since last night."

Amero stopped dead in his tracks. "But how? We are many days' journey from the plains. It's imposs—" The boy cut himself off, once more remembering the ease with which his host had dispatched the yevi.

Duranix offered no explanation. Holding onto the rim of the lower opening, he leaned out toward the waterfall. Spray dampened his short hair. He leaned further and opened his mouth. Water beaded on his face and filled his mouth.

When he'd drunk his fill, Duranix swung back into the cave. His fair skin glistened. He smiled with some secret amusement and said, "Thirsty? There's no sweeter water in the world than my waterfall."

Amero *was* thirsty. He licked his cracked lips and gazed longingly past his host at the tumbling torrent.

"I can't reach out that far," he said, shaking his head.

"I'll help you." Duranix grabbed Amero by the scruff of his neck and thrust him through the opening. The boy let out a shriek of terror as he saw the distant ground between his feet.

"No! No! Don't drop me! Please don't—"

Duranix shoved him into the stream. The water pummeled Amero, and he locked his hands on Duranix's arm, certain he would be dropped over the edge. However, Duranix never lost hold of him, and after a few heart-stopping moments, he was hauled back inside the cave.

Gasping and sputtering, Amero collapsed on the floor. "Why were you screaming?" Duranix asked. "I would not drop you."

"The water—too hard—too hard," the boy choked.

Duranix sighed. "What fragile creatures humans are." He left Amero coughing and spitting. A moment later he was back with a scrap of dry deer hide and one of those shiny oval leaves. He rolled the hide into a cone and crimped the seam shut by folding the leaf around and pinching it with his fingers. He held this odd object in the edge of the flow of water until the hide hollow was filled. He offered it to Amero.

The boy pushed wet hair out of his face and took the proffered gift. The hide held a double handful of water, and he drank it quickly. The water was cold and pure, with a mineral tang missing from lowland streams.

"Thank you," he said, eyes closed as he savored the wonderful taste.

His thirst appeased, Amero turned the unusual object around and around in his slender fingers. "You made this?" he marveled.

"It would be foolish to die of thirst within sight of a waterfall."

Wet through and through, Amero began to shiver, his teeth chattering in the cool air. He returned to his bed of boughs and crawled among them, trying to get warm. The water-catcher he kept firmly in his hand.

Duranix busied himself in the far corner, below the high, larger opening. He returned shortly with an armload of furs and hides.

"Use these as you see fit," he said, dumping the load beside Amero.

"Where are you going?" The boy's voice cracked as he asked the question, and Duranix turned slowly toward him, red eyebrows pressed together in a frown. Amero muttered, "I'm sorry. I didn't mean . . . I'm sorry."

Duranix studied him silently for a moment, and Amero hid his embarrassed face by turning to the heap of furs.

"What did you call the animals who attacked you?" the man finally asked.

Amero pulled a thick white ox hide over himself, up to his chin. "Yevi?"

"Well, boy, I must find out how far the yevi have penetrated into my domain."

"Your domain? Are you . . . are you the father of the whole plains, Duranix?"

He smiled briefly. "Father? Quaintly put. I am the master of the lands from these mountains west to the forest's edge."

"Are there other masters? In the forest?"

Duranix's handsome face darkened. "There is. He is called Sthenn."

"Your . . . brother?"

Duranix folded his arms, looking angry. Then he relaxed and said, "I must remember you have a limited range of expression. Sthenn and I are of the same race, if that's what you mean."

"You look like a man, but you do things I've never seen any other man do."

"I sometimes go abroad in human form."

"Why look like a man if you're not one?"

Duranix was silent and Amero realized he was asking a great many questions. It was a habit that got him in trouble so often with Oto. The boy bit his lip. It was hard not to voice the questions that filled his head.

However, Duranix did not look annoyed, as Oto so often had. He simply looked thoughtful and replied, "It makes traveling easier for me to appear as a man. Besides, humans amuse me. Most of them are no better than the beasts they hunt and kill." He gave Amero a penetrating look. "You're different though. I see signs in you of higher faculties—intelligence, curiosity, and perhaps something more. You heard the yevi speak. When you think clearly, I can hear your thoughts as loudly as I hear the falls outside."

Amero felt oddly embarrassed. "I'm just Amero, the son of Oto and Kinar."

"True, but you are different from your parents and siblings, aren't you?" Amero hung his head, admitting as much. Duranix added, "You have special abilities. It's why I brought you here. I want to know more about you."

Duranix fixed the cape around his shoulders and stood in the lower opening. "I'll return after sunset."

Before Amero could protest being left alone in the cave all day, Duranix leaped into space. He plunged through the waterfall and disappeared. Still wrapped in the white ox hide,

46

Amero crawled to the ledge and looked down. There was no sign of his host. The waterfall was more than an arm's length from the cliff wall, and he could see nothing through the thundering stream but the blue of the sky. While he was gazing down the cliff wall to the boiling pool below, a large shadow passed swiftly over the cave mouth. Amero looked up, but whatever it was had vanished.

He sighed. Though he was pleased at having been rescued from the yevi, Amero thought of his current situation and found himself reminded uncomfortably of a field mouse he'd once captured. He had kept the mouse in a hollow length of cane. He would spend entire evenings playing with the mouse, seeing how it reacted to various things he put in its little home, learning what it would and would not eat. One day he found the mouse was gone—it had gnawed through the bottom of the cane over several nights and run away. Amero, only five at the time, had cried over the loss. Nianki had told him it was only an animal's nature to want freedom. He was beginning to understand how the mouse must have felt.

Thoughts of his future couldn't compete very long with the return of his curiosity. He decided to explore the cavern and see what clues he could glean about his mysterious host. If he found food along the way, so much the better.

He began at the lower opening and worked around the cave wall to his left. The floor here was rougher. Hard stone had been gouged out in some way, leaving long troughs in the floor. Each groove was as wide as his hand, and they occurred in close groups of three at a time.

He found more of the oval leaves along the wall, though most were green with mold. Amero tried to bend one, as he'd seen Duranix do. Arms quivering with effort, he managed to put a slight bend in one. How firm they were! He put one on the floor and stomped it, gaining nothing but an aching foot. With a loose stone, he hit the leaf with all his strength. A clear ringing sound echoed through the cave. The blow left a small dent in the leaf and broke off the tip of the stone cleanly.

These things could be useful, he mused. They were already well shaped for digging. He could scrape away a lot of soil with one.

47

Amero walked slowly along the uneven floor toward the rear of the cave. Aside from loose stones and the odd golden-red leaves, he found little else of interest until he came to Duranix's sleeping place.

In the corner he discovered a heap of bones, many charred and splintered. This explained the sour smell in the cave. Duranix apparently enjoyed a variety of game, as there were bones of elk, deer, and oxen. Then Amero found something that froze the blood in his veins: a fleshless *human* skull.

Oto always said the spirits of the dead clung to their bones. That's why the dead had to be buried. If you left their bones lying around, their ghost would wander the land, doing evil.

Yet there was something pathetic about that dry white lump of bone. Curiosity overcame fear and Amero picked up the skull gingerly. It was big. The jaw had come off, and there wasn't a shred of meat left on it anywhere. On the back were deep, converging gouges. The bone had splintered there.

Amero put down the skull and wished peace to the spirit of the man who had once inhabited it. He decided not to dig further in the bone pile. He didn't want to know if other humans had died here, perhaps—he shuddered to think it—eaten by Duranix. He determined to leave the cave as soon as possible. He would find a way to live, maybe even a whole new family. Anything was better than being eaten by—whatever kind of creature Duranix was.

With renewed vigor he searched the platform and all around it, looking for a passage out of the cave. There was none. All he found in the rest of the chamber were a large heap of hides and skins and piles of the hard red-gold "leaves."

He almost wept with frustration. This high above the ground, how could he get out? He couldn't fly like a bird, bat, or bug. How did Duranix enter and leave without harm?

Amero recalled his captor's exit (how quickly Duranix had gone from host to captor in his mind). The strange man put on his long cape and flung himself through the wall of water, vanishing. The cape—why did he need the cape? To keep the water off, or was there a different reason?

Odd images from his flying dream flitted through his mind: rushing over the ground, the wind whipping his hair, the stars racing by. He imagined Duranix spreading his arms like a bird, the cape billowing out behind him like wings. Could a man really fly like that? Amero thought it unlikely. Was there power in the cape, spirit-power? He had no answer for that.

Yet not everything that flew had wings. In the spring, elms and maples cast their seeds on the wind. These fluttered and spun long distances, but they always came to earth somewhere, unbroken. Was that it? Was that the secret of Duranix's cape?

He scrounged through the hides, looking for a likely scrap. All the pieces were too large. He tried to tear off a portion of pigskin, but it was too tough. He needed a flint knife or some other sharp stone.

The cavern was hollowed out of a sandstone cliff. All the loose pieces of sandstone on the floor, though good for polishing the bark off a spear shaft, were incapable of holding a sharp edge.

The strange leaves, Duranix's so-called rubbish, were certainly hard and fairly thin. Amero tried sawing at a hide with the edge of one, but the leaf was too dull. Taking up a palm-sized chunk of sandstone, Amero scraped one side of the leaf, trying to hone it thinner and sharper.

It worked very well. After a few minutes' work, he cut his thumb on the resulting edge. Bleeding but triumphant, Amero quickly sliced out a piece of hide, which would make a cape for him comparable in size to Duranix's.

Even after his success in cutting the hide, Amero couldn't bring himself to tie on the cape and leap off the cliff. Perhaps he should test his idea first.

He slashed out a smaller piece of buckskin, more square, and cut a few strips of hide as thongs. An elk skull, antlers still attached, would serve to give weight to his experiment. He tied the skull to the hide with four thongs, one to each corner of the buckskin. Amero carried this odd-looking assembly to the opening. Taking a deep breath, he rolled it over the edge.

The elk skull dropped, snapping the four thongs taut. The square of buckskin filled with air and billowed up. Swinging gently back and forth, the strange contraption drifted down the side of the cliff very slowly indeed.

Amero's heart raced. It worked!

Then the floating skull bumped into the cliff wall, swung away, and got caught in the downdraft of the falls. As soon as the plunging water hit the hide, it collapsed and went tumbling into the permanent bank of mist at the foot of the falls.

Amero sat back, shaken. Yes, it could be done, but only if he kept away from the waterfall. That's why Duranix had leaped through the water. He was able to do it because he was preternaturally strong. If Amero tried it and failed, he wouldn't have long to mourn his lack of success.

The cave was growing brighter. Sunlight had crept up the cliff all morning and now was shining through the waterfall into the recesses of the cave. The pulsating, blue-tinged light threw everything in the chamber into strong relief, including the human skull Amero had found. The white bone shell glowed in the midday light, and the sight of it galvanized Amero to action.

With his tool he cut wide strips of hide and tied his ankles and wrists to the ox skin he'd chosen. He gathered the hide to his chest and waddled to the lower opening. At the last moment he stuck the sharpened gold leaf into the waist of his loincloth. His heart thudded painfully in his chest. He cast one look back at the skull. Empty eye sockets gave him the encouragement he needed.

Amero sprang from the rim with all the force his legs could give. He hit the waterfall, and for a fleeting moment felt the power of the roaring column of water. Then he was tumbling through open air, head over heels. He opened his eyes and saw the sun and clifftop career past. He let go of the hide and it fluttered and flopped like a living thing. Down he plummeted. He rolled over on his back to get away from the flailing ox skin. It caught the air and filled. Amero was jerked upward, snatched painfully by his wrists and ankles. His fall slowed greatly, but he was still going down fast enough to make the wind whistle in his ears. Worse, he was tumbling backward and couldn't see where he was going—he saw only the ox hide above him.

It was difficult shifting the hide straps around his wrists, but he managed to flop over on his stomach. He wished he hadn't. Below was the lake of the falls, rushing toward him at sickening speed. Amero opened his mouth and screamed.

He was still screaming when he hit the water. It felt almost as hard as hitting the ground. The air was driven from his chest and water rushed into his mouth and nose. Kicking furiously, he tried to rise to the surface, only to find his progress blocked by the sinking ox hide.

Nianki had been a better swimmer than he, a fact he regretted as he struggled to free himself. A painful poke in the ribs reminded him of his new tool. He drew it and cut the four straps. Kicking away from the confining hide, Amero broke the surface a few paces away.

He dragged himself ashore on a sandy spit. As he lay on his back gasping for air, Amero could see the dark circular openings in the cliff face behind the waterfall. They were so high up, yet here he was, alive on the ground!

Amero sat up and winced. His ribs ached. He had cuts on his hands and chest from the sharp tool, but none of that mattered. He was free again! It was time to put as much distance as possible between himself and Duranix. When sunset came and the strange spirit-man returned, would he come looking for Amero? Or, like a wise fisherman, would he not waste time on one that got away?

Amero hefted the golden tool. What this thing needed was a handle of some kind, some way to carry it so he wouldn't get cut all the time. Maybe a split shaft, like Nianki's hunting club had?

Amero went to the water's edge and waded along the shore. The outflow from the falls would obscure his footprints in the sandy bottom and make it harder for Duranix to track him. With luck, he could be far away before sunset.

Luck was not with him, however. The terrain around the lake was rugged. There were no trails, and in making his own way, Amero had to tread on rocks and gravel washed down the ravine by winter rains. The sharp shards bit into his feet, drawing blood. He'd gone barefoot all his life, and his feet were tough, but he'd never had to contend with conditions like this.

When the sun started to dip below the surrounding mountain peaks, Amero was still within sight of the waterfall. Desperation made him careless. He abandoned the shaded slope of the valley and jogged down to the floor of the ravine.

It was more level there, so the going was easier, but he was in plain sight of anyone on the high ground around him.

The trees in the area were mostly pines and oaks, very tall and widely spaced. A flock of starlings flew over, and the dark shadow they cast frightened Amero into the bushes. When he saw the birds wheel about and return, he emerged from hiding.

"You! Stop!"

He spun around and saw four men rushing toward him. They looked like plainsmen, except they wore more clothing. They were all of an age, four or five seasons older than Amero, and alike enough to be brothers. They ringed him with leveled spears. One, whose dark hair was plaited into a single thick braid, shouted, "Stand still, or we'll kill you!"

"Please!" Amero said. "I have nothing! I've done nothing!"

"You came from the lake of the falls, didn't you?"

"Yes, but—" Amero began, and found four spears pressed into his chest and back.

"I thought so!" said the man with the braid. "You're the monster who lives in the cave behind the falls."

"No, I'm not! I escaped from the cave today."

Another of the men, with a large black mole on his cheek, shook his spear and scoffed, "Oh, yes? And how did you do that?"

"I used an ox hide—" Amero stopped his explanation abruptly. He had floated down beneath an ox hide. It was the truth, but it didn't sound like the truth. Indeed, it sounded ridiculous.

"We've seen you fly in and out of the cave, monster, and we know you can take on human shape. You've killed off all the elk and deer in this range. Our children go hungry!" The man with the braid raised his voice, his face reddening with rage. "And what did you do with our father, Genta? Last autumn he went hunting for you and never came back!"

The skull in Duranix's cave had belonged to a big man, he suddenly remembered. All four of the hunters—all four brothers—were head and shoulders taller than Amero.

"I'm not the monster," he insisted. "I was taken captive by Duranix—that's his name—but I escaped. I dived into the lake and swam ashore. My name is Amero, son of Oto and Kinar."

"Don't lie to us, dragon!"

Dragon? The word meant nothing to Amero. "No," he insisted, "my name is Amero."

Two of the hunters prodded him from behind. Amero staggered forward, stung by the sharp spear points. The angry hunters might kill him at any time. He pointed to his cut and abraded feet and held out his scraped hands.

"Look at me!" he declared. "I bleed, as you do. Does your monster bleed? Is dragon's blood red?"

Mole-face grasped his hand, running a callused thumb over Amero's lacerated palm. "Feels like a girl's hand," he muttered.

Amero snatched his hand back indignantly. "I'm not the monster you seek, but he is returning at dusk from his day's hunt. We should get away from here, quickly, before he finds us."

The brothers had a loud debate over what to do. The eldest, the one with the braid, was called Annom. He wanted to kill Amero just in case he was the dragon. Mole-face, called Hatu by the others, had a sounder idea. They would tie up Amero and hide, watching the cave to see if Duranix returned. If he did, then Amero's story would have more weight. Perhaps he would swoop down and they could capture him. If he didn't return, they would know Amero was actually Duranix and could cut his throat then.

The brothers agreed on Hatu's plan. They lashed Amero's hands behind his back with a length of vine and shoved him into the brush. Hatu cut a leafy bough and used it to erase their tracks in the sand. The two younger brothers, Ramay and Nebo, crouched on either side of Amero, their spears digging into the boy's ribs. Annom scanned the sky a while, then joined the others under cover.

The sun sank behind the western ridge, painting the highest peaks crimson and pink. Twilight came and shadows lengthened. The sky remained clear.

When Soli, the white moon, appeared in a notch between the northern peaks, Annom cleared his throat.

"The dragon has lied to us."

They hauled Amero out and threw him to his knees. Annom drew back his spear.

"Wait!" Amero cried shrilly. "I'm not your monster!"

"Enough lies! Before I kill you, tell me what happened to our father!"

"I don't know. I've never been to this valley before in my life! I am Amero, son of Oto and Kinar, brother of Nianki and Menni—"

Hatu snorted loudly in disbelief. Annom flexed strong fingers around the shaft of his spear and prepared to cast.

*I'm going to die!* was Amero's horrified thought.

Though flushed with terror-driven heat, Amero suddenly felt a chill run down his spine. The cooling twilight air vibrated, as from distant thunder. The boy turned his head, suddenly realizing what was coming.

Annom apparently felt nothing out of the ordinary, but merely stared coldly at him. "Die, monster," he said.

Amero shook his head. "Too late," he whispered.

An invisible hand swept down the ravine, throwing everyone to the ground. Amero found it hard to rise with his hands bound, but the four brothers were up in an instant. They formed a circle, all facing outward.

Duranix came strolling out of the encroaching shadows, his cape draped over one arm. The three younger brothers uttered cries of amazement. Without a word, Annom hurled his spear. Duranix deflected it with a mere wave of his hand.

"You! How did you get down here?" Duranix demanded of Amero. Hatu lined up to charge him while the others covered Amero with their spears.

"I jumped," the boy replied wearily. His fear of Duranix had not abated, but he knew he'd lost his chance of escape.

*Hold your breath.* Duranix's thought reverberated in Amero's head. Wisely, the boy asked no questions but did as he was told.

Hatu, yelling loudly, charged with spear leveled. Duranix awaited his attack with complete calm. When the big plainsman was just six steps away, Duranix opened his mouth and blew in the direction of his attacker.

Hatu staggered and stopped. The heavy spear fell from his hands. He backed a few steps, rubbing his eyes. Duranix inhaled deeply and blew again. Hatu's face went white with fear. He broke and ran. So did Nebo and Ramay. Only Annom remained, kneeling in the dirt, tears of futility flowing down his cheeks.

Duranix hauled Amero to his feet and pulled his bonds apart as though they were nothing. Then he grabbed Annom by his thick braid and pulled him to his feet.

"I'm trying to understand human behavior," Duranix said, "so I won't kill you—this time. But this boy is under my protection, do you hear? If any harm comes to him, I'll kill every human in the six valleys of the lake. Nod your head if you understand me." After an angry, frightened moment of stiffness, Annom nodded once. Duranix flung the big man aside. Annom stumbled away in the direction his brothers had fled.

"You're a great deal of trouble, Amero," Duranix said, planting his hands on his hips. "Why did you leave the cave?"

"I had no food," he replied warily, "and I didn't know what you planned to do to me."

"What do you mean?"

"I found bones in the cave." Amero took a deep breath. "Some of them were human."

"Oh." Duranix picked up Annom's spear and examined the workmanship. "I did eat that man."

Amero's heart skipped a beat. "He was the father of those four hunters. His name was Genta."

"Really? Strange. Even meals have names to you humans."

Trembling, Amero flung a hand out at Duranix. "Are you . . . are you a dragon?"

"So you learned a new word! And what is a dragon?"

"Some kind of monster that eats people!" Amero folded his hands into his armpits, hunching his body as though in pain. "Is that what you have planned for me?"

Duranix pressed his hand to his chest. "I give you my word, Amero, I will not eat you," he vowed solemnly. After a second's hesitation, he added, "At least, not without considerable provocation." He laughed, but Amero found no humor in his words.

Serious once more, Duranix said, "Let me tell you a story, a story about a monster and a human hunter.

"I was born far to the east on another mountain, but I've lived in this mountain range for over three hundred years, as you count them. For a long time I dwelled peacefully in this valley, sleeping in the open, confident no beast would dare disturb me. One day last fall—a magnificent day, too, the morning after the first frost—I woke to find a flint spear in my throat. It was a small wound, but no one had ever hurt me before—no one but another dragon, that is. Surprised, I lashed out and caught the one who was daring and stupid enough to attack me while I slumbered. It was this fur-wearing human. He was big for his race, with copper-colored hair and a beard to match. I was about to bite his head off when I was seized with curiosity. Why had he attacked me? I'd done nothing to him. I held him in one foreclaw and squeezed until he stopped struggling and cursing at me.

" 'What do you think you're up to, little one?' I asked.

" 'Ridding the valley of a monster,' he replied boldly.

" 'Monster? Me?' I'd never been addressed as such. I asked him what made me a monster. His answer was badly phrased, but in essence he claimed I was an unnatural creature, who did not belong in the world of men and beasts.

" 'Men *are* beasts,' I pointed out, with inescapable logic. 'You think because you walk upright and make tools of stone you're better than other animals?'

" 'Men were created by the Great Spirits to be like them and represent them in this world,' he avowed stubbornly. Monsters, he told me, were an affront to the Great Spirits' purpose.

"I earnestly wanted to know more about this belief of his, because if it were widespread, then my peaceful life would soon be over. Packs of smelly, hairy men would be hunting me and my kind wherever we chose to dwell. As I bore no particular ill-will toward humans, I wanted to understand the irrational hatred he seemed to have for me."

"Did he explain?" the boy asked, caught up in the tale.

Duranix jabbed the spear into the stony ground, burying half the length of the shaft. "No, he did not," he said peevishly. "He went back to cursing me. I kept him captive for some days while I enlarged the natural cave behind the waterfall as a safe haven for myself. After it was ready I brought him there and released him from his bonds. The first night, he tried to assault me with a stone. I broke his skull." Duranix sighed. "I didn't really mean to. Humans are so frail."

"And then you—ate him?"

He shrugged. "Later, yes. I was hungry, and it seemed a shame to waste him. If it's any consolation to you, he didn't taste very good. Humans are too stringy. Elk are much to be preferred."

Soli was well up in the star-flecked sky. Its clean, cold light made the sand and gravel look like snow.

"What did you do to the hunters?" Amero asked after a moment of silence. "Why did they run away?"

"I can exhale a gas that engenders extreme trepidation in those who inhale it." Amero regarded him blankly. Duranix added, "My breath causes fear."

The boy nodded slowly. He looked away, staring silently at the landscape and pondering what he'd heard. Duranix remained quiet as well.

At last, the dragon said, "I want you to stay, Amero, but I won't compel you. You can walk away now if you wish, and I won't stop you."

"If I stay, what will happen?" Amero asked warily.

"How should I know? Am I one of your Great Spirits? The future is a day no one has seen yet." Duranix scratched the ground with his foot. "As I said, I think we can learn from each other. More humans arrive on the plains and in the mountains every season. If I'm to live among them, I think we'd better understand each other, don't you?"

After only a moment's reflection, Amero nodded. "I will stay," he said simply.

He started walking down the draw toward the lake. Duranix called for him to wait.

"One more thing. I've used this human form to avoid frightening you. I modeled it after the man I caught—you said his name was Genta? I want you to see how I really look, Amero. Let that be the first step on our path together."

Duranix walked a ways up the ravine and stopped. He spread his arms wide and threw his head back. In the blink of an eye he swelled several times in size and lost his human coloring. Dropping down on all fours, his arms became thick, muscular forelegs with three massive claws and a single rear toe. His torso spread until it was wider than any man's. He had huge, powerful rear legs, bent in a graceful curve like the haunches of a panther. A tail, a good five paces long and ending with a barbed tip, curled up behind his back and scraped the valley walls.

Amero felt a sensation almost like heat. Unmasked, Duranix shed a sort of radiance the boy could feel. It was like the sun on a cold day—a warmth that felt both good and strong. Or was it a cool breeze on a hot day—except the breeze left no sensation of movement? For a moment, Amero was dazed, dazzled. He stepped forward, hand outstretched, numbed by the dragon's presence.

The most arresting feature of Duranix the dragon was his head. More angular than a snake's, the reptilian skull was huge and wide. Barbels hung down from its chin, and yellow membranes flickered sideways back and forth across eyes whose pupils were vertical slits.

Breath from the dragon's nostrils—each as wide as a stout tree trunk—raised swirls of dust at Amero's feet. Across his brow were two upswept horns, matched by a larger set curving back from the broad crown of his head. From nose to tail Duranix was at least fifteen paces long, and he was covered in oval, overlapping, shiny red-gold scales.

When the transformation was complete, Amero staggered, as though released from a powerful hold. He pulled his makeshift tool from his waist and stared at it. His tool, and the strange things in the cave he'd called leaves, were actually the dragon's scales. Duranix must shed a few every day, the way a man left hairs where he lay.

"You're the stormbird!" he exclaimed in awe. "I saw you flying through the clouds the night before you saved me from the yevi!"

Duranix cocked his huge head. "Stormbird, eh?" he said. "I like that. Much more elegant than 'dragon.' "

Duranix's chest heaved. He thrust his serpentine neck forward until his massive head was less than an arm's length from Amero's wide eyes. The effect was so terrifying Amero's knees failed and he sat down hard.

The dragon opened his mouth, revealing wickedly curved fangs. It took Amero a heart-pounding moment to realize that Duranix was actually grinning at him.

"What do you think of me now?" the creature asked. The voice was still recognizably his, but the sheer power of it, even at a whisper, rattled Amero's teeth.

The boy opened his mouth but no sound came out, so he swallowed and began again. "I hope we shall always be friends."

Duranix snorted. Dirt and pebbles flew. He hoisted his head high and said, "Come! I want hear how you escaped from the cave on your own. You have much ingenuity for a human!"

"Could I eat first?" Amero asked faintly.

"Of course! I spotted a herd of mountain goats in the third valley on my way here. Do you like goat?" Amero nodded. He was hungry enough at this moment to eat dragon.

Duranix seized him in his left foreclaw. The grip was irresistible, yet surprisingly gentle. Long narrow wings unfolded from his back. They stretched upward, and without waiting for further comment, Duranix launched into the air with a single massive leap. Amero nearly fainted from the shock of his powerful ascent. The ground dropped away with a rush.

As the dragon flapped his wings to gain altitude, Amero took in deep breaths to calm his pounding heart. The dizziness faded. The stars wheeled overhead and wind whipped at his long hair. Amero knew a sudden urge to shout with joy. He wanted to savor every moment of his first conscious flight.

It was a memory he would long cherish.

# Chapter 5

~

Days passed, then weeks.

With some idea of finding her mother's people, Nianki put the morning sun on her left, the setting sun on her right, and followed ancient trails across plain and woodland. She was going where she had never been, which Oto had taught her was never wise, and she was alone. Walking by night under a vault of stars, she felt at times like the last woman alive. She passed dark campsites under the white moon's gleam, finding nothing in them but broken weapons and scraps of clothing stained with blood. Hidden eyes seemed to follow her progress, but no one attacked her. Pakito's short spear saw to that.

Twenty times she saw Soli rise and set, and on the twenty-first morning she came to a wide river she couldn't easily ford. It flowed west to east, unlike the rivers in her home range. More proof the world was upside down! Nianki tracked along the river bank a full day without finding a place to cross, then gave up and swam to the other side.

The river turned south, so Nianki followed it until she came to the sea. She'd heard about the sea from Kinar, who'd seen it often as a child. Kinar described it as an endless lake, stretching from horizon to horizon, so vast one could not see the opposite shore. She also shared the stories of her coastal ancestors, stories of fearsome monsters that dwelled in the depths, and of massive, deadly tempests lasting for days, scourging the sea and land.

One hot day in late summer, Nianki arrived at a high head-land and beheld the sea. Though it was fully as big as she'd been told, she saw no sign on its calm green-blue waters of sea monsters or storms.

There were, however, many people. She began to encounter increasing numbers of strangers—almost thirty by the time she reached the sea. This was more human company than Nianki had ever seen at one time in her life. The climate was mild, and the local folk seemed placid and accepting. Small bands of centaurs moved among them without rancor, a state of affairs new to Nianki. On the high savanna, plainsfolk and centaurs were competitors, and both were wary of strangers. Unnerved by the crowds, Nianki kept to herself, making contact only when she needed to barter for food.

The coast was rich in forage and game, even with the large number of people about. Much of the provender was strange to her. Fish she knew, but some of the other things the locals ate—like shellfish, crabs, and seaweed—disgusted her. For some days she subsisted on rabbit and wild strawberries, supplemented by fish she obtained in return for mending a local man's nets.

Gradually her wounds healed, her body grew strong, and she was able to hunt. As the seaside sun baked her skin even darker, the scars stood out as bold streaks and splotches. Nianki wore her marks with pride. She'd won them by surviving, surpassing even her father's toughness.

Her harsh appearance proved to be an asset in dealing with others. People saw the scars on her face, neck, and arm and knew they were in the presence of a hunter and fighter, not merely some man's abandoned mate. For herself, the scars also served as tangible memorials of her lost family. Each healed bite, each ragged tear, kept the memory of her father, mother, and brothers alive.

Despite the easy climate and plentiful food here on the coastal plain, every day Nianki saw families large and small leaving, trudging north. At first she gave it no thought, but when she realized they moved even during the punishing heat of midday when sensible folk took their ease, she began to wonder at the reason.

She was sleeping one night within sight of the beach when the sound of footfalls woke her. Snatching up her spear, Nianki rose swiftly to one knee, ready to strike. Instead of marauding four-footed beasts, she found herself faced by a family of four—an old, white-bearded man, a stocky woman of some thirty seasons, and two children—a boy and girl of six and eight. They carried food and water on a pair of willow-withe travois, the woman dragging one, the children the other.

"Peace to you," said the old man, holding up both hands to show they were empty. "We didn't mean to wake you."

"Where are you going?" Nianki asked.

"The mountains," said the woman, eyeing the scarred girl warily. "As we must every summer."

Nianki lowered her spear. "Now? There are beasts abroad in the night."

"We should have left days ago, but the boy was sick with a flux." As she spoke, the woman kept sidling away. Nianki moved in front of her, blocking her path.

"I'm a stranger to these parts," said Nianki. "If there's danger, I want to know."

The woman's eyes darted back and forth. "I don't know what you mean."

"When I arrived, people were thick as tadpoles here. Now everyone's leaving. What are you frightened of?"

"The Good People," chimed the girl child.

"Shh!" hissed the old man. "Don't speak their name!"

"Who are 'the good people'?" Nianki demanded.

The woman tried to barge past. Nianki grabbed her arm. The old man moved to break Nianki's hold, but he found her spear point pressed into his throat. The young boy dropped his side of the travois and started to cry.

"Be still!" Nianki barked. Her fierce shout startled the boy enough that he subsided to a sniffle. The woman remained rooted where she stood, eyes downcast.

"You," Nianki said to the old man. "Talk."

His jaw worked. "Every summer, the Good People come here from the east. They are powerful in spirit, but difficult to deal with. Some use their wisdom to help and heal us. Others treat us like game and hunt us for sport, so every summer we leave the shore and travel to the mountains."

"What do they look like?"

"They are comely people, graceful and lightly made, yet strong. Their color is not like ours—their skin is very fair, and their hair like a dandelion's. They wear strange bright clothing and command beasts to do their bidding."

It sounded like a fable, but they were obviously terrified of something. Nianki moved her spear from the old man's neck.

62

"Be off," she said.

"You'd best leave, too," the woman warned. "The Good People are not to be trusted. They could take your head for a trophy, as they did my poor mate's three summers past."

"I'm fairly warned. Go."

The children picked up their poles and tugged the travois. Their mother bent her back and pushed on ahead, breaking the trail for them. The old man lingered.

"Fifteen summers past I'd have fought you for this," he said, fingering the mark on his throat Nianki's spear made.

"Fifteen summers past I fought only for my mother's milk."

He scowled as he hurried after his family. The old man limped badly, hips rocking from side to side as he walked. He must have taken a bad fall once, and the bones had never set properly.

Nianki moved her camp in case the old hunter decided to double back and visit her while she slept. She laid a circle of twigs on the ground around her, overlapping them. If anyone tried to creep up on her, she'd hear them when they trod on the brittle wood.

The remainder of the night passed peacefully. Dawn broke hot and hazy, and Nianki was awakened by itching all over her body. From the welts on her ribs and legs, she knew she'd been found by a host of sand fleas.

She searched wide and far for a stream to bathe in, but fresh water was sadly lacking in the pine barrens above the beach. Scratching furiously, she resolved to wash in the sea. She had never before dared immerse herself in the sea, but it was the only body of water around large enough to cover her, and she couldn't bear the terrible burning itch—the fleas had even invaded her hair.

Down to the beach she went, shedding her clothes. The cold surf felt wonderful on her tormented skin, and she plunged in head first.

Surfacing, she spat water, surprised by the salty tang. The bites stung a bit, but the itching rapidly subsided. She held her head under for as long as she could stand to drown the miserable insects. When she popped up again, she heard voices coming from the beach.

63

Far down the shore was a sizable party, twelve or thirteen people with animals. The beasts were easier to make out than the people—tall, four-legged creatures, built like elk but less bulky and without antlers. The animals were walking in the midst of the people, tame and docile.

A screech overhead alerted her to the presence of a falcon. It circled the beach in advance of the party, its shrill cry audible above the churning waves. The bird of prey swooped down on the people and animals, coming to land—she was astonished to note—on the arm of one of the men.

Nianki was eight paces from the beach, treading water. Swimming in the surf was tiring, and the cold water sapped the strength in her legs. Early twinges of cramp warned her to seek land. She swam slowly toward shore, keeping her head down and aiming for her pile of clothes. Her short spear was underneath them.

The mixed band of men and animals was approaching rapidly. They were too close now for Nianki to emerge from the water and not be seen. On closer inspection, she counted twelve men and four of the long-legged beasts. Two of the men were actually riding astride the backs of two of the animals, and the creatures didn't seem to mind. Words spoken by the old man last night floated into her head: *They wear strange clothing and command beasts to do their bidding.* Were these the Good People everyone feared?

The strangers' clothing was indeed odd. Instead of faded brown buckskin or tawny hides, they wore smooth, flowing garments, green as leaves. Some wore hoods on their heads of the same green material. Six of the men on foot carried very long spears, and on their heads something shiny caught the light and flashed.

The lead figure pointed and said something unintelligible in a loud voice. Nianki followed his rigid finger to her discarded clothing. The spear carriers ran forward as the foremost figure dug through her pile of clothes, locating her spear in the process.

By this time she was lying on her stomach in very shallow water. Waves were breaking over her head, and a nagging cramp clutched at her right calf. Why didn't they move on? It was just a pile of clothes and a short spear—or were they looking for the owner?

She pushed herself backward into deeper water. Cramp or no cramp, she could swim past the interlopers and leave the water behind them, out of sight. Nianki paddled along slowly, parallel to the shore.

"Ay-ha!" One of the mounted men had spotted her. Those on foot came back on the double. A spearman cast his weapon. It fell harmlessly short. The other mounted man spoke sharply to the spear carriers, who fell into line and remained in place as Nianki swam away.

They weren't pursuing her, but the two riders were. Nianki cursed their ingenuity. They had the use of their animals' longer legs and greater strength. Even swimming as hard as she could, she couldn't outdistance strong animals.

She tried trickery. Diving, she swam a few paces in the same direction, then doubled back. When she came up for air, she saw the two riders had split up to cover both directions. They hadn't left their mother's arms yesterday, these two.

The cramp in her leg was getting worse. Nianki struggled to keep her head up. A few paces in, it was shallow enough for her to stand on her good leg, but the waves kept pounding her. One especially large roller lifted her off her feet and sent her tumbling onto the beach. In a flash, she was up and heading for the trees as fast as her hopping gait could take her. The strangers shouted to each other in their unknown tongue.

Leg burning with every stride, Nianki gritted her teeth and kept going. Halfway to the dunes her right leg seized completely, and she fell. Immediately she was surrounded by slender hoofed legs.

Coiling her good leg beneath her, Nianki sprang up so suddenly that one of the animals shied away, almost tossing its rider to the sand. Before Nianki could exploit this, a heavy net was thrown over her, and she went down again, tangled in its folds.

Somebody hit her with a wooden spear shaft. More blows followed until a clear, authoritative voice rang out and the beating stopped. Several pairs of hands dragged Nianki upright and pulled the net away from her head. Quaking with rage, Nianki found herself staring at a ring of spear points.

"Be still, and no one will hurt you," said a calm voice.

The speaker was sitting atop one of the animals. By his age and demeanor, she decided he was the father of the other louts.

"Let me go!" she demanded angrily. "Why do you attack me?"

The speaker said something to his companions in their incomprehensible tongue. They laughed. Nianki worked her hands through the folds of the net and with a few furious shakes, managed to loosen it enough that it fell to the sand around her. Alarmed, the spear carriers shoved their weapons close to her face and chest.

The speaker raised his hand and bade them stop. In the midst of her peril, Nianki was struck by the fact the man's hands were covered in supple hide, cleverly made to encase each finger separately. His eyes were remarkably large and an arresting shade, bright blue like the sky. He mopped his brow with his sleeve and threw back the hood from his head. Nianki gaped. His ears were bizarrely malformed—tall and pointed. There was no doubt in her mind now. These must be the ones the family had called the Good People. Trouble was, she didn't think they were people at all.

"Do you understand me?" he asked. She nodded curtly. "My name is Balif, of House Protector, first warrior of Silvanos, lord of all the elves."

"Words, words, words," Nianki muttered.

"None of which mean anything to you, I know. Do you have a name?" She maintained a sullen silence. He asked again just as genially.

"Nianki," she said, biting her name into three hard syllables. "You are the Good People."

Her words amused Balif, and he said something in his own language to his comrades. They laughed again and she realized he must have translated the phrase for them. To Nianki he said, "Is that what humans call elves?"

"I don't know 'elves,' but you're the only Good People I've met." She began to feel chilled, sitting naked on the sand. "Well, what will you do? Ravish me, or just take my head as trophy?"

Balif actually looked startled. His sky-colored eyes widened in shock. "Nothing of the sort. Give the human her clothes."

Sandy buckskins were thrown at her feet. Nianki stood up under the strangers' gaze, and donned her clothes. One or two comments were made, and she was just as glad not to know what had been said.

Hardly had she cinched the bone buckle around her waist when her arms were seized and a wide collar clamped around her neck. It was cold, hard, and smooth, and try as she might, she couldn't loosen it. Her captors tied a strong cord to a ring on the front of the collar.

"What is this?" she yelled, pulling at the collar. "What are you doing?"

"I am here on a mission for my lord," said Balif, turning his beast away. "You will not be harmed if you come peacefully."

He spoke in his own language, and the elves on foot formed themselves two by two and walked in step back up the beach. The other riding elf was given the end of Nianki's tether, which he tied to his wrist. He and Balif bumped their heels against their animals' flanks and rode on.

Nianki dug in her own heels. Her determination, though powerful, was no match for the strength of the long-legged beasts. She was jerked abruptly forward and had to flail about wildly to regain her balance.

She was forced to jog to keep up. The cramp had eased, but her right leg was still sore. Cursing loud and long, she struggled to maintain the pace. If she slowed or fell, she knew she'd be dragged.

"Where are you taking me?" she demanded breathlessly.

"To our camp, a few leagues from here," Balif replied.

"What's 'league'?"

"Five thousand, one hundred paces," he said, which was no help at all. Nianki had never had cause to count much above a hundred, so the number meant no more to her than the strange word.

"Why are you doing this?" she said, after abandoning the puzzle of distance. "I've done no wrong to you."

"You wouldn't understand if I told you."

His easy superiority enraged her. "Yes, I would!"

He pulled back on the lines tied to his animal's mouth. It stopped immediately. The walking elves halted as well. Nianki decided this Balif must be a stern father. Men and animals alike obeyed him rigidly.

"This territory has been claimed by my lord Silvanos. It will be added to his realm. You wandering barbarians will be expelled from the land east of the Kharolis River, in order that elves can be settled here. Those humans resisting us will be killed. Those captured, like yourself, will be taken to a camp north of here and held until it is determined whether or not you carry lethal diseases. If you're fit, you'll be marched to the central plain and released, on condition you never return to our land."

She understood the words, but the ideas behind them made no sense to her. Land was what you lived on. It wasn't a thing you could grasp in your hand, like a stone or a spear. How could anyone claim it? The one thing she did clearly comprehend was that they intended to hold her against her will.

The why of it eluded her. Among her people it sometimes happened that men took women as mates against their wills, or a dishonest hunter might covet and take another's weapon, but this capture baffled her. She had nothing of value the elves could covet, and Balif's reaction when she'd asked if he intended to ravish her dispelled any notion of lust on his part. For all she knew, Good People weren't even made like men and women under their clothes.

Still, she had no intention of being led around on a string. Surrounded by the elves with their animals and spears, there wasn't much she could do at the moment, but she wagered that even the Good People had to sleep sometime.

As she jogged along between the animals, she passed the time by studying her captors. The old man's words were true and false. The elves—she decided not to think of them as "Good People" any longer—weren't ugly, though their slenderness and light coloring made them unlike any plainsmen she'd ever seen. They were abundantly clever, with their smooth clothes, bright adornments, and tame animals, but Nianki saw no sign of special spirit-power in them. The spear carriers sweated in the heat as they tramped along behind the riders. They obviously feared her strength and fleetness if they resorted to a collar and cord to restrain her. No, they were strong in cleverness, but not in spirit-power, and that meant she could fight them.

The morning was gone when they reached a shallow valley lined with heavy scrub. On the other side, a dense forest loomed. The ancient trees grew so large and close that it looked like nothing larger than a fox could enter. The elves seemed pleased to see the forest, and Nianki deduced they lived within it.

An animal-borne elf arrived and spoke excitedly to Balif. With broad sweeps of his arm, Balif ordered his sons to follow the new rider as he galloped into the valley. Nianki called to him as he was about to follow them.

"Balif! Where do you go?"

"More of your kind have been flushed from the ravine. We're going to round them up," he said. His animal pranced and snorted, anxious to go. "I leave you with Tamanithas. We shall return shortly."

"Think your son is up to it?" she retorted.

His high brow arched still higher. "Son?"

"These fellows are your sons, yes? That's why they follow you and do your bidding."

Balif steered his animal in a half-circle. "These are my retainers. They are not of my blood." He galloped after the departed spear carriers.

Alone with the other rider, Tamanithas, Nianki promptly sat down. The elf eyed her with a haughty expression. He uttered a short, no doubt uncomplimentary, phrase.

"Don't jabber at me," she said crossly. His response was to wrap her cord around his hand a few more turns. "What kind of hunter are you, anyway, who follows not his father but a stranger? Do you even know who your father is?"

He snapped a single word at her, probably the elf equivalent of "shut up." Nianki noted his irritation and was pleased. She leaned forward slightly and let the cord fall slack on the ground. With a surreptitious shove of her foot, she pushed the cord toward the animal's left rear foot. She didn't think the creature's hoof was sharp enough to cut the cord, but if Tamanithas was a little careless, she'd have the better of him yet.

"Good People? I laugh! You elves are no better than the hunting pack that gave me these!" She waved a hand over her scars. "Look how many of you it took to catch a lone woman swimming in the sea!"

69

The elf glowered, repeating his command. Nianki spat in the dust.

"You think you can possess the land itself? Why, if you got down off that beast and faced me, I'd wring your neck like a rabbit's." She illustrated her remarks by placing her fists one atop the other and making twisting gestures.

Tamanithas shouted and pulled a weapon from a wooden sheath hanging from his waist. The weapon was like a knife, but it was as long as his arm and made of the same hard shiny stuff as her collar and the hard shells the marching elves wore on their heads. There was no mistaking the purpose of the thing's wicked point, which he waved in front of her face with harsh imprecations.

The elf turned his animal a quarter-turn to the left in order to present his weapon. That was the move Nianki had been hoping for. The animal stepped over the slack cord. She took the line in both hands and jerked hard.

Tamanithas's mount felt the cord binding its hind leg and tried to shuffle out of it. Nianki dug in her heels and pulled harder. The elf shouted at her. By now the beast's legs were hopelessly tangled, and with a loud squeal, it toppled over. Tamanithas was thrown face first to the ground.

Nianki tried to leap on the elf's unguarded back, but the cord pulled her up short and she couldn't reach him. The animal thrashed its legs and tried to stand. Braving the broad hooves, Nianki wrapped several lengths of cord around its legs. She looked at the fallen elf. He wasn't moving.

With some stretching, she was able to retrieve his weapon. It was sharper than flint and cut the cord to her neck easily. Nianki rolled Tamanithas over. He'd hit the ground hard. His nose was bloody and he'd probably spit out a few teeth, but he breathed. She thought briefly of dispatching him with his own weapon, but since the elves hadn't harmed her when they could easily have killed her, she spared him.

The animal continued to struggle and bellow. Nianki feared the noise would draw the others back, so she clipped the cord tangling its legs, and the beast reared up, rolling its eyes and looking highly indignant. Nianki spread her arms and shouted, "Hai! Hai!" The creature pivoted on its hind legs and bolted through the trees.

She ran in the opposite direction, east. The elves would expect her to run west or north, toward open country.

Down she went into the scrub-filled valley. Saplings and underbrush were so thick she couldn't work up any speed. The elves' animals couldn't follow into these dense thickets, but pursuers on foot certainly could. She zigzagged through the trees. When fallen logs or hanging vines were available, she traveled across them, leaving a much less obvious trail.

Nianki ran until the land began to rise again. The other side of the valley was the homeland of the elves. She certainly didn't want to go there. Yet her pursuers were likely not far behind, so she needed a place to hide. She found a fallen ash tree that had been hollowed by ants. Both ends were open, and she tested the width to make certain her shoulders would fit inside. They would.

As she was investigating the hollow tree, she spotted a large hornets' nest high up in another tree. That would make an excellent diversion.

She took off her buckskin shirt and climbed near the nest. Hornets as long as her thumb buzzed warily around her. With a length of branch she draped her shirt very, very carefully around the globe of bark and mud. Shinnying down, she went back to her hollow log. If the elves tracked her, they might see her shirt and think she was hidden among the leafy branches. If they used spears or rocks to bring her down, they'd get a face full of hornets for their trouble.

Nianki slipped into the log and lay still. She took slow and deep breaths to quiet her racing heart. Though inside the log was hot and dank, it was far better than being led around by a tether.

She fingered the collar, still firmly in place around her neck. The entire circumference was smooth, save for an oval hole in front. How did this thing work? She tugged and twisted it, but only succeeded in choking herself.

Voices. Heavy footfalls crashing through the underbrush. The elves were coming!

Nianki heard several voices shouting back and forth, and the tramp of many feet came nearer. She thought for a moment she recognized the voice of Tamanithas, speaking loud, unintelligible words to his comrades. No doubt he was cursing the perfidy of his barbarian charge. A cry from nearby brought all other conversation to a stop. They'd found something.

She heard several pairs of feet pass by her hiding place. Nianki held her breath. Something cold touched the sole of her left foot. Had they found her? She bit her hand to prevent herself from making a sound. No cries of discovery followed, and she wondered what was pressing lightly against her foot. No sooner had she thought about it, than the sensation began creeping up her leg.

The open end of the log pointed to the sky. A man of normal height on foot could not see into the log, but an elf on horseback could. Nianki saw Balif ride by, his aquiline profile dark against the bright sky. He didn't see her.

Whatever was crawling on her had reached the small of her back. Nianki resisted an urge to bolt from her hiding place. If she was still, it would leave her alone. If she didn't bother it, it wouldn't bother her. That was true, yes?

Dry and cool to the touch, the thing passed over her right shoulder. The sensation was maddening, made all the worse because she could not squirm, scratch, or reach back to find out what it was. When it brushed Nianki's right ear, she clenched her eyes shut so tightly tears oozed from the corners. Her breath came in ragged little puffs, lips pressed together, nostrils flaring.

Something passed by her cheek. She opened one eye, her right, and saw a blur of green and black. Her stomach knotted. Green and black were the colors of the ground viper, the most poisonous snake in the forest. If its head was by her cheek, and she could still feel it slithering across her heel, the viper must be at least two paces long.

The snake's thick triangular head dipped below her jaw, seeking the bottom of the log. Nianki's hands were clenched into fists under her chin, her arms pinned in place by the tight confines of her sanctuary. She held her breath again as more of the snake crossed under her face. She had one chance of escaping both the viper and the elves. It required absolute accuracy, even by the poor light inside the log. As the snake turned its head left to make room for the rest of its bulky body, Nianki struck. She opened her mouth wide and bit down hard. She had to get close enough behind the serpent's head so that it couldn't bite her in return. If it did, she would die inside this moldering old log.

Scales gritted between her teeth. The snake's pliant bones resisted, then broke under the pressure. Hissing furiously, the snake's body coiled and flailed. Nianki pushed her right hand out and grabbed the angry serpent. A flickering sensation against her left eye was the viper's tongue, lashing in vain. Nianki ground her jaws together, into the meat of the snake. Its struggles diminished. She pulled with her hand against the grip of her own teeth and the viper's head came off. She held on until she was sure it was dead, then she spat it out.

All through her silent battle, the hubbub outside had grown louder. Triumphant cries gave way to screams and obvious maledictions. Nianki heard running and the unmistakable sounds of falling. They must have found her shirt—and the hornets' nest.

Weary, she lowered her head to the lichen-coated wood. She remained in the log until well after the round patch of blue sky at the open end had changed first to purple, then to black.

At last Nianki crawled out. Listening carefully for prowling elves, she stretched her cramped body. All she heard was the normal nightly chorus of frogs and crickets. She saw the pale splotch of her shirt lying on the ground. Shivering from the cool night air, she retrieved it and quickly put it on.

Nianki pulled from the hollow tree the long carcass of the snake she'd killed. Properly dried, viper meat was good to eat. She slung the dead snake over her shoulder and, with the stars as her guide, began the trek away from the elves' country.

As she walked, the words of the old man at the seashore came back to her. *Powerful in spirit, but difficult to deal with.* In her opinion, the elves were a difficulty, but not insurmountable. They seemed less dangerous than the vile beasts that had taken her family, and yet . . .

She grasped the cold smooth body of the dead snake. There were things in the wilderness a good hunter couldn't ignore, things that wouldn't leave you alone even if you were quiet and still.

Plainsmen were leaving the south to escape the elves. Nianki would go, too. Her mother's people would be gone anyway. There was no help for her to be had, no hands to rely on but her own.

So be it.

# Chapter 6

~

Squeezing through the large upper opening in the cave wall, Duranix dropped four smoldering goat carcasses on the floor. In his true shape, he filled the great cave to an alarming degree. Amero ducked and dodged the dragon's feet and tail, yet still managed to catch a stunning blow from one of Duranix's wingtips. Seeing his discomfort, Duranix resumed human form.

Amero picked himself up from the cave floor, grumbling, "It's like being a mouse in a bear's den."

"I see I'll have to remain small for you."

"Is it hard for you to stay in your man-shape?"

"It's confining, but there are some advantages. Being human muffles my senses somewhat, which makes it easier to be around you."

Amero touched a steaming haunch. He snatched his fingers back and blew on them. "What do you mean?"

Duranix wrenched off a charred goat leg. The sizzling meat didn't burn him at all. "Humans smell bad. Odors stick to that soft skin of yours. While I'm in human form, the smell doesn't bother me as much."

Amero could smell nothing but burned goat flesh. He asked the dragon why the animals were so seared.

"I take them down with bolts of lightning," Duranix explained. "That way I don't have to chase them so long. Also, seared meat is more digestible than raw."

Though his skepticism was evident, when the goat cooled Amero tried cooked meat for the first time. At first it tasted dirty, as if it had been dropped on the ground, but under the charred crust the meat was tender and tasted less burned. To his surprise, Amero found himself enjoying the dragon's fare.

Human-sized or not, Duranix had the appetite of his larger form. He ate three of the goats and most of the fourth, leaving Amero to snatch what he could in between. When Duranix was done, only a few bones remained. His stomach ought to have been bulging alarmingly, but he looked no different than before. Amero gathered up the leftover bones and put them on the pile at the rear of the cave.

When he returned, he found Duranix at the lower opening, gazing out. His usual breezy manner was suddenly subdued.

"What troubles you?" Amero asked.

"The yevi have entered the plain in strength," said the dragon. "Though they try to hide from me, I counted more than a hundred between the western forest and the fork of the Plains River. I can only assume even more are roaming the regions I didn't inspect."

"What does it mean?"

"It means hard times for you humans. The yevi will sweep your small hunting bands from the plain before winter sets in." Duranix turned to regard his young friend. "The destruction of your family will be repeated many times."

Amero knew what that meant. His sleep was still troubled by nightmares of his family's destruction. In his dreams, he had to watch helplessly, unable to move, as Oto, Kinar, Nianki, and Menni were torn apart by ravening yevi.

He said urgently, "Can't you stop them?"

Duranix clasped his hands behind his back. "I am only one. They are many."

"Why is this happening?" Amero demanded, pacing up and down behind Duranix. "Where do the yevi come from?"

"They come from the depths of the great marsh that lies on the far side of the western forest. There Sthenn plots to displace free creatures, like you humans, with his own minions. He's a green dragon, my elder by a thousand years, and a clever, vicious character. He's tried to kill me before. When I was but a hatchling, he brought down an avalanche on our nest, killing my two clutchmates and grievously wounding my mother."

For the first time Amero felt a common bond with his fantastic protector. Both of them had lost their families, and both, ultimately, to the same villain.

"Why did Sthenn try to kill you?" Amero asked. "Why does he try to wipe out the plainsfolk?"

Duranix turned away from the dark door. For a moment, Amero saw his eyes gleam in the dim light.

"You've lived long enough to know the world is made up of competing forces. Red ants fight the black ants. Wolves bring down a deer and are chased away from their kill by panthers. Men, ogres, and centaurs rove the plains and mountains, trying to stay ahead of hunger, disease, and one another. Do you understand?"

Amero nodded mutely.

"Even dragons must compete, boy. Sthenn wants this land. I'm not sure why. There isn't much here. It isn't rich by dragon standards. Maybe he wants it only because I have it. Who knows? But I will not let him have it, not one tree, not one peak. I would fight your Great Spirits themselves to keep what is mine."

Amero was silent, not fully understanding what had been said. Duranix pulled some of the dry boughs from the boy's bed and piled them in the center of the cave. He pointed one hand at the pile and a tiny flare of lightning crackled forth, igniting the tinder. Soon the boughs were blazing brightly.

Amero had seen fire in the wild before, but he knew it as a faceless enemy, burning trees, consuming food, terrifying game. When Duranix started the fire the boy kept well back.

"Why are you skulking back there?" the dragon asked. "Come closer. Fire is something to respect, not fear. It's either good or bad, depending how you use it."

Amero approached the flames warily. The heat felt pleasant on his face. Duranix's cave was chilly by night, and the fire dispelled both the somber shadows and the clinging cold.

"How do we stop the yevi?" he asked, staring at the flames.

" 'We?' " said Duranix. He smiled, showing lots of teeth. " 'We' shall try to stop the spread of the yevi packs, somehow. I don't think Sthenn will come out to fight me, dragon to dragon. If we defeat the yevi, that will be enough for the time being."

Again, Amero didn't quite grasp every word, but he knew enough to believe Duranix could be a powerful ally to his people. But the plainsmen were scattered. How to let his people know? And what to do once Amero found them? Most, faced with Duranix in his natural shape, would react like Genta and his sons—they would want to kill the "monster." There had to be a way to let the hunters and plainsmen know that Duranix was actually their friend.

77

"No, boy, I'm not," the dragon said, once more hearing Amero's thoughts. "I don't love your kind. You're smelly, quarrelsome, and violent."

Amero opened his mouth to protest, but Duranix waved away the unspoken words.

"But, tiresome as you are, I prefer humans to Sthenn's mindless beasts. You at least can choose to be good or evil, and that makes you greater in spirit than all the yevi Sthenn commands." He tossed a dry branch on the fire. It blazed up, the flames casting weird shadows on the arching walls. "It puts you in advance of us dragons, too, in some ways."

Amero regarded him quizzically, disbelieving. Did he have a power the dragon didn't possess? If he did, what about other men and women? Would their collective strength be great enough to resist Sthenn?

This time Duranix did not respond to his unspoken question. Still in human form, the dragon had ascended to his broad stone bed and fallen deeply asleep. Eating did that, he'd explained earlier.

Amero watched the glowing embers of the dying fire for a long time. The fire fascinated him. He pushed a dry fir bough into the ashes and watched it catch light. As each needle flamed, it spread its fire to its neighbor, until they were all ablaze. Once burned, the fir bough fell rapidly to ash, crumbled, and disappeared. What if the yevi were like the fire, and the plainsfolk their kindling? If the plains people didn't band together, would they be consumed until nothing remained but smoke in the air and dust on the ground?

\* \* \* \* \*

"There must be an easier way," Amero said. He was standing inside the cave mouth, hundreds of paces above the foaming falls. He'd just asked Duranix how he was supposed to get down, and the dragon's first response was, "Jump."

"I'll carry you," Duranix said patiently.

"Well, yes, but—" He dug his toe into one of the shallow grooves in the cave floor. "Could you cut handholds in the rock for me?"

Fearlessly Duranix leaned out, bracing himself casually with one hand. "Do you really want to climb up and down a sheer cliff face?"

He didn't, but Amero hated being so dependent on the dragon. "I'll think of something else," he muttered.

Duranix wrapped an arm around Amero's chest and leaped through the waterfall. The brief shock of cold water was followed by a prolonged sensation of falling. Amero felt Duranix's arm transform from human to dragon. The great creature spread his wings, and with a snap, their downward plunge ceased.

Amero opened his eyes. They were gliding across the lake of the falls, a long triangle of water whose sharp end curled west and narrowed to become the Six Canyons River, a tributary of the mighty Plains River. Above them the sky was dotted with dull white clouds. The enormous shadow of the dragon raced over the placid surface of the lake, growing larger and faster as Duranix lost altitude. Beating his wings rapidly, the dragon slowed and lowered his hind legs. He landed lightly on a sandy hillock on the north side of the river.

With some effort, Duranix writhed and shrank into human form. He was red-faced and panting by the time he resumed his borrowed shape.

When Amero looked at him quizzically, the dragon said, "Going from large to small is work. From small to large is . . . liberating."

Since searching by air failed to turn up many of the roving yevi, Duranix had resolved to return to the plain on foot. At ground level he could pick up individual tracks, scents, and spoor of the yevi. He could see far when aloft, but the dragon could also be seen from far away. Tracking the hunting packs on the ground was a slower method but promised better results. He set off at a rapid pace that soon had Amero floundering to keep up.

"Wait—wait," the boy gasped, staggering through the waist-high grass. "Don't go so fast!"

"There's a lot of ground to cover. The faster I go, the sooner it will be done."

"I can't keep up! Remember, I'm only a human!" Duranix slackened his pace reluctantly, making no secret of his disdain for Amero's weakness.

The land below the mountains was terraced by flattened hills that widened and lowered as the pair headed west. Clumps of highland pines and cedars thinned until solitary ones stood out like lonely sentinels on the horizon. Striding along with no attempt at stealth, Duranix scattered herds of wild oxen ahead of them and flushed coveys of pigeons from the tall grass.

The boy and the human-shaped dragon made rapid progress. By midday the mountains were only a smudge at their backs. Duranix agreed to a respite when he reached a wide, flat boulder in the midst of the plain. Amero went scouting for water while the dragon perched comfortably atop the sun-baked stone, soaking up the heat like a basking lizard.

A small stream, choked with grass, ran down a gully a few dozen paces from Duranix's sunning spot. Amero parted the grass and dipped out a few handfuls of water. It was poor stuff compared to the waterfall, tasting tepid and weedy. He lifted his head and looked downstream. A fallen twig, boldly white against the green grass, lay half in the water not far away. Wood that white had to be birch, he thought, rising to his knees, but birch didn't grow on the high plains—

On closer inspection, the "twig" proved to be the arm bone of a human child a girl, judging by the scraps of clothing left on the skeleton. Rain had washed away the smell of decay, but the ferocious bite marks on the girl's bones were ample evidence of what had caused her death.

Amero recoiled in horror and opened his mouth to summon Duranix. Before he could form the words in his throat, Duranix was beside him.

"I heard your shock," said the dragon. He knelt by the pathetic remains. "Yevi?"

"Probably. A panther would eat the marrow from the long bones as well as the flesh, and a bear would carry a kill back to its den."

Duranix snapped an arm bone in two and sniffed the marrow inside. Amero grimaced.

"Dead no more than four days," said Duranix. "What the yevi left, the scavengers finished."

"She must have had a family," Amero said sadly. "I wonder what happened to them?"

Duranix stood up. "No trees nearby to hide in, and no caves. I'd say they were killed." He swept the horizon with his powerful senses, trying to locate any living humans or yevi in the vicinity.

His search was interrupted when Amero dropped to his knees and began to dig. With his bare hands he tore up tough lumps of prairie grass. Worms and grubs fled into the earth as quickly as he exposed them. He clawed angrily at the root-infested soil.

"What are you doing?"

"The girl must be buried, else her spirit cannot rest," Amero replied, without slackening.

"Is that true?"

"I believe it."

Duranix went down on one knee. With two sweeps of his hand, he doubled the depth of the hole Amero had started. When the hole was elbow deep, Amero gently placed the dry bones in it. Some of them were missing, but when all the bones present were placed in the hole, Amero said, "Rest now. May your ancestors greet you with joy."

Duranix cocked his head curiously at the boy's words but said nothing as Amero pushed the dirt back and pressed clumps of sod in place.

"There are no large beasts within range of my senses," Duranix said. "The girl's tracks show she was running from south to north when the yevi caught her. A child that young wouldn't be on her own, so we should go south to look for others in her party."

Amero sadly agreed, and they resumed their march.

The land grew flatter, and Duranix began to outpace Amero once more. The boy trudged along, beset by late autumn heat, buzzing flies, and the thoughts churning in his mind.

The child had been perhaps six or seven—older than his brother Menni, but far too young to meet the fate that had found her. He mourned her, though he'd never known her.

*See how the one lags behind. His mind wanders.*

Amero heard the voice in his head, a thin whisper, like the crackling of a dry reed. He looked left and right, ahead and behind. The only thing he saw was Duranix, striding along far in front of him.

*Quiet! It hears you!*

*Never! Two-legged beasts have no ears to hear us.*

Amero thumped his forehead with the heel of this hand. Who was whispering?

*Let him draw a few more paces back, and he will be ours!*

*What of the other?*

*He is too coarse to hear us, and we will be swift. Spread out, brothers.*

Sweat popped out on Amero's face, sweat brought on not by the trek but by sudden enlightenment. He was hearing the voices of yevi! They were near, close enough to see him and Duranix. Where were they? Why didn't the dragon hear them, too?

He feared to slow down too much or to call to Duranix, in case it precipitated their attack. What could he do?

He had a weapon.

The sharpened dragon scale was still shoved into the waist of his loincloth. It rode on his right hip, hard and inflexible. Head down, still shuffling his tired feet, Amero drew the scale. He hadn't yet made a handle for it, but the curved edge was keen enough to cut through the toughest hides in Duranix's cave. He let the tool dangle loosely from his hand.

*Duranix! Duranix, if you can hear me, help! Yevi are stalking me!* he thought as forcefully as he could. The tall figure of his human-disguised friend drew ahead, widening the gap between them.

Grass stems wavered against the prevailing breeze. Something was creeping up on him from both sides. Beads of sweat chilling on his skin, Amero kept his eyes locked on the path ahead, not daring to look right or left. In his mind's eye he imagined three of the gray killers crawling on their hollow bellies through the grass—one behind, one on each side. He gripped the dragon scale tighter. Now, over the hiss of wind in the grass and his own footsteps, he could hear the movements of the yevi clearly. Amero whirled, the sharp scale held horizontally at arm's length.

The yevi launched itself just as he turned, two hundred pounds of murderous stealth against eighty-five pounds of boy. It spied the bright dragon scale but failed to recognize it as a threat. The whetted edge sheered right into the animal's brow, slicing through fur, flesh, and into bone.

The full weight of the animal drove Amero to the ground. He yelled and kicked the creature, trying to shove it off. The smell of dusty fur and filth suffocated him. At any moment, he expected the savage jaws to close on his neck or face. When the yevi drew off him, he threw his hands up to ward off the expected attack.

It never came. Slowly Amero lowered his hands. Astonished, he saw the yevi's sightless, staring eyes and flaccid tongue less than an arm's length from his face. The beast was dead.

He yelled, rolled aside, and leaped to his feet. Duranix was there, holding the dead yevi by the scruff of its neck. Two other yevi, also dead, lay in the grass.

"You killed it," the dragon said, wrenching the weapon from the animal's skull. "What's this? One of my old scales? That's good!" He threw back his head and laughed.

Amero was in no mood to join him. "What took you so long?" he quavered. "I called you and you didn't come."

Duranix tossed the dead yevi to the ground. He dusted his hands with distaste. "I didn't believe you," he said, shrugging. "I detected nothing in the area. Until this one attacked, I thought we were alone." He frowned, his smooth brow furrowing with concern. "You heard them, and I didn't. This human shell of mine is limiting, but not that limiting. Sthenn must have taught them how to veil their thoughts from me. Lucky for us, human senses are different from a dragon's."

Amero picked up the scale and wiped off blood and brains on the grass. His palms were cut again from handling it. "I wish I had a handle for this. It's a good tool, but too sharp to carry in my hand. What I need is a shaft, like an axe handle—"

"Why not a spear shaft?"

Amero shook his head. "I never passed my coming-of-age," he said, regretfully. "I'm not allowed to have a spear. It wouldn't be right."

"Nonsense," Duranix said. "If you can carry and use it, what's not right?" He fingered the honed scale in Amero's hand. It didn't cut his human-looking skin. "What's this coming-of-age anyway? What is required?"

"I must spend four days completely alone on the plain. I have to make my own weapon and kill four-footed game with it, then I bear the trophy-head back to my father and mother."

"You can hear predators talk and killed one with a sloughed bronze scale. There is your trophy." Duranix gestured at the slain yevi.

Amero averted his face so the dragon wouldn't see the tears in his eyes. He cried at the sudden realization he would never be able to present a manhood trophy to his parents, ever. His family was gone, and he was nothing but a wanderer, doomed to pass his life alone.

Feeling Duranix's gaze upon him, Amero brushed aside his childish tears. "Yevi travel in packs," he said. "There must be more nearby. Do we hunt the rest, or search for plainsmen to warn?"

Even as a man, Duranix's pallid eyes were penetrating. "What do *you* say, Amero?"

He considered. "We'll do more good warning hunters. The pack could scatter if we—if you—attacked them directly."

Duranix agreed, and before leaving, he left a macabre message for the yevi pack. He piled the three dead animals in a heap and, with his lightning, set them on fire. Sthenn's creatures would no doubt flee before him, creating a haven of safety in which Amero could warn what plainsmen they met. They set off again, south by west, with a column of dirty black smoke rising from the savanna behind them.

* * * * *

In time the landscape became familiar. Amero recognized several landmarks, like White Elk watering hole and the pine-topped hills called Crows' Haven. The great fork of the Plains River lay to the northeast. Amero and his family had crossed that river three times a year in their circuit of the plain— south in summer, west in autumn, north in winter.

Though it was only days before the onset of deep autumn, they had not encountered a single human since leaving the lake of the falls. Large game was scarce, too. Aside from the occasional solitary antelope or rogue ox, they saw nothing bigger than a rabbit all day.

Towering white clouds sailed slowly across the sky, periodically hiding the blazing sun. Duranix shortened his stride and gradually came to a stop. He turned his head slowly, as though listening to some distant call.

"That way," he said, pointing toward the distant river. "Many men and animals are that way."

Amero felt nothing. "How far?" he asked.

"A half day's walk—or a few moments by air."

"Do you dare show yourself by day? You'll start a stampede if you swoop down on them in your natural shape."

Duranix tapped a golden nail against his chin. "You're right. If only I could observe and not be seen myself."

Amero looked up at the sky. "Could you hide in the clouds?"

He nodded slowly. "I can, though my presence in clouds often precipitates a thunderstorm." Amero regarded him blankly. "I cause it to rain," Duranix said more plainly.

Without further discussion, Duranix unfolded to his winged reptilian form. On the open savanna he didn't seem so overwhelming, but he was a massive, formidable creature nevertheless. Bending his serpentine neck in a half circle, he brought his broad head eye to eye with Amero.

"Do you want to fly with me or walk to the river?" he asked, his voice like fading thunder.

There could be two dozen yevi in the tall grass around them, just waiting for the dragon to depart. Amero truly had only one choice. He took his courage in his hands and declared, "I'll go with you."

Duranix reached out with one foreclaw to pick him up, but Amero backed away, asking, "Couldn't I go some other way?"

"Such as?" rumbled the dragon.

He pointed. "Could I ride on your back?"

Duranix glanced at the expanse of burnished scales and flying muscles standing out prominently on his back. He closed his foreclaw around Amero.

"No," he replied. "At the first gust of wind or abrupt turn, you'd fall off, and I'd have to find a new pet."

Amero would have protested further, but the dragon gathered his mighty rear legs beneath himself and sprang into the air. He climbed rapidly in a tight spiral, aiming for the heavy cloud formations overhead. Amero felt as if his stomach had been left behind on the ground.

They plunged into a cool white pillar. Clouds that looked so solid from the ground, Amero soon discovered, were actually as insubstantial as morning mist. He worked his arms loose from Duranix's grip and tried to see over the dragon's thick claws. Every now and then a scrap of brown earth appeared through holes in the cloud. Amero wondered how high they were.

"High enough," Duranix boomed. "Be quiet. I must concentrate."

His wings beat in quick, steady rhythm. After a short time, blue sparks began to flicker from every downstroke of the dragon's wingtips. The smell of the lightning filled the air, and Amero's hair prickled and stood up on its own. It proved to be more alarming than harmful, and the boy soon got used to it.

A large gap appeared ahead of them. Duranix lowered his left wing and slipped through the opening. Amero caught a glimpse of green water, probably the southern tributary of the great river. Duranix kept below the clouds for a while, then abruptly rose into the bright white mist. Amero's head snapped back, and his stomach did a somersault.

"Did you see them?" said the dragon, his powerful voice tinged with excitement. "Yevi, hundreds of them, just below us."

Amero struggled against his host's impervious grip. "I can't see a thing!" he complained.

"They're massing for an attack. I couldn't tell if they were after elk or humans, but I'm guessing they've driven most of the humans in this area into the fork of the river."

Amero felt his heart pound. Penned on two sides against the swift river, the humans would have to fight or die.

Duranix swung around in a complete circle, losing height as he did. "Hold on, boy, we're going to see and be seen!"

The dragon burst from the underside of the cloud, accompanied by a bolt of lightning. The flash dazzled Amero. When his vision returned, he saw an amazing scene below: Scores of humans were milling around in the riverbend. Mixed in with them were a few centaurs, their heads decorated with colorful headdresses made of feathers. Large numbers of elk, wild oxen, deer, and wild pigs were trapped as well. The more aggressive animals, the boar and bull elk, charged back and forth, conscious they were in a trap. Plainsfolk bunched together in small family groups, warding off half-crazed animals with spears and sharpened sticks. The centaurs, armed with stone-headed clubs, had slain a mighty bull elk and were sheltering behind the bleeding carcass. The yevi formed a great pack just out of spear-casting range.

The sun cracked through the clouds, sending bright shafts of light through the billowing banks of mist. Duranix's shadow swept across the scene. Animals and humans alike looked up in wonder, which quickly gave way to terror.

Duranix hovered, flapping laboriously to remain in one spot. Lightning played about his wings, head, and tail. The prickling sensation on Amero's skin grew almost unbearable.

"Now what?" the boy asked.

"Time to land!"

The dragon folded his wings and plummeted to the ground. He aimed for the empty ground between the trapped plainsmen and the yevi. Oxen, elk, centaurs, and humans scattered, some throwing themselves in the river to escape. The current was very strong, and the panic-stricken were swept away.

Duranix alighted hard, shaking the earth beneath him. Lightning played about him, striking the ground with explosive force. The milling throng at his back raised a dense cloud of dust, but above this, Duranix could see the yevi advancing.

Duranix threw back his horned head and let loose an ear-shattering bellow. Amero was astonished by the sheer volume of his mighty companion's cry. He clapped his hands over his ears until the roar died away.

"I am Duranix the Bronze, master of mountain and plains! Who dares challenge me?"

"What are you doing?" Amero stammered. He was facing rank upon rank of snarling yevi. It seemed impossible they couldn't bury even a great dragon under a mass of lean, gray bodies.

Walking a bit awkwardly on his hind legs, the dragon advanced a few steps.

"Begone!" he roared. "This is your only warning!"

The gray horde shifted forward in a single, rippling motion. Duranix extended his neck and opened his mouth wide. A searing column of blue-white fire erupted from his throat. It played back and forth on the front ranks of the yevi, who exploded when the dragon-fire touched them. Duranix closed his jaws and drew in a breath. The unhurt yevi surged over the smoldering bodies of their own dead. They were just forty paces away.

The dragon brought his barbed tail around and used it to scratch behind his left horn. The yevi had closed to thirty paces.

"Duranix?" Amero said nervously, tapping the dragon's claw for attention.

"What?" was the mild response.

"Do something!"

"What did you have in mind?"

Several hundred raging beasts were now only twenty paces away. Amero shouted, "Anything! Do anything!"

With his free foreclaw Duranix gestured at the onrushing pack. The air shook, and dust whirled into the air in front of the dragon. An invisible swath was torn through the yevi ranks, scattering those on either side and pulverizing those in the center. The yevi checked their attack, milling about in confusion. Duranix gestured again, and another hole was torn in the pack. Animals at the edges and rear began to run away. The trickle of desertions became a torrent until only the front ranks remained.

"This range is mine, from the lake of the falls to the southern sea!" Duranix bellowed. "Tell Sthenn I will not allow his creatures to poach on my land!"

"You cannot hold!" muttered the remaining yevi. "You cannot hold! You tire! We will have the plain as our own. That is the promise of our master!"

Duranix let loose a blast of lightning, milder than before, but which nonetheless tore the ground asunder and ignited grass and scrub among the yevi. Singed, the beasts fled yelping.

A mild, warm rain began to fall. Duranix set Amero on the ground. When he was sure the yevi had all fled, he and

Amero walked back to where the trapped plainsfolk were crouching behind hastily erected barricades of stones, logs, and twists of thorny vines. At their approach, a hail of spears landed around Amero.

"Stop!" he shouted. "I'm human, like you!"

"Showering you with gratitude," Duranix said dryly. He stood behind Amero, looking a bit unsteady on his feet.

"You're scaring them," the boy said. "Can't you change to human form?"

"I'm tired," he said. The dragon dropped on his belly and rested his chin on his crossed forelegs. His tail curled around his body. He sighed and closed his eyes. "You explain things to the silly creatures. I'll remain here."

Amero picked his way through a welter of rocks and logs. Deer sprinted to and fro, and wild pigs dashed about, grunting.

"The yevi are gone!" Amero called. "It's safe! You can come out!"

Slowly, a thickset man emerged from a heap of logs and stones, spear couched on his shoulder. He climbed atop a fallen log and pointed at Amero with his weapon.

"Who are you, who commands the stormbird?" he asked hoarsely.

" 'Commands?' " said Amero. He glanced back at the slumbering dragon. *Forgive me, mighty one, but if it calms them, let them think so!*

Amero approached the lone hunter. His beard was strongly flecked with gray, and his broad shoulders were scarred with the marks of a long and strenuous life. Amero held up his hands, palms out, the plainsman's gesture of peace.

"I am Amero, son of Oto and Kinar," he said.

"Valka," the man replied, tapping his chest with his spearhead. "What do you want with us?"

Amero was taken aback. He'd expected, at the very least, grudging thanks. Stifling his annoyance, he said, "I want nothing. My friend and I saw your trouble from the air and came to help you."

Valka's black brows rose. "The stormbird is your friend?"

"Yes. His name is Duranix."

Gradually more hunters appeared, along with their mates and children. Amero had never seen so many people together

89

at one time. They were plainly curious about the boy they'd seen fall from the clouds in the grasp of a mythical storm-bird. They pressed in, trying to get a glimpse of him and the fantastic creature lying so quietly on the same ground where he'd routed the yevi host.

Valka said, "Who are you, boy? Where did you come from?"

"As I said, I am Amero, son of a hunter like you. Some weeks past my family was killed by the yevi—the same creatures who were stalking you. I was saved by Duranix, and since then we've been trying to warn others about them."

"We've been running from the near-wolves for a full change of the moon," Valka said. "They killed my son, Duru." Fathers and mothers in the crowd took up the refrain, listing the names of family members claimed by the remorseless yevi.

"Duranix has scattered them," Amero said. "A few may lurk about for a while, but I don't think they'll mass again, for fear he will destroy them."

"How can he destroy them?" said a yellow-haired woman, her faced streaked with tears. "Are they not evil spirits sent to plague us?"

Amero shook his head. "They're flesh, hide, and bone, like any other animal," he said firmly. "Come, look at the slain." He started toward the battle site. "Come," he said again to the reluctant hunters. "Don't be afraid."

Though Amero walked within arm's length of the dozing dragon, the other humans gave him a wide berth. Rain had put out the fires Duranix had started, but steam hung in the air over the blasted soil. Three centaurs had already gone out to inspect the bodies of the burned and smashed predators. The centaurs watched the plainsmen approach with tense expressions.

"Peace to you," Amero said. Up close, centaurs stank. He tried not to wrinkle his nose in disgust, remembering what Duranix had said about the smell of humans. Valka and some of the bolder hunters poked and prodded among the dead yevi.

"Huh," a centaur grunted. "Like wolf, but bigger."

"They have hands," said one of the humans, startled. "What unnatural beasts!"

The tallest centaur approached Amero. He held out a swarthy, black-nailed hand to the boy. "You save *miteera*. Now, friends."

"Miteera" must be either the centaur's name, or the name of his band, Amero decided. The boy did not hesitate but clasped the creature's rough, callused hand. Not long ago he would have been terrified to be so close to a centaur, but after living with a dragon, he found that centaurs weren't so frightening after all. They certainly showed a lot more gratitude than the plainsmen.

"Friends," he said, gripping the centaur's hand as hard as he could.

The creature released him and gestured at the yevi with his club. "These people?"

"They're smart as people," Amero said. "They were sent to drive us off the plains."

"Sent by who?" asked the blonde woman sharply.

"Another dragon—a stormbird—the enemy of Duranix. He lives far to the west, in the forest."

They mulled this over, and Valka said, "What's to prevent this enemy from sending more beasts to attack us?"

"Duranix will fight them," Amero said proudly.

"He's a mighty beast, but he can't be all places at once."

"My children are dead!" cried the blonde woman. "Three of them carried off! How can my man and I live, knowing any other children we have can be killed by these creatures?"

"My family was destroyed by them, too," Amero replied, "but Duranix saved me." He wanted to ask her how safe any of them were, with panthers, vipers, drought, starvation, disease . . . their lives were an endless struggle for survival. He wanted to ask all of them, but he didn't. There was no answer to her question, or to his.

The centaur leader said it best: "Help now, and live. Help later, and live. *Alala!*" With this exclamation, he and his brethren raised their clubs in salute and galloped away.

Amero trudged through the slackening rain to where the dragon slept. Before he reached the slumbering giant, a hand caught his arm.

Valka asked, "Where do you go now, boy?"

"I go home with Duranix."

"What is 'home?' "

"The place where Duranix lives." He pointed eastward. "There, at the edge of the mountains, at the lake of the falls."

"And he protects you from the yevi?"

Amero nodded. Valka looked back at the other people. Some had taken up their meager possessions and were already moving on. Others, among them the angry blonde woman, remained a few paces away, waiting expectantly.

"Would he protect us?" asked Valka.

Amero hesitated. "I think he would," he said. "Let me ask him."

Valka hung back as Amero approached the sleeping dragon. Though his heart hammered at his own temerity, Amero decided to put on a bold front. The folk watching were all older and more experienced than he. If he betrayed any fear of the dragon, he'd forfeit the influence he had as Duranix's friend.

"Hey," he said loudly, "Duranix, wake up!"

The dragon's leathery nostrils flared. A gust of hot breath almost swept Amero off his feet. The dragon opened one eye, the eyelids splitting vertically to reveal a huge gold-flecked pupil. The eye focused on Amero, narrowing.

"What do you want?" said the dragon testily. The edge in his voice caused the small crowd of humans to shrink back.

"I have an idea," Amero said brightly. "These people would like to place themselves under our protection."

"Our protection?"

Amero lowered his voice. "Your protection."

"What am I going to do with a herd of humans? One makes an interesting pet, but twenty are an infestation."

"They won't live in the cave with us," Amero said, his voice rising. He spread his hands apart, sketching out his new vision in the air. "They can live on the shore of the lake below the cave. They can go about their own lives there. You need not do anything for them, unless the yevi come back."

Duranix lifted his head so suddenly the group of waiting humans stumbled backward in fearful surprise, half tripping and falling to the ground. He eyed them coolly.

"I'm not feeding them," he announced.

"Of course not! They'll feed themselves."

"And when I'm sleeping, I want it quiet. None of their shouting and squawking."

"Yes, Duranix."

He heaved himself to his feet with a yawn. "Very well," the dragon said, "but they're your responsibility, Amero. I expect you to keep them in line. It's one thing to save wildlife from slaughter. It's another thing entirely to invite a herd into your home." He yawned again prodigiously. "Fighting makes me hungry. I don't suppose any elk are left on this side of the river?"

Before Amero could reply, Valka called, "We will find them!" He gestured to the other hunters in the group. They took up their spears and fanned out in the direction of the riverbank. There was a rumble of hooves and shouts from the plainsmen, and in short order they returned dragging the carcasses of three large elk. They presented these to the dragon from a respectful distance.

"Well," said Duranix, blinking. His eyelids made loud clicks when they came together. "Perhaps we will get along after all."

He stretched his mouth wide. Amero shouted a warning, and the hunters and their families scattered before the lightning erupted to roast the elk to the famished dragon's taste.

## Chapter 7

~

Nianki ran across the moonlit plain, knees rising high, arms pumping in time with her legs. The spring night was warm, and the white moon played hide-and-seek with high clouds made pink by Lutar, the low-hanging red moon. Sweat poured down her face, stinging her eyes. A few paces ahead, a yearling buck darted, its bold white tail flicking with fright. She'd flushed the deer by accident as she crossed the high plain by night. It sprang up so close in front of her that she couldn't ignore the opportunity.

Had she owned a full-length spear, she could have brought the yearling down by now, but Pakito's cast-off weapon was good only for short throws. After eluding the elves, she had doubled back to the beach and found the truncated spear unclaimed on the sand.

Snorting, the deer twisted sharply to the right. Nianki yelled at the animal. Her blood was up, and she meant to have this young buck. She stretched her long legs and gained a step on her prey. The deer was too young to know it could outrun her. It knew pursuit only by panthers or wolves, which it could evade but not outrun. It kept changing direction, dodging from side to side, in an attempt to escape, but she wasn't fooled. She closed to within a pace of the buck. Each step made her legs burn, each breath now felt like a flint knife in her ribs. The yearling was panting, too, its long tongue lolling from the side of its mouth.

Nianki raised the spear to her shoulder. The next time the buck bore right—

He did, making a lightning turn right across her line of sight. Nianki hurled the short spear. It grazed down the deer's ribs, drawing blood. The head buried itself in the ground, and the shaft tangled the yearling's feet. It tumbled to the ground in a welter of flailing legs and wide, rolling eyes.

With a ferocious cry of triumph, she leaped upon the fallen animal. It struggled to rise, but she caught it around the neck with both arms. Bleating with terror, the young buck tried to roll her off, but she held on, tightening her grip on the animal's throat. Nianki got a knee in the deer's side and wrenched backward with all her might. Bones in its neck snapped, and the deer ceased struggling.

She fell back on the matted grass and gasped for air. The collar the elves had put on her chafed. Worse, though her wounds had healed cleanly, the scars still ached when she exerted herself.

Recovered, Nianki found her spear and used the flint head to butcher her kill. She gutted the carcass, wiped it out with dry grass, and then slung the yearling across her shoulders. It was essential to keep moving. The smell of blood would draw scavengers from far and wide, and she didn't want to have to fight them off.

She made for an outcropping of boulders near the horizon. Bowed under the weight of the carcass, Nianki kept her head down until she was quite close to the boulders. When she finally looked up, she was startled to see two human figures in the shadow of the rocks. She tossed aside the deer and presented her spearpoint.

"Who's there?" she demanded.

"Peace to you, spirit of the night! We mean no harm!"

"Show yourselves!"

Two plainsmen, young enough to be beardless, emerged from the darkness and stood open-handed before Nianki. They were naked but for scrap-hide kilts. Their faces were gaunt with hunger, and their ribs stood out like reeds, even in the dimness of the soft moonlight.

"Who are you?" she asked.

"I am Kenase," answered the taller boy, "son of Ebon and Filar, and this is Neko."

"Your brother?"

"No, I am the son of Sensi and Myera," said Neko.

"How come you to be here?"

The boys exchanged looks. "We escaped from the Good People."

Nianki tapped her spear against the hard collar. "I escaped from them as well. When did you break free?"

"We left their camp near sundown," said Neko haltingly.

"That way." He pointed east. "The Good People are powerful, but I didn't think they could capture a spirit!"

Nianki frowned. "What are you talking about? Who's a spirit?"

"You!"

She laughed. "The moons have addled your heads! I'm no more a spirit than you."

Kenase pointed at the deer. "We saw you. You ran down a deer and slew it with your own hands! Who but a spirit of the night could do that?"

"A hungry woman, that's who," Nianki replied. She hoisted the carcass back on her shoulders. "How long has it been since you two ate?"

Neko licked his lips. "Three days, Great Sp— Uh, what shall we call you?"

"Nianki, daughter of Oto and Kinar."

"Oto the panther killer?" said Kenase.

Nianki nodded.

"I know tales of his prowess as a hunter. You're his daughter? That explains much!"

Nianki climbed atop the lower boulder and set to work skinning the buck. She nipped off morsels for the two young men. Kenase, she reckoned, was about her age, maybe a season older. Neko was a year or two behind her. They ate greedily, and Nianki had to admonish them to chew long and swallow little. Fresh meat was hard on a starved stomach.

Kenase explained he had been visiting Neko's family to meet Neko's younger sister, Nefra. Their parents were considering Nefra taking Kenase as her mate. While with Neko's family, they were captured by a band of the Good People, eight on foot and four riding those strong, four-legged animals, which he called "horses."

"The Good People breed them to serve as beasts of burden," Kenase explained.

"Go on," said Nianki, chewing slowly.

"There were six of us," Neko said, "and they drove us to a hilltop near the boundary of the eastern forest. The Good People have made a sort of hedge of tree trunks at the top of the hill, so close together no one could pass between them. There were many, many plainsfolk there, inside the hedge."

"How many?"

Kenase counted on his fingers, then on Neko's as well. "More than our hands can count."

"So how did you get away?"

"Some of the women made a noise and drew the eyes of the Good People to them. The men boosted me and Neko over the tree trunks, and we ran away. We meant to find my family, return, and free the rest." Kenase's shoulders slumped dejectedly. "In the time we've been running from the Good People, we've seen no plainsmen at all, until we saw you."

Nianki sighed. She thought herself favored by the spirits to have gotten away from the elves. The last thing she wanted to do was steal into a camp full of them, but her heart ached to hear this. She couldn't bear the thought of so many plainsmen being held captive.

"How many elves—Good People—were at this camp?" she asked finally.

More counting on fingers. "We saw twelve in all," said Kenase.

"If they have the chance, will your kinsmen fight for their freedom?"

"Yes, I am sure of it!"

"Good." Nianki stood on the boulder and wiped her hands on her buckskin shirt. "I'll help you."

Neko and Kenase jumped up, ready to return, but Nianki ignored them and dragged the rest of her kill to the highest point in the outcropping. As the boys watched, she climbed down a few steps and stretched out on the rock.

"Aren't we going right away?" asked Neko.

"Not now. It would be light by the time we reached the camp. Better to go tomorrow afternoon and arrive after the sun has set."

"But they hunger and thirst!" Kenase protested.

"They're plainsmen," Nianki replied. "Hunger and thirst are familiar companions. They'll endure another day. If you want my help, you'll have to do as I say, and I say we can best help them after dark."

She put an arm across her forehead, covering her eyes. Oto used to do that when he was through talking, and it had the

97

same effect on Neko and Kenase it always had on Nianki, Amero, and Kinar. They fell silent.

Nianki was glad they'd seen her run down the yearling buck. It was an unusual kill, and it awed them enough to accept her counsel.

"Great Spirit of the Night," they had called her. The longer Nianki lived, the less she believed in spirits. The elves were supposed to have mystical powers, and she'd seen little of it. Kenase and Neko took her for a spirit, yet she was flesh and blood. Were all the stories she'd heard of ghosts and spirits just lies or dreams? The hard world Nianki was coming to know seemed to have little room for spirits.

* * * * *

She awoke to find bright sunlight streaming on her face, and she heard low voices conversing close by. Nianki sat up abruptly. The two boys were sitting on the ground with their backs against the boulder, eating and talking. A pile of wild celery lay between them. From the stems and strings heaped alongside, it looked like Kenase and Neko had already eaten about half of what they'd gathered.

Nianki checked her deer. It had not been touched, she noted with satisfaction. One of the oldest tenets of the hunters' code was a kill belonged to whomever brought it down. The boys' respect of her kill was a positive sign.

She scrambled down the rock. Kenase stood up.

"Good morning," he said. "Sleep well?"

"Well enough."

Neko also rose, though more slowly than his companion. A stalk of celery stuck out of his mouth.

"Hungry?" he mumbled, offering her the unchewed end.

"I need water," Nianki replied. "Is there any?"

Kenase offered to lead her to a nearby spring, but she declined. He gave her directions, and she went to the water hole alone.

After she drank her fill, Nianki splashed the tepid water on her face. She thought about Pa'alu and his hollow gourd for carrying water. Maybe it wasn't such a strange idea. Never knowing where the next water hole might be, carrying your own supply on a long trek made a lot of sense. Next time she came across a suitable gourd vine, she would save one.

While trudging up the hill, Nianki decided to test the young men's mettle. Instead of walking straight back to the boulder, she circled around the low side of the hill and came up on the far side, with the rock between her and the boys. She crept up on the warm stone and lay flat, pushing herself along with just her fingers and toes.

". . . until she gets back," Neko was saying.

"What do you think of Karada?" asked Kenase.

"Strange," said Neko, "and dangerous."

"Karada" in the plainsmen's tongue meant "Scarred One." Nianki had no doubt whom they were talking about.

"Do you think she can get my family out?" Neko continued.

"She's strong and fleet, and no matter what she says, I think the spirits are strong in her. You saw how she brought down the deer with her hands?"

"Uh-huh." Neko picked celery string out of his teeth. "She moves like a panther. If anyone can free my family, she's the one."

Kenase looked down the hill toward the spring. "She's taking a long time."

"Women are like that."

Nianki quietly withdrew. She considered jumping down on them from her hiding place, but that seemed childish. Besides, it was useful to know what other people thought, especially if they didn't realize you knew.

She ran back around to the spring and ascended the hill in plain view. Again Kenase stood when Nianki approached, and again Neko remained where he was, slouching against the boulder.

"We've enough food for the day, so there's no need to tire ourselves hunting," Nianki said. "I say we stay here and rest a while, so we'll be strong tonight." The boys readily agreed.

They slumped in the shade of the boulder. Kenase offered Nianki the wild celery they'd gathered. She munched a few stalks, all the while evaluating her new comrades. Kenase was earnest and talkative. He was plainly impressed with Nianki and kept trying to do things for her, to her secret amusement. Neko was different. He was quiet and observant—in fact, he watched Nianki as intently as she watched him. His interest wasn't as openly friendly as Kenase's, and he seemed more detached.

She told them without elaboration about the loss of her family, and how she'd received the scars she bore. More detailed was her recounting of her meeting with Balif and his band of elves near the coast. Both youths were puzzled by Balif's declaration that the elves would take all the land from the Khar River east to their forest home.

"Take it? Take it where?" Kenase asked.

"The elves mean to live here and drive all the plainsfolk out," Nianki explained.

"They can't do that," Neko replied. "Where will we go? West of the river is the land of the ox-herders. The hunting is bad there. There's no room for us!"

"All the more reason to free your family, and any other humans we find. The people of the plain must work together, like the elves do, to resist this invasion."

Nianki curled up on her side, pillowing her head with one arm. "Rest now," she said. "When night falls, we go."

* * * * *

When twilight faded to the black of night, Nianki and the boys made ready. No moons were up yet. It would well past midnight before Lutar rose. By then, Nianki hoped they would be on their way to freedom.

Neko led the way. He set an easy, loping pace that Nianki had no trouble matching. Pausing only to take his bearings from the stars, Neko bore due east for a long time. To the north, foothills stood out against the glittering sky. Ahead, the fringes of the vast eastern forest loomed.

Halfway to midnight, Neko stopped and fell to one knee. Nianki came up on his left, while Kenase knelt on his right.

"Between those two hills," Neko whispered. A faint glow lit up the hollow between the indicated hills.

"What's that light?" Nianki wondered aloud.

"Fire," said Kenase. "The Good People command flame."

She didn't like that. Fire was not something a sensible hunter fooled with. It did not care whose hide it burned, and its illumination would make their task that much harder.

"Follow me. No sound." Nianki moved forward at a slow, crouching walk.

The trail wound between two round-topped hills into a steep ravine. Atop the ridge to the right was a row of tree trunks, just like the boys had described. They were so close together not even a rabbit could have passed between them. Somewhere inside this line of tree trunks a bonfire blazed. By its glow Nianki saw an elf on horseback, riding slowly around the outside of the camp.

With gestures, she conveyed she wanted to circle the camp and view it from all sides. Kenase took her hand and led her off to his left, away from the horse and rider. She was a bit surprised at his touch.

The terrain along the foot of the ridge was all briars and knifegrass. Nianki took the lead, pushing aside the thorny growth with her spear. Every few paces they stopped to study the camp. So far they'd spotted no easy way in.

"There's a gap on the other side," Neko whispered, "but it's closely guarded."

They climbed the steep slope toward the dark end of the camp. Nianki used her spear as a handhold—she drove it into the ground, used it to haul herself up, yanked it out, repeated the process. She held out a hand to Kenase, who in turn pulled Neko along. The ridge had steep sides, but it wasn't that high, and before long all three were lying on their bellies, staring at the blank wall of logs.

"A rider circles the camp," Kenase said. "Elves on the inside keep people away from the trunks."

"And you escaped from here?" Nianki said. "How did you manage? Did they pursue you?"

"It was dark. I guess they couldn't see us."

She looked to Neko for confirmation, but he was too busy gazing at the wall. She nudged him, and they continued their circuit.

The firelight grew stronger, and it quickly became apparent the elves had a large fire going in front of the opening to the camp. Four of them, armed with spears, stood between the fire and the gap in the logs. Nianki tried to see beyond them into the camp, but the glare of the fire was too bright.

"What now?" Kenase hissed.

"Back," she muttered. "Back to the dark. We'll get in the way you got out—climb over the trees."

"But the rider—"

"We'll wait till he passes. Come on!"

The enclosure was roughly oval shaped, with the bonfire at the center of one of the long sides. Nianki got as far from the firelight as she could. She crept out of the bushes and listened. The clop-clop of the approaching horse's hooves caused her to flatten herself into a chink in the trunks. The horse walked by, its bored rider's head bobbing with every step his mount made. When he was well past, she waved for Kenase and Neko to join her.

"This is not good!" Neko said with surprising fervor.

"Have you got a better idea?" Nianki replied. He looked at his toes. "All right, lift me up!"

They boys braced themselves against the logs and Nianki climbed their backs. The tree trunks were about twice her height, so with one foot on each boy's shoulder, she was able to see over them.

The dark end of the camp was dotted with sleeping people lying in family groups of five and six. She guessed there were thirty or forty people. At the other end of the enclosure the elves made their camp. They had hides stretched over frames of tree branches to keep the rain and sun off. She counted eight to ten sleeping elves. A pair of horses was tethered to the wall.

Nianki swung first one leg then the other over the tops of the tree trunks. The ground was a good three paces distant, but she slid off her perch and landed lightly on her fingers and toes. She crept up to the nearest sleeper—a woman—and clamped a hand over her mouth. The woman opened wide dark eyes and gave a cry muffled by Nianki's hand.

"Quiet!" Nianki said. "I'm here to help you!"

The woman nodded her head, showing her understanding, and Nianki removed her hand. She sat up, and Nianki saw she wore a hard collar, identical to the one that encircled Nianki's throat. A cord ran through the collar's ring to the collar of the next sleeper, and the next, eventually ending at a large stake pounded in the ground in the center of the camp.

In her travels since leaving the coast, Nianki had availed herself of a piece of sharp obsidian as a cutting tool. It was brittle stone, but easy to knap to a keen edge. She flicked the obsidian blade over the cord, cutting it cleanly.

"Wake the rest, carefully," she whispered. "Pull the cord through and you'll be loose. I'll help the others." The woman nodded vigorously, turning to wake her companion.

Nianki crept to the next group of sleepers. Before she could awaken anyone else, a cry went up from the elves at the fire. At first Nianki thought they were just carrying on among themselves, but then she saw the sleeping elves were rising and taking up their weapons.

Without bothering to wake the boy she'd approached, she cut the cord on his collar. Two elves mounted their horses and the rest ran to the opening in the wall. To her consternation, Nianki saw they had Kenase and Neko.

"Listen, human!" shouted one of the elves on horseback. "You can't get out. We have your friends! Stand up and let yourself be seen!"

Sleeping plainsfolk stirred all around her. Some got to their feet, rubbing their eyes. Nianki joined in, mixing with them while gradually working her way toward the way out.

"Can you see her?" called a man's voice in the plainsmen's language.

"Not yet," replied the mounted elf. "*Cha!* They all look alike to me!"

"This one has a scarred face and long brown hair."

Who was speaking? Most of the captives were on their feet now, making it hard for Nianki to see ahead. She bumped into a burly hunter with fierce black brows and curly beard. She pressed the obsidian knife into his hand.

"Free as many as you can," she said. "If we all move as one, they can't stop us."

"Aye," he said, black eyes shining. "Stampede. Good plan!"

She worked her way to the front of the crowd and found herself looking up at a familiar face. The mounted elf was Tamanithas, the elf she'd knocked down and left unconscious.

103

His eyes widened in shocked recognition as his gaze fell upon her. "You!" he spat in passable human-speech.

"I thought you would've gone home by now," she said calmly. "Learned to talk like a real person, have you?"

"I knew your barbarous tongue when last we met," he sneered. "I just hate to soil my mouth by speaking it!" He ordered the elves on foot to take her.

A concerted shout went up from the humans at Nianki's back. As fast as they could, they whipped the confining cord from the rings around their necks. The man with the curly black beard rushed to Nianki's side and returned the obsidian knife to her.

The sight of their prisoners freeing themselves paralyzed the elves for a moment. They were only twelve against forty. The elves closed ranks and presented a hedge of spears to the angry mob. Tamanithas paraded his horse up and down behind the line of guards.

"Get back to your places!" he shouted. "Get back and you will not be harmed!"

"It's you who should flee," Nianki shouted back. "This is not your land! Return to your forest, and we won't kill you!"

Tamanithas drew his long-bladed weapon and started to ride over his own spear carriers, but he was restrained by two comrades on horseback. They argued loudly in their own language while the unruly mob of plainsfolk drew closer and closer, forcing the elves into the narrow end of the oval camp. Hands found stones in the dirt, and lengths of wood cut by the elves to feed their fires made handy clubs.

A shower of stones fell on the mounted elves. The pair restraining Tamanithas went down, and one of the horses bolted from the scene. One stout rock struck Tamanithas in the shoulder. He shrugged it off and urged his animal forward. The spear carriers parted ranks to avoid being trampled. He rode straight at Nianki, who awaited his charge calmly.

She was unarmed, save for her knife. Her spear she'd left with Kenase. Tamanithas rode with his weapon held high. Just before the horse would have collided with Nianki, she leaped to the side, throwing her right arm and right leg around the horse's neck. The beast reared and bucked. She held on tightly and drove the heel of her foot into Tamanithas's chest. His hands flew up, and he slid off the horse.

A swarm of furious men and women descended on the fallen elf. He was kicked and pummeled and dragged to his feet. By the time Nianki managed to get off the spinning, bucking horse, the rest of the elves had withdrawn to the opening, leaving Tamanithas in the hands of the humans.

Sudden quiet fell over the scene. Nianki strode through the crowd and saw the elves had reorganized at the bonfire. On one side, the humans held Tamanithas, bruised and bloody. On the other side, the elves had Neko, kneeling, with a spear to his back. Standing with the elves, unguarded, was Kenase.

"So, you're with them," Nianki said, the truth dawning on her.

"I serve the Good People," Kenase replied. "Let Lord Tamanithas go, and we'll serve them together, you and I."

She spat in the dirt. "I serve no one."

"They'll kill Neko."

She stepped out further, planting her hands on her hips. "Listen to me! Tell your people what I say, Tamanithas." He sullenly agreed. "We will release Tamanithas if you give up Neko and leave this country. If you harm Neko, we'll kill the elf, hunt you all down, and kill you, every one." She glanced back at Tamanithas. "Tell them."

He translated her threat. The elves drew closer together. There was some conferring among those on horseback. At last, one gave a command, and Neko was prodded to his feet. He limped across the open ground to stand by Nianki.

"Let him go," she said to the people holding Tamanithas. There was some growling from the crowd, but they relinquished their hostage. With as much dignity as his battered appearance could support, Tamanithas rejoined his people.

"Depart now," Nianki said. "You'll be followed until you leave the plain. If you try to come back, everyone in your band will be slain."

Tamanithas's horse was sent to the waiting elves. The former hostage mounted and rode out in front of the wary spear carriers.

"This is not over," he vowed. "This land will belong to my lord Silvanos."

"Land belongs to the spirits, not to those who live on it," said Nianki, "but we'll not be driven from our hunting grounds. The plainsmen will know of your deeds, and how we turned you back. If you return, we'll be waiting for you."

The humans raised a cheer. Stung by her declaration, the elves formed ranks and started marching away. Then only the mounted elves were left with Kenase standing between them. He looked at Nianki fearfully and reached up to clasp the mane of Tamanithas's horse.

"Take me with you, great one!" Kenase said. "I can still serve you!"

"Begone, wretch. You would lick the hand of whoever feeds you." Tamanithas pulled his animal free. With a single cry, he kicked his horse to a gallop. The other riders were close behind him.

Kenase was quickly ringed by vengeful hunters.

"You led my family to the Good People!" Curly Beard cried, punching Kenase on the jaw with his fist. Others echoed his accusation. Kenase was hauled to his feet only to be beaten down again. Nianki watched silently until Neko appeared at her side. He handed her the short-shafted spear.

"Thank you," she said. The ring of betrayed hunters parted for her. Her face was as hard as her voice when she spoke to Kenase. "I fed you. I gave you meat. You lied to me."

"I did it for all of us!" he exclaimed. "The Good People are wise and great! They can bring many wonders to us, wonders of comfort and ease!"

"Like this?" Nianki said, yanking at the cold collar at her throat. "Wonders like starvation and slavery?"

"The collars come off!" Kenase edged away from Nianki, toward the interior of the camp. "There is a tool that makes them come off."

The plainsfolk allowed him to ransack the bedding left behind by the elves. He found a large bright ring made of the same hard, smooth substance as the collars. "Bronze," Kenase called it. It was "metal," he said.

A curious worked rod of metal hung on the ring. Kenase pushed one end of the rod in the hole in Nianki's collar and twisted. The collar popped open and fell to the ground. With a roar, the crowd surged over Kenase and the rod was torn from his grasp. The camp resounded with cheers as collar after collar was removed.

Curly Beard, who said his name was Targun, asked Nianki what should be done with Kenase, who was cowering as he awaited his fate.

"Why ask me?" she replied, still rubbing her neck. Her skin was peeling from days of chafing.

"He betrayed us," Targun said, "but you saved us. Decide his fate. It will be done as you say."

Heavy silence fell over the camp, broken only by the crackle of the dying bonfire. Nianki cast a cold eye over the boy. He was crying now. His weakness disgusted her.

"Turn him out," she said at last. "Let him fend for himself. Tell the story far and wide so that no plainsman lends him food or comfort. If he lacks for anything, let him seek his masters in the forest."

Targun and the others man-handled Kenase to the path taken by the elves. Head bowed, the whimpering boy shuffled away, terrified of exile but relieved to be alive.

Someone pushed Nianki aside and jerked the spear from her hand. He ran forward a few steps and cast the short spear at the retreating Kenase. It struck him in the small of the back. He uttered a cry and fell facedown in the dirt.

The spear-thrower faced Nianki. It was Neko.

"Why?" Nianki demanded.

"Kenase led the Good People to my family," said the boy. "They killed my brother because he wouldn't submit to capture."

Nianki removed the spear and rolled the dead boy over. She closed his eyes and wiped the spear head on the grass.

"It is done," Targun said solemnly. "Let no more blood be shed."

The plainsmen drifted away, eager to put distance between themselves and the elf camp. Most of the families were gone by the time the red moon appeared over the horizon. A few remained, Targun's among them.

Nianki poked among the elves' abandoned gear. She found a bronze dagger in a wooden chest and slipped it in her waistband. While she was rummaging, she noticed the remaining men, women, and children were watching her.

"I'll not take everything," she assured them. "Get what you want."

"No," said Targun. "We're waiting for you." She stared at him blankly. "We want to follow you."

"I don't seek a mate," she said flatly.

"That's not what I mean." Targun gestured, and a short, smiling woman of ample proportions led four children to stand at his side. He obviously had no need of a mate. He said, "You bested the Good People and saved us all. There is a power in your presence, like the nearness of a panther. The spirits are in you, and we want to follow you."

"Let the spirits who protect you protect us as well," added Targun's mate.

Bewildered, Nianki was about to tell them they were all crazy, when she spotted Neko sitting on a stump near the fire. He looked numb, vacant. Though she'd never killed a man, she had seen that dazed reaction in others.

"What about you, Neko?" she called.

Slowly he looked up at her. "I've no blood kin left. I follow you."

Many pairs of eyes stared hopefully at her. As she looked around at the expectant faces and considered what was being asked of her, Nianki was reminded how they had defeated the better-armed, supposedly more powerful elves. A band of hunters who were not blood kin—such a band had not existed on the plains before. Perhaps there was something to be said for the safety and strength of numbers. If elves could do it, so could humans.

Nianki scrubbed a hand through her hair and sighed gustily. "I'm unmated, yet I've acquired a family," she muttered, then added more loudly, "All right, you can follow me."

"Where should we go?" asked Pirith, Targun's mate.

Nianki frowned at her, though it was a frown of thought rather than of displeasure. Pirith posed a very good question. Where should they go? East lay the domain of the elves, and the land to the south was also infested with the invaders. The western plain was where the killer pack had wiped out her family.

"North," Nianki said firmly. "Good hunting up north, this time of year."

They stripped the camp of everything useful, then waited for Nianki to lead them away.

Targun asked, "What is your name?"

Before Nianki could answer, Neko spoke.

"Karada," he said. She looked at him and smiled.

"That's right," she said. "Call me Karada."

# Chapter 8

~

Years passed. Ten times the trees blossomed, and ten times winter sheathed the cliffs surrounding the lake of the falls in white mantles of snow. Twenty-two plainsmen followed Amero to the lake—six women, four men, and twelve children. In ten years they became six hundred, partly from natural increase, partly from the arrival of new settlers. Word spread across the plains of the marvelous village on the lake where people came to live instead of spending their lives roaming the endless savanna. Some people came to see the settlement and went away puzzled. Others saw and remained to swell the growing population, and like tinder heaped on a glowing coal, the more the population swelled, the brighter the flames of progress.

The people who lived there called it Yala-tene, or "Mountain Nest," though most outsiders called the settlement Arkupeli, which meant "Place of the Dragon."

Unburdened by fears of attack, the people of Yala-tene devoted their energy to peaceful pursuits of hearth and field. The hide tents of the first settlers gave way over the years to real houses, stoutly built of local stone. There was little good timber in the vicinity—most of the wood available was soft pine and cedar—but stone was abundant. The villagers built their houses in the style of their old tents: round with high, domed roofs covered by slabs of slate or cedar shakes. The peak of the dome was left open to allow smoke from the hearth to escape. Each house was like a miniature fortress, with thick stone walls and no opening other than a single door. As families grew larger and more prosperous, some houses acquired second floors, and these were often pierced with long slit windows.

People who stayed in Yala-tene brought with them their own skills and ways of living. From the northern plains came gardeners, who taught the plainsmen how to cultivate crops instead of having to gather them in the wild. On the west shore of the lake, ground was cleared of thorny scrub and turned over to planting onions, cabbages, carrots, and even grapes. To make passage across the lake easier, the untamed river was bridged late one winter by a plan ingeniously conceived by Amero. Because of the lack of strong timber, a flexible plank bridge was held up by thick strands of vine rope that were anchored on each end by a squat stone tower. The bridge was completed in time for the spring planting of the settlement's fifth year.

In the seventh year of Yala-tene, herders arrived from the far south, driving flocks of goats and oxen before them. They came to barter for fodder as they passed through the desolate mountains, but some of the herders, too, remained behind when the flocks moved on. Enough herders chose to stay to provide fresh meat to the settlement the year round. Rock-walled pens were built on the north side of the sandy hill on which Yala-tene stood.

Twice a week the villagers slaughtered an ox or a pair of elk for the dragon. Knowing Duranix liked his food cooked, they learned to offer the meat on a blazing pyre of logs. The smell and sight of roasted meat attracted the attention of many people, and in time the fashion of eating cooked food became a firm habit.

After many weeks, bones and ashes began to pile up. To contain the growing mound of debris, villagers laid the beginnings of a rectangular wall of rock around the fire pit. Eager to show their appreciation of Duranix, everyone in Yala-tene gathered an armload of stones for the project. Before long, a large flat-topped cairn of smooth lake stones rose in the center of the village.

It became a sought-after honor to present the dragon with the twice-weekly offering, one the families in Yala-tene vied for. To keep the peace and determine fairly which family could serve the select haunches of beef and venison, Amero had to institute a rotating schedule, fixed by the positions of the white moon.

It was an arrangement that suited Duranix perfectly. At first the dragon had maintained his stated lack of interest in the humans that accompanied Amero back to the lake. Gradually, over many months, he found himself intrigued by their

111

activities. It was as though the very shortness of their lives imbued them with a sense of urgency. Duranix still came and went according to his desires, but he acceded to Amero's wish that he not absent himself for extended periods, since the fledgling settlement had come to rely on him completely for protection.

Duranix seldom went among the people himself because, even in his human form, most of the villagers feared him and wouldn't speak or act freely in his presence. Amero, who still lived in the great cave, became the dragon's go-between, and through him, Duranix kept up with the villagers' affairs. He knew them all by name, their rivalries, their passions, their triumphs and travails.

In the second year after the founding of the village, Amero devised a hoist by which he could be raised and lowered from the cave to the lake. At first this was a simple rope of vines tied to a man-sized basket made of woven willow wands, and it required Duranix to haul the basket up or lower it down. By year three, Amero had added a counter-weight and a windlass to the hoist so that he could raise or lower the basket without the dragon's help.

Though still a young man, Amero was generally recognized as the chief of Yala-tene, by virtue of his special relationship with the dragon. At twenty-three, he was a lean young man of middling height. He was pale for a plainsman, a consequence of spending so much time in caves and tents. After getting his long hair tangled in the windlass one day, Amero had gone to Konza the tanner and had his hair cut short. Elder plainsmen were shocked—they thought the length of a man's hair reflected strongly on his virility—but boys in the village took heed of the change and began cropping their hair in imitation of Amero. In time, only the most elderly men still wore traditional plainsman's braids or horsetails.

One evening in early summer of the eleventh year of Yala-tene, as shadows lengthened and the first fires began to gleam in the village below, the timber frame attached to the lower mouth of the cave creaked, and the thick vine rope piled up in a heap on the cave floor. The basket arrived bearing Amero, who leaped out and tied off the hoist.

Amero hailed Duranix as he entered the cave. The dragon, in his natural form, was lying atop his platform at the rear of the cave. He held a stone in one foreclaw and rubbed and scratched it with the other claw. The stone's surface glittered in the dimly lit cavern. Duranix's tail was wrapped around an oblong slab of granite, and he repeatedly lifted and lowered the slab. Amero knew what that repetitive motion meant—the dragon was bored.

"What do you have there?" Amero said, climbing the steps to the platform.

"I found it on my last flight east," said Duranix, squinting with one enormous eye at the stone in his fist. "It's extremely hard. I've been trying to work it into a more pleasing shape."

He paused his scratching and held the glittering stone on the points of two claws for Amero to see. It resembled a ball of ice the size of a child's head and was almost completely clear. Amero could see through the stone to Duranix's eye. The globular stone distorted the image, making the dragon's eye seem even larger than usual.

"It's beautiful," said Amero. "What kind of stone is it?"

"Diamond." He tossed the bright rock aside. "How go the storage caves?"

"Slow. The diggers hit a vein of black stone that's stopped them."

The villagers had decided to emulate Duranix and carve a series of tunnels in the cliff face—not to live in, but to store their supplies of dried and smoked meat, vegetables, and other foodstuffs. Early work went rapidly, and three galleries had been sunk into the mountain, but after forty days, the diggers met tougher rock. All three passages were blocked by the same impenetrable black stone, and their deer-antler picks and stone hammers could make little progress against the impervious wall.

"Do you need my help?" Duranix said.

"Not yet," Amero replied. "There's no better way to wake a lazy mind than to put it to work. Mieda will figure out some way around the problem."

Mieda was their chief digger, a man of many unusual talents. He'd walked into Yala-tene a year ago, starving and unable to speak. With patience and many good meals, he'd recovered, though he remained a taciturn, enigmatic figure. He had many skills, but his black skin and tightly curled hair marked him as being from a far different place.

Amero had been thrilled to meet Mieda, remembering the glimpse he'd caught of the two black men the day his family was attacked by the yevi. However, any questions Amero and his fellow villagers had about his origins were doomed to remain unanswered. Mieda would not talk about where he was from or about his past, but he did work hard and well, winning the trust and respect of the plainsmen.

"Speaking of problems, how's yours?" Duranix asked.

"Oh! My fire!"

Amero ran down the steps to the great hearth in the center of the cave. He used the leg bone of an ox to rake the ashes away from the morning fire. Buried under the ashes were several bronze dragon scales. Amero was trying to find a way to work Duranix's bronze into forms the villagers could use. Gingerly, with much waving of singed fingers, Amero snatched the blackened metal from the ashes.

Duranix slipped off the platform in one sinuous movement and came to the hearth. He found the notion of formulating tools from his hide peculiarly human. His wide reptilian head hovered over Amero's shoulder.

"Well?"

Though warped and blackened by heat, the scales had not melted. "Failed again!" Amero cried. "I was sure it would work this time!"

"What did you do differently?"

Amero threw the hot shards of bronze back in the firepit and dusted his sooty hands. "I wrapped the scales in wet river clay. I thought it might hold in the heat and melt the bronze."

"You laid an ordinary fire?"

Amero ran a hand through his cropped hair. "Yes. I've already tried using different kinds of wood in the fire. That had no effect. Are you sure your scales can be melted?"

"So I was told, long ago. It's not something I've given much thought to, you understand," said Duranix, rapidly losing interest. He flowed under the larger cave opening and reared up, resting his foreclaws on the rim of the hole and stretching his wings slightly. "I'm leaving the valley tonight. I may not be back till dawn."

Amero yawned, stretching his arms wide. "I was in the diggings all day, breathing dust and smoke from torches. I think I'll just wash up and go to sleep."

Long ago, at Amero's request, the dragon made a rent in the outer wall of the cave. A steady trickle of water from the falls flowed down this crack and filled a deep basin Duranix clawed out of the rock.

Amero stripped off his buckskin shirt and dipped his hands in the cool water.

"Where will you go?" he asked.

"South by east."

Amero stopped, water dripping from his cupped hands. "You've scouted that direction twice in the last five days. What's out there?"

"I don't know. Something. I've seen large clouds of dust hanging in the air at twilight. I've seen swaths cut through the grass by some large, moving formation. The tracks I've found are of four-footed creatures."

Amero dipped his hands in the water again and splashed a double handful on his face. "Yevi?" They'd periodically had to hunt down and destroy small yevi packs, but there'd been no massing of Sthenn's minions in almost ten years.

Duranix shook his head. Several loose scales fell from his neck, ringing when they hit the stone floor.

"It's the wrong direction for yevi unless they moved east in large numbers without my detecting them," the dragon said. "Whatever it is, they don't want to be seen. They move by night and hide by day. Game animals flee before them but follow after them, if that makes any sense."

The dragon thrust his head through the cave opening and sniffed the evening air. "Nothing seems amiss, yet something is," Duranix rumbled. "I'll find out what. Nothing on the plain can hide from me for long."

With his back feet gripping the rim, Duranix squeezed his bulky shoulders through the hole and unfurled his wings. A single push of his massive rear legs launched him skyward.

"Be careful!" Amero shouted. It was a silly thing to say to a creature as powerful as a dragon, but Amero meant it. He'd

grown extremely fond of Duranix, slowly coming to understand the dragon's odd sense of humor—and developing a
sense of humor himself in the process. He enjoyed their com-
panionship greatly. It still amazed him that he had such a fantastic creature for a friend.

He pulled a fur blanket around his shoulders and sat down
on the warm hearthstones. Scratching a piece of scorched
bronze with his fingernails, he pondered his problem. He
needed more heat if he was ever to melt the bronze. What
made one fire hotter than another? Women in the village
would sometimes hurry a pot to boiling by blowing the flames
with a reed fan. Would such a technique work on metal?
Maybe he could get one of the town basket weavers to make
him a big fan for the experiment.

Amero lay down on the hearth. Sleep claimed him, but
his rest was not peaceful. For the first time in many years he
dreamed of the day the yevi had killed his family. In his
dream he kept looking back over his shoulder to see Nianki
running behind him. *Faster! Go faster!* She mouthed the
words, but no sound came out. Amero raced for the nearest
tree. By the time he reached it and looked back again, Nianki
had vanished under a seething mass of fanged, gray-furred
bodies. He woke calling her name.

\* \* \* \* \*

Duranix cruised slowly at a great height, buoyed by
warm updrafts rising through the cold, high air. Far below,
the valleys were deeply shadowed clefts where any number
of enemies could hide. The valleys opened onto the plain,
which by night resembled a featureless sea of gray grassland. The dragon gazed down, trying to detect movement.
Individual creatures would be invisible from this height.
Even the heat of their blood wasn't discernible. It would
take a hundred creatures moving in unison to register in
Duranix's vision.

He floated for some time, bearing south and east from
home. Far to the south was the homeland of the elves, a
region he could safely ignore. They were no danger to him.
The elves were too civilized, too powerful to succumb to the

influence of Sthenn. The host moving across the eastern plain by night, slowly closing on the mountains, could be an elf band, but he discounted the idea. He'd found signs in the Khar River region that the elves had been fighting a formidable foe there. Daylight investigation revealed half a dozen elven strongholds burned to the ground since the red moon last waned.

Duranix had landed at one such site. The log stockade had still been smoldering when he arrived, but the only bodies he'd found were of slain elves. There had been no clues left behind to identify the marauders. Whoever had attacked the outposts carried away their own dead and scoured the battlefield for lost weapons.

The dragon hadn't shared this with Amero or the villagers. The settled life of the plainsmen was still precarious. One wrong word and many frightened humans would flee for the imagined safety of dispersal on the open grasslands. Amero had worked long and hard to win the trust of his people. He cared deeply that the village succeed. Duranix was too fond of his friend to allow his great project to fail, so he'd decided to hold his tongue until he had more certain knowledge of the possible danger.

A red glimmer broke the monotonous gray expanse below. It was only a momentary flare, but it caught the dragon's attention. Wings beating hard, he held his place and watched for a repeat of the telltale light. It did not appear again.

He spiraled down as quietly as possible, slowing his speed by letting his feet dangle. The savanna gained more detail. A strip of silver water running east-west, probably the river the elves called the Thon-Tanjan, appeared on Duranix's left. The ground was dotted with a few very large, widely spaced trees, burltops and vallenwoods. Scores of men or beasts could hide under a single one of them. He'd have to get closer still to investigate. At least the hilly terrain afforded him a concealed place to land.

The dragon alighted in a narrow draw and shrank to human guise. By the time he climbed the highest of the near hills, the denizens of the night had recovered from his intrusion. Crickets chirped in the grass, and clouds of mosquitoes filled the air.

He ran down the hill toward the spot where he'd seen the crimson gleam. When the pungent smell of burning pine reached him, Duranix flattened himself against the ribbed trunk of a giant burltop. He'd hardly taken up this position when a pair of animals trotted past. Mounted on the animals were riders carrying long spears.

Duranix froze. Grand as he was, as a dragon he was still cousin to the lizard and the snake, and when he wished he could remain perfectly motionless. The riders passed within arm's length of him. Their shape and smell was unmistakable—two humans riding two horses. Duranix knew elves tamed and rode horses, but he'd never heard of humans doing it until now.

He considered snatching one of the men and forcing him to answer questions, but paused when he heard them conversing in the tongue of the plainsmen.

". . . so I said, 'The best flint is the black kind from Khar land,' but you know Nebef, he thinks he knows everything, so he says, 'The yellow flint of the east mountains makes the best points . . .' "

Interesting, Duranix thought. Whoever they were, they were wide-ranging if they knew both Khar and this eastern plain.

After they'd passed, Duranix stepped out from behind the tree and watched the riders continue down the draw. He was so distracted by his discoveries that he didn't hear a second pair of riders steal up behind him.

Suddenly, a rough hide net was thrown over his head. Two horsemen, shouting in triumph, tried to sweep by on either side and scoop him into their net. They hadn't reckoned on snaring a dragon in disguise. Though he looked no bigger than a sturdy man, Duranix weighed as much as full-grown bronze dragon. When the net snapped taut, he merely planted his feet, and the riders were yanked off their horses.

Duranix pulled the net apart as easily as a man can tear a cobweb and stood over the two dazed riders. One was a rangy fellow with yellow hair, a flowing mustache, and a smoothly shaven chin. His companion was a short, dark female, clad in a strange outfit consisting of a buckskin tunic with short lengths of twig sewn on. The twigs had been peeled of their bark and matched to length. The female's arms and chest were covered in tight horizontal rows of white wooden pegs.

He picked up the woman by the collar and held her off the ground. She shook off the effects of her fall and stared at Duranix.

"Uran! Uran, get up!" she yelled. The yellow-haired man only groaned. The woman yanked a sharply pointed flint dagger from her waist and slashed at Duranix with it.

He caught her wrist with his free hand and squeezed. She screamed and let the knife fall to the ground. Duranix dropped her.

"You broke my arm!" she gasped, collapsing to the ground.

"I haven't broken it yet, but I can," said Duranix

"Who are you?"

"I'll ask the questions, though I can't improve on yours. Who are you?"

The woman glared at him fiercely and wouldn't respond. He picked up the stone knife and snapped it in two with one hand. His great strength caused her anger to dissolve into shock. To further intimidate her, Duranix allowed his eyes to flash with contained lightning.

"Forgive me, Great Spirit! Forgive us! We thought you were an elf!" the woman said.

"What is your name?" asked the dragon.

"Samtu."

"And him?"

"Uran. We are of Karada's band."

Duranix folded his arms. "And who is Karada?"

"The greatest hunter, the bravest warrior, the keenest tracker, the cleverest—"

"Yes, yes," said the dragon, interrupting a no doubt lengthy list of superlatives. "Where is this Karada? I would like to meet him."

All at once something gripped Duranix's ankles. There was a sharp tug and he lost his balance and fell backward. This is why four feet are better than two, he thought in disgust.

Samtu yelled, and her companion, Uran, leaped on the fallen Duranix. It was a brave deed, but entirely futile. With only the slightest effort, the disguised dragon hurled Uran aside. The plainsman flew some distance and landed heavily in the grass.

Duranix rose, irritated at being tripped by such a puny creature. He grasped Samtu by the hair and dragged her to her feet.

"I should pluck the head from your shoulders like a ripe cherry," he said coldly, "but first tell me where I can find this Karada."

"Spare me, Great Spirit!" she begged. "I'll take you to the camp! It isn't easy to find in the dark! Please let me live!"

Duranix released her, embarrassed he'd caused such terror. Humans, with their spears and stone knives, were far too weak to present a serious danger to him. He might as well torment a rabbit.

"Look to your companion," he said gruffly, gesturing at the fallen man. "He landed hard."

Samtu went to Uran, who hadn't moved since landing. She found him wide-eyed and staring, dead of a broken neck. She reported this to Duranix.

"My apologies," he said.

He was surprised when Samtu shook her head and declared, "It was a fair fight, though not an even one." She closed the dead man's eyes and removed the flint knife from his belt. Favoring her injured arm, she managed to heave Uran's body onto his horse. Samtu tied the reins to her mount's bridle.

"Come, Great Spirit. I will take you to Karada."

He expected to find the human chieftain camped beneath a spreading vallenwood, but the truth was more subtle. The plainsmen had cleared a large area of the shoulder-high grass in the midst of the open plain. Nets, supported by poles, were spread across the clearing. The cut grass had been layered on top of the net, which kept the camp from being spotted from above and gave shade to the artificial clearing beneath.

Leading her own and Uran's horse, Samtu allowed Duranix to precede her into the clearing, which was lit by a few small, smoky fires. That's what he'd glimpsed from the air, one of these veiled campfires.

Tough-looking warriors leaped to attention when they spied the stranger. Samtu tied the horses and warned her comrades off. As he passed them, Duranix slowly increased the height of his human form, so that he soon overtopped the tallest plainsman by a full span. He hoped his imposing size would forestall any more rash attacks.

Samtu announced, "Tell Karada a mighty spirit wishes to speak with her."

A runner was dispatched, and all awaited the arrival of the chieftain—the warriors with much muttering and fingering of spears, Duranix with utter calm. They did not have long to wait.

The chieftain entered the clearing alone and on foot. She was a woman, a bit older than twenty-five, rawboned and red-brown from the sun. Aside from her piercing eyes, Karada's most striking feature were the jagged scars that crisscrossed her throat, left arm, and right leg. She was clad in a knee-length, divided kilt of pigskin, tanned a soft gray. Her torso was covered with a ribbed breastplate of carved twigs, similar to the one Samtu wore, except the twigs were studded with carved teeth taken from various predators. Karada carried an unusual short-handled spear. The shaft was only half the usual length.

"Who are you?" she asked. Her voice was clear and firm, the tone of a woman used to being obeyed.

"My name is Duranix."

"Samtu says you killed one of my men."

"An accident. My regrets. I should have been more careful."

"Uran was a stout fighter," she said. "How did he die?"

Samtu related how they'd spied Duranix in the dark, apparently skulking on the trail of two of their other riders. She described their failure with the net and Duranix's amazing strength.

"Are you a spirit?" Karada asked, nonplussed.

"I am a living, flesh-and-blood creature, I assure you, but this shape you see is not my real one. I am a dragon—what you call a stormbird."

This revelation set off a loud hubbub in the clearing. Plainsmen left their campfires and filled the clearing around Duranix while he spoke, eyeing the body of their fallen comrade. When he announced the truth about himself, there were many loud denunciations.

"Shut up," Karada said without raising her voice. The crowd fell silent at once. "That's a tall tale, stranger. I'm known to be a blunt woman, but I won't call you a liar. What I want to know is, why are you here?"

"I dwell some distance from here, in the mountains. There are humans there living under my protection, and when I detected your band hiding by day and advancing by night, naturally I wanted to find out whether you were dangerous to my people."

Karada rested the short spear on her shoulder. "You live with humans?"

"A modest settlement," Duranix said.

Someone in the crowd said, "Arku-peli!"

The dragon surveyed the faces of Karada's plainsmen. They were very different from Amero's villagers, and different from the small family groups who still wandered the western savanna. There was pride in their faces, a sense of their own independence and toughness. Despite Duranix's words, his appearance, and the corpse of their comrade, they were not intimidated. The dragon found this interesting and disturbing at the same time.

"I see you've heard of our village," Duranix said. "Those who live there call it Yala-tene."

"It's said a stormbird lives at Arku-peli, in the cliffs above the lake," Karada replied. "Are you him?"

"None other."

She smiled thinly, sitting down on a fallen log. "I saw a stormbird once, many years ago, high in the sky. It was riding the crest of a storm, and I watched it slay half a herd of elk with its fiery breath."

Her words triggered a memory. Duranix hadn't hunted elk in years, not since the villagers began supplying him with choice sides of meat. An image surfaced in his mind: a bedraggled and bloody human waif, standing in pouring rain, watching him devour his food on the hoof . . .

"Are you listening?" Karada was saying.

Duranix pulled himself back to the present. "What?"

"I said, let me see you as you really are."

He considered the request briefly, then said no.

"Why not?" she asked. "You allow the people of Arku-peli to look upon you, don't you?"

"They're used to me. I wouldn't want to scare your men."

Duranix's remarks brought on a shower of boasts and threats from the plainsmen. Karada let them rant.

The dragon ignored their posturing. "What are you doing here, Karada? Are you headed for Yala-tene?" he asked.

"What if we were?"

"You're welcome, so long as you come in peace."

She jabbed the butt of her spear into the dirt. "Peace is not our concern just now! Silvanos, lord of the elves, is trying to push us back across the Tanjan. We're fighting back, as we did in the south. My scouts tell me he's moving a large war band up the Thon-Thalas on rafts. I intend to meet them. We'll crush them where they step ashore."

This declaration stirred fierce cheers from the warriors.

Karada continued, "When we've defeated the elves and sent them back to their forest, maybe then we'll pay a friendly visit to Arku-peli. Does that answer your question, dragon-man?"

"Well enough, Scarred One." The mutual witticism made them both smile. He touched his right hand to his forehead in salute, allowing a small snap of lightning to pass between his fingertips and head. The plainsmen pressing in on the scene grunted in surprise and drew back.

"I'll tell the people of Yala-tene you're only interested in fighting elves. Good luck to you, Karada, and be cautious. Elves are not to be trifled with. They're a force of nature, like a cloudburst. Their fury can be endured but not turned aside."

"Keep your advice, dragon. Silvanos is learning we humans are a force as well. We ask only the right to go where we will, to live as we will. If Silvanos would grant us that, there would be no fighting."

Tired of the belligerent band, Duranix said farewell and departed on foot. Karada's nomads parted ranks for him, and he strolled away into the night.

\* \* \* \* \*

When the dragon was gone, Karada called, "Pakito, Pa'alu, I want you."

The two brothers, long members of Karada's band, pushed their way through the throng and stood before their chief.

Pakito had grown into a huge man, heavily muscled from balding head to bare toes. Pa'alu cut an impressive figure as well, less massive than his brother, but with a formidable width of shoulders and powerful limbs.

"What's your will, Karada?" asked Pa'alu.

"Follow him," she said, indicating the departed Duranix. "Find out where he goes, and see if he is what he claims."

"And if he's not?" rumbled Pakito.

"If he's a fool or a liar, let him be. If he's a scout for Silvanos, bring back his head."

"Aye, Karada. That we'll do." Pakito cracked the joints of his enormous hands for emphasis.

The plainsmen dispersed to their beds. Pa'alu lingered in the clearing until he was alone with Karada.

"What is it?" she asked.

"I still think your plan is wrong," he said, kneeling beside her. "We can't face an elf war band on equal terms. Most of our men still use flint-head spears and stone axes. We have horses now, and a few elven blades, but it's not enough."

She regarded him coldly. "Is it because you are afraid, Pa'alu?"

"I've hunted and fought at your side for nine seasons. What's at stake is not my life or yours, but the whole band. You know I speak from the heart."

"When the gray killers destroyed my family, I survived because I fought back," she said. "I've hunted down and slain more of them than I can count. When the 'Good People' tried to drive all humans from the southland, I brought the families and single hunters together to fight back. Now we're five hundred strong. We have horses and can cover ten leagues a day, hunt and fight on the move . . ." Karada paused, tracing a line in the dirt with her toe. "I know the elves are powerful, Pa'alu. They have metal. Their shamans have spirit-power none of our wise men can match. It's said they can change the weather, command the winds, talk to beasts of the air, land, and water . . ." She slammed the butt of her spear on the ground. "So, do we throw down our spears and run away, hoping the great Silvanos doesn't decide to take the land north of the river away from us?"

She stood up, hair falling loosely into her face. "We will

fight, Pa'alu. We will hit them as they try to leave their rafts, and the river will run red with elf blood. Then Silvanos will know we are not rabbits, but plainsmen!"

She stalked away. He followed, catching her arm.

"You've been alone too long," he said in a low voice. "You see only with the eyes of a hunter. Put down your spear, Nianki. Take me as your mate."

She pried his hand loose. "You take a chance," she whispered. "I've killed men who laid hands on me. Do you remember Neko?"

Pa'alu stepped back. "I meant no disrespect. I love you, Nianki."

Her expression did not change. "I've no time for such things. Pakito is waiting. Go."

When Pa'alu remained, she gave him a level look and departed. He watched until darkness engulfed her, cursing himself for saying too much and for loving a woman he could not reach. He might as well love the stars in the sky—like Nianki, they could lead you through the darkest night, but they were impossible to touch and gave no warmth. So it was with his chief. Many men had tried to win her or take her, but she'd bested them all. Through it all Pa'alu remained at her side, glad to be a friend and comrade, if nothing else.

Pakito's bull voice echoed across the clearing, calling him. With a deep sigh Pa'alu shouldered his knapsack and went to join his brother.

Out from under the protective canopy of grass, the sight of the stars mocked his heart. Pa'alu had never thought much about spirits and powers, but faced with an impossible goal, he decided it couldn't hurt to reach out to them in case there were forces greater than humankind who could intervene on his behalf.

Pa'alu looked up at the sparkling firmament and made a solemn vow. Some day, Nianki would be his. Whatever the cost, he would have her.

# Chapter 9

~

It didn't take long for Duranix to discover he was being followed. This did not mean Pa'alu and Pakito were clumsy stalkers, merely that the dragon's senses were far more perceptive than any normal prey. He heard their footfalls behind him within a league of leaving Karada's camp. Once he knew they were there, it was easy to spot them. The warm blood in their veins gave their silhouettes a dull luminosity against the cooler background of trees and grass. After ascertaining his trackers numbered only two, he moved on.

Duranix could have reverted to dragon shape and taken to the air, leaving the humans far behind, but that wouldn't have been nearly so interesting. Instead, he began to walk faster and faster until he was covering ground in huge bounds. His pursuers faded in the distance. Once his lead was comfortable, Duranix searched for a convenient spot to turn the tables on the plainsmen.

He found what he wanted in a field of boulders. Hundreds of upright stones littered the grassland, most of them slabs of black granite. Their regularity, and the fact that no other outcroppings of similar stone occurred in the vicinity, puzzled the disguised dragon. The stones appeared to have been arranged purposefully, but who could have done such a thing? They were well outside elf territory, and the backward local humans lacked the means to move so many heavy boulders.

Duranix stopped at the edge of the field of standing stones. His run across the savanna hadn't winded him. A quick glance behind failed to reveal Pakito or Pa'alu in sight.

The dragon entered the outer circle of stones. He trailed his fingers over the rough surface of one angular boulder. His senses tingled strongly. Surprised, he pressed first his palm, then his cheek against the cold granite. The stone fairly hummed with contained force. There were hundreds more stones around him. He touched those nearest him and found them charged as well. Much power had been expended here in the distant past—power greater than a hundred dragons. The stones radiated it invisibly, like heat stored up from a hot summer day.

The deeper he went into the formation, the more disturbed Duranix became. He'd been looking for a spot to stage a playful ambush. Instead, he'd stumbled across a place of vast, captive spiritual energy. It was neither benign nor malign in flavor, but the sheer amount of power pent up in these stones made Duranix's mock-human skin crawl.

He'd wasted enough time with these savages. He resolved to get out of this strange forest of stones, resume dragon form, and fly back to his lake. On his way out, he heard movement among the standing stones—a jingle of metallic links, the flex of heavy leather.

A tiny blue spark appeared in the air before him and rapidly grew into a spinning globe of light three spans wide. It was harmless, Duranix knew, merely a source of illumination, but it meant someone mortal was drawing on the power of this place.

Folding his arms, Duranix said loudly, "You've made yourself known. Who are you, and what do you want?"

Two-legged figures emerged from behind the stones—more than a dozen in all. Duranix readied himself to fight or flee. Some of the hidden watchers gathered under the blue light, and he saw they were elves, not humans. They surrounded Duranix with a ring of bronze-tipped javelins.

Eleven were dressed in warrior garb. The twelfth was visibly older than the rest, wore a long blue robe embroidered with arcane hieroglyphs, and had a feathery mustache and beard. Duranix was intrigued by this last detail. Elves did not possess facial hair. They regarded beards as a bestial human trait. Sparse though it was, this bearded stranger could not be a full-blooded elf and, surprisingly, he chose to flaunt the fact.

He leaned on a tall, stout staff, studded with raw, unpolished gems. "I am Vedvedsica, high sage to my lord Balif, first warrior of the host of our great master, Silvanos." Vedvedsica raised his staff, pointed it at Duranix, and declared in ringing tones, "You are not what you appear to be!"

"Who is?" said the dragon pleasantly. "What brings you so far from your native forest? Aren't you afraid of the plainsmen?"

"I am well protected," the robed elf replied, with a nod to his escort.

Piercing the night with his dragon's eyes, Duranix perceived each of the armed elves was weighed down with a pair of hide bags draped across their shoulders. The bags were obviously heavy and clinked when the elves moved. Vedvedsica himself had a small drawstring bag around his neck.

"You've been prospecting," Duranix surmised, "chipping fragments from the standing stones."

One of the warriors shifted nervously, saying, "He knows our business, Master. Shall we silence him?" The other elves tensed, ready to strike with their javelins.

"No!" the priest said sternly. "This is no wandering barbarian! Keep still, or he may slay us all!"

Duranix had to smile. "You're wise for one so small."

A shrill whistle split the air. Half the elves turned about, scanning the ill-lit stones for the source of the noise. A similar whistle rose from the darkness on the other side of the stone field. The senior warrior snapped commands, and four elves ran off into the shadows to investigate.

Duranix stood very still. He detected motion above and behind him. His peripheral vision discerned someone jumping from the top of one standing stone to another. The elves hadn't noticed.

"What will you do with them?" Duranix asked as the drama unfolded around them.

"Do with what?" Vedvedsica asked, frowning. There was something unnatural about his eyes. With those whiskers under his nose, he had the face of a panther.

"Those stones." A second shadowy figure leaped across the high rocks on Duranix's right. Still the elves saw nothing. "The ones you and your retainers carry."

The priest fingered the little bag hanging down on his chest. "These will make powerful amulets," he said. "The high lords of Silvanost will reward me richly for them."

Just then a fist-sized rock hit the warrior nearest Duranix in the face. He went down hard, blood spurting from his nose.

The rest of the elves exploded into uncoordinated action—running, yelling, trying to minister to their fallen comrade. One angry elf ported his javelin and tried to shove Duranix back against one of the boulders.

The dragon felt he had been more than patient, but his forbearance was wearing thin. He grasped the offending javelin with one hand and snapped it in two places with a twist of his wrist. The astonished elf leaped back, clawing for his bronze short sword. Duranix blew lightly in the warrior's face. The elf dropped his sword and ran screaming into the outer darkness.

Duranix turned his attention to the priest's light orb. With a sweep of his hand he shattered the fiery blue ball into ten thousand sparks, which winked and went out. Night engulfed the scene.

Someone large and heavy landed in front of Duranix. He grabbed the intruder by the front of his buckskin shirt.

"It's me—Pakito!" his captive said.

"So it is." Duranix hoisted Pakito off his feet and flung him at the group of elves guarding Vedvedsica. They all went down in a flailing, cursing heap. Pakito recovered first and laid about him with his massive fists.

"Pa'alu! Brother, I'm here!" he shouted. Duranix couldn't tell if he was calling for help or asking Pa'alu to join the fun.

The priest, seeing his guards scattered, turned to run. He was preternaturally fleet, but Duranix was on him in two long bounds. The disguised dragon snagged the elf priest by the back of his robe. Suddenly, there was a choking aroma of flowers, as if Duranix had been buried under a mountain of roses and lilacs, and he found himself holding an empty robe.

The smell was overwhelming. Coughing, Duranix threw down the robe and tried to find the fleeing priest. His eyes swept the horizon but saw nothing.

Pakito had subdued five of the elves by sitting on them. When one struggled to escape, Pakito whacked him with the butt of a javelin. One brave elf charged out of the dark with his weapon leveled. Duranix stepped in front of him. The bronze spearhead struck the dragon square in the chest, and the elf thrust hard. His javelin bent double, leaving Duranix unharmed. Uttering a terrified oath, the warrior dropped his weapon and fled.

Quiet descended. Pa'alu joined them, casually wiping blood from an elven sword.

Pakito looked up from his awkward position atop the unconscious elves. "Well, dragon-man," he said genially, "I'm glad we didn't try to take you back at camp!" He told his brother how the elf's spear had hurt Duranix no more than a soggy reed.

Pa'alu listened intently then shoved his sword through his belt and surveyed the area. "Lucky thing we happened along."

"Luck? You two have been trailing me since I left Karada's camp."

"Not us!" Pakito insisted, but his open expression easily betrayed the truth of the matter.

The dragon shook his head. "No matter. What concerns me most is the elf priest who escaped."

"We first thought you came here to meet them," Pa'alu said. "It wasn't until we heard you talking that we realized you were as surprised as we were to find them here."

"What is this place, anyway?" asked Pakito.

"I'm not certain," said Duranix. "It feels like . . . a graveyard."

Pakito jumped to his feet. The elves he'd been sitting on groaned but remained quiescent. "Who's buried here?" the big man asked, eyes wide.

"No one."

Pa'alu ran a hand lightly over a nearby stone. "What do you mean?"

"This formation is not natural," Duranix told them. "These stones have stood for untold years, yet they still resonate with great power."

"I've heard stories," Pa'alu said, lowering his voice, "tales of the days before men and elves. It's said the spirits fought a great war over who would rule the world."

"True enough," Duranix said.

"Maybe these are some of the losers."

The dragon was struck by the plainsman's surprising acumen. He knew from his hatchling days of the All-Saints War, when the spirits aligned themselves with Good or Evil, or tried to remain neutral. After some defeats, the forces of

Good and Neutrality allied themselves and defeated—but did not destroy—the forces of Evil. What greater punishment could there be for defeated spiritual beings than to be confined to the material world, imprisoned for eons in a matrix of unfeeling stone?

Pakito broke the silence. "What about them?" he asked, gesturing toward the limp pile of bodies.

"Take their metal and leave 'em," Pa'alu said, squatting by his brother's unconscious victims. "It's a long walk back to the forest. Maybe a wolf or panther will get them on the way."

"Karada should know they were here," Pakito insisted. "There aren't supposed to be any elves this far north. What if there are more?"

"What indeed?" Duranix shook off the oppressive aura of the stones. "Your chief should be warned. This was a small party, but if a sizable band of elves is about, your people could be trapped between it and the force ascending the Thon-Thalas."

"Who'll warn Karada?" Pakito wondered, looking confused. "We were ordered to follow you."

"I return to Yala-tene. One of you can come along; the other can go back and warn Karada."

The brothers saw the sense in this. Pakito, knowing his brother's feelings for their chief, offered to go with Duranix. Pa'alu declined.

"I haven't been to the mountains since I was a boy," he said. "I'll go with the dragon-man."

"But—"

"Go on, Pakito. You're the only one who can carry all this metal back anyway." He filled his brother's arms with elven javelins, swords, greaves, and helmets. "Start now. You'll reach camp before noon."

Pa'alu hung a few extra waterskins—taken from the elves—around his hulking brother's neck and, with a hearty slap on his back, sent him on his way. While the brothers were parting, Duranix went to where Vedvedsica's robe lay. A dense odor of flowers still clung to the empty garment.

Pa'alu approached. "Find something?"

"I'd hoped to find the bag of stone chips he carried," said Duranix. "It appears he took them with him."

"How are such things done?"

"It's a talent, and a rare one among flimsy creatures like yourselves. I think the priest has somehow learned to tap the latent power of the stones. It's a dangerous ability for savages."

Duranix stood, tossing the robe aside. When he did, a single small stone fell from the folds. Pa'alu picked it up. It was a smooth, heavy nugget, no bigger than a walnut, and of a richer yellow color than bronze.

"Heavy," said the plainsman, handing the stone to Duranix. "What is it?"

"Gold." What felt like cold stone to the plainsman almost burned Duranix's hand. The nugget was saturated with power.

To Pa'alu's bewilderment, Duranix put the yellow nugget in his mouth. Without further explanation, he struck out due west for Yala-tene, leaving Pa'alu hurrying on his heels to keep up.

* * * * *

Smoke poured from the mouth of the tunnel. Amero and his chief digger, Mieda, stood back from the opening with strips of wet birch-bark over their noses and mouths. Deep inside, they could see a red flicker of flame. More diggers emerged, coughing and soot-stained. When they reached open air, they doused themselves with handy buckets of cold lake water.

"How goes it, Farun?" Amero asked anxiously.

The digger, his face blackened by soot, coughed and said, "It's still burning, but no one can stay in there long."

"That's all right," Amero replied. "As long as we can run in and feed the fire, there's nothing else to do right now."

Fire had been Mieda's idea. The storage tunnels had progressed well as long as there was sandstone to burrow through, but when the diggers found a strain of hard black stone, the project stopped dead. They tried various tools on the black stone, including shovels fashioned from the dragon's cast-off scales, but nothing made an impression. Then one morning Amero found Mieda by the shore of the lake. He'd built a small twig fire and was watching it intently.

"Catch a fish?" Amero asked.

Mieda tapped the black object in the fire with a stick.

"What's that?"

"Black stone, like in tunnel." Mieda's command of the plainsman's language wasn't complete. Many villagers still thought he was slow-witted because he didn't talk much. Amero knew better.

"You're cooking a stone?"

"Yes." Mieda remained cross-legged on the sand, staring at the fire.

Amero dropped down on the other side of the flames. He said nothing for a long time, then impatience stirred his tongue.

"What are you doing, Mieda?"

"Learning to break rock." He leaned forward and spat on the black stone shard. Satisfied with the hiss that it produced, Mieda dipped his hands in the lake and dumped the water squarely on the stone. Smoke and steam rose. The little fire sputtered and died.

"What did that accomplish?" Amero asked.

Mieda raised his stick—a limp pine branch, plucked green from the tree—and struck the black rock smartly. To Amero's amazement, the rock cracked and fell apart.

"How did you do that?" he exclaimed.

Mieda smiled. "Seen it before. Cooled fast, hot stone breaks." He met Amero's eyes. "Understand?"

"Yes! We can do this in the tunnel!"

So they did. It wasn't as easy as cooking a rock on the beach. The tunnels filled with smoke when the first dry pine boughs were set alight. The diggers ran out for fresh air, but someone had to go back at intervals to feed the flames. Every bucket, gourd, and bowl in Yala-tene was filled with water, ready to throw on the heated rock face. Normal work in the village came to standstill as everyone waited to see if Mieda's technique worked as well in the large scale as it did in the small.

The fire had been burning all morning. Farun reported the heat inside the tunnel was unbearable. Amero looked to his chief digger.

"What do you say, Mieda?"

133

"Water."

Amero held up his hands. "Take the water now! Two at a time, go!"

He and Mieda were the first to enter. Still holding soaked bark to their faces and waddling under the weight of full buckets, they entered the smoky passage. The heat was overwhelming. Sweat coursed down Amero's face as they neared the fire. In addition to the pine boughs, the diggers had stacked oak wood against the wall. The hardwood had burned down to a glowing drift of coals.

Mieda dropped his mask and picked up his bucket in both hands. He flung the water high, so it would run down the rock face. Amero did the same, then both men retreated, coughing hard. As soon as they were out, the next pair ran in, and the next, until forty pails had been dumped on the fire.

Amero, Mieda, and the diggers stood around the mouth of the tunnel, wrapped in steam and smoke. A gentle breeze helped clear the mist away.

"Now, we'll see." Amero started for the opening. Farun held out a long-handled stone mallet. Amero smiled and rested the heavy tool on his shoulder.

The others trooped in behind Amero. The carved stone floor sloped downward, so the farther they went the more standing water they encountered. By the time they reached the black stone wall, water, ashes, and rock dust had combined to make a soupy black mud. Some of the men slipped and fell. A few others snickered. Amero let the mallet hit the floor, and the resulting clunk silenced the crowd at his back.

"Give it a whack," said Farun.

"It ought to be your honor," Amero said, offering the handle to Mieda.

The dark-skinned man pressed the mallet back into Amero's hands. "Honor's yours," he said. He gestured to Farun and the others. "My life, their lives, are owed to you. You hit."

Amero swung the hammer high and brought it down smartly on the obstinate wall. The hammer head was granite, and many granite tools had been broken on the black stone before, but this time the obstruction shattered. Grit flew, and hand-sized flakes fell to the muddy floor. The diggers roared with satisfaction.

Outside, the waiting villagers heard the cry of success and echoed it. Men ran out of the tunnel calling for baskets to haul away the debris. More mallets were brought, and soon the cliff side rang with the blows of stone on stone.

Amero and Mieda stood outside and watched a continuous line of diggers emerge bearing baskets full of broken rock. These were emptied on a large pile of leavings that rose by the side of the lake. As more black stone was thrown on top of the sandstone debris, tiny avalanches cascaded down the pile into the lake.

"We'll have to find a better place to dump that," Amero mused. "We don't want the lake tainted with rock dust."

A young woman emerged from the tunnel with a basket on her back. Amero quickly lost interest in the rock pile when he recognized Halshi, eldest child of Valka, one of the first plainsmen to settle by the lake with his family. Halshi had jet-black hair, smooth, tanned skin, and a ready smile. Amero had hinted to Valka he was interested in becoming Halshi's mate, but with one thing and another, this task and that, nothing was ever settled between them. Still, Amero always found himself watching her whenever she was around.

Halshi added her burden to the pile. She'd started for another load when Amero called to her.

"How goes it?" he asked. "Are they breaking through?"

"Oh, yes," she said, hitching her basket on her hip. "The rock's flying apart now. You did a good job, Mieda."

The chief digger acknowledged the compliment with a nod. Amero found himself wishing he'd earned Halshi's praise.

A scattering of red glints in the rock pile caught his eye. Amero squinted to see them better. It wasn't a trick of the light. As he drew nearer, he saw the debris was flecked with hundreds of small red beads.

"What's this?"

He knelt and picked a larger nodule out of the pile. Roughly globular, the bead was shiny and hard, like Duranix's scales, though a different color.

"That stuff?" said Halshi, looking down at him. "I don't know, but the pit's full of it." She returned to the tunnel.

Amero found himself intrigued by the strange red beads. He dug through the coarse slag with his hands and found most of the black stone was dotted with them. Even odder were the larger slabs of rock that had red beads oozing out of them.

A shadow fell across Amero. Mieda had come to see. "Ever seen this stuff before?" Amero held up a handful of red beads.

Mieda examined the pellets closely, holding them up to the light, even putting one between his teeth and biting on it. At last, he replied, "It's copper."

"What's copper?"

"It's strong. It's—" Mieda groped for a word the plainsman would recognize. "The dragon, his hide is like this." He made two fists and banged them together. "Strong. Hard. This is copper."

"Metal? It comes from rocks?" asked Amero, amazed.

"I've lived long, been many places, seen it before. I never saw it made. It makes tools and pretty things, if you have enough of it."

Amero was lost in thought. "There were no beads in the black stone before the fire," he muttered to himself. "Somehow the fire sweated the copper out of the rock."

His mind was racing. For years he'd sought to make use of Duranix's cast-off scales, but aside from bending or sharpening them, he'd found no way of changing their shape. All his experiments with fire had failed to melt a single bronze scale. If a substance with scale-like hardness could be extracted from the earth around them, couldn't it be worked into more useful forms, into any form they wanted?

He set a gang of children to work sifting through the tunnel slag. All the red pellets were to be collected and saved.

By sunset the tunnel had been extended five paces deeper into the mountain. They'd planned to go twenty paces in each tunnel. That would guarantee cool, safe storage for a long time. The villagers were tired but happy with their success.

Amero was too excited to sleep. He had a basket full of copper beads and a head full of ideas. Other tunnels could be extended through the black stone blockage using Mieda's heating method. If each one yielded similar amounts of copper, Amero would have enough raw material to begin experimenting with it. He wished Duranix were here to advise him. The dragon found the human predilection for toolmaking amusing, and he was a fount of useful ideas.

Thinking of the dragon raised a new question: Where was Duranix? His flight to and from the east should have taken only one day. The sun was now setting on the dragon's second day away.

Amero realized Duranix might have been diverted by any number of things. Who could know what would interest a dragon? Still, he found himself staring at the eastern range, a frown on his face, as the setting sun turned the sky at his back crimson. He kept hoping for a glimpse of the dragon flying home, but the darkening sky remained empty

# Chapter 10

A strange and ominous calm hung over the banks of the Thon-Thalas. Cold river water, collected in the mountains to the west, chilled the warm summer air, creating patches of mist slowly flowing along with the current. Half of Karada's band, almost two hundred-fifty men and women of fighting age, crouched in the bushes a pace or two from the water's edge. Further up the hill, the rest of the plainsmen waited on horseback, their position screened by a hedge of freshly cut saplings.

Now and then a horse snorted or tried to eat the tender leaves of the camouflage just in front of them. Karada glowered at these indiscretions, and the riders quieted their mounts quickly.

Pakito came up the hill, moving with remarkable stealth for a man his size. He'd been appointed to lead the warriors on foot, partly because of his great strength, but also because they had no horse that could carry him.

He ascended by way of a path carefully screened with vines and replaced undergrowth. When he reached the hedge Pakito waved to his chief.

"Any sign?" she whispered.

"They were at the deer ford last night," Pakito replied huskily. "Our scouts counted thirty-two rafts, sixteen with warriors, ten for horses, and the rest laden with supplies."

Karada nodded, satisfied. The elves never traveled without what seemed to plainsmen like copious, unnecessary supplies—food, tents, tools, and assorted mysterious gear whose purpose was known only to elves. Their equipment allowed them to do many things the plainsmen couldn't, but carrying it also slowed them down. Karada intended to exploit this weakness to the fullest.

"Go back to the river," she told Pakito. "Make ready. They'll be here about dawn."

He grinned widely. "I wouldn't want to be an elf this morning!"

"I wouldn't be an elf ever," she muttered, dismissing him. Pakito hurried back down the path to his waiting men.

Gradually the violet pre-dawn gave way to the rose of daybreak. Karada took off her heavy headband and wiped her forehead. The band was made of bear teeth, bored through and strung together on a backing of black ox hide. Her people had contributed all the bear's teeth gathered in a year's hunting to make the headband for Karada. She clenched it tightly in her hand as if to take the power and ferocity of the bears into her own spirit.

A distinctive three-note whistle rose from the riverbank. The signal! The elves were in sight!

Karada replaced her headband and drew the sword she'd taken from the elf Tamanithas so many years ago. All along the line the mounted warriors stirred restlessly. She glared them into silence again.

Through the leafy hedge she spied the first raft. It was a square platform of logs lashed together, about two paces by four. A crowd of twenty elf warriors stood in the center of the raft while bare-chested rafters walked back and forth along both sides, pushing the craft along by means of long wooden poles. Mist on the river parted in front of them. The raft moved slowly down the center of the stream, making deliberate progress against the current.

Karada and her scouts had reconnoitered the Thon-Thalas for eight leagues in both directions and had picked this spot as the place the elf expedition would likely disembark. The riverbank was wide and firm here. Farther south the banks were too steep, and farther west the current was too swift for poling. This was the spot and no other.

A shout, and the rafters reversed their poling pattern. Karada flexed her fingers around her reins. With much scrambling, the pole-carriers collected on the left side and in unison drove their poles hard into the water. The awkward craft nosed for shore.

No sooner had the hewn ends of the logs touched the bank than the elf warriors sprang ashore with weapons drawn. They formed a line, their chief shouting a series of commands. They moved inland a few paces, poking the underbrush with their spears and swords. Karada held her breath.

139

Her warriors were not far from where the sharp bronze points probed. She knew her fighters would keep cool. They were as much afraid of her and Pakito as they were the elves, but she worried the elves would discover the trap before it was ready to spring.

The elf chief called a halt, assembling his troop at the water's edge. The rafters pushed their craft away and made room for the next one. It too was loaded with armed warriors. These filed off and awaited the next raft.

Karada shaded her eyes from the morning sun and looked downriver. The expedition was piling up, the rafts bumping each other. The current was just strong enough to require constant effort to keep the rafts in place. As she expected, the warriors were concentrated in the first rafts. After them came the horses; the supplies would be landed last. By then the river would be a solid, chaotic mass of rafts, balky animals, and struggling rafters. That would be the time to attack.

And so it happened. Elf warriors filled the dry ravine leading from the river's edge to the open plain above. It was the obvious, easy place for them to muster once they'd left their rafts. They stood alertly for a time, watching the trees with disconcerting intensity, but as the morning grew hot and nothing happened they began to grow careless. Some even took off their helmets and sat down on the mossy ground.

The last of the three hundred and sixty warriors came ashore, and the first raft of horses nosed forward. Pens had been erected on the rafts to keep the animals in order. Karada was glad to see the horses arrive. Their smell covered the odor of her band's horses.

An elf on the front of the first raft of horses threw a line to waiting comrades on shore. Four elves took hold and hauled the raft in. Empty troop rafts bumping against them made the process awkward and tedious.

Karada gave a signal. It was relayed down the line, and a gray object, a little bigger than a man's head, was tossed out of the trees to land at the feet of the four elves pulling in the horse barge. In an instant wasps spilled out of the gray object and attacked the rafters. Yells and much slapping ensued, and some of the unfortunates threw themselves in the river. Warriors nearest the shore stood and laughed at their comrades' ill luck.

They stopped laughing as three more wasps' nests landed among them. A lordly chieftain, recognizable by his elaborate helmet and fur-trimmed mantle, drew his sword and pointed at the trees where Pakito's men were hiding. One nest might be a misfortune; four constituted an attack.

The elves formed ranks even as the wasps swarmed over them. Karada had to admire their discipline under such conditions. She doubted even fear of her would keep her own band steady under such an onslaught.

More nests were lobbed at the horse rafts. Crazed by the stings, the horses burst their flimsy pens and floundered into the river. Rafters were thrown down when the animals swamped the log platforms. Soon the river was filled with elves and horses. Over all hung a cloud of angry black wasps.

The front ranks of the elf force stormed up the bank to Pakito's position. The giant plainsman stood up and roared defiance at the enemy. He had painted his face with white clay, soot, and berry juice. When Pakito was joined by two hundred and fifty comrades, the charging elves wavered and stopped, but only for a moment. The rear ranks flung javelins at the wildly painted enemy, and Pakito's men replied with their last batch of wasps' nests.

Karada wanted to cheer when she saw Pakito holding his men in place. Plainsmen all too often wanted to rush their foes, yelling and waving their spears. A headlong rush would strike terror into the hearts of most foes, but the elves were too well trained to succumb to panic. This time Pakito, holding his people firm, forced the elves to climb the slope. All the while the plainsmen pelted their enemy with rocks and heavy splits of wood.

The line of elves extended past the plainsmen's position, so those on the extreme right broke formation and ran to hit Pakito's men on the flank. When they did, they exposed their backs to Karada's hidden horsemen. She raised her sword high. The eye of every horseman was on her. Wordlessly she whipped her blade down and urged her mount forward.

From the river it appeared as though a wall of mounted human warriors had burst through the trees, and a wail of confusion went up from the elves.

141

Karada charged ahead, running one elf down and impaling another with her sword. The shocked troops tried to turn to counter her attack. As they did Pakito let loose his bull-like battle cry, and the humans fighting on foot surged down the hill.

The trap was sprung, and the fight quickly became fierce. Karada laid about her on every side, trading blows with any elf in reach. A javelin flew at her face. She batted it aside, but an elf came up close on her right and upended her by grasping her foot and heaving her off her horse. She landed heavily in the trampled ferns and rolled quickly away to avoid being stepped on by her own animal. Rising, she was immediately attacked by a sword-armed elf. They traded cuts. He was trained in this art, and Karada was not. She received a ringing blow on the side of the head. Her bear's tooth headband saved her life, but she went down hard, losing her weapon.

Karada scrambled to her feet, snatched up an elven spear, and fought her way to her comrades. She climbed atop a stump and saw that most of the elves had been pushed back to the river. Some had been driven into the water, and others clambered onto empty rafts. Bundles of javelins were being passed hand over hand from the supply rafts to where the battle raged. Karada decided to put a stop to that.

She rallied sixteen mounted plainsmen and ordered one to give up her mount to the chief. The woman climbed down. It was Samtu, who'd brought the dragon-man to camp not long ago.

"Take care of Appleseed," Samtu said, handing the reins to Karada.

"No promises," the chief replied. "Warriors, with me!"

They swung away from the main fight and galloped down the riverbank. The elven rafts had bunched together, filling the river from side to side. Without a word of explanation or warning, Karada rode to the water's edge and urged her horse to leap. The horse sprang and landed solidly on one of the rafts. The craft bobbed hard, causing Appleseed to scramble for footing, but the animal kept his feet and Karada kept her balance too.

She speared a rafter who tried to fend her off with his pole. Two other elves tore into the bundle of javelins they'd been trying to pass, seeking to free some to use against Karada. She slid off Appleseed and killed them both before they could get weapons in their hands.

By now many elves were standing in water up to their knees. The rearmost ranks were climbing across rafts to reach the south shore. The plainsmen higher up on the bank, with no one left to fight, began throwing stones or javelins at the fleeing enemy. The last rafts in the convoy, the ones laden with the expedition's supplies, began to retreat. Rafters poled frantically downstream, eager to escape the ferocious onslaught.

"Go!" Karada shouted after them. "Go! Come no more to our land!"

Her triumph was cut short by a blast of noise—the sound of ram's horns. Startled, she remounted Appleseed and rode to the shore. The rumble of massed hooves filled the air.

A cry rose from the throats of the elves on the riverbank. "Balif! Balif!"

She couldn't believe it. Balif, the elf lord who'd captured her on the beach so many years ago? She led the remaining mounted plainsmen up the draw, reining up when she reached the edge of the plain. What she saw brought a lump to her throat.

Elves, hundreds and hundreds of them, all on horseback. Sunshine glinted off their bronze lances. Two standards waved in the breeze over this magnificent host—the first was the hated emblem of Silvanos; the second, a device Karada didn't recognize. It was a narrow pennant of bright blue, slashed with slanting red and black bars.

The band behind her milled about uncertainly. There were no more than one hundred and fifty plainsmen on horseback to receive the charge of five hundred or more elves. Samtu, now astride another horse, worked her way to Karada's side.

"We can't stand against that!" she cried.

Karada looked back at Pakito's force on foot, still fighting the few elves left at the river. "If we don't, Pakito and all those with him will die!"

She ordered her horsemen to group together in a tight circle. At a deliberate trot, they rode away from Pakito, crossing toward the approaching elf host. As Karada hoped, she drew the elven army's attention away from the vulnerable plainsmen on foot.

"Ready?" she called to her band. "If we die, we die free!"

The plainsmen managed a cheer, but it sounded hollow. Karada took her place in the front rank of horsemen and put aside her sword in favor of her old short-handled spear, which she always carried slung on her back. She was just about to order the charge when a surprising movement among the elf riders stopped her.

The block of five hundred riders turned to the right in one simultaneous movement. It was then Karada and her followers saw that behind the mass of elf warriors was another army of equal size. This army turned their horses left on command, revealing a third contingent.

The plainsmen sat and gaped. None of them had ever seen so many elves at once, much less so many armed, mounted elves. The rear of Karada's band fell apart, warriors galloping away as fast as they could. Karada pushed her way through the ranks, yelling and striking her own men with the shaft of her spear.

"Cowards!" she raged. "Craven dogs! Where are you going?"

"We are lost!" they cried, scattering out of her reach.

She saw Sessan, one of her best horsemen, urging his comrades to follow him, retreating to safety. Karada screamed curses at him, damning him for his treachery.

"We'll fight another day!" Sessan whirled, declaring, "Die if you want, Karada, but don't expect us to die for nothing!"

She reversed her grip on her spear and made ready to hurl it at Sessan. Samtu rode up beside her and tried to stay her hand. Blind with fury, Karada slashed at her comrade. White-faced, Samtu dropped her sword and rode away.

In scant minutes Karada was alone, facing fifteen hundred elf warriors. Her anger burned itself out, leaving her surprisingly calm in the face of imminent death. She wrapped her reins tightly around her fist and thumped her bare heels against Appleseed's ribs, and the horse cantered through the bloody grass toward the foe. When the gap had closed to thirty paces—javelin range—Karada stopped to savor her last breath of life.

Facing her was a splendidly outfitted band of elite outriders in sky-blue mantles. Twenty strong, they wore tall bronze helmets and carried round shields, burnished until they shone like gold. The shields bore the emblem of the sun, the symbol of Silvanos's throne.

In the midst of these magnificent warriors she spotted one elf flanked by standard bearers and another, older elf in civilian clothes. The younger elf was clad in a gilded breastplate and plumed helmet, greaves, and a brilliant blue cape. She recognized him. It was Balif, her old enemy.

\* \* \* \* \*

From under the visor of his helmet Balif saw a lone human on horseback, confronting his entire host. Her gray chaps were streaked with blood, and a barbarous headdress of yellow teeth held down a mane of sun-bleached hair. When Balif finally realized who this human was, he couldn't help himself. He smiled.

The line of elves stood still behind him, awaiting the order to attack. Instead of launching his whole force at Karada, Balif rode out followed only by four standard bearers.

Karada raised her spear.

"Hold!" Balif shouted. "Do not throw your life away with that spear!"

"My life is mine," she shouted back. "I'll do with it as I please!"

Balif reined up an arm's length away. "Greetings, Nianki."

"You remember me."

"How could I forget?" He looked past her as the last of her mounted warriors disappeared over the hills. "You seem to have run out of army."

"They were unworthy."

"I don't think so. Your band has wrought great havoc in the south, burning outposts. They simply know when not to fight." Balif pulled off his helmet and cradled it in front of him. Wind caught his long blond hair. "I give you leave to withdraw, Nianki."

She shook her head. "Never."

"Your life will be spared if you go."

145

"A few elf lives too, I reckon, but I won't live by your charity."

"I have only to raise my hand and you'll be trampled into the weeds."

"So what's stopping you?" she replied harshly. "Are you afraid to fight me in single combat?"

Balif laughed. "You're a strange foe, Nianki!" he said. "Your bravery here today confounds the claim that humans are merely grunting savages who deserve nothing better than to be driven from the plain. You're resourceful, gallant, and have a certain rough grace."

"If you truly believed what you say, you would not persist in driving us from the land," she told him.

He shrugged. "I think there is room for all. Unfortunately, mine is but one voice. There are many in my lord's council who prefer to exterminate humans rather than live with them." With a little shake of his head, he recalled himself to the current situation. In a loud voice he declared, "Withdraw, Nianki."

"I offered you single combat," she said grimly. "Do you refuse?"

"So you did. Yes, I'll fight you, if you wish."

One of his retainers cried out, "No, my lord, you cannot!"

"This barbarian is no honorable opponent!" said another.

"I'll stake my life on this human's honor," he said curtly. "Stand back, and do not interfere."

The unhappy standard bearers turned their animals back and rode slowly to the waiting elf host. Balif drew his sword and slung his bright golden shield over his shoulder.

"Since you have no shield, it would be unfair of me to use mine," he explained.

"Use whatever you like," Karada replied. She shifted her spear from an overhand, throwing position to an underhand thrusting grip. "Hah!" she cried, urging Appleseed forward.

Balif likewise launched his mount into motion. They met with a loud clang of metal and stone. A shout went up from the elf army.

The fine flint head of Karada's spear showed a deep chip where Balif's bronze blade struck it. Another blow and the flint would shatter.

Karada shifted her grip to present more of the hardwood shaft and lunged again. His sword hilt slammed into her jaw. Dazed, she raked her spear upward, opening a jagged cut on his forehead, below the rim of his helmet. Balif caught her spear arm with his free hand, pinning it back, and brought his sword down hard on Karada's shoulder. Her wooden armor saved her from a serious wound, but it fell apart as the sharp edge of the elven blade cut the thongs holding it together. Karada twisted her horse around to shield her exposed side, then she hit Balif in the chest with the butt of her spear. He grunted, falling backward off his horse.

Unbidden, the elf army surged forward, eager to save their stricken commander. Balif jumped to his feet and waved them off. Karada took her horse back a few paces to gather room to charge. Shouting, she bore down on Balif. He stood awaiting her attack impassively, sword at his side. At the last moment, he raised his empty hands, fingers spread, and intoned two words in his own language. Appleseed stopped and rooted his hoofs to the ground. The stop was so sudden Karada had no time to prepare, and she went flying forward over the horse's neck. She landed hard at Balif's feet. By the time her head had cleared, she found herself staring at the point of Balif's sword.

In spite of the blood trickling down his face from his forehead wound, his expression was calm and his sword was steady.

"Yield," he said.

"I will not!"

"By my ancestors, you're stubborn!" He sheathed his sword and extended his hand. "Come on, get up."

She sullenly refused his help and stood on her own. The standard bearers, flanked by the elite riders from the center of the elf host, quickly surrounded Karada and their commander. One of the elves handed his commander a cloth, which Balif tied around his head to stanch the bleeding.

The older elf, who had a high, domed forehead and thin, unelven whiskers, sat silently on his horse, fingering a long wooden staff studded with colored stones.

"What will you do with the human, my lord?" he asked.

"A good question," Balif said. One of his retainers found his helmet and offered it to him. Balif tucked the conical bronze helmet under one arm and said, "I could take her back to my lord Silvanos, as a captive."

"I'd rather die," Karada spat.

"I thought you would." Balif sighed and gestured to his soldiers. The ring of javelins surrounding her lowered.

The older elf, his posture deferential, said something to Balif in their own tongue. Balif shook his head, saying, "No, Vedvedsica. I have a better idea." Then he spoke to Nianki. "I think a better message would be sent to your people if I spared your life and sent you on your way."

"Not a wise choice," warned Vedvedsica quickly, all deference gone.

"No one asked you." The sharp retort shut the elder elf's mouth and brought satisfied grins to the faces of Balif's retainers.

"You're letting me go?" demanded Nianki.

"Just so."

Karada tore off her bear's tooth headband and hurled it to the ground. "No! Damn you, a warrior doesn't let a dangerous enemy go free! Do you think I'm so harmless, I'm not worth killing?"

"On the contrary," he replied, swinging back onto his horse. "You've caused much trouble to my lord Silvanos. Neither my lord nor I wishes to pursue a war against the plainsmen in our territory. By sparing you I send a clear message to your comrades that Silvanos's rule is just and temperate. You'll be deprived of your arms and your horse, and you'll have to leave this province before the next conjunction of the red and white moons. After that time, if you attack subjects or property of my lord Silvanos, you'll be declared an outlaw. You'll be hunted down and killed without mercy. Is that clear?"

She did not reply. When the silence lengthened, the elves around her slowly recovered their javelins and broke ranks. Balif, Vedvedsica, and his retainers rode past her, down to the river to relieve the battered elf force there.

\* \* \* \* \*

Line after line of elf warriors rode by Karada, inspecting her with cool indifference. She felt her face burn with impotent fury.

148

Appleseed was led away, and her spear was taken as a trophy by Balif's squire. Seething, Karada turned her back on the elf host and walked away, toward the distant mountains.

She followed the trampled grass trail of the plainsmen who'd abandoned her. Before long she came upon a group of her people on foot, led by the towering Pakito.

"Karada! You live! The day isn't totally lost!" said the giant.

"I live, if I can bear the shame of this day." Balif hadn't even left her a sword to fall on. "I'm pleased you made it and led these good men to safety," she said, clasping Pakito's burly arm. The remaining plainsmen who'd fought on foot gathered round her. She told them how she'd fought Balif and lost, and how he'd outlawed them all from the province.

"What'll we do?" asked Targun, one of her oldest followers. "Where do we go?"

"Away," she said. "We've lost, and all we can do is gather our strength and fight another day."

"You mean we're not giving up?"

She looked over all that remained of her once-proud band of followers. Tired, sore, bleeding from a handful of superficial cuts, Karada managed to smile in her old, fierce way.

"The land where our ancestors roamed will be the land where our children live," she declared. "So long as we live, we can rise and fight again. Is that not so?"

"Aye!" Pakito shouted.

"Aye!" echoed the others.

"For now, we'll go over the mountains," she said, pointing northwest. "There are no elves there."

# Chapter 11

In winter the mountains slumbered under a thick layer of snow. The passes were filled with deep drifts, ice formed on every surface, and the cold air cut through the heaviest furs like a fine bronze blade. Summer was more agreeable, though often strange. Warm, humid air from the lowlands got trapped in the high passes, filling them with dense white fog that could linger for days.

This was the situation when Duranix and Pa'alu arrived at Vulture's Beak, the highest pass in the mountains. On the eastern side of the peak the sun shone, and a dry wind flowed down the slopes to the plain. As soon as they crossed over to the western side, the world was wrapped in chill, damp mist.

"I should've flown," Duranix muttered, rubbing his arms.

"Why didn't you?" Pa'alu asked. He pulled a fur cloak from his pack and threw it around his shoulders.

Duranix did not reply. Of course, he could have changed to dragon form and carried Pa'alu along, as he did Amero, but he wanted time to get to know this barbarian better. There was an aura of menace about Pa'alu that Duranix couldn't quite fathom. He needed to take the measure of Pa'alu before introducing him to the peaceful, sheltered world of Yala-tene.

Their rate of progress slowed as the fog closed in, leaving them to work their way along a narrow ledge. The drop-off might have been two steps away or two hundred; the fog made it impossible to tell. Even the dragon's powerful senses were of little use. Between the muffling effect of his human guise, the cold, and the fog, he could discern little about their surroundings.

As they crept along, they played a game of questions to pass the time. The plainsman began.

"Why do you protect humans?"

Duranix slid his right foot forward, feeling loose gravel give way when he put his weight on it.

"Oh, to be on all fours," he grumbled.

"Well, what's your answer?" prodded the hunter.

"I protect what is mine," Duranix said, moving forward a few inches. "I have rivals, other dragons, who would steal my territory away from me. The worst of these is a green dragon named Sthenn. He thought to extend his influence at my expense by sending a horde of predators to attack the humans living on my range."

"The yevi."

"I see the name has penetrated beyond the mountains. Yes, using the yevi to exterminate free-roaming humans, Sthenn hoped to bring my lands under his control."

Duranix's progress stirred up a flock of raucous crows. They burst from a rock ledge above the disguised dragon's head, cawing loudly. Both Pa'alu and Duranix flattened themselves against the cliff as the birds flew off into the mist.

"Damn noisy birds. Another question, dragon-man—"

"No, it's my turn," Duranix said. "How long have you been in love with your chief."

Pa'alu flinched as if speared. "Who told you that?"

"No one. The signs are obvious. I've studied humans, you know. When you're near her, your face glows with hot blood, and your heart beats faster."

Pa'alu said nothing. He let the interval between Duranix and himself widen. Duranix looked back and raised an eyebrow.

"I take it from your silence that your feelings are *not* returned?" the dragon said, waiting for Pa'alu to catch up.

"I won't discuss this. Ask a different question."

Genuinely curious, Duranix would not be dissuaded. "Have you confessed your feelings to her?" Pa'alu said nothing and the dragon misread his silence. "You haven't. Well, then, perhaps she does love you. How can you know if you don't—"

"I *have* told her, for all the good it did me!" the plainsman said.

"She rejected you."

"Karada is a hunter and a fighter, the leader of our people. She has little time for aught else."

Pa'alu looked away into the featureless fog. Duranix let him think for a while, then resumed his inquiry.

"Does she love someone else?"

151

"No. Other men have pursued her. When I joined the band nine seasons past, she had a close friend, a fellow called Neko. He was like her shadow, never far from her side. She treated him like—a brother, I guess. Karada is a keen tracker and a bold leader, but she doesn't look deeply into people's hearts. She never knew Neko loved her and wanted her as a mate. One day, the two of them went out to hunt together. This was before we learned to ride horses. They should've returned after two days, yet four went by before Karada came back, alone. She refused to say what had happened, or where Neko was. Pakito, me, and a few others searched the bush and found Neko's body. His throat had been cut."

"Now that's rejection," said Duranix.

Pa'alu glared. "Don't speak ill of her! We brought his body back to camp. He was one of us, and deserved a hunter's burial. The entire band sat in judgment of Karada. She told us what had happened. On the first night out, Neko tried to force himself on her after his spoken overtures were refused. She rejected him and went her separate way, but he wouldn't be denied. He tracked her down and attacked her." A look of savage satisfaction darkened Pa'alu's face. "So she killed him."

"And you believed her?"

"All of us believed her."

The ledge widened into a broad path slanting down toward the west. Duranix and the plainsman paused there, sharing swallows from Pa'alu's water gourd.

"My turn to answer," said the dragon, leaning back against a boulder. "Ask a question."

Pa'alu shook his head. "No, I weary of talking." He excused himself and walked off into the fog.

The golden nugget Duranix had taken from the field of standing stones suddenly awakened and throbbed against his jawbone. Curious about sudden activity in the stone after so many quiet days, he took it out and examined it. It looked just the same as when he put it there. There were no visible changes, yet even as he looked at it, the nugget seemed to pulsate between his fingers.

"Pa'alu!" he called. When there was no answer after a few seconds, he called again.

"What is it?" said the plainsman, emerging from the fog. "I was only gone a moment—"

The dragon displayed the nugget. "It's come alive. I can feel it vibrating."

Pa'alu turned a half-circle, surveying the trail in both directions. "Would it do that on its own?"

Duranix stood up. "Unlikely. It must be reacting to some other source of power."

"Are there rings of spirit-stones in these mountains?"

Duranix shook his head. He had been through this pass many times before.

They picked up their gear and hurried on. The path widened until the towering peaks were shrouded in fog. Heavy mist closed in behind them, cutting them loose from all visible landmarks. Duranix walked ahead, the nugget lying on his open palm.

"Wait," he said in a low voice. Something about his tone made Pa'alu draw his elven sword.

Noiselessly, Duranix began to swell. His flesh darkened to reddish bronze and his limbs elongated dramatically. Pa'alu stepped back in wonder to make room for a formidable length of tail snaking back to where he was standing. He'd spent four days with Duranix and had accepted his claim that he was a dragon in disguise. However, merely hearing the words had not prepared Pa'alu for the actual sight.

Fifteen paces long, Duranix was four paces tall at the shoulder and seven from the ground to the top of his long, bronze-scaled neck. Fog swirled about his enormous, horned head.

"By all the spirits!" Pa'alu gasped.

Duranix bent his neck around and glared at the astonished plainsman. His vast nostrils flared. "Shh!" he said, and Pa'alu thought it sounded like all the snakes in creation hissing at once.

Arcs of blue light flickered through the mist. Duranix opened his wings and flapped them a few times. The resulting wind parted the fog just enough to reveal a lone figure standing on a patch of level ground not far ahead. Wrapped head to toe in a long garment the color of the fog, the stranger was almost invisible. Duranix advanced slowly, his great four-toed claws driving deep into the rocky soil.

"Priest!" the dragon demanded in a thunderous tone. "Why are you here?"

The stranger came toward them slowly. He raised his hands to shoulder height, parting the pale gray cape he wore. Pa'alu finally recognized him. It was Vedvedsica, the elf priest they'd bested at the field of standing stones.

"You have something of mine," said the elf. He seemed unaffected by Duranix's overpowering presence. "I want it back."

"I don't think I'll give it to you," the dragon replied. "Children and savages shouldn't play with fire."

Vedvedsica brought his hands together. A beam of blue light lanced out from them, striking Duranix in the chest. The dragon grunted and slid backward a step. Shaking his horned head, he opened his mouth and exhaled at the elf. Vedvedsica crossed his arms and stood unflinching in the stream of fear-inducing gas.

"I'm not so weak as to succumb to this child's-play," he said, smiling benignly.

Pa'alu worked his way around the dragon's left and crouched behind a low boulder. Closer now, he saw the priest wore a breastplate of shiny white metal, studded with rough gems and chips of striated black granite—just like the boulders where he and the dragon first encountered him.

Duranix snapped his jaws shut, staring with increased respect at Vedvedsica. His huge, panther-like pupils raked the elf priest up and down.

"We seem to be at an impasse," he said finally. "Your spells cannot hurt me, and my powers will not affect you so long as you wear that breastplate." Duranix displayed his fearsome teeth. "I could just bite your head off. It's crude, I know, but it would solve the problem of your being here."

At that moment Pa'alu stood out from his hiding place and hurled a pair of rocks at Vedvedsica, one from each hand. They never reached their target but fell to the ground a few steps away.

"Keep out of the way, human, or you might get hurt," said Vedvedsica blandly. "Your barbarian chieftain and her band have already been destroyed by my lord Balif. If you value your life, you'll keep clear of me."

"Liar!" Pa'alu started forward, only to find his way blocked by the dragon's tail.

"Stand away," ordered Duranix.

The dragon gathered his four legs beneath himself, coiling his back to spring. The elf stood his ground, coolly watching his mighty adversary preparing to attack. When Duranix sprang, however, Vedvedsica whipped his cape around his body and vanished. The dragon landed with a crash on all fours where the cleric had been standing. Looking momentarily astonished, Duranix whirled around.

Pa'alu caught a twinkle of azure from the corner of one eye. Vedvedsica had reappeared behind Duranix. Swiftly the elf threw open his cape and brought his hands together for another blast of that spirit-light he commanded. Silently, Pa'alu lunged. The captured elven sword caught the priest's left wrist, and Vedvedsica screamed. There was a brilliant flash of light and a thunderclap that hurled Pa'alu to the ground.

Deafness and blindness followed, then Pa'alu felt himself being hauled to his feet. By the time he recovered his senses, he saw Duranix had resumed human guise and was helping him to stand.

"Wh-what?" the plainsman stammered. His head was throbbing, and the ground seemed to spin beneath his feet.

"My thanks," said the dragon. He steadied Pa'alu until he could stand on his own then added, "I underestimated Vedvedsica. He's very powerful. His first blow was just a test. The second might actually have injured me." Duranix closed his human hand around the gold nugget. "Strong as he is, though, he has limitations. You stopped him, Pa'alu. I thank you."

"What do you mean?"

Duranix pointed to the spot where the elf had disappeared. Lying on the ground was a slender white hand, severed raggedly at the wrist. It was pale as wax, as if it had no blood in it. There was no blood on the ground either.

Duranix picked up the hand. The stump was seared dry, cauterized by the very power Vedvedsica had tried to use against them.

Pa'alu found his sword, knocked from his grip by the powerful blast. The blade was bent and partly melted at a point two thirds of the way from the hilt. Awed, he touched the ruined blade, then snatched his hand back when he discovered how hot the bronze still was.

"That shaman is evil!" he declared, rejoining Duranix.

"No, not evil. He probably serves his lord quite loyally. But he is ambitious, hungry for power, and careless of how he gets it." Duranix replaced the nugget in his mouth. "This encounter will give him something to think about."

"Do you think he spoke the truth about Karada?"

The disguised dragon shrugged. "Your chief is a tough woman, but I doubt she can stand against the might of Silvanos."

Pa'alu slipped the ruined sword into his belt, as it would no longer fit the wooden scabbard. "Then I must go back and find her!"

"Go if you must, but consider!" Duranix called after him. "We're closer to Yala-tene than to Karada's last camp. It would be better to go on to the village. Once there, you can get tools and supplies for a return journey, while I fly back and search for your comrades."

Pa'alu hesitated. The dragon added, "If the battle is over, there's nothing you can do."

"I should have gone back with Pakito!"

"Then you might be dead or captured now, too. Come, let's go. You cannot change what has been, but you can shape what will be."

Pa'alu turned around, and they marched down the ravine another league, finally breaking through the omnipresent fog. Below the white mist the sun shone brightly on the valleys and lower peaks spread out before them. Duranix pointed to a distant green summit.

"Yala-tene lies below that mountain," he said. "We should be there by tomorrow afternoon."

"It will be good to see people again." No sooner had he said it, Pa'alu apologized.

"No need," the dragon said. "Humans are herd animals, after all. They're happiest in a flock of their fellow beasts. But you, Pa'alu, are due a reward. You dealt bravely with Vedvedsica and did me a good turn. I want to repay you."

"I can't imagine how."

"Well, think on it. I am in your debt."

They continued their descent to the lower valley. The long-hidden sun was warm on Pa'alu's face. He accepted it without complaint, along with the gratitude of his strange and powerful companion.

\* \* \* \* \*

"All right—fan!"

Six children from the village were kneeling around a stone-lined pit. Each child held a reed fan. At Amero's command, they began waving the fans vigorously over the fire. Orange flames leaped up, and the dry cedar firewood filled the air with aromatic smoke.

Amero had spent half a day building this pit, digging a shallow hole in the sand near the base of the cliff and lining it with small stones. In the center of the pit he'd piled up a ring of smaller stones and plastered the resulting bowl with clay. He'd filled this inner bowl with beads of raw copper collected from the tunnel debris. He had then carefully laid a fire in the outer pit and marshaled his helpers to fan the flames.

Duranix had been gone four days and four nights. The dragon had been away from Yala-tene for longer periods in the past, but Amero usually knew why and where Duranix had gone. The twice weekly offering of meat had been placed on the cairn the previous day and was still there, gathering only flies. The family of Konza the tanner had the honor of providing the dragon's meat, and its apparent rejection didn't sit well. A family of five could live for two weeks on one offering. So, where was the dragon? Amero had tried to explain Duranix was away on an important reconnaissance, scouting for possible dangers to Yala-tene. The village elders had accepted this in stony silence and departed to their daily work. The rotting meat continued to lie in the open.

It was a hot, sunny morning. As Amero toiled over his copper experiment, lines of villagers led by Farun and Mieda headed for the tunnels. Mieda's stone-cracking technique was such a success that he and Farun planned to duplicate it in the two other tunnels, finishing the excavation in short order.

Mieda rose at dawn and supervised the laying of firewood at the blocked ends of both passages. About the same time Amero was lighting the fire in his pit, Mieda was putting the torch to the tunnel fires.

"Keep fanning," Amero said, as some of the children tired. He'd brought a bucket of melons along to reward his helpers, and when anyone faltered, he handed them a sweet wedge of fruit. Some minutes—and some melons—passed, and the beads of copper began to shimmer with heat. Amero poked them with a long stick, which quickly succumbed to the heat and flickered into flame. He'd forgotten how hot the fanned fire would be to his tools as well as the copper.

The children slid back from the pit as the heat grew. Amero sent around a gourd dipper of cold water. Most opted to pour the water over their heads rather than drink it. Knowing a good idea when he saw one, Amero soaked not only himself but another stick. The damp stick survived the heat long enough to prod the beads. To his delight, Amero found the metal bits had grown soft as tallow.

"Keep it up!" he said. "Something's happening!"

Just then a loud rumble reverberated through the valley. Amero felt it strongly through the soles of his feet. He looked down the shoreline and saw a tall cloud of dust and smoke rising from the mouths of the two tunnels under construction. At first he thought nothing of it, remembering how much smoke had come from the tunnel he'd helped dig. Then he heard screaming.

"Douse that fire!" he said. They stared at him in disbelief. One boy froze, and the flames caught his reed fan. He dropped it, blazing, into the pit.

"Go on, douse it!"

Two boys picked up buckets and poured water over the fire. It died with a loud hiss and much smoke and steam. By then Amero was already running toward the tunnels.

People were crowding around the tunnel mouths, shouting, crying, climbing over each other to see. Amero had to shove his way through the mob to reach the center tunnel. The air was full of acrid, resinous smoke and grit. Lying on the ground were eight diggers, covered in dust and bleeding from gashes on their heads and backs.

Amero spotted Farun through the dirt and soot. He dropped to his knees and clasped Farun's hand.

"What happened?" he demanded. "What went wrong?"

Coughing, Farun replied, "The roof fell. We had the black stone hot enough, and Mieda sent for water. I was in the first pair to dump water on the rock face—" Another fit of coughing seized him and blood flecked his chin.

Amero ordered everyone back and called for travois to take the injured away. Eight men were removed from the center tunnel. The north tunnel had also collapsed. No one had managed to get out.

Amero looked around wildly at the sooty, coughing men and cried, "Who was in there? Does anyone know?"

Konza the tanner regarded him with a dull, shocked expression. "Mieda, Talek the mason, Halshi—"

"Halshi was in there?" Amero exclaimed.

Konza nodded slowly. "So was my eldest son, Merenta," he said. Tears trickled down his face, cutting tracks in the dust on his cheeks.

Amero tried to think of something comforting to say, but his tongue felt wooden and useless. He could only stare at the blocked tunnel. Halshi was in there, and Mieda, and so very many others.

Suddenly, a tall stranger appeared among the dazed crowd. Dressed in buckskin trews and a sleeveless hunting shirt, his long chestnut hair gathered in a thick knot at the back of his neck, the stranger ran by the grieving Konza and the paralyzed Amero to the pile of fallen stone blocking the tunnel mouth. With his bare hands he took hold of a large chunk of sandstone and rolled it aside. Several smaller rocks he tossed out of the way.

His industry freed Amero from the paralysis gripping him. He fell to his knees beside the stranger and started digging, too. The two men joined forces to dislodge a large, flat boulder. With much grunting and a few skinned knuckles, they got the slab out of the way. Others overcame their shock and horror and joined in the digging.

"Thank you," Amero panted. He suddenly realized he had no idea who he was speaking to. "I don't know your face. Who are you?"

"My name's Pa'alu," the man said.

"You're a plainsman. Where did you come from?"

"I'm one of Karada's band. The dragon, Duranix, guided me here."

Amero seized the muscular newcomer by the shoulders. "Duranix! Where is he? We need him—he could tear down the whole mountain and free those buried!"

Firmly but gently, Pa'alu broke Amero's grip. "Duranix isn't here. He brought me to the valley and showed me the trail here, then he flew away."

"But why?"

Pa'alu hesitated. Under the circumstances, how could he explain? Duranix owed him a debt, so he'd asked the dragon to fly back to the Thon-Thalas to look for Karada and the rest of his people.

He said simply, "He went to search for survivors of a great battle. Karada and my people fought the elves and lost."

Amero looked away briefly, searching in vain for a glimpse of his friend, as Pa'alu turned and rejoined the rescue dig. Bare-handed progress was slow, but tools were brought and the furious work organized. The sun bore down on the scene as the men and women of Yala-tene toiled to free their trapped friends. Many of the rescuers worked until the pitiless heat wore them out. The exhausted were carried to the shade.

Besides being hot, the work was bedeviled by constant secondary landslides. Rocks ranging from fist-sized pebbles to veritable boulders rained down on the tunnel mouth. The entire face of the sandstone cliff was shattered, and the cracks ran all the way back to the collapsed center tunnel. Mieda's technique had worked too well.

The sun had sunk behind the western peaks by the time they reached the buried diggers. One by one they were brought out—Mieda, Talek, Merenta, Halshi, and the rest. None were alive.

They were carried to the nearest open ground, below the cairn that had held the food offerings of the dragon. It had been a long time since Amero had lost someone he cared about, and gazing at the still faces of Mieda and Halshi left him feeling empty inside. Hollow. He didn't understand why he felt so betrayed. There was no one to blame. Mieda hadn't known the rock was fissured over the tunnels when he built the fires. He had died leading his diggers, an honorable death. No, the betrayal lay elsewhere.

A foul smell assaulted his nostrils.

"Get that rotten carcass out of here!" Amero shouted. A maggot-ridden ox haunch was dragged off the cairn. As family members gathered to claim the bodies of their loved ones, Amero's aching emptiness grew larger. An idea formed to fill the void in his heart. He called for firewood—lots of it.

Farun, his head bandaged and his arm in a sling, limped up to Amero. "What do you intend?" he asked.

"Our lost friends were working to make the village a better place," Amero said. "They died together. We should honor them together." His head swam. He wiped cold sweat from his brow. "The mountain treacherously crushed them. We will free their spirits and send them to the sky, where the mountain cannot touch them."

He ordered cords of pine and cedar laid atop the cairn. The eight victims were then laid on the stacked wood, and Amero called for a torch.

No one moved to comply. The villagers, like all plainsmen, believed burial was the proper way to treat the dead. They were paralyzed between loyalty to their young leader and anguish at his flaunting of one of their ancient traditions.

It was Pa'alu, the stranger, who brought Amero a blazing torch. He took it with a grateful nod and held it high above his head.

"Don't be afraid!" Amero declared. "We have all lost friends we've loved. I give them the honor, the dignity of fire! Let their spirits remain ever more watching over us!"

He thrust the torch into the lowest course of logs. The dry pine caught fire rapidly. In minutes, the cairn was a lake of flame.

The people of Yala-tene stood silently around the pyre, watching the thick smoke rise to the stars above. Amero tossed the torch into the flames and stood back beside Pa'alu.

"Thank you," he said.

"It's nothing," the hunter replied. "I hope someone does as much for me someday."

Paul B. Thompson & Tonya C. Cook

*Duranix, where are you?* was Amero's miserable thought. The words had barely formed in his head when the sky was shattered by the dragon's terrible roar. Already overwrought by events, the crowd shifted and wavered. Some fell to their knees as the black shadow of the winged dragon passed overhead.

In a rare display of his true shape, Duranix alighted on the shore of the lake, some paces from the blazing cairn. He furled his leathery wings and approached the pyre, scales gleaming in the firelight. People scattered before him, many more dropping to their knees as the dragon's flashing eyes swept over them. By the time he reached the cairn, only Amero and Pa'alu were standing.

"What is this?" asked Duranix, raising a claw to the fire.

Tersely, Amero told of the disaster, the rescue attempt, and his inspiration to honor the dead with a funeral pyre.

Duranix extended his long neck and put his head in the flames. A wave of horrified gasps flowed from the villagers and several of the women shrieked. Seeming not to notice their reactions, the dragon looked around in the fire for a moment, then withdrew his head. "Mieda," he said with unusual emotion. "He'll never see the northern seas again."

"Where were you?" Amero demanded. Words caught in his throat like stones. "We needed you! You could've dug those people out of the mountain faster than the whole village, but you weren't here!"

Duranix sat back on his haunches. His booming voice carried over the crackle of the fire. "I was scouting for enemies. I found a band of warrior nomads, led by the woman Karada. She's fighting the elves for control of the eastern plain. Two days ago she lost a battle, and her people are scattered. This man," he said, pointing to Pa'alu, "came with me to see Yala-tene. He's one of Karada's band."

"Are we in any danger?" asked Amero, wiping tears from his face.

"Not from the elves. They've come no farther than the headwaters of the Thon-Thalas."

"Any news of Karada?" asked Pa'alu anxiously.

The dragon shook his massive head. "I could find no one brave enough to converse with me," he said, sounding vexed. "The nomads are hiding in fear of elf retribution."

Duranix backed away from the cairn. The flames had subsided a bit, and the balmy wind off the lake was blowing smoke and hot ashes. He moved off a few paces and unfurled his wings. Without another word, he leaped into the air and flew back to his lair behind the waterfall.

Amero took a deep breath and faced the crowd. "I don't know what to say," he said. "Duranix might have been able to save our people if he'd been here. He was away, working on our behalf, and he's only one creature. He can't be everywhere at once." He searched the faces of the stunned, anguished people. "If any of you are unhappy with me, with what I have done, speak now. I will listen."

For a moment no one said anything. Then Valka, father of Halshi, tottered to the front of the crowd. He was elderly, lame from old hunting injuries. Despite his gnarled limbs and twisted hip, he stood as straight as he could before Amero.

"I've lived twice as long as my father," he said in a wavering, tired voice. "I've seen more of my children survive in the last ten years than in all the years before. I have a warm house, a bed, and much family around me. These things I owe to the great dragon and to his son." When he used the word "son," Pa'alu turned to stare at Amero.

Old Valka went on. "Halshi was my only daughter, a good girl, hard-working and cheerful. I'll miss her, but I would rather she died in a cave at Yala-tene than out in the wild, poisoned by snakebite or torn to pieces by the yevi. Here, a hundred families knew her and can mourn for her. That's as good a rest as any plainsman can hope for."

Valka doffed his buckskin cap and bowed his head. "Be content, Amero. You've made my life more than I ever expected."

By threes and fives and tens, the people of Yala-tene bared their heads and expressed sentiments like Valka's. In the end, Amero found their gratitude as hard to bear as their grief. Weeping, he walked off alone into the darkness beyond the dying pyre.

Amero remained in the village until the fire was out. By then it was very late, and the crowd had dispersed, save for a few, like Valka and Pa'alu, who slept on the ground by the cairn. As Amero walked slowly through the quiet village on his way back to the cave, he passed by the remains of his copper experiment. He took a moment to kick apart the clay bowl. Instead of a cascade of separate copper pellets, the bowl contained a single mass of metal, all melted together. At least the day had one success, though he had no heart to celebrate it.

# Chapter 12

~

By the time Karada reached the western slopes of the mountains, her band of followers had grown from forty-odd warriors on foot and horse to over a hundred. All along the route plainsmen left the line of march to collect their mates and children, most of whom lived in solitary camps in the eastern foothills. In the wake of their defeat, they feared the Silvanesti would sweep the countryside clear of humans, so they packed up their families and followed Karada west.

It was raining as the long, straggling procession of nomads wound its way along the twisting mountain passes. Most of them, Karada included, had walked all the way from the Thon-Thalas. What horses they had were given to a few trusted scouts, who rode ahead looking for potential trouble and locating the best trails.

The habit of leadership was strong in Karada. Though this ragtag collection of families was a far cry from the hundreds of warriors she had so recently led, they still saw her as their chief, and it was a role she could not easily relinquish.

She was constantly on the move, going from the head of the line to the back, encouraging the wounded and whipping the laggards into line. It became clear four days into the march that the elves were not pursuing, but still Karada wouldn't allow her people to dawdle. She drove them over the mountains through the low, easy southern passes, and not until they reached the great open plain did she allow any rest.

The skies cleared, and while the younger hunters scoured the savanna for food, Karada held a council with the surviving leaders of the band. There weren't many—Targun, Pakito, Hatu the One-eyed, and Samtu.

No one was surprised Samtu remained in Karada's band despite being threatened by her own chief. Samtu owed everything to Karada. Her family had died when she was only five. Karada had found the girl wandering like a fox cub, naked and filthy, and raised her in a stern but caring way.

Karada's seconds ranged themselves around a modest fire, sitting on whatever rocks or logs were convenient. Karada took a chunk of trail bread from her knapsack—the last bit of food she had—broke off a piece and handed the rest to Pakito. The trail bread went around the circle until it was gone, then Karada started a gourd of fresh water in its wake.

"Here we are, back again on the plains of my birth," Karada said. "I wish it were for better reasons."

"I can't think of a better reason than being alive," Targun said. Though Karada had never stopped to consider it before, he was the oldest man present and was showing his age. His once black hair was shot through with gray, his squat, powerful frame now seemed wasted and hollow.

"At least there's good fishing here," he added. "Nothing bigger than a minnow ever got up the blasted Thon-Thalas!"

They laughed a little. The water gourd came back to Karada. It was still heavy and sloshing. Her comrades had left much of the water for her.

"It's late in the season," she said. "We don't have the time or the horses to hunt down enough game to feed the band." She spat on the flattened grass. "Balif thinks he's shown himself to be a generous conqueror by letting us go. The fact is, if we don't do something, few of us will survive the winter."

"What can we do?" Samtu wondered.

"That's what I'm asking you."

Silence reigned. Finally, Pakito said, "We could find Pa'alu."

"How will that help?"

The big man reddened. "He's smart. He could think of something," he said lamely.

"He's smart all right—smart enough to run off and not come back," jeered Hatu.

Pakito jumped up. "Watch your words, One-eye!"

"Have I said something untrue?" Hatu was no weakling himself, the last survivor of a family of four strapping brothers. His manner was always outwardly mild, but he was a tough, sometimes ruthless character. Even Karada respected him as a fighter.

"My brother never ran away," Pakito said. "The chief ordered us to follow the dragon-man."

"So where did he follow him to? The red moon?"

Pakito took a step toward him. Karada stopped the giant with a word.

"Sit," she said. Pakito flexed his battle-scarred hands into fists, but he obeyed his chief and sat down.

"Fighting each other is worse than stupid," she told them. "I won't have it, do you hear?"

"I wonder about Pa'alu," Targun said. Pakito glared, but the old man went on. "Pa'alu and the dragon-man, I mean. Did they go to the Place of the Dragon?"

"So what if they did?" asked Samtu.

"What of the settlement there? Might they help us?"

Karada slowly sat up straight. "I pondered that when Pakito told me how the dragon-man helped defeat some elves at the place of standing stones." She made a fist. "I put away the idea because I thought we could beat the elves without help."

"Things have changed," said Targun.

"A dragon would make a powerful ally," Pakito remarked.

"How can you bargain with such a monster?" said Hatu. "Long ago my brothers and I fought a dragon in those very mountains. He killed my father! For all I know, it's the same beast."

"It may not be. Should we pass up a useful ally for such a slender reason?" Karada said. Hatu did not reply. "You know the mountains, Hatu. Can you find Arku-peli?"

Long ago, a wounded elk had gored Hatu, costing him his right eye. He wore a patch on his headband that hid the empty socket. When he was very troubled, he would rub the patch absently. He was rubbing it now with his thumbnail.

"I'll do as my chief commands," he said at last. "To me there seems little difference between serving an elf or serving a dragon, but if Karada says 'dragon,' then I obey."

"Thank you, Hatu." Everyone shifted uncomfortably. It was not a phrase Karada used often. Her saying it was a grim measure of their plight.

They estimated they were four days from the Place of the Dragon. None of them, not even Hatu, knew exactly where the settlement lay. Common repute said the village was on a lake at the foot of a high waterfall. Hatu remembered such a lake from his youth. Once back in the mountains, he felt sure he could find his way there again.

The nomads rested a full day on the savanna. Their meager food dwindled, and they resumed the march under a cloudless blue sky, the last hot days of the season. The scouts returned and reported no signs of pursuit by Balif and no other sources of trouble in sight.

\* \* \* \* \*

Unknown riders began appearing in the valleys south and east of the lake. Foragers from Yala-tene were alarmed when they encountered the first humans they'd ever seen on horseback. They'd heard tales of plainsmen who had adopted this elf habit, but it was strange to see men and women astride long-legged beasts. And what strange humans they were—tough, sinewy people, cured by wind and sun until they resembled the leather gear they wore. They moved in groups of eight or ten at a time and were armed with spears or long-handled clubs. They were polite enough when bartering for food and water, but there were scores of them roaming the high passes, and their very numbers made the villagers nervous.

The first riders arrived at the lake five days after the tunnel disaster. They were first seen on the cliffs overlooking the village and were mistaken for elf warriors. A panic ensued until Pa'alu identified the horsemen as members of Karada's band, his comrades.

Amero heard the commotion and descended from the cave to see what the matter was. He found a congregation of village elders in the square before the dragon's cairn. Pa'alu was with them.

"What's the alarm?" asked Amero wearily. He was hollow-eyed and pale, having slept little the past few nights.

"Riders have been seen atop the cliffs," Pa'alu said. "Some of my people have arrived."

Amero glanced back at the cave where Duranix was sleeping off his recent meal of ox meat. In his current state, the dragon would be hard to rouse, but if there was trouble . . .

Pa'alu read Amero's thoughts on his face. "Why all the worry?" the plainsman asked. "Wanderers come to the village all the time, don't they? Why are you all so scared?"

168

"Plainsmen on horses," said Konza, "like warrior elves."

"They mean no harm," Pa'alu vowed. He looked away to the cliff wistfully. "My brother Pakito may be with them." And Karada.

Now it was Amero's turn to read Pa'alu's thoughts. "Your people are welcome," he said, as much for the elders' benefit as Pa'alu's. "Go and meet them, Pa'alu, so there's no mistake about our good will. If you find your chief, bring her here and we will do her all honor."

A smile flickered across Pa'alu's face. He saluted Amero with his javelin, saying, "I go gladly. Please tell the villagers not to challenge Karada's band. They're seasoned fighters who've lately lost a battle. They'll likely be in a foul mood."

He departed at a jog. Once he was out of earshot, the elders peppered Amero with their fears about the newcomers. Amero let them rant for a while then waved for silence.

"Why do you worry so much?" he asked. "They are plainsmen like us. If we treat them kindly, we're more likely to make them strong friends than enemies." He let that sink in for a moment, then added, "And you forget who we are. We're not exactly sheep."

"Maybe not, but we do have a powerful shepherd," Valka said wryly. The dragon was an asset not easily trumped. Amero decided not to tell the worried elders that Duranix probably would be out of action for several days at least.

"Go back to work," he advised them. "Act as if this were any day, and receive the strangers with kindness."

Despite his words, Amero himself was anything but calm. As he returned to the cave to study his copper melting experiments and await events, he felt a shiver of fear. Pa'alu had described Karada's band as being five hundred strong. Yala-tene had had trouble in the past with lone outcasts or small bands of thieves, kidnappers, and killers. In most cases they hadn't needed Duranix's assistance, but they'd never faced so large a force of strangers before. Amero was no warrior, and neither were the people of Yala-tene. Could Duranix defend them against so many?

His fears were magnified as he ascended to the cave in his basket. As he rose, Amero could see more and more of the plateau behind the cliff. It was dotted with moving figures, all approaching Cedarsplit Gap, a steep ravine that led from the heights down to the valley of the lake. By late afternoon, for good or ill, Karada's band would be here.

Then his anxiety doubled when he saw Duranix was not in the main chamber. Amero ran up the steps to the dragon's sleeping platform and saw him there—in human form. Duranix's slow, regular breathing filled the cavern. Still asleep? Had he changed to human form in his sleep?

The thought must have been a strong one, because it disturbed the sleeping dragon. Duranix turned over in one of those sinuous motions impossible for a true man to make and opened his eyes. Without saying a word, he held a hand up in front of his face.

"Bizarre," he said, and sat up abruptly. "How long have you been gone?"

Amero was still at the edge of the platform. "Not long. It's not yet midday."

The dragon held out his human hands. "I must have transformed in my sleep. That's very strange."

Duranix stood up, spread his feet apart and held his arms out. Usually this signaled the beginning of his change back to dragon form. This time nothing happened. The dragon looked disturbed.

"What is this?" he said wonderingly.

Amero had no idea and said so.

Duranix whirled, pointing both hands at the pile of old bones at the rear of the platform. Lightning arced from his spread fingers. Bones shattered into dull white shards that flew in high arcs, falling to the sandstone floor. He followed this demonstration by hurling a web of incandescent lightning against the wall. The crash and flash were stunning. When Amero lifted his head, Duranix was standing, staring at the smoking holes in the wall.

"I'm not totally powerless," said the dragon slowly, and Amero detected relief in his voice. It crackled to anger when he added, "But this is intolerable! Why can't I revert to my natural shape?"

"Are you ill?" asked Amero.

"I feel buried in this feeble body," Duranix snapped.

"Could it be your enemy?"

"Sthenn? No. I would sense him long before he could get near enough to place such a spell on me."

Amero racked his brain for a helpful thought. "Maybe it was something you ate?"

Duranix blinked, then burst into bitter laughter. "Don't be stupid, boy. This isn't a bellyache!"

Amero recoiled. Though he had lived with a dragon for ten years, he knew next to nothing about the creature's inner thoughts or workings. His sudden anger, coupled with the imminent arrival of Karada's band, brought home to him the tenuousness of his life, and of Yala-tene itself.

"Calm down. I'm not going to eat you," said Duranix, interrupting Amero's anxious reverie. "Your thoughts are muddled. *Who* is coming?"

"Pa'alu's people—Karada's band—at least, some of them. Riders have been spotted on the plateau and in the outlying valleys. They seem to be converging on Yala-tene."

"I see." Duranix sat down on the edge of the platform and let his bare feet dangle. "You're worried the warriors will attack your people?" Amero admitted as much, and Duranix nodded. "You're wise to think so. Karada is hard and harsh, and her band takes her as their model. Does Pa'alu know they're coming?"

"He's gone to meet them."

Duranix thumped his heel against the cool stone. "That's good. He's in love with Karada. That may give him some influence over her."

"Good influence, I hope," Amero muttered.

The dragon hopped down to the floor. "Fear not, Amero. Though I may be confined to this shape, I'm still the dragon of the lake. No one need know otherwise. If the problem is some allergy or influence, it will pass."

A trio of ram's horns blared from below. Amero raced to the door and looked down. Dust rose from the direction of Cedarsplit Gap, and a small column of riders could be seen entering the valley between the cattle pens and the bridge.

"How does this thing work?" Duranix was examining Amero's hoist. "If I can't spread my wings, I'll have to descend like you, won't I?"

Amero frowned. He explained the hoist system, with its counterweight and pulleys made of the heartwood of the burltop tree. The basket attached to the hoist was roomy enough for two. However, he said, the counterweight was too light for Duranix, who still weighed as much he did in dragon form.

"So am I stuck here, a prisoner in my own cave?"

Amero recalled the dragon's advice from years ago when he, Amero, had asked the same question. With pleasure, he repeated that advice now. "You could jump."

"I'm in no mood for your insolence!"

His fury was genuine, and Amero backed away. "It was a jest!"

"A poor one. There must be a cause for this malady—"

The horns sounded again. Amero climbed in the wicker basket and prepared to drop the counterweight. "You'll have to work it out yourself. I must go," he said. Grunting, he yanked on the strap and the hide sack of stones rolled off the timber shelf and started down. On the ground, a second sack started to rise, as the basket sank slowly.

The hoist gathered speed and Duranix disappeared above. It was all very well to tease the dragon about being marooned in the cave, but without him the village was practically defenseless. Under no circumstances could Karada's band be allowed to know this—nor could the people of Yala-tene.

As Amero crossed the sandy lanes between the villagers' houses, doors thumped shut around him. The paths through the village were empty of people. Homes with two stories had their upper windows open, as curious and anxious families peered out at the approaching horsemen. Tools and work were left in place as everyone fled inside and bolted their doors. By the time Amero reached the outer edge of the settlement, he was alone, completely exposed and vulnerable.

A ragged line of horsemen, no more than a dozen in all, trotted over the sandhill. Rather than walk out to meet them, Amero halted and struck what he hoped was a confident pose. The lead riders spotted him and came toward him at the same lazy trot. When they got closer, they spread out in a line six horses wide. At little more than spitting distance, the rider in the center of the line held up his hand, halting his comrades.

"Greetings," said the dusty, fair-haired nomad.

"Peace to you all," replied Amero, clearing his throat to avoid any quaver in his voice. "I am Amero, headman of Yala-tene."

The horsemen's leader looked surprised. "Are you the Arkuden we've heard of?" In the plains tongue *Arkuden* meant "dragon's son."

"Some have called me that. I am simply Amero, founder of this village and friend to Duranix, the bronze dragon of the lake."

The horseman smiled widely, showing bad teeth. "My name's Sessan. This is Tarkwa, and this, Nacris." These were the man and woman flanking him, respectively. Like the rest of the riders, they were grimy, sunbrowned, and hard-eyed. Amero greeted them.

"You're part of Karada's band?" he said.

Sessan betrayed surprise. "We were, not so long ago. How'd you know?"

"One of your comrades has been with us for a while, Pa'alu by name. We saw you coming, and he identified you as being of her band."

"Pa'alu, here? Where is he?" Nacris said.

"He left on foot this morning to meet you," Amero replied, scratching his head. "I'm sure he went up Cedarsplit Gap. I can't think why you didn't see him."

"It's a dusty day," Sessan said. "We may not have seen him if he was walking. Truth to tell, we don't pay much attention to you stray root-pickers on foot."

A few of the other riders laughed. Amero smiled through the insult and said, "How many of you are there?"

"What you see here, plus whoever else makes it this far."

"Is your chief with you?"

Tarkwa exclaimed loudly, "Karada? She's dead!"

Sessan and Nacris stared at him with as much surprise as Amero. Abashed, Tarkwa said, "She must be dead, I mean— she stayed behind to fight the elves alone. No one's seen her since, have they?"

An awkward silence ensued. Amero broke it by saying, "On behalf of my people and the great dragon Duranix, I welcome you. Please, follow me."

Nacris steered her horse in front of Amero and extended a dirty, callused hand to him. "Climb on," she said cheerfully.

Amero had never ridden a horse in his life, and he sensed this was a test of his mettle. How hard could riding a horse be for a fellow who'd flown through the air in a dragon's claw? He clasped Nacris's hand, and she hauled him up. He slid onto the horse behind her. It was hard to say who smelled worse, Nacris or the horse.

Sessan raised his hand and shouted, "Let's go!"

The nomads stirred their horses to gallop. They yipped and yelled as they raced down the hill toward the silent houses. Amero clung to Nacris's waist and bounced up and down with the motion of the horse. It was punishing, but he was proud he remained on the creature's back. He called instructions to Nacris, and she guided her horse toward the lakeshore.

At his direction, she stopped on the open ground between the cairn and Amero's hoist. Here the ground was all rock ledges, lightly dusted with sand washed down by the falls. The waterfall was close by. Amero had long since gotten used to its thunder, but the nomads were as excited as children by the roaring column of water. They walked their horses into shallow water and let the fine spray cover their faces. Amero slid off the horse, went back to dry land, sat down on a slate ledge, and waited.

When he tired of playing in the water, Sessan slogged ashore, wringing out his long hair as he came. Dripping, he dropped beside Amero and began peeling off his sodden sandals and leggings.

"Nice spot," he said, squeezing the excess water from his suede footgear. "I can see why you chose to live here."

"I didn't choose it," Amero replied. "The dragon did."

"Oh, the dragon. When can we see him?"

"Any time he decides to show himself. He doesn't come among us too often."

"I thought he took on the shape of a human? He came to Karada's camp looking like a big man."

"He takes human form sometimes," Amero said carefully, "but he does not do our bidding."

The other riders whooped and splashed in the cold lake. Amero watched them, smiling. At least they would smell better after their wet roughhousing.

"We'd like to stay for a while," Sessan said suddenly.

"I understand. You can live here if you want, so long as you agree to obey the village elders."

"Oh, we won't be staying that long." Sessan slung his damp sandals around his neck. "We're wanderers. We can't dig a hole and live in it, like some rabbit."

"No, you're more like wolves, aren't you?"

Sessan wasn't offended. He laughed at Amero's comparison. Jumping to his feet, he swept his arm in a wide half-circle. "Yeah, us wolves'll camp here, by the lake."

"You'll find it damp," Amero said. "The mist from the falls will soak your tents before nightfall."

He waved away the young headman's warning. "We're used to it. Any night on the savanna it rains is damp for us. Thanks, boy!" He clapped Amero on the back and went to unpack his horse.

Hide tents sprouted on the rocky ledge, and a picket line for the horses stretched between some boulders rolled over from the cliff base. Before departing, Amero told the nomads they could barter with the villagers for whatever they needed—food, fodder for their animals, and so on. He warned them against stealing, then bade them a good evening.

By the slanting amber light of an early autumn afternoon, he saw more dust, more riders filing down the gap. Wearily, he set out to greet them. Amero wondered how many visitors the valley could take before the villagers and the nomads found it too close for comfort.

# Chapter 13

❧

When he left Yala-tene, Pa'alu's step was light. The news Karada might be close by put power and speed in his stride.

When he reached Cedarsplit Gap, he started the climb. Within a few score paces the ravine divided into northern and southern branches. Having spotted his old comrades atop the plateau south of the village, he assumed the southern course would take him to them.

As Pa'alu walked along the red rock ravine, his head filled with thoughts of Karada and the hope that he would find her well. Pakito also figured in his hopes. Surely nothing could ever harm his foolish giant of a brother. The feel of the sun on his face finally broke through Pa'alu's busy thoughts.

When he'd left the village the sun had been at his back, very low in the eastern sky. Now it was in front of him and over halfway toward its zenith. How long had he been walking? When had the ravine doubled back? Most annoying of all, why had he met none of his fellow plainsman?

Pa'alu shook his head. Perhaps he should go back the way he had come—

Even as the thought formed in his head, he came around a curve in the ravine and found that the narrowing gorge opened into a bowl-shaped canyon perhaps twenty paces wide. Pa'alu squinted. The rock walls here were not the dark red of the ravine but were made up entirely of a light-colored stone. The creamy rock reflected the sun's light dazzlingly.

The plainsman moved farther into the bowl-shaped canyon. Its floor was strewn with loose rocks that varied from fist-sized chunks to boulders twice as wide as he was tall. The canyon's rim was completely bare of foliage. Two other passages led out of the deep bowl—one due east, directly ahead of him, the other to his left, on the north side.

By now it was obvious to Pa'alu he'd taken the wrong way. Grumbling at his foolishness and angry at the wasted time, he turned to retrace his steps back to Cedarsplit so he could take the northern fork in the ravine.

The opening that had been directly behind him was gone.

Pa'alu stopped, surprised. Deciding that he must have moved away from the opening while looking at his surroundings, he searched along the curving wall of the canyon to locate the passage.

He found nothing but solid rock.

Perplexed, Pa'alu continued on around the edge of the canyon intent on finding the northern path out. It, too, seemingly had disappeared. He went to the center of the canyon, climbed atop a medium-sized boulder, and scanned for the openings.

His annoyance became shock. There were no openings at all in the canyon's walls. They had disappeared, and he was trapped in a steep-sided, rock-filled hole in the ground.

"This is madness!" he exclaimed to the high walls. His voice ricocheted around and came back to him, mockingly. "Madness . . . adness . . . ness."

Pa'alu picked up a stone and threw it at the canyon wall. It had no more effect than his spoken protest, but the action made him feel a little bit better.

"That won't get you out."

He whirled to face the unexpected voice. A few paces away, seated atop a low table of fractured shale, was a strange, gaunt figure dressed in green. Pa'alu brought up his javelin, ready to attack or defend.

"Peace to you, friend," said the stranger in a mild, calm voice. "I mean you no harm."

He was sitting with one leg tucked under him, the other drawn up to his chest. His leg seemed strangely long, his bent knee reaching up as high as his head. The weird man's arms were also outlandishly proportioned—the forearms too short, the fingers incredibly long. His clothes added to his freakish appearance; he wore a tight-fitting leather garment in various shades of green.

Pa'alu slid off his own rocky perch and watched the stranger warily. "Who are you?"

"A friend. A friend, Pa'alu."

"You know my name."

"I've heard it said." The stranger unfolded his legs. His dangling feet touched the ground—some three paces below the rock ledge on which he sat.

"Who are you?" Pa'alu repeated, staring at those weirdly long legs. "How did you get to this place?"

"My name is . . . well, call me Greengall. I've been watching this path for a long time, waiting for the right fellow to come along. I think you're that fellow."

"Did you trap me in here?" asked Pa'alu, gripping his javelin tightly in both hands.

"Yes."

Pa'alu raised the weapon to his shoulder to cast. Greengall's hairless brows knitted together in a fearsome frown at the javelin aimed unwaveringly at his chest.

"Don't be stupid! If I can divert you to this place and close walls of stone, do you think I can be hurt by such a trivial weapon as that?"

Pa'alu lowered his weapon sullenly. "What do you want of me?"

"You came from the place called Arku-peli, did you not?"

"I did."

Greengall smiled, and Pa'alu flinched. The smile had drawn the corners of the stranger's mouth up until they were even with the outside corners of his jade-green eyes. The plainsman swallowed hard.

Seeming not to notice Pa'alu's discomfort, Greengall said, "A pleasant habitation! Such a picturesque location, too. How many people live there, would you say?"

The back of Pa'alu's neck prickled, as it did when he heard the night cry of a wolf. "I don't know," he replied slowly. "I've only been there a few days."

"They say a dragon lives there, too."

"That's true."

"His name is. . . ?"

"Duranix," replied Pa'alu.

Greengall clapped his hands together. "Duranix, that's it." His expression abruptly went from extravagantly merry to deadly serious. "Have you seen him?"

"I've seen him."

"It must have been very frightening for you."

"No, most of the time I spent with him, he was in human form."

Greengall's head tilted to one side. He sighed loudly. "He's so good at that. Me, I look like an overgrown grasshopper."

The comparison was apt, and it prompted Pa'alu to ask, "Are you a dragon, too?"

Greengall snapped to his feet, causing Pa'alu to back quickly, hand flexing around the shaft of his javelin.

"What did you say?" Greengall snarled. Unfolded, his legs were enormously long and tightly muscled. His green leather breeches fit him like a second skin. At full height he towered over Pa'alu, who was tall for a plainsman.

"What did you say?" Greengall repeated.

Pa'alu did not reply but hurled his javelin at Greengall's narrow chest. It was a good cast, well aimed and propelled by all of the nomad's considerable strength. Even so, Greengall's long-fingered hand lashed out and grabbed the elegant elven spear in mid-flight. The green-clad stranger laughed, deep in the back of his throat.

"A poor decision," he said lightly. Saliva dripped from the corner of his too-wide mouth. "Here I am, trying to be polite, and you throw a sharp stick at me! Poor, poor choice. After I'm done with you, you won't be throwing anything, little friend."

He advanced, covering the ground between them in two vast strides. Pa'alu snatched a bronze dagger from his belt and prepared to sell his life dearly. Before he could strike, however, Greengall caught him by the wrists. He stretched his hands apart, pulling Pa'alu's arms out straight. With no effort, Greengall hauled the stout warrior's arms over his head and lifted until he stood on tip-toe. Pa'alu's knife hand went numb, and the dagger fell to the ground.

"Humans are so loosely made," Greengall said matter-of-factly, pushing his caricature of a face close to Pa'alu's. "I wonder how long you can live without your arms?"

His lips parted enough to reveal his teeth. They were awful, serrated, and like nothing in any human mouth. Greengall lifted one long, narrow foot and rested it on Pa'alu's feet, pinning him in place. Then he pulled on Pa'alu's arms. With agonizing slowness, the creature increased the tension. The plainsman resisted as long as he could, then groaned in pain. His shoulders began to ache, then burned as though they were on fire. The remorseless Greengall pulled harder. Something in his shoulders gave. Pa'alu's eyes filmed over with red agony.

The haze of pain was penetrated by an intense blue flash. The tension on his arms slackened, then ceased. The weight of the stranger's foot on his feet disappeared. Pa'alu dropped heavily to the ground. His eyes were still clenched shut in pain, but he heard a loud, tortured hiss. Then an acrid odor filled the air, searing his throat. His arms flopping uselessly, Pa'alu rolled away, gasping for air.

When he opened his eyes, Pa'alu saw Greengall was backed up against the canyon wall. The chest of his taut leather shirt was scorched, and a sickly yellow fluid dripped from a wound there. Pa'alu followed the monster's line of sight. He gasped when he realized who his rescuer was.

It was Vedvedsica, the elf priest. His severed hand had somehow grown back, for he was pointing two hands at the bizarre green-clad monster who cringed against the shadowed rock wall.

Greengall's inhumanly wide mouth howled obscenities at the elf, who stood on a boulder ten paces away. A cloud of greenish gas blasted from Greengall's mouth and swirled around Vedvedsica like a gale of vile smoke. The tiniest wisps of the gas strayed over to Pa'alu, causing him to cough and gag, yet Vedvedsica stood unmoved by the full blast of it.

"You should not have come out," Vedvedsica told Greengall loudly. "Your powers are weakened when you leave your swamp. If Duranix or his kin catches you here, your life will be forfeit."

"So why do you do their dirty work, elf?" Greengall snarled. "Have you come to worship little Duranix as the stupid humans do?"

"Duranix and I have business to settle that doesn't concern you," replied the priest. He pressed his hands together and blue light began to emanate from them.

Realizing another attack was imminent, Greengall screamed horribly and launched himself upward. He vanished in a blur of motion, leaving behind a whirlwind that sucked all the greenish vapors out of the bowl-shaped canyon and into the sky.

Pa'alu got up slowly, still unable to use his arms, which hung limply at his sides. To Vedvedsica he croaked, "I thank you, but why did you rescue me?"

"Troublesome as Duranix is," said the priest, casting a distasteful glance skyward, "things would be infinitely worse if that creature usurped his place."

"But I—". He swallowed with shame to say it. "I cut off your hand!"

Vedvedsica shrugged. "An annoyance and a setback, but I have no time to waste on matters of petty revenge. How badly are you hurt?"

Pa'alu tried to move his arms. His hands tingled, his shoulders burned, and he couldn't make the limbs work. Vedvedsica stepped down from his boulder. His hand dipped into a hidden pocket in his robe and came out with a large green leaf, rolled into a tube. He took Pa'alu's hand. The plainsman turned white with agony at the forced movement, but he couldn't pull away. Vedvedsica shook out of the leafy tube a small round berry, the size and color of a black cherry.

"Swallow it," ordered Vedvedsica. With much effort, the plainsman got the berry to his lips. Within seconds a warm sensation spread through his injured limbs. The terrible pain ebbed, then vanished altogether. He fell to his knees before the priest.

"I am yours to command," he said humbly. "That monster would have killed me for sure if you hadn't come. How can I repay this debt to you?"

The elf tucked his hands into his sleeves and assumed a thoughtful expression. "If you truly mean to repay me, there is something you can do for me," he said.

"You have only to name it, great one."

Vedvedsica lowered his eyes. "What if I asked you to kill someone?"

The answer hung in Pa'alu's throat for a moment. "Then they would die," he said haltingly.

"Don't be such a fool," the elf said. "Don't give away your conscience so readily. The world is full of beings who are stronger, smarter, or more ruthless than you—your will is the only thing these powerful ones cannot take away from you, as long as you don't let them!" Pa'alu looked confused, so Vedvedsica continued, "What I want is simple, plainsman. No one need die for my wishes, least of all you. I want the yellow stone Duranix took from me. You know the one, don't you?"

"Y-yes," Pa'alu said tentatively.

"Get the stone from him and bring it here, to this place." Vedvedsica pressed his thumb into the ledge on which Greengall had been sitting. His finger made a deep hole, as if the hard stone was merely wet clay.

"Leave the yellow nugget in this hole. I will find it."

He turned to go. Pa'alu, feeling fully recovered from his one-sided fight with Greengall, followed after the priest, saying forlornly, "How can I get out of here? The passages in and out are gone!"

"That was simply one of the monster's illusions," Vedvedsica said, waving a dismissive hand. "Look again."

Sure enough. The three paths were right where Pa'alu had expected them to be. He blinked a few times, but the clefts in the canyon wall remained.

Vedvedsica was already picking his way over the sloping ground to the east. Pa'alu called after him. "What is this yellow stone? Why is it so important?"

The strange elf paused, stroking the sparse hair on his pointed chin. "It's part of a larger answer," he said. The plainsman obviously didn't understand, so Vedvedsica offered this explanation. "When hunting, if you find large footprints, you know you're on the trail of big game, don't you?"

Pa'alu nodded.

"Well, consider the yellow stone the 'footprint' of something much larger, so large your human mind can't conceive it. It has touched a great font of power—perhaps the source of all power in the world." His eyes grew distant, looking at some vista only he could see. "When I have it," he mused aloud, "I'll know for sure."

His golden, almost feline eyes focused on Pa'alu once more, impaling him with a glance. "Get the stone, human. Get it soon, and your debt," he said the word almost with amusement, "will be paid."

* * * * *

Karada's straggling band found the first signs of habitation when they reached the river of the falls. All along both banks were stumps of trees, cut down with stone axes. Wandering plainsmen never cut down whole trees; they used only dead or windfall limbs.

Karada squatted by the stump of an oak. She scooped up a handful of wood chips and sniffed them.

"Sap's still fresh," she remarked. She dumped the chips, dusting her hand on the leg of her chaps. "Can't have been cut more than three or four days ago."

"There are drag marks, here," Pakito said. The dark loam was deeply indented where the felled tree had been dragged to the river and rolled in.

"I don't understand. The stream flows away from the mountains. How could they float logs against the current?" asked Samtu.

"They must haul them from the riverbank," Karada replied. "It would be easier than dragging them all the way back to the mountains."

Eighty-eight survivors of Karada's once mighty band stood quietly behind their chief, waiting for her word to move on. Their numbers had diminished in the last days of their journey. Each night a few slipped away, no longer believing Karada was leading them to safety. Autumn was in the air—mornings broke crisp and cool—and the plainsmen's instincts were to head north, following the game herds as they migrated before winter set in. Karada's trek east into the inhospitable mountains seemed like folly.

Karada paid no attention to the lessening muster. Their strength as a people lay in their unity. Leaving the band was a step backward for the deserters, a return to the hard, desperate days of lonesome hunting and gathering. If there were those in the band too weak to trust her, then she didn't want them around anyway.

"Hatu," she said, rising to her feet, "how far to the lake?"

He surveyed the gray peaks with his good eye. "Half a day," he said. "Certainly by nightfall." He pointed to a trio of nearby mountains. "The river passes through them on the north side of the low ridge. The lake of the falls is on the other side."

"Good. Let's get moving."

Hatu had not been to the lake in ten years, and his memory played him false. By the time the sun had begun to dip below the western horizon, Karada's band was barely in the shadow of the first major peak in the mountain range. They paused on the riverbank and ate cold rations from their vanishing supplies, not bothering to build campfires or forage for fresh food. This was usually the time of day the nomads made camp for the night, but Karada insisted they push onward.

She formed a mounted patrol of six, including herself, and rode ahead into the darkening valley. The rest were left under the leadership of Targun and Samtu, to follow at the best possible speed.

The sound of their horses' hooves rattled loudly off the walls of the narrow valley. Signs of human life continued: tracks in the mud on the riverbank, signs that outcroppings of rock had been hammered away to make wider trails. By the side of one trail Karada and her scouts found a pile of stinking garbage—fruit and vegetable peelings, offal, and the like. It was becoming more and more obvious they were approaching a sizable settlement.

The valley walls closed in, and the river made a sharp bend to the right. The low thrumming sound they'd been hearing became a steady booming noise, heralding the great waterfall. The night was very dark, with only occasional glimpses of the stars through scudding clouds. Karada ordered her companions to halt at the river's bend and stay out of sight. She rode forward slowly alone.

Even by filtered starlight the waterfall was a stunning vista. The river poured down the mountainside, fed by a thousand clear springs and the snows of a long winter. It gathered force and hurled itself over the cliff, losing a third of its volume to mist. What remained churned up a bright, clear lake, which narrowed once more into the river they'd been following.

The lake was bound by a narrow shoreline on the right, thickly covered with low plants and slender trees growing in unnaturally straight rows. The wider, left bank was even more surprising. A cluster of tall, beehive-shaped houses filled the land between the lake and the cliff wall. Smoke rose from every rooftop, orange firelight glinting from many of the second story windows. The wind changed, bringing to Karada the odors of pine smoke and cattle dung.

Hatu edged forward on horseback to Karada's side. He looked over the scene and whistled softly.

"This is it! Sure has changed," he said in an awed voice.

"Ride back to the main band, and tell Targun to bring everyone on. We sleep in Arku-peli tonight."

Pakito and the other scouts rode up. After admiring the sights for a moment, Pakito said, "We're on the wrong side of the river. It's too deep to ford. How do we get across?"

"I don't know. Maybe there's a ford upstream." Karada wrapped the reins around her hand. "Let's find out."

They didn't have to travel far before they found the bridge. The plainsmen crowded around the end of the bridge, marveling at its construction.

"Is it a plant? Did it grow here?" Pakito wondered. "It's made of wood and vine—"

"Human hands made it," Karada said. "See the blade marks on the planks?"

Karada and the scouts waited until the column of people appeared, headed by Targun, Samtu, and Hatu—the latter on horseback.

Karada and Pakito rode across the bridge. It swayed under their weight but held up fine. The rest of the band followed, many of the younger members clinging to the supporting vines and moving nervously from handhold to handhold until they were on solid ground again.

"What do you suppose they're like, these people?" Pakito murmured as they rode slowly toward the first line of houses.

"They're very clever," offered Targun.

"That they may be, but living under piles of stone is for lizards, not plainsmen," Karada stated flatly. "And where are their scouts, their watchmen? We could be a war party of elves for all they know."

"We've been seen." Hatu pointed to the looming houses. "There are people moving inside those stone piles. They know we're here."

He was right. Karada watched the upper-story windows and saw heads and bodies silhouetted again the inside glow of firelight. Suspicious, she slowed her horse, and the rest of

185

the band did likewise. Just as they were about to enter the shadowed lane between the lines of houses, the wail of a ram's horn filled the night.

The tired, edgy plainsfolk on foot recoiled from the sudden alarm. Hatu and the mounted warriors drew swords or leveled spears, but Karada called for calm and ordered everyone to stand still.

A glow appeared between the houses. As they watched, it came nearer, bobbing gently. It soon resolved itself into a solitary figure on foot, carrying a blazing torch. It was a young man, whose hair was cut short in a strange kind of fashion. Hatu fingered his own long braid of hair and gave the shorn villager a disparaging sneer. He made a rude comment to Pakito about a bald goat he'd once seen. The big man laughed.

The light was poor enough the young man did not seem to notice their disdain. He stopped a safe distance away.

"You're the largest group so far," he said in a genial voice. "Welcome!"

"You don't even know who we are," Karada said coldly.

"More of Karada's band, yes? Your people have been arriving steadily for the past few days."

The plainsmen exchanged looks of surprise. Pakito asked, "How many of Karada's band have come here?"

The torchbearer considered the question silently, tilting his head in thought for a few seconds, then replied, "Over two hundred, so far. How many are you?"

"Eighty-eight."

"Quite a crowd! Well, follow me. I'll take you to your comrades."

The pale-faced, short-haired man started back the way he'd come.

Hatu muttered, "Our so-called comrades—those who abandoned us on the battlefield. How will they take to seeing us now?"

"That's my problem," Karada said quietly. "Whatever happens, don't let the old folks or children come to harm."

The mounted plainsmen followed the torch bearer in single file, Karada leading. They passed silently through the quiet village. A small wolf sprang out of the shadows and barked at them. Karada raised her spear to strike, then noticed the wolf was tied to a stake with a rope around its neck. Their guide came back and quieted the beast with a few soothing words and a pat on the head.

"You command beasts here?" asked Samtu.

"A few. They guard our homes and fight off their wild brethren."

"Why should they do that?" Pakito asked from over Karada's shoulder.

"We've tamed them. Settled life agrees with them, as it does the rest of us."

The torch bearer went on, Karada's people following him. Each one passed under the scrutiny of the tame wolf, who watched them with unblinking yellow eyes.

The copse of houses came to an end. A patch of sandy, open ground followed, in the midst of which was a tall, square pile of stones, quite unlike the domed houses. The top layers of stone were soot-stained.

"What's this?" asked Samtu.

"Our place of offering. Here we give oxen and elk to our protector, the dragon."

"Duranix," the chief said.

Their young guide halted. "You know of him?"

"He came to our camp in human guise," Karada explained.

"My brother followed him here. Do you know if one named Pa'alu is here?" asked Pakito.

"He was, but he isn't now." The torch bearer scratched his head and explained. "Pa'alu was here, but he left yesterday to meet small parties of your band arriving then. He was hoping to find Karada. He hasn't returned yet. Actually, we're quite worried about him."

"This is Ka—" Samtu began, but a glare from her chief stilled her tongue.

"We all have friends and comrades we hope to see again," Karada said.

In contrast to the quiet, orderly village, the camp of the nomads was a riot of haphazard tents, lean-tos, and wind-breaks of sand and loose stone. The young guide left Karada for a moment and ducked into a rambling tent made from spotted cowhide. He returned with Sessan and Nacris in tow then slipped away quietly.

Both nomads staggered as they walked, and their clothes were awry. They'd worked in the ox pens all day in exchange for two jugs of wine, most of which they'd already drunk.

Sessan looked up at his chief. "By my blood!" he swore in surprise. "You're alive!"

Karada had noted the departure of their young guide, now she spat at Sessan, "I am. Why are you?"

He pressed the wineskin on Nacris and drew himself up as straight as he could. "I'm alive because I left!"

"You admit it, do you? You ran away from the battle!"

He swept his hand in a wide arc. "We had no chance," he said solemnly.

Nacris upended the skin, gulping down more wine. She wiped her mouth and said, "How did you survive, eh?"

"I fought until captured. Balif stripped me of arms and turned me loose."

"How can you live with the shame?" asked Sessan harshly. "I'm surprised you didn't throw yourself from the cliff top!"

"Yes, I chose to live with our defeat. Any fool can kill herself, but I will rebuild the band and strike the elves again! I'll make Balif curse the day he sought to shame me into quiet exile!" Karada stormed. "You want to speak of shame? Look at you, cowards and traitors, standing there! And addled with drink like a pair of loons! Is this the end of our band, our dream of a free land for our people?"

"The elf lord spared you," Sessan replied heatedly, "but the rest of us would have been trampled into the grass had we stayed."

Karada mastered her anger. "You disobeyed my command."

"You've no right to judge us, no right to lead us. You would've let us all die in a lost cause!" Nacris retorted. She cast about wildly. "Ask him. These are sensible people here. Where'd he go—the Arkuden?"

"Who?"

"The village headman, the fellow who led you here."

Karada said, "He left. And why should I ask a short-haired villager anything?"

More nomads came out of their shelters to watch the confrontation. Tarkwa, the other leader of the breakaway band, joined Sessan and Nacris.

"If we are to be one band, strong and united, there must be one chief," Karada said. "The chief's word must be obeyed. Anything else is chaos."

Tarkwa, who was sober, said, "I cannot follow you, Karada. You speak of freedom for all plainsmen—that is my desire, too. But we can't be free *and* be your children, trembling at your every order. What difference is there between serving elf lords or serving you?"

"I am one of you."

"Not good enough!" Sessan sputtered.

"You care nothing for our lives," Nacris cried. "You'd sacrifice us all for your own glory!" Many of the nomads behind her shouted approval of Nacris's hard words.

Karada flinched, but she swung down from her horse and walked up to Sessan. She stood nose to nose with him, shoving Nacris away when the woman tried to wedge herself between her man and Karada.

"Will you fight me?" she whispered fiercely.

His reddened eyes betrayed fear, but he said, "Yes. Any time. Tomorrow!"

Her laugh was sharp and ugly. "Make it the day after tomorrow. I need rest and you need to sleep off your foolishness."

Sessan stepped back and slammed his foot on the sand. "Daybreak, then. Here."

Karada turned on her heel and remounted. "Look to your horse, Sessan. We'll fight mounted, with spears, as plainsmen should."

There was a murmuring behind her as she rode on to claim the high ground by the cliff wall for her tired band of loyalists. Samtu and Targun went to find food for the children. Hatu and Pakito were delegated to organize the raising of tents and tarps. Pakito tried to say something to her about Sessan, but he was banished with an angry gesture.

Karada flung her skimpy baggage to the ground and pulled the blanket off her horse. Without a further glance or a word to anyone, she strode down to the lake.

A wall of mist swirled up from the falls, enveloping her in a silver cloud. She stood up to her ankles in the chill water and removed all her gear and clothing. Kneeling, she threw handfuls of water on her face and neck. The dust of many leagues washed away.

She wished her many worries could be as easily lost.

# Chapter 14

~

It had been a restless couple of days. Amero had had to go out after dark each night and lead in party after party of stragglers from Karada's band. The last was a particularly large and pathetic group, made up of old folks, children, and a few warriors who seemed worn out and ill-fed. Their appearance reminded Amero of the hard life that still existed outside the comfortable confines of Yala-tene.

As if these interruptions to his sleep weren't bad enough, his days were disrupted as well. Duranix had been ceaselessly pacing and prowling the cave ever since he found himself unable to change back to dragon form. As time passed, he became more and more irritable. For long periods he would sit, motionless, staring at the cave walls. Then, in a sudden burst of action, he would circle the room over and over, muttering and gesticulating. Tiny bolts of lightning arced from his hands, and after a few hours of this, the air in the cave seemed alive with crackling energy. Everything Amero touched gave him a shock.

He tried to concentrate on his copper experiment. Men in the village had constructed an anvil to his specifications, hewn from a single block of rose granite. Amero placed the ingot he'd cast the day the tunnels collapsed on the anvil and pounded it with a sandstone maul. The spaces between the half-melted beads closed up, and the ingot gradually became a flat, thin plate.

As Amero worked in the early hours before dawn, on the second day after the arrival of Karada's band, the mussel shell chimes at the top of the hoist rattled. Amero didn't hear it at first and kept hammering. Duranix left the path he was wearing in the sandstone floor and went to the lower door.

"Pa'alu's returned," he announced. Amero kept pounding, so Duranix shouted the news. Amero looked up distractedly. Sighing, he set aside the maul and went to the opening. All he could see was the ever-present waterfall disappearing into the dark depths below.

"It's him," Duranix insisted, then added testily, "I may be crammed into this tiny body, but I haven't gone blind yet!"

Amero started the counterweight down. Rope hissed over the wooden pulleys. The basket appeared. He saw Pa'alu, gazing up at him. The broad-shouldered plainsman filled the small basket completely, and his ascent was slow.

The top of the basket frame bumped the pulley and stopped. Amero tied off the hoist and Pa'alu vaulted over the side, landing lightly on his feet.

"Greetings, Amero, and to you, great Duranix." The dragon grunted something unintelligible and resumed his angry pacing.

"What ails him?" asked Pa'alu.

Amero considered speaking the truth, then said, "Who can say? Pay him no heed." He put aside his newly made copper sheet and sat down on the anvil. "I'm glad to see you, Pa'alu. Where have you been? Many of your comrades have arrived during your absence, including a big man who says he's your brother."

"Pakito's here! That is good news!" He clapped Amero on the shoulder. The well-intentioned blow was enough to knock Amero off his perch.

"Any word of Karada?" Pa'alu asked anxiously, lending the young man a hand.

"No word as yet."

By this time Duranix had circled the cave and come back. "What kept you?" asked the dragon. "We worried you were lost in the mountains." Amero was curious to hear Duranix express concern about a mere human.

"That's what I came to tell you. I was waylaid in the mountains." Pa'alu related his encounter with the monstrous Greengall—up to a point. He carefully avoided any mention of Vedvedsica. The dragon would not knowingly give up the nugget if he knew it would go to the elf priest.

"Describe this Greengall!" Duranix said grimly. "Leave nothing out!"

Pa'alu described the weird fellow: long legs, short arms, spidery fingers, hideously oversized head and mouth. When he began to describe Greengall's clothing, Duranix folded his arms and lowered his head.

The dragon muttered, "I should have expected this. He's been quiet too long."

"Do you know this creature?" asked Amero.

"Sthenn." The name was an evil hiss. Duranix locked eyes with Pa'alu. "You met the green dragon Sthenn and lived to tell about it. How did you manage that? You're a stout fellow for a human, but you're no match for a dragon of any hue. Why did Sthenn let you go?"

It was Pa'alu's turn to fold his arms and look grave. "He spared me to be a messenger," he said. "He sent me back to tell you he wants the nugget, the gold nugget you took from the elf priest."

The dragon was speechless for a moment. Amero, who knew little of the unusual nugget Duranix had brought back from his travels, asked, "Why does he want a mere stone? What value is it to him?"

"It's a cache of pure spirit-power," interjected Duranix curtly. "Sthenn must have some idea of tapping it, though I don't understand why. We dragons have our own sources of power. What is Sthenn planning? Does he think to offer such power to his followers?"

"What is he talking about?" Pa'alu asked Amero.

"Be still," the dragon said. He put a thumb and forefinger into his mouth and took out the nugget. He placed it on Amero's granite anvil. All three looked at it with new curiosity.

"There is a hierarchy in the universe," Duranix explained. "Some of your people already know of the higher beings and worship them as gods. Below them in power are dragons, who exist midway between the pure spirits and the lower animals." Amero didn't have to be told who the "lower animals" were. Pa'alu still looked mystified.

The dragon continued, "With proper concentration and training, elves and even humans could release the power contained in this stone."

"Could the yevi?" Amero said under his breath.

Pa'alu reached out to grasp the dull golden nugget. His hand froze just above it.

"Go ahead, pick it up," said the dragon. "You'll feel nothing from it."

Pa'alu found the stone warm to the touch—no doubt from being in Duranix's mouth all this time. The nugget was weighty for its size, but as the dragon had said, Pa'alu could feel nothing emanating from it.

"It's just a stone," he said, disappointed.

"Keep thinking that," the dragon replied. "When humans start coveting spirit-power, the world is in for more grief than it can bear."

Pa'alu carefully replaced the nugget on the granite block. He expected Duranix to reclaim it instantly, but the disguised dragon had wandered away, a hand to his head.

"Duranix?" Amero said.

The dragon's steps faltered. He clutched his head in both hands and stumbled through the hearth. Ashes and charred wood went skittering across the floor. Amero hurried to him, leaving Pa'alu by the anvil.

"Duranix? Duranix, what is it?" Amero called, alarmed.

The dragon-man threw his arms wide suddenly and let loose a roar of—what? Agony? Fear? Amero couldn't tell.

As he stood there, shaking, his screams reverberating off the hard walls of the cave, Duranix's arms began to bleed blue-green blood. The skin along the back of his arms split open. Under the tearing human skin were the red-bronze scales of Duranix's true flesh.

The dreadful sound of skin splitting was not quite drowned out by Duranix's continuous roaring. He doubled over and, before their eyes, his human body burst apart. His true self stretched outward and upward. The roar increased to full dragon volume. Amero fell to the floor, covering his ears with his hands while Pa'alu, trembling in amazement, ducked behind the weighty anvil. Amero thought the ceiling would surely crack apart under the terrible noise.

Then, as suddenly as it began, the transformation was complete.

"It's good to be full size again!" Duranix shouted, extending his wings. The dragon shivered with obvious pleasure. "How do you creatures live in such small bodies?"

"We manage," Amero grunted, as he hauled himself out

from under an outstretched wing. Coming up on the dragon's left side, he reached out and gave the great creature an affectionate thump with his clenched fist.

"Are you all right? What happened?" Amero asked as Pa'alu came crawling out from his hiding place.

"It's hard to describe. Pressure built inside me—I thought I was going to burst!" Duranix sniffed at the shreds of his human shell lying on the floor. "It appears that I did."

"You don't usually shed your skin when you transform," Amero mused.

Dragon eye met human eye in a flash of shared thought, and they turned to Pa'alu. "The stone!" they cried in unison.

Pa'alu picked up the nugget and fingered it wonderingly. "This yellow rock kept you from shapeshifting?"

The dragon clomped forward, furling his wings. "That must be it!" he said. "The stone somehow kept me in the shape I was in."

"Then we must get rid of it," Amero said firmly.

"I'll do it," said Pa'alu quickly, closing his fingers around the stone.

"I must keep it out of Sthenn's hands," Duranix said. "Give it to me."

Pa'alu walked slowly under the dragon's arching neck. He held out the nugget to Duranix.

"Are you sure you want to handle it again? Who knows what ultimate effect it may have on you? Let me destroy it. I have no sensitivity to its power. To me, it's just a lump of rock."

Duranix had extended two claws to take the nugget off the plainsman's palm. He suddenly thought better of it and withdrew.

"Very well, Pa'alu," he agreed. "You have good instincts. They saved me some trouble with Vedvedsica not long ago. Take the stone. Put it some place neither elves nor dragons can easily find—a deep lake, a bottomless cave. Take it away, and tell no one where you leave it."

Pa'alu tucked the nugget into the pouch on his belt. "Fear not," he said confidently. "You won't see it again."

The cave had grown steadily lighter. A gray dawn, filtered by clouds and the waterfall, had arrived. Weary from his labors, Amero went to the water basin and tried to awaken his numb face. Duranix, his serpentine grace restored, sprang to the upper cave exit and put his head out.

"I must stretch my wings," he stated grandly. "I'll look around for Sthenn while I'm at it." A rumbling sound, like a distant avalanche, filled the cave. The dragon's keen eyes fastened on movement farther down in the valley. The eyes narrowed, and he hissed a single word. "Prey!"

With a flip of his barbed tail, the dragon vaulted through the wall of water and disappeared. Pa'alu hauled the hoist into the cavern and threw a leg over the side of the basket.

"I'd best get rid of the stone now," he said.

The sound of many loud voices penetrated the cave—a massed shouting. Pa'alu couldn't see through the waterfall. Amero came to the opening. "That's coming from the nomads' camp," he said with a pang of foreboding.

Another shout went up. It had a feral, bloodthirsty sound, like the cry of yevi. Amero climbed in the basket with Pa'alu.

"Something's happening," he said, rubbing his brow tiredly. "Something bad."

"Hold on," Pa'alu advised. He loosened the descending counterweight, and the basket lurched free. Bowed by fatigue, his eyes shadowed by dark circles, Amero gripped the sides of the basket.

Pa'alu put two fingers into his belt pouch and touched the yellow stone. So near his moment of triumph, it wouldn't do to let the nugget fall out and be lost.

\* \* \* \* \*

Karada slept soundly her first two nights in Yala-tene. She spread her elkhide blanket at the foot of the high cliffs and rested better than she had in many days. On the second morning, Pakito had to shake her hard to wake from her deep slumber.

"Chief," he whispered, "Sessan waits."

She sat up, yawning. "Let 'im. If he gets thirsty, he'll drink more wine. The more time he has to drink, the better." In a show of bravado, Sessan and Nacris had spent the time since the challenge drinking and gaming with their cronies. Karada had kept clear of them, eating sparingly and re-knapping her flint knife.

The whole camp was awake when Karada strolled down to the lake to wash her face and neck. The nomads were astonishingly quiet, not at all the boisterous tribe Karada had created and led for ten years. She noted with satisfaction the sight of Sessan kneeling on the shore, pressing a cold, wet piece of buckskin to his aching head. Nacris hovered over him, massaging his shoulders. If her expression was any indication, her head hurt at least as much as his.

Karada spared them only a glance as she headed for the water. When the challenge had been made, she had given the stupid man a day's grace to recover from the effects of his drinking. If he chose to spend that time getting himself even drunker, then so be it.

She washed her neck and face, savoring the feel of the chill lake water, then donned her chief's headband. Sessan and Nacris, pointedly ignoring her, left the lakeshore to finish their own preparations for the coming contest.

Samtu brought her horse, and Karada slung a dusty blanket over the animal's back. Vaulting easily astride, she took the reins from Samtu and kicked the horse into a trot. She rode down the hill to an open piece of ground along the water, which was closed in on three sides by nomad tents and a growing crowd of onlookers.

Sessan appeared at the other end of the strip. His horse, a fine roan stallion, pranced and snorted at being hemmed in. Nacris was dancing around beside him, trying to give her man last-minute fighting advice. Sessan kept nodding, but his eyes were closed.

"Karada."

She looked down as Pakito handed her a flint-headed spear. "Here," he said. "Tarkwa and I compared weapons, and this one matches Sessan's length."

"Thank you, Pakito."

"Chief, I don't like to tell you how to do things, but . . ." His voice trailed off.

"But what?"

"Beat him, but don't beat him too hard. You'll win more by being fair than by being harsh."

"I didn't start this," Karada answered. "Sessan and those who follow him need to learn who the real leader is and always will be."

She thumped her heels against the horse's flanks and trotted away. The big man shook his head and returned to the sidelines with Targun and Samtu.

Tarkwa stood between the combatants with his hands upraised. The rolling murmur of the crowd faded. He declaimed, "We are here to see the contest of Karada and Sessan. You all know the reasons for this fight. Do you accept it and pledge to follow the victor?"

"Yes!" the assembled nomads cried.

A flurry of wind scoured the shoreline, driving dust in the eyes of the spectators. All eyes rose skyward in time to see the dark shape of the dragon climb into the low hanging roof of white clouds. Their first glimpse of Duranix in dragon form set the nomads to chattering again, until Tarkwa shouted for their attention.

He picked up a stone from the beach. "When this stone strikes the water, the fight begins!" he said. He went to the edge of the crowd, faced the lake, and lobbed the stone into the air.

Karada wasn't watching it. She looped a thong around her wrist and used it to tie the spear shaft securely to her hand.

*Splash!* The sound of the rock entering the lake was immediately followed by a clatter of hooves. Sessan had launched into a headlong gallop. Still unmoving, Karada busied herself with her weapon, her seat, her reins.

The open strip was only twenty paces long by eight wide. Sessan bore down on the motionless Karada, his spear leveled. He uttered a sharp cry. Some of his friends in the crowd cheered, but most of the nomads held their breath.

Karada turned her horse slightly to her right and rested the spear shaft against her shoulder. Only then did she look up at the horse and rider thundering toward her.

"Now, Karada!" Sessan yelled. He aimed his spear at the center of her chest. When the flint head passed the ears of Karada's horse, she bent herself backward at the waist, twisting slightly away. Sessan's eyes widened in surprise. His spear passed harmlessly over her shoulder. When he was past, she sprang up and swung her weapon sideways in a wide arc. The hardwood shaft, as thick as Karada's wrist, struck Sessan at the base of the neck. Part of the crowd howled with delight at her tactic.

Sessan reeled but kept his seat and his grip on his spear. Karada swung her horse around in a tight left turn and cantered after him. He parried her first thrust and tried to maneuver away to get some fighting room. She crowded him, and when he blocked the sharp flint head, she used the butt end of her spear as a club, landing a hard blow to his ribs.

The crowd melted away as the two riders pressed against them. Sessan, bleeding from the nose, saw an opening and drove through, galloping through the water toward the center of the strip. Karada checked the thong on her wrist and rode sedately after her foe.

This was the scene when Amero and Pa'alu arrived. The first thing Pa'alu saw was his brother, towering over everyone else in the crowd. He shouted a greeting, and the big man plowed through the press to reach his elder brother. With much hugging and back-slapping Pa'alu and Pakito were reunited.

Pa'alu's joy vanished when he saw what was happening by the lake. He thrust Pakito away and said, "Karada? Alive? Here? What is she doing?"

"It's a duel," said Pakito. "She's fighting Sessan to see who'll be chief of the band."

"What?" The idea that anyone would challenge Karada was insanity to Pa'alu. Did Sessan truly understand what he was up against?

Amero slipped in beside him and asked, "Is that woman Karada?" Pa'alu nodded vigorously, and Amero said, "That's the woman I led in two night's past."

Sessan wrenched his horse around and galloped back, again trying to impale Karada by a full charge. This time she lowered her head and urged her mount to a gallop, too. She kept her spear low, on her right side, away from Sessan's rush.

"What's she trying to do?" Amero asked, spellbound.

Pa'alu knew. He'd seen her maneuver before. Grimly he said, "Sessan's a dead man."

The gap between the riders closed fast. Karada steered left, crossing in front of Sessan. The nomads gasped with surprise.

Still she kept her spear low. Sessan let his point droop until it was aimed directly at the crouching woman.

The two horses flashed by each other. Karada raised her arm, deflecting Sessan's spear head. At the same time, the flint tip of her weapon caught him just under the ribs. It went in until the head emerged from his back. The thong binding the weapon to her wrist should have betrayed Karada, perhaps breaking her wrist or snatching her off her speeding mount, but the leather was no longer tied to her. She opened her hand and the loose ends of the thong flew free.

Karada sat up and slowed her horse. By the time she turned around, the roan was trotting riderless toward Sessan's tent.

A woman screamed. Nacris ran out of the crowd. She picked up a pair of stones and threw them at Karada. The chief batted one away, but the other hit her horse on the side of the head. The animal reared, and to avoid being thrown to the ground, Karada slid off his rump. A bronze elven dagger gleamed in Nacris's hand. Karada had only a flint hunting knife.

Pa'alu had a bronze dagger of his own. He forced his way through the excited crowd until he was a few paces from where Karada and Nacris now circled each other.

"Karada!" he shouted, holding up the elven blade. She couldn't pick out his voice amid all the others screaming her name, so he cried, "Nianki! Take this!"

Her old name reached her. She cast a quick glance over her shoulder at him. That was enough for Nacris, who lunged at her. Karada grabbed Nacris's arm and spun around, using the force of her spin to propel Nacris away.

"Nianki! Take the dagger!" Pa'alu flipped the weapon at her. It landed point first in the sand. Karada snatched it up just in time to parry another furious rush. Nacris used her blade like a short sword, slashing underhand and lunging at Karada's belly. At one point the bronze blade scored a bloody line down the length of Karada's right forearm. Nacris paid for her success when Karada backhanded her across the face. The furious challenger spun away, falling to her knees in the sand. With astonishing speed, Karada was on her back. She grasped Nacris by the hair and jerked her head back, baring her throat to the keen bronze blade

The yelling, milling crowd instantly fell silent. The change was so abrupt even Karada noticed. She paused, crouching over her opponent, knife pressed to Nacris's throat just enough to crease her skin but not enough to draw blood.

"Stop!" yelled a man's voice. "Stay your hand!"

Nacris struggled a little, but Karada pricked her to remind her how close to death she was. Karada looked this way and that, trying to see who dared give her orders.

The nomads parted ranks and a young man emerged. His short hair and tidy clothes marked him as a villager, not one of her nomads.

"Don't kill her!" he said, horror evident on his pale face.

"Why not? She meant to kill me!" Karada snarled, panting.

"She's mad with rage because you killed her mate," the man insisted.

Karada looked down at Nacris. She could feel her foe trembling and see tears running off her face to the sand. Karada removed the knife, stood up, and planted a foot in middle of Nacris's back. The latter collapsed facedown in the dirt. Karada kicked Nacris's dagger away. It skittered to the man's feet. He picked it up and offered it butt first to Karada.

Pa'alu ran forward and took his own knife back. Karada was sweating heavily, and blood dripped down her fingers from the cut on her arm.

Pa'alu offered her his water gourd. She took it, saying, "You made it."

He smiled. "So did you."

She took a long swig from the gourd. When she finally lowered it, she wiped her chin with the back of her hand and looked at the villager. "Why did you try to stop me?" she asked him.

Amero said, "You won the fight. There was no reason to kill her."

"Maybe not, but I heard a lot of people shouting her name. There can't be two chiefs in this band. Either I am chief, or there is no band."

"You won. You are the chief," said Pa'alu firmly.

Amero opened his mouth to speak but he was jostled aside as Pakito, Targun, Hatu, and Samtu worked their way to

Karada's side. Pa'alu took his brother's hand and raised it high. He cried, "Hail, Karada! Hail, Karada's band!"

The nomads took up the chant with enthusiasm, repeating it so loudly the valley thundered with their cry.

Sessan's body was cleared away, and Nacris was carried off to a shelter on the edge of the camp. Karada strode up to Sessan's large tent and sat down on the chief's stool. Targun set to washing and binding her wound as warriors lined up to attest their renewed loyalty to her.

Standing in a half circle behind Karada were her stalwarts, Pa'alu, Pakito, Samtu, and the rest. Amero worked his way to Pa'alu's side. The young villager's face reflected a jumble of emotions, impossible to read.

"Pa'alu, I must speak to you." Amero said.

"Aye, Arkuden. What is it?"

"What was it you called Karada during the fight?"

The plainsman kept his eye on the line of warriors saluting and passing his chief. "Her true name," he said. "Everyone was screaming 'Karada, Karada,' and she couldn't hear me among the hundreds."

"Karada is not her true name?"

Something in Amero's tone caught Pa'alu's attention, and he looked down at the smaller man. Shaking his head, he replied, "Ten years ago, when I first met her, she was just a wandering hunter like Pakito and me. Only later, when she was gathering the band together did she take the name Karada."

Amero tried to calm the excitement rising in his breast. He'd heard what the plainsman had yelled, but he kept telling himself he'd heard wrong. It simply couldn't be.

"What is it? What is her birth name?"

"Nianki."

Amero blinked. He tried to speak, but his words came out as a croaking whisper. He cleared his throat. The noise of jostling, celebrating nomads around him seemed to grow louder in his ears. He swayed slightly. "Did you say 'Nianki?' "

Pa'alu nodded. His eyes were on his chief and he didn't notice the young headman's evident distress.

Amero left the loyal circle and stepped into the chief's line of sight. He stared at her, this stranger called Karada.

Could it be? He stared hard, trying to see past the sunburn and the scars, calling up in his mind the face of his lost sister.

His strange expression caused the chief's smile to drop away. She returned his glance sharply and demanded, "Now what, village-man? First, you had me spare a foe who would've killed me. Do you want me to forego the oaths of my loyal people now?"

"What is your name?" Amero asked. His voice trembled.

"What? Can't you hear? The sky knows my name today!" To Targun, almost done wrapping her injured arm, she said in a phony whisper, "These rockpile villagers seem a little slow-witted."

"Is your—" Once more Amero had to clear his throat before he could resume. "Is your name Nianki?"

Conversation around the chief's tent died. Karada shrugged. "That was the name given me by my mother and father."

"Were their names Oto and Kinar?"

"So they were. Who told you that?"

Amero took a step toward her. "Did you have a brother named Amero?"

Her amused expression vanished, and she frowned at him. "I did," she said. Her hazel eyes were as hard as gemstones. "He was killed many years ago, along with my parents and another brother. How do you know his name?"

Amero's mouth opened and closed. As Karada watched him with growing wonder, he looked straight at her and announced, "Because *I* am Amero, Nianki. I am your brother."

# Chapter 15

~

The plainsmen had a saying: "Swift water grows the biggest fish." It was their way of saying change brought danger and hope in equal measure.

In the days that followed, Karada and Amero became brother and sister again. The cooling nights were passed at the chief's tent, where the story of Nianki and Amero's survival were told for all to hear. The knowledge that Karada had a family was something of a revelation to the warrior band. Many of them considered their chief almost a spirit, a demigoddess of the hunt. As they listened to brother and sister speak, the change in their chief was startling. The stern, vengeful Karada became talkative. She even laughed. Few of her people had ever seen Karada smile widely, much less laugh out loud.

Pa'alu was enchanted by Karada's transformation. He had long cherished every line of her face—wide cheekbones, high forehead, small, straight nose, pointed chin—and every scar on it. Yet the face he knew had always been hard as fieldstone and cold as mountain snow. This new feature—a tooth-baring grin that crinkled her eyes—was totally astonishing, and he silently loved her all the more.

Yet even as he watched the reunion of sister and brother, his delight slowly gave way to something unsettling and ugly. Why did she bestow the favor of her smile and good humor on a man she hadn't seen in more than ten years? Brother or not, Amero hadn't fought at her side, hunted and scouted the trackless savanna with her. Was an accident of birth enough to justify this injustice? When she clapped an arm around Amero's shoulder, Pa'alu felt as if a knife had been shoved into his ribcage.

Two days after the fight between Karada and Sessan, Pa'alu slipped away from the chief's tent and lost himself in the crowd. It was easy to do. The people of Yala-tene were also turning out to see Karada, the famous nomad chief. Word she was blood kin to their own headman only heightened the villagers' curiosity and relief. Surely no harm would come to them and their village now, not if the chief of the wild nomads was the long-lost sister of their founder.

Pa'alu drifted through the excited surge of villagers, buffeted this way and that as they flowed around him. He found himself behind the high cairn of the dragon altar, deposited there like a leaf in the eddies of a swiftly moving stream. He came to rest slumped against the sloping side of the cairn. Some time passed before his surroundings breached his melancholy thoughts.

The smell of soot and burned meat roused him. He looked up at the stone pile where the villagers placed their offerings for the dragon. Thinking of Duranix brought to mind Greengall and Vedvedsica. It had been many days since he thought of the task given him by the elf priest. Digging a hand in his belt pouch now, he found the yellow stone.

This golden nugget held power, enough to affect the mighty Duranix, enough that Vedvedsica should crave the stone for himself. Why should Pa'alu give up such power? Why couldn't he utilize it for himself?

You owe a debt to the priest, he reminded himself. The elf had saved his life. Besides, Pa'alu was no wise man, stewing herbs or plotting the courses of the stars. In his hand, it was just a piece of stone. It wasn't the way to Karada's heart.

Pa'alu put the nugget back in his pouch and stood up, thinking. He might not know how to use the power in the stone, but he knew how to get what he wanted in other ways. The price of the yellow stone had gone up. Once it had been worth Pa'alu's life—cheap for so miserable a soul. If the elf priest still wanted the stone, Vedvedsica had better be willing to bargain, because the price was now Pa'alu's happiness.

\* \* \* \* \*

Amero declared a feast in his sister's honor. Oxen would be slaughtered, fruit would be brought from the orchards across the lake, and the red wine of Yala-tene would flow. Not to be outdone, Karada organized a hunting party to provide the feast with rabbit, gamecock, and golden trout from the highest mountain streams. The day of the feast was set for Moonmeet, the night when the moons Soli and Lutar would meet at the peak of the vault of heaven—by tradition, the last day of summer. Moonmeet would happen three days hence.

His initial shock having passed, Amero was filled with excitement at finding Nianki alive. She and her trusted companions were taken on a tour of Yala-tene, the villagers proudly showing off the storage tunnels, the gardens and orchards. All went well until Nianki asked if she could visit Duranix's cave.

"Certainly," said Amero after a moment's hesitation, "but only you and I may go."

"Why's that?"

"The cave is the dragon's home, and though I've lived there for ten years, I must consult with him about the visits of strangers." Seeing Nianki's men look disappointed and a bit offended, he added, "You will all meet him in due course. Besides, the hoist can carry only two people at a time."

Hatu fingered his eyepatch. "Don't go, Karada," he said warily. "This is the valley where my father died, and that dragon is the one who killed him. You can never trust a monster."

She laughed caustically. "What, after ten years the dragon is going to go berserk and bite our heads off? Too much food and wine has made your head soft!"

He bristled, drawing himself up and squaring his shoulders. "I speak what I feel to be the truth, Karada," he said stiffly.

"You need exercise," she said, laughing. "Join Kiopi's fishing band. Use your vivid imagination to catch us some trout."

Amero shifted his feet, embarrassed by his sister's taunting. He didn't like her high-handed, insulting manner with other people. He tried to think of something soothing to say to Hatu, but the one-eyed nomad departed in mute anger. Nianki didn't seem to notice, or if she did, she didn't seem to care.

At the hoist Nianki grabbed the frame and levered herself into the cramped basket. Her brother tugged on the ready lines and the counterweight started down. With a jerk, the basket began to rise.

"Karada!" Targun called up to her. "Don't forget! The time of mourning is past. Sessan will be buried at sunset!"

She leaned both elbows on the basket rim and looked down at him. "So?"

"You should be there!"

She waved the notion away. "I've no time for traitors," she replied.

As they rose out of voice range of the ground, Amero said, "It will cause bad feeling if you slight Sessan's funeral, Nianki."

"He was a fool and a coward," replied Karada shortly.

"He fought bravely. You killed him. You should go."

She lost the smile that had been on her face since their reunion. "Amero, I killed Sessan because he tried to steal my people from me. He paid for that with his life. I won't dignify his burial with my presence."

There was no budging her, so he let the matter drop. As they climbed out of the basket underneath the waterfall, Amero pointed out the system of pulleys he and Duranix had mounted in the sheer cliff face. The pulleys allowed the basket to rise, descend, and even traverse sideways a distance of a few paces to clear the waterfall.

Nianki looked where he pointed and nodded when he spoke, but the mechanism didn't interest her. As the basket slipped behind the thundering falls, she put out her hand and let the edges of the torrent briefly tear at her fingers. She smiled again. Here at least was a force she could admire.

Amero tied off the basket, and they entered the cave. The thick stone walls muted the roar of the water enough to allow for normal conversation. Nianki, gazing upward, boldly walked into the center of the cavern. Hands clasped at his back, Amero followed her.

"The dragon made this?"

"He clawed this room out of solid sandstone," was Amero's proud reply.

"Amazing. I wish we'd had him with us at the Thon-Thalas."

She wandered here and there, admiring the water pool and hearth and examining his various tools and experiments with polite curiosity. Amero watched her explore for a while, then said, "Nianki, we have to talk."

She turned his copper sheet over in her hands. "About what?"

"We've found each other after all these years. You have a life on the plains, while I—"

She dropped the copper carelessly. It clanged on the floor. "Why don't you join us? It's a great life—riding, hunting, seeing the wide plain unroll beneath your horse. There're the elves, of course. I've not given up the fight to free the south and east from Silvanos's hands."

"Nianki, my life is here." Amero sat on the edge of the stone hearth. "This is my place. These are my people."

Her smile faded. "I thought you'd say that."

"You're welcome to stay as long as you like."

"Thanks, brother. We may stay a while to gather supplies and our strength before we move on."

Amero looked away to where the stream flowing down the wall pattered into the pool. They'd found each other after almost eleven years, and already they were speaking of separating again.

"Where will you go?" he asked.

She considered a moment. "North. The hunting's better there, come winter. We'll cover the northern plain, maybe even follow the coastline to the far northeast. I hear tales of other humans there, living in treetops. They also say the black-skinned folk cross the sea in great dugout canoes and trade along the shore. Maybe some of them will join us."

"I think you should stay here, Nianki," Amero said urgently, "We'll combine our people into a single band. We've a lot to teach each other. Why, I'm close to learning how to make my own copper tools! Once I've mastered that, I'll make bronze. The mountains are full of minerals, and the valleys are good for crops and flocks. Your people can teach us your way with horses."

She dipped a hand in the cold pool. The hard face of Karada had replaced the smiling visage of Nianki.

"And who will lead this united band?" she scoffed. "You? Me? Both of us? Think again, brother. Your villagers won't stand for orders from a wanderer like me, and my plainsmen won't listen to a soft-handed foot-walker like you." He opened his mouth to protest, but she said more softly, "Even

208

I wouldn't follow your orders, Amero, and I don't think you would follow mine."

He nodded sadly. "Will you come to visit now and then?"

She grinned. "Every Moonmeet, if I'm able, I'll come—so long as you hold a feast each time!"

He rose and embraced the sister he once thought he would never see again. As she felt his fingers tighten against on her back, scarred Karada was briefly big sister Nianki once more. "Cheer up," she said. "Knowing you're alive makes a difference."

"And to me," he said.

A shower of water announced the return of Duranix. Amero and Nianki stepped quickly apart, embarrassed by their mutual affection, and to escape the torrent of water flung off by the huge dragon. Duranix shook his head. His barbels jangled metallically against his chin and muzzle. Nianki was taken aback. She had never seen Duranix in his true form, and her hunter's instincts were aroused by the looming creature. She tensed to fight or flee.

"Ha," said Duranix, grinning. "I leave for a while and Amero brings a mate to my cave. What next? Pups?"

Nianki threw back her head and laughed. She laughed all the harder at seeing her brother's face turn brilliant crimson.

Furious and more than a little embarrassed, Amero exclaimed, "This is my sister! The one I thought long dead!"

"Ah," Duranix said. "Karada is your sister. How can that be?" Duranix studied them. His pupils narrowed to slits. "I don't see the resemblance." Amero's face showed anger again and the dragon added, "Humans look so much alike to me, you might all be siblings. I'm sure you know your own sister."

Nianki gave a snort of smothered laughter.

Duranix clomped heavily to his platform, each ponderous step intended to shake the water off his back. He climbed smoothly onto the dished-out ledge and idly picked up an ox leg bone lying nearby. All the flesh had been eaten off already, but the dragon gnawed the ends of the bone. His wickedly curved teeth scraped against the bone.

"Does he always eat like that?" Nianki muttered.

Amero rolled his eyes and climbed the steps at the front of the platform. He cleared his throat. Duranix bit through the bone with a single snap of his jaws. Nianki flinched. Amero, used to his companion's habits, said eagerly, "Did you find anything?"

The dragon's casual manner vanished. He tossed the bone aside. "Sthenn was here. I could smell his trail from five thousand paces high."

"Who's Sthenn?" asked Nianki.

"Is he still around?" Amero asked gravely.

"No—or if he is, I can't find him."

Amero's anxiety was evident and Nianki demanded again, "Who's Sthenn?"

Her brother explained about the green dragon, the yevi, and his ongoing rivalry with Duranix. She listened with a grim expression.

"This green dragon created the yevi?" she said. Amero nodded. She made a fist, pressing it to her lips. "Elves in the east, dragons in the west . . . Is there anyone who doesn't want to drive us off the land?"

Duranix exhaled sharply, and the resulting whirlwind blew Nianki's hair across her face. She regarded the bronze dragon warily and said, "I have to wonder—maybe I'm fighting the wrong foe. The elves, arrogant as they are, are beings not unlike us. Some of them have notions of honor. This green dragon sends packs of unnatural beasts to do his dirty work for him. Maybe he's the one Karada's band should be fighting."

"I wouldn't recommend it," said Duranix. "Sthenn is more than two thousand years old, by human reckoning. He's clever, cruel, vindictive, and unpredictable. He never forgives a transgression, no matter how slight. As long as you are nomadic savages, wandering the plains, he will take little notice if you kill his pets. But if you show up at his lair with an army, he'll use every trick and tool at his disposal to destroy every last one of you in the most unpleasant fashion he can think of, and in his long life, he's thought of many."

Amero felt suddenly cold. Unconsciously, he stepped closer to Duranix.

"You talk like you're afraid of him," Nianki said to the dragon.

Duranix raised his head. "I am afraid of him. He killed my mother and my clutchmates—my siblings, as you would say—for no other reason than it pleased him to do so."

"How did you escape?"

Duranix's claws flexed, scratching loudly on the stone platform. "I didn't," he said. "Sthenn spared me on purpose. He deliberately killed my family then let me live."

"Why?" asked Amero. Duranix seldom spoke of his own past, so this was rare information to him.

"I spent a few centuries wondering that myself. I believe Sthenn let me live so that he could terrorize me. Over the course of his long life, Sthenn has grown jaded. One thing he still savors is fear. He loves being the object of dread and goes to elaborate lengths to instill it in others. It's easy enough to frighten lesser creatures, but there's little for dragons to fear except another dragon. Making me afraid of him is a powerful pleasure."

"Why don't you seek him out and kill him?" said Nianki.

"Eighty-six years ago I tried to bring him to battle. He set fire to an entire forest and escaped under cover of the smoke. For all the years since, he has taunted me. His avalanches made my first home uninhabitable. He drives off herds of game in hope that I'll go hungry. He attacks humans and elves to make them fear all dragons and hunt me."

Nianki pounded a fist into the palm of her hand. "If I were you, I'd find this green monster and settle him once and for all!"

Duranix glanced at Amero. "Are you sure you two are related?"

Amero ignored the gibe and told Nianki it was time they departed. He had work in the village below. Nianki bid the dragon good-bye, but as her brother tugged at her elbow she continued to urge Duranix to deeds of bloody vengeance against his mortal enemy, Sthenn.

"Yes, yes," the dragon answered her dismissively. "Amero, have the elders set up an ox or two for me, won't you? I'm famished."

While they descended in the hoist, Nianki shook her head saying, "With an ally like Duranix, I could defeat the elves in a single season!"

211

"He won't fight elves for you," Amero replied. "The struggles of we lesser creatures are not his concern."

"He helps you."

"I'm his friend. Also, our village is a thorn in Sthenn's claw. The more humans settle here, the harder it will be for Sthenn to harm Duranix."

Nianki considered this as the basket emerged from behind the waterfall. Below, Samtu and her retainers were waiting.

"Nianki, I understand why the villagers listen to me," Amero said. "The dragon protects them, and I speak to Duranix. Living here has made their lives easier. But why do these people follow you? Why do they obey you?"

"I give them a name," she said, her voice almost inaudible against the roar of the falls. "They are Karada's band. It's something to belong to, to believe in, to be proud of. There are so many enemies in the world, brother—faceless ones like hunger, cold, storms, sickness, wild beasts. We fight them every day, knowing we can't really win. I gave my people a new enemy: the elves—an enemy we have a chance of defeating. So my people have something to belong to, an enemy they can defeat, a leader to fight for. For that they will follow me to the end of my days."

The basket came to rest with a thump. Karada climbed out and was immediately surrounded by her comrades, all eager to hear about the lair of the dragon. She strolled grandly back to the camp with them hanging on her every word.

Amero stood in the wicker basket and watched his sister—no, she was not Nianki any more, but every bit Karada, leader of her band. Though life had taken them down different trails, Amero realized he and his sister were not so far apart after all.

* * * * *

In a cleft in the mountains a quarter-league from Yalatene, the plainsmen buried Sessan. As the sun sank lower in the western sky, Nacris made the burial party wait while she selected a spot for her mate's final rest. The soil was too hard and stony for them to dig a proper grave. They would have to pile rocks atop Sessan's body. Nacris chose a wide ledge near the crest of a hill. As the diggers covered her mate, she stared out at the expanse of hills and valleys laid out before her.

It wasn't right, she thought dully. They didn't belong in this place. The sky seemed closer and smaller than it did on the vast grasslands she was accustomed to. At least here, near the top of this mountain, Sessan's spirit might not feel quite as imprisoned as it must in the narrow confines of the valley.

As soon as their task was done, the nomads sent by Karada to bury the dead man promptly departed. The few plainsmen who cared enough to grieve remained a short while, then one by one, left the melancholy scene. Soon only two remained, Nacris and Hatu.

After a period of silence, Hatu said softly, "A terrible loss."

Nacris glared at him, the red light of the setting sun giving her face a ruddy cast. "What? Why are you here?" she demanded coldly.

"To pay homage to a brave warrior," the one-eyed plainsman replied.

Nacris reached out to touch the heaped-up stones. "You're one of Karada's," she spat.

"When it comes to fighting elves, I'll follow Karada, but this village, this dragon . . . it's a dangerous sham."

Nacris raised her reddened eyes.

"Did you hear? The village headman is Karada's brother."

"No!" Nacris exclaimed.

Hatu nodded. "It's true. She was grinning like a panther when she found out. Sessan wasn't even cold yet, and Karada was laughing."

"Someday I'll kill her," Nacris whispered.

"Not an easy task," said Hatu. "For one person, that is."

Nacris stood up. The last of the sun's light vanished behind the high peaks and a chill wind whistled across the ridge. She drew her sheepskin vest close around her. "Are you turning against her?"

Hatu walked slowly around the pile of stones. Nacris began moving too, keeping her distance from the one-eyed warrior. He paused at the head of the grave, and she stopped at the foot.

When he spoke, Hatu avoided her question. "Did you notice the pile of stones in the village?" he asked. "That's where the people of Arku-peli sacrifice oxen or elk to the dragon, twice a week. In return for his meals, the dragon supposedly protects Arku-peli from attack."

"So?"

"Did anyone try to stop you and Sessan from leading half a hundred riders into the valley?"

Nacris rubbed her cheek, trying to remember. "No, no one. The headman—Arkuden?—he met us unarmed."

"Some protection the dragon gives, eh?"

Hatu started walking again, circling the grave. Nacris continued to keep her distance. When he reached the foot of the grave, he halted.

"I tell you what I think," he said finally. "I think these people have sold themselves into slavery. They feed this dragon out of fear, not because he protects them. And what happens when the oxen run out, and no elk can be found? How long will it be before the villagers are setting their own beloved children on that altar?"

Nacris laughed. "What a mind you have! No plainsman would—"

"No plainsman would sacrifice his child to a dragon? Do you really believe that? Our own comrades abandoned a good warrior, Sessan, out of fear of Karada. You saw how few of them came to honor his death. Do you think these strange, *settled*—" he sneered as he said the word— "folk of Arku-peli would be any better?"

The scorn faded from Nacris's face. "What do you propose?"

"Nothing for now. I will speak to others, quietly. You should too. Start with Tarkwa. He's a clear-thinker. Then, when the time comes, the band will leave that accursed valley, but it won't be led by Karada."

He picked up a stray stone and placed it on Sessan's grave. "And if the Arkuden tries to defend his sister, he will be destroyed, too."

\* \* \* \* \*

Pa'alu placed the golden nugget in the hole Vedvedsica had made in the rock. Since there was no way to know when the priest would appear to claim his prize, the plainsman settled down to wait.

Night fell. The canyon was draped in deep shadows, and still Pa'alu kept his vigil. He stayed awake the entire night, sometimes singing out loud to keep his mind alert, other times striding around the perimeter of the canyon and stamping his feet on the rough ground until they were bruised and sore. His only companion was the sound of his own voice. Any night creatures that lived in the canyon gave the noisy human a wide, wary berth.

At last, the milky wall on the west side of his prison took on a tinge of pink as the rising sun finally made an appearance. The indigo sky lightened to azure. Still, there was no sign of Vedvedsica.

Near midday, his stomach empty and his patience exhausted, Pa'alu picked up the stone and prepared to leave. A shadow passed over the sun. Strange, since the sky was cloudless. Pa'alu looked up, shading his eyes. The sun's glare seared his vision, and for several heartbeats he could see nothing. The air grew heavy, dense. It was hard to force it into his lungs. When his eyesight resolved again, he saw the priest standing by the rock, probing the hole with his slender fingers.

"Where is the stone?" asked Vedvedsica. "Give it to me."

"I have it," Pa'alu said, his voice sounding oddly distant and flat.

The priest held out his hand. His arm elongated in a weird fashion, extending all the way from where he stood to where Pa'alu was, a good three paces away.

The plainsman recoiled in shock. "The price has gone up," he said.

Vedvedsica came closer. His outstretched hand remained near Pa'alu and the rest of his body caught up to it. He looked concerned.

"The stone is more powerful than I thought," the priest said. "It is affecting you. It wants to remain with you, but you must give it to me. Only I can control it. If you keep it, it will control you."

"I'll give it to you, but you must do something for me," stated Pa'alu, anxious now that the elf priest was so near.

"Wasn't saving your life enough?"

Pa'alu had a strange urge to laugh. He opened his mouth and tiny crystals, like snowflakes, flew out. When they struck

215

the rocky ground, they shattered, and the sound of a hundred tiny chuckles escaped. Shocked, he looked at Vedvedsica. The elf seemed to see nothing amiss. He regarded the plainsman with obvious vexation.

"What does my life matter?" Pa'alu continued warily. No crystals flew out of his mouth this time. "What does anything matter without Karada?"

"The woman? She loves you not."

The elf's words were like blows. Pa'alu lifted his chin and said, "No, but with your power you can change that."

"You would compel her affection?"

"Yes!" The word echoed off the sun-washed canyon walls.

Vedvedsica sighed. "Elves and humans are so alike! While I search for knowledge and wisdom, others crave only petty wealth or love. I spend half my time making love philters for the nobles of Silvanos's court." He shook his long, narrow head contemptuously. "What a waste!"

"Will you do it?" Pa'alu said.

The priest stroked his sparse beard. He had hair sprouting between his fingers, and his nails were long and narrow, like a panther's claws. "It would serve you right if I walked away and let the stone eat your soul, but I need that nugget far too much. Yes, I will cause this barbarian woman to love you."

Pa'alu felt in his pouch for the stone. He could see it, yet for some reason, he couldn't grasp it. He plainly saw his fingers pass through the yellow stone as if it were smoke. What strange things were happening!

"Concentrate," said Vedvedsica sternly. "Use all your senses, not just your eyes!"

Sweat dripped from the plainsman's nose as he carefully closed his fingers around the phantom nugget. At last, he felt the rough edges of the rock. Sighing deeply, he handed the stone to Vedvedsica.

"There'll be none of that, now," the elf said, apparently speaking to the stone. "In you go." He placed the rock in a small agate box with a sliding lid then tucked the box in his robe.

"How will you do it?" Pa'alu asked. Already his hearing was back to normal, and the distortion in his vision was rapidly clearing.

"Do what? Oh, your true love." Scorn dripped from his voice. "I don't have my flasks and alembics, so I can't brew a philter. I'll have to give you an amulet. They're not as precise, but you'll have to make do."

From another recess in his robe, the priest took out a handful of small bronze disks. They were blank on both sides, merely smooth metal. He chose one about the size of a daisy blossom and returned the rest to his robe. As Pa'alu looked on, Vedvedsica pressed the disk between the palms of his hands, holding them high over his head. His lips moved in a silent conjuration.

This went on for some time. Pa'alu grew tired and retreated to the shady side of the canyon. He mopped his brow and watched the priest stand in the full glare of the sun with not a bead of sweat on his translucent skin.

The sun was halfway to its western bed when Vedvedsica at last lowered his hands. He stared at Pa'alu, a smile on his thin face. The plainsman got stiffly to his feet and approached. When the elf opened his hands, Pa'alu leaned over to see. The disk was unchanged.

He was about to say something when the elf took out a shard of rosy rock crystal. Vedvedsica placed the shard on top of the disk and stood back. He clapped his hands five times and shouted a single-syllable in Elvish. The crystal shard vanished in a pinpoint flash of light.

Folding his arms, Vedvedsica said, "It's done."

Tentatively, Pa'alu picked up the disk. He expected it to be hot or at least warm to the touch. In fact, it was as cold as mountain spring water. It was also no longer blank. The whole surface, front and back, was covered with incredibly fine lines, swirling in an intricate pattern. He rubbed a finger over the images. The metal was smooth, so the lines weren't engraved on the surface, but neither did they smear under his rubbing.

"Listen well, human," said the priest. "This amulet works only once. You must touch it to the skin of the one whose love you desire. It must touch yours at the same time. A common method is to place it in your palm when you clasp hands with the object of your affection. Once touched to both persons, the spell discharges and cannot be repeated or repaired. Do you understand?"

"I do. Thank you, great one!"

Vedvedsica smiled unpleasantly. "Passion is easy to compel," he said. "It may not be so easy to live with."

But Pa'alu wasn't listening. Exhaustion and hunger had made him lightheaded. He gripped the amulet tightly and spun around, dancing with joy. At last, at last! he exulted. At last Karada would be his!

A shadow crossed the sun's face again. When the plainsman looked up, Vedvedsica had vanished.

# Chapter 16

~

Preparations for the Moonmeet feast had been vigorous and were now nearly complete. Children had collected armloads of kindling, gleaning every fallen twig and branch from the valley of the waterfall. Loggers had supplied larger trees from the supply they'd floated upriver. The area between the dragon's cairn and the nomads' camp had been cleared, and a large bonfire laid. The fire was lit, allowed to burn down to a shimmering bed of coals, and whole oxen were set up to roast.

The nomads were astonished that the villagers chose to ruin good meat with fire. Karada, though she also found the idea shocking, allowed herself to be persuaded by her brother that cooked meat could be tasty. However, she approved Pakito's quiet suggestion that the feast also include some animal flesh not seared by the villagers' fires.

Apples and pears from the orchard were wrapped in clay and baked in the ashes, and smaller game—rabbits, fowl, and two wild boar—were spitted and cooked at the edges of the great fire.

Village women pounded a ring of stakes into the sand and rigged a large hide vat. Clay jugs were brought from the houses and storage tunnel and emptied into the vat. Before long it was brimming with scarlet wine, and the smell of the new vintage saturated the air.

Not to be outdone, the nomads brought out an array of drums, wooden flutes, and rams' horns. Positioning themselves with their backs to the lake (so the setting sun wasn't in their eyes), the nomads began to play. There was no structure to their music. They generally followed whoever displayed the most energy at the moment. If a pair of drummers were moved to pound a fierce rhythm, then the other drummers and pipers followed them. If a horn player stood up to sound a melancholy air, the drummers fell silent and let the lone player soar.

The valley reverberated with the sounds of the feast. Children—from both the nomads' camp and the village—ran between the houses, shrieking with delight, chasing each other, engaging in mock fights, or capturing fireflies. Long trenchers made of white pine planks or pinned birch bark carried steaming ribs and cutlets to the hungry crowd.

Higher up the hill, just below the cliff face, an open tent had been raised. There, Amero and Nianki sat side by side, eating from a common tray. On Nianki's left were Targun, Samtu, Pakito, and Hatu. An empty place was left for Pa'alu. No one had seen him for almost three days, but Nianki wasn't concerned, and Amero was getting used to his strange absences.

On Amero's right were the village elders: Konza the tanner, Valka, Farun the stonecutter, Hulami the vintner, and Menefer the master potter. Everyone was eating and talking. A steady stream of boys circled from the vat and firepit back to the tent bearing fresh supplies of food and drink.

"Great stuff, this," Nianki exclaimed at one point, swirling her cup around. "Where did you learn to make this?"

"Some of our people knew how to make wine when they arrived," Amero said. He didn't care for it himself. It distressed his stomach. "Northerners, from Plains' End. They brought vines with them in pots of dirt."

"Sometimes we took drink like this from elves we captured. Theirs is lighter in color, almost clear. They call it 'nectar,' " said Pakito. A huge pile of gnawed beef bones lay in front of him. "Drink enough of it and it sneaks up and hits you on top of your head!" He banged a broad fist against his own forehead to illustrate the sensation. Samtu and Targun laughed.

"Where is that brother of yours?" Hatu asked from the end of the row. "He should be here."

"I don't know," the big man said, the edges of his words growing soft with wine. "He won' stan' still at all."

"A true nomad," said Targun, his face red as a berry.

"I'm old enough to remember growing up on the plain, moving every day, trying to live off roots and lizards and the odd deer now an' then," Valka said. "That life was hard. Why do you still do it?"

"Are you talking to me?" said Targun.

"You're the eldest here, yes. Why keep roaming?"

"It's what I know," Targun declared fervently. "I feel nervy if I stay in one place too long, like a snared rabbit."

"We're free," added Samtu, dark hair falling across her round face. She was leaning on Pakito's enormous shoulder with evident contentment. "We go where we will, when we will."

"Except to elf land," Hatu muttered. Alone among the nomads at this table, he had made a point of refusing to sample the cooked meat.

Nianki glared. Amero cut off any awkwardness by saying, "Tell me of this warlord, Balif. What sort of fellow is he?"

Everyone fell quiet, looking expectantly at Nianki. They were all curious. She was gnawing a pheasant's leg. Lowering the morsel she said loudly, "What are you all gawking at?"

"You know Balif well," said Pakito impishly. "Tell your brother about him."

"I tried to kill him a few times and failed. That doesn't make us comrades," Nianki said matter-of-factly.

"But what's he like?" her brother insisted.

Nianki sighed and tossed the now clean pheasant leg over her shoulder. "He's a clever, arrogant fellow, like most elves. A bit skinny, but made of sinew and whit-leather, and his eyes are strange." Some of them regarded her quizzically. "Very pale blue," she explained.

"Sounds like quite a man," said Hulami the vintner. She'd outlived three mates herself and had an eye for capable men. "I'd like to meet him."

"He's not a man, he's an elf," Nianki retorted, annoyed. "And if I meet him again, I hope he's on his knees, suing for peace!"

Shouts of greeting rose from the crowd. Torches were lit from the dying bonfire, and by their warm glow Amero and the others could see Pa'alu approaching up the hill. Amero rose and gave his hand to the plainsman.

"Peace be with you, Pa'alu! Welcome to the feast at last. Is everything well?"

Pa'alu nodded curtly and replied, "Very well, Arkuden. Very well."

He half-turned and offered his hand to Nianki. As she was busy downing a cup of wine, his gesture went unnoticed. Pa'alu lowered his hand.

A boy offered the plainsman a trencher of roast. Pa'alu accepted it gratefully and took his place between Pakito and Hatu. His younger brother regaled Pa'alu with stories of the doings of the past couple of days—the bird hunts, fishing expeditions, building the bonfire, and the various reactions to the taste of roasted oxen, which Pakito declared to be far superior to raw. Pa'alu listened idly while eating.

On his left, Hatu said pointedly, "Sessan was buried yesterday."

Everyone ignored the remark—everyone but Pa'alu. He said simply, "I'm sorry I wasn't there."

"Thank you," Hatu said, his single eye gleaming.

The nomad drummers struck up a brisk rhythm. Samtu jumped up and tugged at Pakito's unresisting arms.

"Dance with me, dance with me," she teased.

"I dance like a bull elk," Pakito told her, shaking his head.

"I don't care. Come."

He rose unsteadily, but Samtu ducked under one of his arms and braced him up. They weaved slightly as they went down the hill toward the torchlit festivities—Pakito because the wine was affecting his head, and Samtu because Pakito's weight was affecting her balance.

Nianki leaned back in her stool, one hand patting her leg in time to the beat. Pa'alu put aside his trencher and stood, asking her to dance.

"A chief doesn't dance," she answered lightly. "It isn't dignified."

"No one will judge you, " Pa'alu said. He smiled and held out his hand. "Please."

Amero watched this little scene unfold with great interest. Despite the many intervening years, he still had much residual affection for his sister. He worried about her. She was too hard, too much apart from the world, and he found himself wishing she'd take Pa'alu's hand and dance.

Something glinted in the plainsman's cupped hand, catching Amero's eye. He looked again. A gleam like that meant metal. On second glance, he saw that Pa'alu's hands were empty. Had he imagined it?

The tall plainsman's hands stayed empty as Nianki rudely

ignored him. He finally returned to his platter with a chas-
tened expression and devoted himself to his food.

Hulami set her eye on Targun and dragged him away to
the growing crowd of dancers. The plainsmen were dancing
in large circles, men on the outside, shoulder to shoulder,
and women on the inside, facing out. Most of the action con-
sisted of stomping and kicking to the rhythm of the drummers, twists and turns punctuated by high-spirited yelps.

Into the uneven circle of torchlight came a stranger. It
was Duranix, once more in human shape, but his build and
coloring were different than before. Now, strangely, the
dragon resembled a slightly taller, brawnier version of
Amero. He paused by the end of the tent, gazing at the merry-
making.

Though the nomads didn't recognize this newcomer as the
dragon, those nearest him found themselves moving back,
giving this unknown fellow room. Nianki also didn't recognize him, but the young man they called "Dragon's Son" did.
Amero beckoned to Duranix to join them, calling his name
heartily.

A stool was brought and placed between brother and sister.
The serving boys brought trenchers of beef and a lengthy jack
of wine. Duranix dismissed the drink but accepted the meat.

"I had an ox this afternoon," Duranix said, "but now I'm
hungry again." Everyone except Hatu laughed. He was glaring at Duranix, Amero, and Nianki, and did so for a long
time, until he realized they were paying no attention to him.
The one-eyed plainsman knocked over his cup and stalked
away into the darkness.

"He's Genta's son," Amero explained privately to
Duranix. "He's never forgiven you for what happened."

Duranix shrugged. "I've never forgiven the slayer of my
mother and clutchmates."

"He's a whining child," Nianki stated a little too loudly.
"Ignore him!"

Duranix gestured to the ring of dancers. "What is this?
Some kind of ritual?"

"This dance? They're just feeling their blood," said
Nianki. She drained the last drops from her cup and, to everyone's amazement, clamped a hand on her brother's forearm.

"I'll show you, dragon-man," she declared merrily. "Come, brother!"

Amero allowed himself to be dragged away by his tipsy sister. He looked over his shoulder at Duranix and Pa'alu, his face showing—was it amusement or puzzlement? Duranix couldn't tell.

The disguised dragon glanced at Pa'alu to see how he was taking Nianki's playfulness. When Duranix asked if he was jealous of Amero or annoyed with Nianki, he denied it with remarkable calm.

"Karada makes her own choices," Pa'alu said in a low voice. "As her loyal comrade, I accept them." So saying, he put aside the remains of his dinner and departed in the direction of the wine vat.

As the wine level went down, the feast grew louder and the music more fevered, more ragged. A few fistfights broke out on the fringes of the crowd, but none of them lasted more than a few blows before one of the combatants went down. Once a blade flashed, but Amero was on the spot in an instant. He stopped the fight brewing between a nomad and a villager, shaming them into settling their dispute peaceably, but the incident left him uneasy. Where had Duranix gotten to?

Craning his neck, the young man saw that the dragon was standing in the center of the women's circle. The women—both nomads and villagers—dancing in the circle had turned to face him rather than the men still moving in the outer circle. The women were whirling around the bemused dragon. Karada, very much the tallest woman there, had her arms linked with two of her nomad sisters, and her joyous face was flushed, her long, tawny hair flying.

A muscular, bearded nomad, his ropy arms sheened with sweat, called a loud cadence and resumed the beat on his goatskin drum. The others gradually joined in, slowly building the volume and tempo.

Amero spotted Nianki standing alone near the heaping embers from the ox roast. She too was sweating heavily from her wild dancing, and she was gulping down drink from a full-sized leather bucket. Amero hoped there was only water in the pail. His sister had already had too much wine.

"What a feast, eh?" he said, touching her lightly on the back. Her buckskins were sodden, her hair plastered to her head. She lowered the bucket. Thankfully, it was water.

Pa'alu appeared with three cups and a tall clay amphora brimming with wine. "You look thirsty," he said, pouring Nianki a cup. She took it, drained it, and held it out for more. Pa'alu smiled at her.

"Hold still," he said, reaching out toward her cup hand as though to brace it. "I don't want to spill."

Laughing uproariously, Pakito and Samtu came up behind Pa'alu. The cheerful giant slapped his brother on the back, a blow to rattle any man's teeth. Pa'alu lost the amphora, which crashed to the ground and shattered, spraying them with sticky wine and clay shards. He also failed to catch hold of Nianki's hand as she cursed the spilled wine and strode away to the lake to wash her hands and legs. Pa'alu turned on his merry brother and grasped the front of his sheepskin vest.

"Drunken idiot!" he hissed. Pakito, who could've flattened his brother with the back of one hand, blinked a few times and leaned back away from Pa'alu's incomprehensible display of temper.

"Shut up, 'Alu," Samtu said genially. "There's more wine!"

Pa'alu broke away and ran down the beach to the water's edge. Amero too had noticed and was puzzled by the plainsman's harsh reaction to such a minor accident. He went after Pa'alu.

The crowd was sparse by the lake. A chill rose from the water, and this discouraged most revelers from tarrying by the shore. Formidable piles of dirty trenchers lay heaped up along the shoreline. There would be much work to do in the morning, cleaning up after such a celebration.

Nianki was squatting on the sand, splashing cold water on her arms, legs, and face. Pa'alu slowed to a walk when he spotted her. Amero lingered at the edge of the crowd, anxious not to appear too intrusive.

"Karada."

She didn't look up. "What do you want, Pa'alu?"

"I have something to give you," Pa'alu said softly.

"More wine? Good."

225

"No, not wine." He stood over her, one fist clenched.

She finally looked up, her sodden hair covering half her face. "Speak plainly, man. I can't stand it when you drift around behind my back with that doe-eyed look."

He held out his closed fist. "It's here."

"What is it?"

"Stand up and I'll show you."

Distant lightning shimmered behind her when she stood. Nianki wiped her hand on her legs, then planted her fists on her hips expectantly.

"Well, what've you got?"

"Something very rare. . . ."

Over his shoulder she spied Amero watching them. Nianki let out a yell. "Hey, brother, come here! Pa'alu has something to show us!"

He jerked his hand away. "It's not for anyone but you!" he said through clenched teeth. Pa'alu was about to flee when Duranix also appeared, walking along the shore toward him, blocking his way.

Lightning played about the western sky, and muffled peals of thunder echoed overhead, mixing with the pulsing rumble of the drums.

"What do you have?" asked the dragon. His voice was casual but plainly suspicious. "It's the stone, isn't it? You kept it, didn't you?"

"No." Pa'alu was hemmed in on three sides. The only escape was the lake.

"Show me what you have," Duranix ordered.

"It's not for you!"

"I can see it glowing through your foolish flesh. I smelled it on you earlier at the tent, but I thought it was just an aura, a remnant of the stone, but it's not. You never got rid of the thing, did you? Do it now—throw it in the lake. It will poison you, as it almost poisoned me."

"What he's talking about?" asked a groggy Nianki.

"A nugget, charged with dangerous spirit-power," Amero explained, his eyes watching Pa'alu with new seriousness.

"You're wrong," Pa'alu said, backing away from the dragon. "It's not the yellow stone, I swear!"

Duranix closed within arm's reach. Pa'alu drew his knife

to fend him off. Nianki also advanced a step toward the pale, shivering plainsman, but Amero caught her by the arms, holding her.

A blade of elven bronze was no threat to a dragon, but Duranix didn't want to harm the plainsman. He raised a finger near the tip of Pa'alu's knife. A tiny arc of lightning flashed from his finger to the blade. There a was a loud snap, and Pa'alu flew backward into Nianki and Amero. All three went down in a heap on the sand.

"Get off me, you fool," Nianki snarled, pushing the stunned Pa'alu away. Amero squirmed out from under the bigger man and saw something shiny and golden glittering on the sand.

Nianki saw it too and reached for it. Her hand brushed Amero's, and their fingers touched the warm metal disk at the same moment.

Nianki drew in her breath sharply and flinched as if struck. She snatched her hand back and stared at it with distaste.

"Did it shock you?" asked Amero, stooping to pick up the mysterious object, but she continued to stare, saying nothing.

Amero examined it. It was a flat round piece of bronze. The light was poor, so he held it close to his face to see it, turning it over and over, examining it. Nianki was staring strangely at him, not at the disk.

"What is it?" asked Duranix, looking over Amero's shoulder.

"A disk of metal. Bronze, I think." The disk was blank on both sides, with no engraving or marks whatsoever. He handed it the dragon, who scrutinized it with diminishing curiosity. "He was telling the truth after all. It's not the nugget." Amero looked regretfully at Pa'alu, who was staring fiercely at Nianki.

Duranix flipped the disk over and over in his hands. "Strange. I could've sworn he was carrying the stone. I thought I sensed an aura of power hanging over him like the stink of an unwashed human."

All of a sudden Nianki shuddered so violently she tottered into Amero. He put an arm around her to brace her up. "Too much to drink?" he asked gently.

"Uh . . . that must be it."

"Let me help you back to your tent."

Amero helped her stand. When he let go, Nianki shivered so hard she almost fell down. Amero grabbed her arm to steady her.

"What's wrong?" Duranix asked.

The dragon folded the bronze disk in half with his powerful fingers and tossed it toward Pa'alu. The plainsman dropped to his knees, fingers scrabbling through the sand to find the disk. With a shout he stood bolt upright, staring at his empty hands.

"Where is it?" he cried hopelessly. His eyes darted between Nianki and Amero with a terror that none of them understood.

Then, with an agonized cry, Pa'alu picked up his knife, reversed the blade and raised it high to plunge into his own chest. He never made it. His hand was caught in Duranix's unbreakable grip.

"Let me go!" Pa'alu screamed. "My life is over!"

Without a word, Duranix wrung the elf blade from the plainsman a second time and tossed it in the lake. He released Pa'alu, who stumbled backward and fell to the sand.

At that moment a fork of rose-colored lightning, bright as the moon, lanced down from the clouds and struck the mountaintop above the waterfall. A shattering thunderclap sounded, silencing the drums and pipes of the feast.

"By all my ancestors!" Pa'alu said hoarsely. "Forgive me, Karada. I never meant—" He scrambled to his feet and started to run toward the village. Once he spun around and cried, "Forgive me! I never meant it!" Then he ran on, crashing against the revelers in his path.

Amero exchanged a puzzled look with Duranix. "Strange," said the dragon, watching Pa'alu as he disappeared into the crowd. None of what happened had registered with Nianki, who seemed dazed.

A sheet of warm rain fell suddenly, lashing the crowd of celebrants. With much yelling and coarse laughter, the feast broke up as people sprinted for house and tent. Amero hurried through the hubbub with Nianki on his arm. Torches died in the downpour, and the stony flat above the beach became dark and confusing, with much running, falling, cursing, laughing. Steam and smoke curled up from the ashes of the bonfire, and village women struggled to get the uneaten portions of the feast into the storage tunnel.

Amero reached Nianki's tent with some difficulty. The cowhide shelter flapped and lashed in the wind, threatening to blow away. Amero left Nianki on her bed roll and grappled with the whipping flaps. He tied them off, one by one, until the open shelter became a dark, dry, enclosed room.

Rained drummed on the roof. Amero snugged down the center flap. In the dark he could hear Nianki moving.

"I'm almost done. Feeling any better?" he asked. There was no response but her even breathing. Was she asleep? "Hulami's wine is good, but it creeps up on you like a viper."

With the tent secured, he wiped the rain and sweat from his face. "Sleep well, Nianki."

"Amero."

He paused at the door flap. "Hmm?"

"I love you."

Though he'd always known she cared about him in her own rough way, he'd never heard his sister speak such tender words before. She sounded tired, a little lost.

"I love you, too," Amero said before he ducked out into the storm. "Sleep well."

\* \* \* \* \*

Soon after the storm broke, the shore was empty, the feast over. A single towering figure remained outdoors, close to the water's edge. Rain pelted Duranix in his true reptilian shape, running in thick streams down his massive face and off the scales on his back. He didn't bother to unfurl his wings and use them to protect his eyes. A dragon's vision was more acute by night than by day. He could see just fine, rain or no rain.

High above Yala-tene, at the very edge of the cliff overlooking the nomad camp, stood a solitary onlooker. To Duranix, his warm blood painted him against the night in a rose silhouette. He and the dragon stared through the night and the storm at each other.

"Vedvedsica." Duranix's rumbling whisper was swallowed by the wind.

Looking down, the elf cleric smiled to himself. The nugget, wrapped in fine gold wire, hung from a slender chain around his neck. He turned away, laughing.

# Chapter 17

~

After their night of indulgence, the villagers had to rise with the new day and go about their work. Cattle had to be fed and watered, the gardens weeded, and ripe vegetables harvested. Summer was over, and cool-weather crops like cabbage and onions had to be planted. In addition to all these chores, there were pots to throw, timber to harvest, and hides to tan. Red-eyed and yawning, the villagers rose from their beds and silently went to work.

Not so the nomads. It was their custom to sleep in the remains of their revelries until thirst and hunger forced them to face the day. When they feasted a good hunt or a victory in battle, they got up only when their heads stopped throbbing, then mounted their horses and moved on. In the days after the Moonmeet feast, Karada's band continued to carouse after dark. The only one who might have stopped them, Karada herself, was strangely absent from the scene.

Amero, like the rest of the villagers, had been busy. Three days went by before he found time to visit his sister. By then, the nomad camp resembled the scene of some terrible disaster. The thunderstorm on the night of the feast had collapsed most of their carelessly pitched tents, and the plainsmen had been too inebriated to do much about it. The most hard-drinking nomads slept where they fell, spending their nights exposed to the elements.

The only good-humored nomad Amero met was the amiable giant Pakito. He spotted the big man sitting outside his lopsided shelter, pouring rainwater out of his boots and smiling. A less violent, but no less dampening, rainstorm had rolled over the valley the night before.

"You're in good spirits, considering," Amero said, hailing him.

"Considering what?" asked Pakito.

"Considering your boots won't be dry for days."

Pakito sighed happily. "What do wet feet matter on a glorious morning like this?"

Amero was about to inquire what made it so glorious, but
he was interrupted by Samtu. The dark-haired plainswoman
poked her head out of the tent, squinted her eyes against the
feeble morning light, and croaked, "Oh, help! Is there water?
By all my ancestors, I think I'm dying."

Still grinning, Pakito handed her a waterskin, and she
ducked back into his tent. Amero had to laugh. "Now I understand. You've taken a mate!"

"Been taken, more like. I've always been a stumbling ox
when it came to women, but Samtu wouldn't let me go." He
flung a boot high in the air and yelled for the simple joy of
it. The boot came down on a nearby sleeping nomad, who
bounced up, cursing. From inside the tent, Samtu groaned
and told Pakito to shut up.

"Sounds like love to me," Amero said, and with a wave,
moved toward Nianki's tent.

With much groaning, coughing, and cursing, the nomads
roused themselves from their latest stupor. A general cry for
water went up, and this time there wasn't enough to go
round. Several blinking, stumbling plainsfolk made their way
down to the lake, where they fell on their bellies and lapped
up the cold water.

Reaching his sister's tent, Amero called out to her.
Nomads lying nearby cursed at him. He ignored them, saying,
"Nianki, are you here?"

"Yes," was her low reply.

He lifted the flap and squatted down to look inside. Nianki
was sitting up, her back to the opening. She wore only a thigh-
length doeskin shirt. Her long hair was tangled and matted.

"Nianki?"

"Amero." She did not turn to greet him.

"Are you well?"

She hung her head. "I had a strange dream," she murmured. "I thought it was a dream, but I'm awake and it's still
going on." She looked over her shoulder at him. Her tanned
face seemed quite pale, and he could see dark circles under
her eyes, even in the dimness of the shelter.

He knelt in the opening, his back holding the flap up and
letting daylight in. "Your people were at it again last night,"
he said. "Are you well? I haven't seen you since the feast."

"Come inside, Amero. Let the flap down."

He crawled in. It was close and steamy inside the small tent, and very dark. A few narrow beams of light penetrated through small holes in the hide.

"Something happened to me," Nianki said. She still sat with her back to him.

"What? Are you ill?"

"Not . . . not in the usual way." She drew a deep breath, held it, then let it out slowly. "Amero, do you believe we are brother and sister?"

A strange and surprising question. "Of course," he said.

"Is it possible our memories are wrong, that we're not related at all?" Her voice sounded taut, almost desperate.

He settled down on the ground and stared at her hunched shoulders, barely visible in the sultry shadows. Her questions confused him, but her tone told him this was important to her. "Our memories match," he said. "Our experiences are the same up to the day the yevi attacked us, all those years ago."

"But suppose we're not really siblings—suppose you were a baby found abandoned on the savanna. What if that were true, and Oto and Kinar just the people who raised you and not the parents of your body?"

Confusion became shock. "What are you telling me? Am I not your brother?"

She turned suddenly and seized his hands in her own. Her eyes were dark and troubled as she whispered, "What if it were true?"

He looked down at her rough hands, gripping his with fervor. "I'd be very surprised," he said lamely. "All I remember from my childhood is Oto, Kinar, Menni, and you. If I were a taken-up babe, I wouldn't know it unless I was told." He slowly raised his eyes to hers. She was weeping, soundlessly. He'd never seen Nianki cry before, not even as a child.

"You're only two years older than me," he went on. "How could you remember when I was born, much less found?"

Nianki dropped her hands and turned away again. "You weren't found, Amero," she muttered. "You are my brother."

His head was spinning. He felt like the victim of a prank, only the prankster was weeping at him instead of laughing.

"What's this all about?" he demanded. "Why are you acting so strangely?"

She scrubbed her cheeks with the backs of her hands, taking in deep draughts of air as though to clear her head. "It's nothing," she said, sounding stern again. "Too much wine and too many bad dreams."

Amero got up on one knee. "I'd say the same things were afflicting your band," he said. "All but Pakito." He explained how the strapping warrior and Samtu had come together.

"Good," she said, quite clearly. "A man needs a good mate."

Shouts erupted outside, hoarse male and female voices. Amero stood and flung back the tent flap. Nomads were running past Nianki's tent toward a small crowd gathering at the edge of the village. The loud, angry voices came from there.

Sighing, he said, "There's been nothing but trouble between your people and mine, since the feast. If this keeps up . . ." He left the thought unfinished and hurried away to the disturbance. Nianki followed, still clad in the long, doe-skin tunic, shading her eyes against the hazy daylight.

Amero worked his way through a hostile crowd of nomads. They were massed around the house of Hulami the vintner. At first Amero thought they were blaming Hulami's wine for their pounding heads and raging thirst, but when he got closer, he discovered they were besieging her with requests for more wine.

Hulami was backed up against her own door. Her two apprentices stood on either side of her, stout stirring paddles held up like clubs. Amero recognized the man yelling at her as Tarkwa, one of Nianki's leading warriors.

"Whatta ya mean, you won't give us wine?" Tarkwa bellowed. "You gave away a vat full three days ago and now it's gone!"

"That was a feast!" Hulami replied hotly. "I expect the villagers to send me food and goods for the wine I make. I can't afford to give it away every day! If you smelly fools want more of my wine, you'll have to barter for it like everyone else!"

Amero winced at the vintner's harsh words. Karada's band shouted insults right back. "Bloodsucking viper" was the kindest one he heard.

Tarkwa stepped forward from the crowd. The apprentices presented their paddles, pressing the grape-stained ends against Tarkwa's chest.

Someone shouted, "Kill 'em Tarkwa! We'll take what we want over their dead bodies!"

Amero ran to the front of the mob, yelling and waving for attention. The shouts of the crowd drowned him out and no one paid him much heed until Nianki appeared and stood close beside him.

"What's the problem?" she said loudly.

"This sour wench thinks she can fill us with wine one day and keep it back from us the next! We're going to teach her different!" Tarkwa snarled. The mob at his back howled approval of his words.

Nianki turned and shoved the two young apprentices aside. Hulami looked to Amero for help, but before he could say anything, Nianki whispered something in her ear. White-faced, Hulami stood away from her door.

Tarkwa gave a rousing cry. The mob echoed his cheer and surged forward. Nianki put her hands on the doorjambs, bracing herself and blocking their way.

"What're you doing, Karada?" Tarkwa said.

"I'll get out of the way," she said calmly, "and you can drink up everything you find—drain the chamber pots, if you want—but if you take away this woman's livelihood today, there won't be any more wine in Arku-peli. Ever."

She dropped her arms. Her angry followers hesitated.

"It's some kind of trick," said a woman in the front ranks. "Karada's playing with us."

"No trick," Nianki replied. "If you pick all the apples off a tree one day, you know there won't be any apples tomorrow. If you guzzle all the wine in the village, it'll be gone, and you'll be just as thirsty and heavy-headed tomorrow." She moved out of the doorway, folded her arms, and leaned against the wall. "So go ahead."

Some of the nomads took halting steps toward the door. Nianki eyed them. "It's not just the wine you're giving up you know," she told them in the same matter-of-fact tone. "You start robbing the villagers, and there won't be so much as an ox tongue for you tomorrow."

"But we're thirsty!" someone cried.

"There's a whole lake over there, or didn't you notice?" she snapped.

Slowly, grumbling all the while, the mob of nomads receded from Hulami's door.

"What's the matter?" Nianki called. "Lose your taste for wine?"

The crowd broke up sullenly as the parched nomads headed for the free water of the lake. Tarkwa lingered a few steps behind. Out of the press appeared Hatu, looking surprisingly well compared to the others. He spoke to Tarkwa, and they fell to talking.

Hulami went into her house and returned with a clay jug of wine. "Karada, this is for you," she said, beaming. "You saved my life!"

Amero joined them. "You handled that well," he said.

Nianki set the brimful jug of wine at her feet and smiled faintly. "Fierce as they are, they're like children. They want what they want, and they want it now. You can either beat them into obedience—which I'm too tired to do this morning—or you can try to point out what they'll lose if they do as they want." She shrugged. "It usually works."

Tarkwa and Hatu watched them from twenty paces away. After a short exchange, they left, following the others to the lake.

Nianki picked up the wine jug and gave it back to Hulami. The vintner was puzzled.

"Don't you want it?" she said.

"I'd better not. I can't pay the price of it either."

She walked away, slowly and rather stiffly. Amero and Hulami watched her go.

"She's different today," said Hulami. "She seems—I don't know—more like a woman and less like a war chief this morning."

The vintner's words trailed off as she watched Nianki walk away. "What do you think it is?" Amero prompted, worried about the sister he'd so recently regained. "She's been acting strangely this morning, even crying, and she seems so distracted. Do you think she's ill?"

Hulami gave him an quick sideways glance. "Ill? Not

exactly," she said. "If I didn't know better, I'd swear Karada was in love."

That was a notion Amero had never considered. "You really think it possible?" he asked her.

"Certainly. I've lived long enough to recognize that look on a woman's face when I see it."

Amero thought of Pa'alu and of Nianki's strange behavior at the feast. Perhaps a few nights' reflection, aided by Hulami's vintage and his news about Pakito and Samtu, had caused Nianki to consider Pa'alu anew. Amero wondered where Pa'alu was. The plainsman should be told about Nianki's change of heart.

*     *     *     *     *

Pa'alu woke, certain he was dead.

He'd run off from the feast just as the thunderstorm broke, fleeing headlong into the rain-swept night. His only thought was to find the elf priest and demand the spell be broken. Though he waited in the bowl-shaped canyon for two days, Vedvedsica never appeared. Despairing, his mind still reeling from what had happened, Pa'alu returned to the fringes of the nomads' camp and was taken up by several of his reveling comrades. He accepted their repeated offers of wine.

When the wine and food had at last run out, Pa'alu had left his compatriots. A part of his benumbed, wine-sodden brain still seethed with thoughts of finding the elf priest, so he thought to search elsewhere. Late one night, he crossed the rope bridge and staggered up the logger's path, tripping constantly on the deep ruts left by dragged logs. Exhausted at last, he collapsed on an outflow of tiny pebbles.

When Pa'alu woke, this third morning after the feast, his face and arms were numb from lying on the stones all the night before. Thinking for one crazed moment he was dead and in his grave, he swallowed hard and tried to move his lifeless limbs. When his feet twitched and tingled painfully—though his arms remained numb—he decided he might not be dead after all.

He rolled over, and the brightness of the ivory-clouded sky burned his face like a flaming brand. After an effort that brought beads of sweat to his brow, Pa'alu managed to get one limp arm over his tortured eyes. Too much wine. Far too much.

The amulet.

The thought brought him upright with such violence, his stiff muscles shrieked in protest. He sat, wavering from side to side, as his foggy mind tried to recall the events of the past—how many?—days, especially those of the feast night. Where was the amulet Vedvedsica had given him? He patted through his muddy clothing and found nothing.

Some of the fog wrapping his brain lifted. He'd already used the amulet, hadn't he? At the feast, he'd held it out to Karada. The dragon tried to take it from him. Pa'alu drew his knife. There was a flash of lightning from the dragon. Then Pa'alu was lying on the sand, and he no longer held the amulet.

Nianki had picked it up. Nianki and Amero.

*Nianki and Amero.*

"Oh, my ancestors," Pa'alu groaned, covering his face with his hands.

"Don't the blame the dead for the faults of the living."

Pa'alu flinched at the sudden intrusion and tried to push himself to his feet. When his bleary eyes adjusted, he saw Nacris sitting cross-legged on the ground a few steps away. Her horse was tethered to a handy pine sapling. He'd been so involved in his memories of that horrible night that he'd not heard her arrive.

"Why are you here?" he groaned, too lost in his own misery to really care.

"I've been looking for you," Nacris replied. She looked well-scrubbed, her hair pulled back tightly and tied. Her buckskins had been buffed with pumice to whiten them.

"So you found me."

Ignoring his unwelcoming tone, she handed him a full waterskin. It dangled from her hand for only an instant before the painfully parched Pa'alu grabbed it. Upending it, he drank deeply, the excess water trickling over his neck and chest.

Wiping his lips with the back of his hand, he said, "Thanks."

Nacris said nothing but continued to watch him intently. He suddenly felt uncomfortable under her flinty gaze, and unconsciously he began to comb his hair and beard with his fingers, trying to look more presentable.

"Why are you here?" Nacris said at last.

"I drank too much and lost my way."

"No, I mean, why are you in the band?"

He paused in his grooming. "To follow Karada," he said.

"Is that the only reason?"

"What other reason do I need?"

"And when Karada falls in battle or dies of sickness? Will you remain with the band then?"

Feeling was returning to Pa'alu's limbs. The sensation was agonizing—like the bites of a thousand horseflies at once—but Pa'alu hardened himself and addressed Nacris's question. "I would stay by my brother," he said. "I would stand with Pakito."

She nodded slightly. "A sensible answer. Did you know Pakito has gained a mate since the feast?" Pa'alu's expression showed his ignorance, so she added, "Samtu."

"He's fortunate." His tone gave the lie to the simple pleasantry. Knowledge of his brother's happiness, when he himself was so miserable, was like bitter ashes in his mouth.

"You're one of the finest hunters and scouts in the band, Pa'alu," Nacris said. "If Karada and the band part ways, who will you follow?"

He was beginning to understand the cast of her words, and he shook his head. "You can't be trying to take the band away from Karada again. Did Sessan's death teach you nothing?"

"It taught me no one of us is strong enough to defeat Karada. To succeed, the best of us must join together."

Pa'alu stood up, dropping the waterskin on the pebbles in front of Nacris. "You're a fool," he told her flatly. "Karada *is* the band. There is no band without her."

He started to walk past her, and Nacris said, "And if Karada betrays the band? What then?"

"You're talking nonsense. Because you brought me water, I won't mention this to Karada—"

Nacris stood quickly, took Pa'alu by the shoulder, and whirled him around. "Karada is betraying the band right

now! She sided with the mudtoes this morning!" Pa'alu recognized the derisive term for the villagers that was gaining
popularity among the nomads.

"What are you talking about?" he said. Nacris related the
events that had taken place outside the house of Hulami the
vintner. "Karada sent her own people away thirsty then
accepted a jug of wine for herself! She's so taken with her
own power, she forgets the welfare of her people!"

"Liar! How many times in the past has she gone without
food so that others could eat? Gone without sleep so that
others could rest? Karada cares nothing for her personal comfort. She lives like a mountain goat, guiding her flock through
treacherous places, surviving on only the sparest food and
water."

Nacris folded her arms. "That was before we came to this
strange valley. Now there's meat and drink in abundance and
a man for her to love."

The last words pierced Pa'alu's aching head. His fist knotted around the front of Nacris's whitened buckskin shirt. He
lifted her till she was swaying on her toes.

"What did you say?" he hissed.

Unresisting, she said, "Arkuden, the headman. Her brother."

His grip slackened, and Nacris stepped back. Eyes wide in
horror, Pa'alu hissed, "Why do you say that?"

"Isn't it obvious? Her long-lost brother turns up alive,
offers food and comfort in abundance. Why shouldn't she
side with him against the rest of us?"

Pa'alu relaxed, realizing Nacris knew nothing about the
amulet or its effect. The rage and frustration he felt over the
failure of his stratagem resurfaced.

"Pa'alu, are you listening?" He looked at her and she added
gravely, "Join me or not, as your spirit commands, but I have
to know: Will you tell Karada what has passed between us?"

Misery welled up in his breast. Tell Karada? How could
he even look upon her again?

"No," he said. "I won't tell her."

Nacris regarded him warily. "Swear by your ancestors."

His head throbbed unmercifully, and a tendon in his neck
felt like it was going to jump through his skin. Compared to
his current pain and anguish, the wrath of his ancestors'

spirits was as remote as the great gray sea. Without hesitation, he said, "I swear. By the spirits of my ancestors."

He departed, leaving Nacris standing by her horse. Once he was well out of sight, two men emerged from the rocks farther down the draw and approached Nacris.

"Well?" said Hatu.

"He won't join us, at least not yet," Nacris reported.

"I told you he wouldn't," Tarkwa said.

Hatu fingered the handle of his flint knife. "But will he betray us?"

"I don't think so," Nacris said. "Drunk or sober, his word is still granite."

"They say he tried to gut himself in front of Karada, Arkuden, and the dragon," Tarkwa said with a smirk.

"If his mind is weakening, so be it," Hatu said. "That could be a boon for us. Alive and silent, he's still dangerous. Alive and mad, he may be the best weapon against Karada we can get."

\* \* \* \* \*

Duranix had left the valley only moments after seeing Vedvedsica atop the cliff at Yala-tene. Searching for the elf priest, the dragon flew south as far as the vast woodland claimed by Silvanos, yet he found no sign of Vedvedsica. The priest was probably already back in the elf city, trying to work his will with the help of the yellow stone.

The dragon flapped hard to gain height, climbing so high that even his impervious bronze hide shuddered with the extreme cold. Peering southward, he could see—very faintly—the pale, golden glow on the horizon that heralded the city of Silvanost.

Remarkable. To think there could be a gathering of the creatures so large that the combined light of their fires stained the night sky. A part of him would enjoy making the long flight to see such an amazing sight. Instead, he made a wide, sweeping turn, speeding his strokes.

Now that he'd determined Vedvedsica was beyond his reach, he wanted to get back to Yala-tene as fast as he could. It was apparent Pa'alu had made some kind of bargain with the elf priest. The bronze disk had contained so much power it glowed in the dragon's vision, even when clenched inside the man's hand. By the time Duranix had gotten hold of the metal, it had given up its power somewhere, for some purpose. He needed to discover exactly what had happened.

The landscape slowly unfurled below the flying dragon. The dense forest home of the elves gave way to grassy plains, which in turn began to swell and roll as he drew near the mountains that held the Lake of the Falls. Those mountains loomed larger and larger before him, clouds thickening on their slopes. Soon he was gliding in their silent heights, alone save for the tallest peaks poking up through the clouds.

It was irksome that Vedvedsica had succeeded in getting the stone, but it was much to be preferred over Sthenn or the humans having it. The elf had some limited knowledge and experience of higher powers, but he could be in for an unpleasant surprise should he try to use the stone. It was a whole order of magnitude greater in strength than any fetish or object of power he would have encountered before. It could consume him in the end.

Vedvedsica reminded Duranix of the thirsty centaur in a story Amero had told him. The centaur had stood under a thundercloud, eyes closed, mouth open, expecting a refreshing shower. Instead, he received a white-hot bolt of lightning. As the humans said, "Thought rain, got pain." The elf priest hoped to bend the stone to his own ends; instead, he might end up being the one bent—or broken.

Duranix smelled the waterfall from twenty leagues away and descended through the clouds. He circled the mountain once, morning sunlight flashing from his scales, then dived for the cave. His hind claws caught the rim of the opening, and he hung there for an instant, shaking the water from his long face. He smelled a human in his cave. It didn't smell like Amero.

He leaped to the floor, and his landing made the mountain shake. The cavern was dark, but his eyes noted a glimmer of body heat, far off to his left, near the small lower door.

"Come out, little mouse, come out," Duranix rumbled, in a very undragonlike, sing-song manner.

Nianki stood away from the hoist basket, hands clasped

in front of her. "Ah, no mouse after all," said Duranix. "A wolf, more like."

"Save your humor, dragon," she said. "I have something important to ask you."

He lowered his belly to the floor and folded his tree-trunk size legs under him. "Speak, Nianki," he said.

"Karada," she said sharply. "Nianki is an old, empty name. It only sounds right coming from my brother's lips."

"Speak then, Karada."

She stepped forward, and he saw her cheeks were damp with tears, her eyes red-rimmed. His barbels twitched with surprise.

Drawing a deep breath, she said, "You're a creature of great power, I know. I've seen some of it these past days. Just how great is it?"

"It's the measure of myself, no more, no less." Karada gave him a disgusted look, and he snapped, "I'm not being coy or poetic, woman. I don't know how to quantify my own strength. How powerful is the sun? How forceful is the wind?" He lowered his chin to rest on the stone floor, bringing his eyes more or less to the level of her own. "Why do you ask?"

"I need your help," she said, her voice tinged with real pain. "I . . . I'm going mad."

"For most humans, a short journey."

Karada was in no mood for levity. She whipped a flint knife from her belt waved it under the dragon's vast eye. "I'll not be made a fool of!" she cried, her voice ragged with emotion. "Listen to me or I'll start that journey right now!"

It was absurd, threatening a bronze dragon with a span of sharp flint. Duranix was unmoved, and the click of his blinking eyelids was loud in the quiet cave. However, her obvious sincerity moved him to say, in a kinder tone, "Please continue, Karada, but calmly."

She returned her knife to her belt and ran a hand through her gilded brown hair. "I have . . . I have a . . . sickness of the mind," she faltered. "I don't know where it came from, and I don't know how to get rid of it."

"What are the symptoms?"

She swallowed, her mouth suddenly dry. Her voice was barely audible. "I think about a man, all the time. I hear his name when I draw breath. I see his face whenever I shut my eyes. If I let his image linger, my face grows hot and my legs and arms feel weak."

"That's not so mysterious. Humans are so afflicted all the time. You're in love. Haven't you ever been in love before?"

Nianki turned quickly on her heel. "No, never! There've been men in the band I admired—Pakito is strong and loyal, Hatu a fine tracker, even Sessan was good fighter when he wasn't listening to the venom Nacris poured in his ear. . . ." Her voice trailed off. "But, it's nothing like that. I feel sick . . . here." She pressed a hand to her belly. "And I have thoughts. Strange thoughts."

"I'm sure you do," Duranix said quickly. The last thing the dragon wanted to hear were this warrior woman's inner thoughts. "In my years observing humans, I've learned love is an extremely potent feeling. It makes people happy and miserable, often at the same time." He cocked a flaring metallic eyebrow at her and added, "You seem no different than the rest, except you're not used to it."

His bantering tone was lost on Nianki. Arms hanging limply at her sides, she stared dully at the floor and said, with no emotion at all, "I'm in love with Amero."

The smoldering question in Duranix's mind suddenly flared to brilliant life. The disk Pa'alu had been concealing the night of the feast must have caused this. He'd tried to get Karada to take his hand while he held the disk. He must have intended the spell (most certainly cast by Vedvedsica) for her and himself. *This* outcome had surely been an accident.

Or was this exactly what Vedvedsica had intended?

"Did you hear me?" she demanded.

Duranix pulled his attention back to her angry, worried face. "Yes, I did," he assured her. "Humans don't mate with their siblings, do they?"

"No!" Her eyes widened in self-loathing, and she clutched her head in both hands. "The very thought is a horror! How can I, born of the same spirit and flesh as Amero, possibly be so unnatural?"

Duranix gave no reply, but instead reared up on his haunches. Shuddering, he shrank himself into human form.

Eyes downcast, wrapped in her own misery, Nianki didn't notice his transformation. She started when his human hand touched her shoulder. When she looked up at him, she flinched even more violently.

Duranix wore a completely new form. He was a tall, muscular plainsman with glossy, waist-length black hair and deeply tanned skin. "Be calm!" he told her. "I took on this form to make a point."

"What point?"

"Outward appearance is an illusion. Every being is unique because his or her spirit is unique. I could, if I chose, take on the appearance of Amero, but would that make me Amero? Of course not."

With her mind in such turmoil, Nianki could not understand the reasoning behind his demonstration. "Are you telling it me it's all right for me to feel this way?" she said, astonished.

"No." He sighed at the obtuseness of humans. "I believe you're the victim of a plot, Karada." He told her about Pa'alu and the amulet. As he watched her face redden alarmingly and her body begin to shake with anger, he chose to keep the name of Vedvedsica to himself. She was capable of any foolishness just now, even embarking on a quest for vengeance that would most likely end with her death.

When Nianki finally spoke, her voice was a hoarse, furious whisper. "Do you mean that I'm suffering this unnatural love because of Pa'alu?" Duranix nodded. She clenched her fists and said, her voice rising with each word, "Oh, the filth-eating dog! The crawling, cold-blooded, wretched—!"

Duranix held up a hand. "I don't believe Pa'alu meant you ill. I think he traded the nugget for some kind of spirit-token, which was meant to loose its power on you and make you love him, but there was a mix-up, and the spell discharged instead on you and Amero."

Nianki breathed hard, forcing herself to master her anger. Her deep red color faded to normal tan. She could not escape the bounds of her compulsion, so her next question was, "Does Amero feel for me the way I feel for him?"

"He does not seem so affected. We'll have to find Pa'alu and question him on the way the token was supposed to work."

From towering rage, Nianki fell into despair. She wept uncontrollably at the mere thought that Amero might be suffering as she was. It was unbearable, the idea the one she loved could be in pain.

Duranix watched her cry silently, but with some sympathy. He could think of nothing to say to her.

"The old question returns," she said, sniffling and dabbing at her nose with her sleeve. "Can you help me?"

Duranix faced her, his black, more-than-human eyes sweeping her up and down. "I cannot," he said at last. "If the power was forced into you, it would leave a spirit wound on you I could see, and I might be able to draw it out into a likely receptacle—a crystal or metal object, but I sense nothing out of place. That's the black subtlety of it. Every human has the capacity to love. Yours has simply been directed along an unnatural course. There's nothing I can do about it."

"Can't you use your power to change *who* I love, at least?" she asked wildly.

"I'm not a practitioner of such arts. If I tried blindly, I might harm you, or worse, even kill you."

Nianki laughed bitterly. "Death couldn't be worse than this." Her countenance convulsed in deep anguish for a few seconds, then suddenly cleared. She strode to the lower door, bypassing the hoist basket, which was lying on its side. Standing in the opening, her long shirt rippling in the breeze from the waterfall, she cried, "I can do something a dragon can't! I can cure a lovesick heart!"

She jumped.

Duranix's tall human form crossed the distance to the opening in two bounds. Without pausing, he hurled himself after her. A heartbeat later he hit the wall of plunging water. As he fell, he flung his arms outward and expanded to his true shape.

The force of the torrent was driving him toward the lake below. Through the icy blast of falling water he spotted the warmth of Nianki's tumbling body, already halfway to the foot of the falls. Duranix folded his wings tightly to his back and plummeted after her.

Head down, neck outstretched, nose pointed at his own imminent death, the dragon overtook Nianki and grasped her in one foreclaw. She was limp and did not resist. He flung out his wings to slow their descent, but the force of the waterfall was so great, it snapped his left wing bone where it was joined to his body.

*Pain.*

He hadn't felt pain in a long time. Genta's spear thrusts, even Vedvedsica's spirit-blast, had been playful buffets compared to this. The last time the dragon had felt anything this excruciating was the day the avalanche had covered the nest. A whole mountain had fallen on him, and he'd lain there, entombed with his mother and siblings, gasping in the darkness as his bones were crushed, his body smashed.

He had to slow their fall. He threw his shoulders back, forcing his wings open. Bone scraped on bone in the broken wing, and the dragon roared in agony. The updraft around the churning falls lifted and slowed him just enough for him to put his three unencumbered claws down before he hit the ground. The shock of his landing was enough to bring blood to his mouth. Yet, through the red haze of pain, Duranix remembered what he held in his left foreclaw. He leaned to his right, put his claw down gently and opened it. Nianki rolled senseless to the ground. Duranix toppled over, trembled, and lay still.

The sound of Amero's voice penetrated the roar of the water and the fog in the dragon's head.

"Duranix! Duranix!"

"Don't shout," the dragon rasped, "you're standing by my ear."

He opened one eye. Amero and a score of nomads were clustered around. Several of the nomads knelt by Nianki's limp body, working over her. Amero, his face white with concern, said angrily, "What were you trying to do, kill yourself?"

"Humans are so much trouble," muttered Duranix. "Besides being stupid, they're clumsy. That one missed your basket contraption in the dark and fell from the cave."

Amero hurried to the circle where Nianki was being tended. He knelt beside her, pressing his hand to her throat. Her pulse beat strongly.

"She passed out," said Targun, who was kneeling on the other side of her. "Let her rest a minute, and she'll come back."

247

Amero was about to rise when Nianki's eyes snapped open. She half-rose and threw her arms around his neck.

"Amero! Amero! Don't let me go!" she gasped.

Embarrassed and relieved at the same time, her brother pulled her trembling hands apart and lowered her back to the hide blanket Targun had brought for her.

"You're all right," he said soothingly. She turned her face away and wept. Misunderstanding the cause of her distress, Amero added, "It's all right, truly. Duranix saved you. He's had a hard landing, but you can't kill a dragon so easily."

As if to prove the truth of those words, Duranix had gotten to his feet. He clumped over to them, his broken wing dragging on the ground. His wide, serpentine head hovered over them, eyelids clicking open and shut.

Amero held his sister's cold, wet hand. "You and I have something more in common now," he said cheerfully. She said nothing, her face still turned away. "We're the only two people to have leaped from the dragon's cave and lived. I guess clumsiness runs in our blood, eh?" The gathered nomads chuckled. "What do you think, Duranix?"

The dragon glanced from Nianki to Amero and back to Nianki again. "I think humans make terrible pets," he said.

# Chapter 18

~

Autumn arrived. The days grew short and dark, but the darkness was not confined to the sky. Once the dragon was known to be injured, the atmosphere in the valley changed.

Nomad and villager had been getting along tolerably well, with occasional disagreements between individuals offset by frequent incidents of cooperation. Several of the younger nomads had actually begun teaching their village counterparts to ride horses. At first the elder villagers scoffed at those taking the lessons, but the young of Yala-tene knew riding could be an extremely useful sill. The lessons were marked by much raucous roughhousing, but the gibing was good-natured, and no one got hurt.

Now trouble between nomad and villager was on the rise—name-calling and theft became more frequent and escalated into shouting matches and fistfights. Riding lessons came to a halt. The once-friendly sessions had become untenable after several violent melees.

Amero and the village elders moved from one crisis to another, separating angry nomads and villagers, smoothing over confrontations, trying to resolve a growing host of simmering disputes.

"I don't understand it," Amero complained one evening. He was in the home of Konza the tanner. He and his host had gulped a hasty meal by the circular fireplace while waiting for the next outbreak of trouble.

"I thought things would work out better than this," he continued, poking the fire with an aromatic cedar stick. "Our people and Nianki's—we're all plainsmen. We've learned so much from each other and can learn a lot more. So why is there so much trouble?"

"You believe too much in the goodness of people," Konza said. The firelight etched the lines of weariness on his face with deep shadows. "These wanderers are lazy, good-for-nothing savages. What they want, they steal. What they don't understand, they destroy."

Amero looked up from prodding the flames. "I thought Nianki could keep them in line."

Konza sighed, pouring hot water over a pot full of mashed dewberries. He let this steep a few moments, then poured off the resulting tea for Amero and himself.

"You'll forgive me for saying so," Konza said solemnly, "but your sister is mad."

Amero stared at the flames. No anger showed on his face, for Konza was saying only what Amero had secretly feared for some time. Hearing the words from the sober, hard-working tanner made them seem all the more true.

Following her fall from the cave, Nianki had sunk into a strange, withdrawn state. She wandered through the valley, laughing or weeping for no obvious reason. Her hands, feet, and face grew dirty, her hair was tangled with bits of straw and leaves from sleeping in the open. She remained fierce, however, and thoroughly thrashed a pair of young bucks from the village who cornered her in the orchard one day and taunted her about her wild appearance. Amero had a terrible time keeping the boys' families from retaliating.

The only time Nianki ever seemed to regain clarity was in the presence of Duranix. The dragon, his broken wing rendering him temporarily unable to fly to his high cavern home, remained on the shore of the lake. The village healer, a young sage named Raho, designed a massive leather harness for the dragon to wear which supported his folded, broken wing as it healed. Village delegates brought Duranix offerings of meat, but none of them, nor any of the nomads, would remain near the crippled creature for very long.

Only Nianki and Amero would spend much time with Duranix, and they rarely appeared together. Her brother's presence seemed to provoke wild extremes of emotion. When Amero complained of this to Duranix, the dragon flicked his forked tongue several times and said cryptically, "The hardest stone in this valley is your skull, human."

Now, facing Konza across a flaming hearth and hearing the tanner's comment about Nianki's state of mind, Amero tried to reason out the cause of all the trouble between the nomads and their settled brethren.

"We've had a lot of bad luck lately," he mused. "The tunnels collapsed, Duranix got hurt, my sister's ill, the nomads are restless, and I haven't had any time to work on my copper experiments."

Konza shrugged. "The answer to our bad luck is simple. It started with the arrival of the nomads, and it will end when we rid ourselves of them."

Amero flinched at his blunt words, which stung like a lash. "They're valiant and useful people," he said. "They can add to our strength."

Konza snorted. "They're violent and dangerous," he insisted. With a sidelong look at the younger man, he added, "I'm not the only villager who thinks so."

Shouts and a loud crash outside forestalled Amero's reply and underscored the tanner's claim. Wearily, Amero rose from the hearth and went to the door. Konza got up to follow, but Amero waved him back.

"Take your ease," he said. "I'll see what's up."

Two houses over he found a boy lying in the dirt, his head bleeding. The travois he'd been dragging was wrecked, and broken pots lay scattered about. A thick, sweet smell filled the cool night air. Honey.

Amero helped the boy sit up. His name was Udi, second son of Tepa, the beekeeper. Tepa had a cache of beehives in the apple orchard, and he traded his honey in the village at considerable advantage. Udi groaned a bit when he felt the bump on his head, but groaned much louder when he saw the damage done to his father's supply of honey.

"Who did this?" demanded Amero.

"I never saw them," said the teenager, a hand to his head. "I heard footsteps behind me, but I thought it was just a neighbor. There was a yell, and when I turned to see who it was, something hit me on the back of the head."

"Can you tell what's missing?"

The boy counted jars. Eight were intact, four broken, and only one was missing.

"Someone attacked you to take just one jar of honey?" asked Amero, incredulous.

"It's the riders," Udi muttered. "They steal for the rough jest of it."

"You don't know that," Amero replied, with more conviction than he felt. He helped reload the travois and sent Udi on his way. A cursory examination showed three pairs of footprints in the dust around the site of the robbery. Two pairs headed toward the lake. The third went north, toward the cattle pens.

He tracked the solo marauder straight to the walled corral. Sure enough, a single figure sat atop the stone wall, looking over the herd of brown and white spotted oxen.

"You there! Stay where you are!"

The fellow didn't even turn around. Amero climbed onto the wall and was surprised to see that the lone figure was Pa'alu.

Pa'alu had been acting oddly ever since the night of the feast. He disappeared for days at a time and had not been seen now for over a week. Amero wondered at the epidemic of strange behavior.

"I thought perhaps you were gone from the valley," he said, sitting beside the warrior.

"I've been away," Pa'alu replied. "I've been hunting in the nearby valleys by myself, on foot. Haven't done that in eight seasons."

"There was a robbery back there." Amero pointed to the row of dome-shaped houses.

"Robbery? What was stolen?"

"A jar of honey."

"Ha, a robber with a sweet tooth."

"He came this way. See anybody run by?"

"I wasn't looking."

The cattle stirred sleepily, crowding around piles of fodder that had been left for them. Amero watched the long-horned animals silently for several minutes, searching for the words he wanted.

"Pa'alu?" he said at last.

"Hmm?"

"What happened, the night of the feast? Why did you try to stab yourself? We've never talked about it."

The other man turned his head, and for the first time Amero saw how hollow-eyed he'd become. "Too much wine," Pa'alu said calmly. "I should thank the dragon for stopping me."

Amero flashed a smile. "Duranix says living with humans means stopping a hundred stupid things a day."

Both men laughed briefly. Amero threw his legs back over the wall and slid down to the ground outside the pen.

"I must keep looking for the thieves," he said. "Good night, Pa'alu."

"Peace be with you, Arkuden."

Amero departed and was soon swallowed by the darkness around the village houses. Pa'alu waited to a slow count of thirty, then took a squat jar from under his cloak and broke the beeswax seal. Making clucking sounds in his throat to attract the hungry cattle, he poured a stream of golden honey on the dirt. Before long the oxen were lapping at it with their fleshy red tongues. Pa'alu wiped the rim of the empty jar with his fingers, then stuck them in his mouth.

\* \* \* \* \*

Back in the camp, Nacris and Tarkwa were panting from their run. They ducked into a large tent, with triumphant grins. Hatu, inside the tent, was waiting with a small lamp burning.

"Well?" demanded Hatu.

"He wouldn't strike a blow, but he took a jar," Nacris reported.

"Good. Pa'alu will soon be one of us. Next time, we must make sure he strikes the first blow but not the last."

Hatu bent forward and blew out the lamp.

\* \* \* \* \*

Nianki was not sleeping in the orchard.

Though she lay in the soft grass at the base of an apple tree, she could not rest. She stared up through the tree's twisted branches at the patches of night sky visible through its remaining leaves.

*It was a tree that saved me.*

Amero's voice drifted through her mind. He'd climbed a tree to escape the yevi all those years ago.

253

Thoughts of Amero kept Nianki from sleeping. Each time she closed her eyes, her brother's face seemed to rise up before her like a spectre that wouldn't be banished.

"Go away," she muttered. "Leave me be. Go away."

Her brother's face smiled at her.

"Leave me in peace!" she screamed and sprang to her feet, drawing her flint knife as though she could fight off the strange, unnatural feelings assailing her.

With a shock, she found herself facing a stranger. A tall, thin figure with a high forehead stood only a few steps away from her blade. He recoiled so sharply that the long robes he wore whipped around his ankles.

"Stop!" he commanded.

Nianki kept her knife between them and demanded to know who he was.

He recovered himself quickly and adopted a calm, superior air. "Savages have short memories," he said. "Don't you know me, Karada?"

She still didn't relax her posture, but it was obvious that her mind was working to place him. With a small smile, he lifted his hands and pushed back the hood he wore. The moon's light limned his features with silver, including a wispy beard and tall, sharply pointed ears.

Surprised, Nianki backed away a step. "Elf!" she spat. "You were with Balif the day we fought on the plain. He called you . . ." Her troubled mind wouldn't obey her. The name escaped her utterly.

"Vedvedsica," he said coolly. "My name is Vedvedsica."

Nianki wasn't listening. Her head darted violently left and right. "Where are your troops?" she demanded. "Does Balif think to attack us as we sleep?"

"There are no troops," he said. "There is no one but me."

After a few more moments peering into the dark, she had to accept his words. "What do you want?"

"You."

Her expression was so outraged the priest gave a dry laugh. "Calm yourself, savage," he said. "I merely wish to take you on a journey."

She backed away. "I'll go nowhere with you."

Vedvedsica shrugged. "You would cast aside an opportunity

to know your enemy better? You aren't much of a leader, are you?"

"What do you mean?"

"I offer you the chance to learn more about the Silvanesti. It will cost you nothing, not even time."

She obviously didn't understand, and he sighed. Slowly, as though speaking to a particularly dim-witted child, Vedvedsica said, "I will not harm you. I merely wish to show you the city of your enemy." Stroking his wispy beard he added, "A true leader would not miss such an opportunity. Unless she were afraid to see the truth."

His taunt penetrated her clouded thoughts. It was true her mind was a whirl of conflicting impressions and impulses, and she often found herself in places with no memory of how she got there. For all of that, she understood the elf's slight to her courage, and it angered her.

Stiffening her spine, Nianki shoved her knife back into its sheath, pushed her tangled hair from her face, and said, "Show me, then."

"Take my hand."

She nearly balked again, but his expression—so condescending!—caused her to clench her jaw and obey. She wrapped her hand around his wrist. The cool dryness of his skin made her flinch, but a sudden blast of icy wind in her face was much more shocking. She squeezed her eyes shut to keep the dust out. It felt as though she were falling.

"Home."

At his spoken word, Nianki opened her eyes and gasped. She was suspended in midair, hundreds of paces above the ground. The elf was by her side, and she still held his wrist. She was immensely grateful for the touch now. It seemed the only thing between her and a horrible death.

"Amazing, is it not?" Vedvedsica said calmly, looking around.

Nianki squinted in bright sunshine, though only seconds before it had been night in the orchard. Once her eyes had adjusted, she gathered her courage and turned her gaze slightly downward. It was enough to set her heart to pounding, and she closed her eyes.

"You won't fall, savage." His sarcastic comment forced her to open her eyes again.

"Where—?" It came out as a croak, so Nianki swallowed and tried again. "Where are we?"

"Silvanost. The city of my master, Balif, and his master, the great Silvanos. You may be the first human ever to see it. Don't squander the opportunity."

Taking a deep breath, Nianki vowed to do as he said. She looked down. She was standing on stone so white it nearly blinded her to look at it. The marble was cool beneath her bare feet and just ahead of her it curved downward. Behind her the white stone stretched for a good distance, probably twenty paces at least.

"What is this?" With her free hand she gestured at the glossy marble platform.

"The Tower of the Stars."

"Tower?" Nianki carefully edged her feet forward, toward the downward curving edge of the marble. Peering beyond the edge, she gasped.

She and the elf were standing atop a structure that must surely reach halfway to the sky. Its white marble sides stretched for a dizzying length to the ground far, far below.

Nianki slowly and carefully straightened herself again, fighting against the urge to clutch the elf's arm with her free hand. When she was upright once more, she turned her gaze outward to take in her surroundings.

Now that she'd grown accustomed to the great height, her first impression was one of light. It glinted and sparkled and flashed from a thousand surfaces. All around this tower were other, smaller structures. They appeared to be made from white or milky stone and the sun's light scintillated off them as though from a thousand polished blades. Quite a few of the structures looked complete—Nianki stopped counting after thirty—but nearly twice that number seemed to be still under construction.

It was astonishing. Amero's village of Yala-tene represented the largest gathering of people Nianki had ever seen, yet this place, this Silvanost, was easily ten or more times the size of the humans' village.

Looking past the ring of spires, Nianki saw the city was built on an island. Beyond the surrounding water lay a forest. It stretched away, green and dense, as far as the eye could see.

Strange—too strange. Not only had it been dark before and now was bright day, but the season had changed as well. It had been cold in the valley of the falls. She remembered the chill night air in the orchard. Had not the apple trees' leaves turned brown already and fallen around her? Here the trees were clothed in their mid-summer foliage, not the bright colors of autumn.

Vedvedsica seemed to sense her growing confusion. With his free hand he squeezed her arm, saying sharply, "You tax my concentration! Be calm! There is great disorder in your thoughts."

"You have no idea," she muttered. His words acted as a tonic though, and her surroundings sharpened into focus.

Nianki saw the streets below fill with movement. The figures were made impossibly small by distance.

"Shall we move among them?"

She had no chance to reply to his question before they were dropping like stones. Though her fingers tightened convulsively on his wrist, Nianki stifled an urge to cry out. Vedvedsica, she was sure, would not let them be hurt.

Their plunge suddenly halted a few steps above the ground. Her heart pounded in her throat, and she threw the elf a furious glare. He paid her no heed whatsoever.

Three male elves nearly walked into Nianki. She stepped back out of their way, but they gave no sign they'd seen her.

As a pair of females approached, Vedvedsica planted himself directly in their path. Nianki was astonished to see the females pass through him as though he was made of smoke.

"How—?" she began, then gave a violent shake of her head. Why question what was so obviously the work of great spirit-power?

They were graceful-looking people, she had to give them that. No taller than she, and many of them shorter, they somehow gave an impression of height. Their movements were easy and fluid. Their skin was paler than hers, their hair was mostly light-colored, ranging from sandy blond through pure snowy white. They wore flowing robes in a rainbow of bright colors.

Though she saw their lips moving, she could not hear what the elves were saying. In fact, she realized, she could hear nothing at all from her surroundings. The elves walking or riding on horseback made no noise, and there was no sound of birds or insects.

"Why don't I hear them?" she asked.

Vedvedsica looked a bit strained. "It isn't necessary," he told her, and that was all he would say on the subject.

Nianki went back to watching the Silvanesti. There were so many! The streets teemed with life, young and old, male and female. She caught sight of two children—a boy and girl—jogging toward her. The girl, taller of the two, was obviously teasing the boy, and even Nianki could see the family resemblance between them. When the girl turned her back, the boy reached out and yanked a long golden plait of her hair. He then turned, laughing, to flee as she gave chase.

"At least children are children everywhere," she said.

"Really? That girl will likely outlive your great-great-grandchildren."

Looking at him as though he were the one whose wits were addled, she snorted. "I'm not that far gone in my head, shaman."

Vedvedsica's eyes glittered with a strange inner light as he turned to look her full in the face.

"Do you suppose all the races have the same pitifully short lifespan as humans?" he said in that same calm, certain tone. "We elves live for hundreds of years. My Lord Balif has seen ninety-eight springs come and go, and he will still be a strong, valiant warrior when your grandchildren are nothing more than dust."

Nianki opened her mouth, but no sound came out.

"How can you hope to best an enemy," Vedvedsica continued, "who will still be vigorous when you are twisted with age, who will still be hale and hardy when your grandchildren are bowed down with the weight of years? Don't you see how foolish your resistance is?"

Movement above her head caused Nianki to look up quickly. The white stone structures on each side of the street loomed above her, their tops seeming to draw closer and closer together, blocking out the sky, blocking out the light.

She felt a painful tightness in her chest. As yet another elf moved through her, unseeing, unknowing, leaving not even a whisper of air in his wake, she swayed on her feet.

"What have you done to me, shaman?" she gasped. "Can't breathe—"

Faster than thought, Nianki found herself back atop the Tower of the Stars. The strange breathlessness faded, and she inhaled and exhaled deeply, relief coursing through her.

"You're hexing me," she accused.

He regarded her thoughtfully. "In truth, I am not. You're unaccustomed to the presence of so many beings, so many structures. For one raised under the open sky, it would be a shock."

Nianki was rubbing her temple with her free hand. It pounded as though a drummer was beating on her head. "Can it be true?" she muttered to herself. "Ninety-eight years? *Ninety-eight?*"

"It is but a brief moment, after all."

The plainswoman looked up quickly. The priest was no longer there. In his place stood the warlord Balif. The wind blew through the elf's shoulder-length blond hair, and his sky-colored eyes regarded her with a strange intensity.

She took a step backward in surprise but found herself brought up short. Just as her fingers were releasing his wrist, he deftly caught hold of her arm, maintaining the contact between them. Nianki looked down, staring dumbly at the long, pale fingers encircling her sunbrowned arm.

"Do not fight me, Nianki," he said. "There are greater rewards to be had as my friend than as my enemy. To fight the Throne of the Stars means only death for you and your followers."

"Stop!" she cried. Nianki moved as far away from him as his hold on her arm allowed, though that brought her perilously close to the edge of the marble platform. "This is a trick! You aren't Balif, and I will not give up what is mine!"

So saying, she yanked her hand violently out of his grip.

As soon as their hands parted, Nianki felt herself fall backward off the tower. The last thing she saw as she plummeted into the void was Vedvedsica's surprised face staring down as her as he stroked his wispy beard.

Nianki woke with a violent start, her angry shout still echoing in her ears. Casting about wildly, she saw the faint outlines of the Yala-tene orchard, but atop this was overlaid the phantom elf city—bright towers, impossibly high, reared out of the silver waters of the lake. Crowds of transparent elves passed to and fro among the white marble columns.

She shook her head, but still the ghostly images lingered. Nianki struck her forehead hard with her fist. The ghostly scene blurred and thinned slightly, the dark outlines of the orchard growing stronger.

So, pain countered the spell? Very well. She was no stranger to pain. Nianki drew her knife.

* * * * *

Duranix squirmed fitfully, trying to find a comfortable position. His left wing ached, so he had to lie on his right side exclusively. Trouble was, his weight tended to cramp his good wing if he lay on it too long. Pain and annoyance combined to ignite an angry blue aura around his head. When his blood was up, the air around him tended to crackle with lightning.

He gave up trying to sleep and went down to the lake for a drink of water. He trod as lightly as he could so as not to disturb the sleeping humans around him. When humans were disturbed there was always noise—babies crying, dogs barking, men cursing when they stubbed their toes on the way to the latrine, women complaining about the babies crying, the dogs barking, and the men cursing. Duranix preferred his nights quiet.

He waded out a few paces and dipped his long neck down for a sip of cold water. It didn't taste as sweet as it once had, before the humans started living here. Water from the falls was as pristine as ever, but the lake had lost its purity long ago.

The dragon turned and slogged back to shore. He spied a lone, lanky figure coming down the pebbly beach toward him. For once his eyes deceived him. He thought it was Amero, but when the stranger began humming tunelessly in a high, hoarse voice, he realized it was Nianki.

"Greetings, mighty one," she said.

"Thunder and lightning, woman!" Duranix said. "What have you done to yourself?"

260

Nianki had cut her hair—rather violently, from the looks of things. Long tendrils still hung to her shoulders, but the rest was sheered off so closely that less than a fingerwidth of hair remained. In a couple of spots, her pallid scalp actually showed through and cuts on her head showed dried beads of blood.

"I was in the orchard," she said simply. "My hair got tangled in a tree limb, so I cut it off."

"You look like you've been in a fight, one you didn't win."

"Oh, no," she said, smiling. "I won."

Duranix sensed that the haze in her mind seemed thinner now. Had she succeeded in chasing the shadows away?

"How's your wing?" she asked.

He worked his left shoulder in a circle, hissing from the resulting pain. "Still hurts, but I'll fly again."

She ran a hand over the stubbly crown of her head. "Did I thank you for saving me?" Before he could answer, she frowned and added, "I can't remember. So much has happened that I can't remember."

The dragon's voice cut through this thought. "Do you recall your brother, Amero?"

"Do you know the sun and the wind?" she said sarcastically.

They both heard footfalls among the loose rocks higher up the shore. Two men paused on a rocky outcropping and one called out, "Karada! We must speak to you!"

She squinted into the darkness. "Who's there?"

"Tarkwa," Duranix said, "and the one-eyed man—what's his name?"

"Hatu." Raising her voice again, she asked, "What do you want?"

"Karada, we need to speak to you!" came the call again.

She started up the hill and Duranix followed, but the men waved the dragon off. "We only want to speak to our chief!"

"Rude animals," said the dragon. He settled down on his haunches. "Watch yourself, Karada."

She looked back at him. "Why?"

"I sense those men are not your friends."

She laughed in her old way and seemed almost her normal self. "No, they aren't my friends," she agreed, "they're my followers. Besides, Hatu doesn't hate me; it's you he loathes. He thinks you killed his father."

"I did. Ate him, too." He waited for shocked exclamations.

There were none forthcoming. Instead, she asked, "Really? How was he?"

"Treacherous, like most humans."

Amero didn't like jokes about eating people, but Nianki laughed heartily and strode up the hill to meet her men. When she drew near, both Hatu and Tarkwa recoiled at the sight of her ragged hair.

"Who attacked you?" exclaimed Tarkwa.

"Forty angry centaurs, but I bested them," she replied. "What do you want?"

"We want to leave, Karada."

"So go."

"He means the whole band," said Hatu.

"I'm not ready to leave," she answered.

The two men exchanged looks. Tarkwa said, "Karada, we can't stay here forever, living on scraps from the villagers and idling our days away. We're getting to be like those fat oxen they keep in pens, dull and lifeless. We need action! What about the elves? What about your plan to drive them off the southern plain?"

Memories of her bizarre dream echoed in Nianki's mind. She shook her head hard, dismissing them, and said flatly, "We're not ready yet. We need to build up our numbers, rest, get strong."

"And how long will that take?" asked Hatu.

Nianki folded her arms. "As long it takes."

"Some of the band are restless," Hatu retorted. "Nacris has been talking to the warriors—"

"That poisonous wench had better keep her mouth shut! I spared her because of what happened to Sessan, but if she crosses me again, I'll have her head!"

Nianki's voice had risen to a shout. From twenty paces away, Duranix heard her and lowered his head to ground. He could hear better that way, as the rocky soil transmitted noise to the sensitive barbels on his chin.

"It isn't just Nacris," Tarkwa said. "Others are grumbling too. Even Pa'alu."

"Where is Pa'alu?" she demanded.

"I can't say for certain, Karada," replied Hatu. "He seldom stays in camp but roams the valleys by night and the high peaks by day."

"Hiding from me, is he? Next time you lay eyes on that pig, you tell him I want to see him. No, better still, bring him to me! Drag him, if he won't come on his own! I have much to pay him back for!"

Both Hatu and Tarkwa were edging away from her. The sight of their chief, red-eyed, hair ravaged, screaming at them, was fearsome even to the seasoned warriors. She might have gone on denouncing Pa'alu had not Amero appeared, drawn by the sound of her loud voice.

"Nianki? What's the matter?" He stared at her, aghast. "What's happened to you?"

Her rage evaporated like mist in the hot morning sun. In the space of a few breaths, Nianki's face mirrored a whole gamut of emotions—delight, relief, anguish, shame. The display wasn't lost on Hatu. He made careful note of it.

"Amero," she said, "forgive me, I didn't mean to shout."

"Is there trouble?" He stepped forward, hand out, but his sister evaded his touch.

"No trouble, Arkuden," said Tarkwa quickly. "We were talking about the day our band leaves Arku-peli."

"Oh? When is that?"

"Soon," said the two men in unison.

Nianki's jaw worked. "I haven't decided yet. There are still things to be done here."

"You're welcome to stay as long as you want," Amero told her, putting a hand to her back. She swayed and shut her eyes briefly.

"Spread the word," she said to her followers. "Karada's band will move when Karada says so—not before."

Hatu said nothing, but Tarkwa nodded, saying, "Yes, Karada."

They left.

"Did you fall off the mountain?" asked Amero, perfectly seriously.

She touched her head self-consciously. "It was tangled in a tree limb. I couldn't free it, so I cut it off."

263

"What with, a hatchet?"

"No, a flint knife."

He looked her in the eye. She avoided meeting his gaze momentarily, then let herself be fixed by his concern.

"I am well," she said firmly. "For the first time in many days, I am well."

"Are you sure? Forgive me, but you look like you just finished battling a panther with your bare hands!"

"A panther would be easy compared to what I've been wrestling with."

"Was it a fever of the brain?" he asked.

"No. The affliction lay . . . in other regions."

Hearing Duranix snort nearby, Amero moved toward the dragon. Nianki followed closely.

A warm breeze struck their faces. Amero halted, peering into the darkness. He held a finger to his lips and pointed. Duranix had fallen asleep at last. The breeze was his breath.

Amero took his sister's hand, and they tiptoed away. Nothing was said as Amero led Nianki past the falls to the waiting hoist. Remembering her last visit to the cave, Nianki dug in her heels and balked.

To be heard over the roar of tumbling water, he had to put his lips close to her ear. "It's all right," he said reassuringly. "You won't fall out this time."

He righted the basket and helped her in. With a stout heave on the rope, Amero started the counterweight on its downward journey. The basket stretched under their combined weight then, with a groan, lifted off the ground.

The cave was dark when they arrived. Amero knew his way and crossed to the hearth. He poked in the embers of the afternoon fire and found some coals still glowing. Tossing a handful of grass on the embers, he quickly had a smoky red fire blazing. He laid on a few larger pieces of kindling. When the firelight bloomed, vast shadows were thrown upon the high walls.

"Come, warm yourself," he said, beckoning her to the fire. "Are you hungry?"

Nianki sat down stiffly on a pile of furs. Amero stirred the small fire, laying on a few larger splits of oak to keep the autumn chill out of the cave.

"Hatu is right," Nianki said suddenly. Her voice echoed off the distant ceiling. "The band should leave, and soon."

"Really? Why?"

"It's not good for us to stay."

Amero held his hands up to the crackling fire. "Winter will be here soon. I thought you came here to shelter your people from the cold."

"We'll go to the north country, where it's warmer. There'll be game there. We'll do all right."

"Do as you think best, but I, for one, wish you'd stay."

She regarded him longingly. "Do you mean it?"

"Of course," he replied, surprised by the fervor of her response. "You're my sister. I've only just found you, and I don't want to lose you again."

Nianki withdrew to the shadowed end of the hearth. For a time there was no sound in the cave but the snap of burning wood. She finally broke the silence by saying, "Are you happy with your life, Amero?"

"Yes. I think so. It's hard sometimes." He wove his fingers together and hooked his hands around one knee. "The villagers expect me to know what to do all the time, to have an answer whenever they ask a question. There's a hundred questions today, and a hundred the next day, and a hundred the day after that. People think Duranix tells me what's what, but he really doesn't help me much. He likes to hear gossip, but he isn't interested in the real work of the village. I keep trying new ideas—I want to make our lives better, easier. Lately I've been working on a way to get copper metal out of cliff rocks—"

"What about the rest of your life?" Nianki said, interrupting.

He shrugged. "Only the spirits know what will happen then."

"That's not what I mean. What about the part of your life you share with another?"

"Duranix is my friend—"

She rolled her eyes. "A mate, idiot! Have you ever had a mate?"

"No. I haven't had time. There was a girl in the village, Halshi . . ." Amero's hazel eyes clouded with the painful memory of the cave-in. "But she died, not long before you came."

"Did you love her?"

Amero considered, then decided if he had to think about it so hard, the answer must be no. "I liked her. There wasn't time for more," he said. Shifting uncomfortably, he changed the subject. "What about you? Any man caught your eye?"

She shook her head violently.

"What about Pa'alu? He seems a fine fellow."

Nianki's eyes glittered in the half-light. "Pa'alu is the biggest fool on the plains. Soon, he'll pay for his foolishness."

The quiet savagery of her tone sent a chill through Amero. He put another split on the fire.

"I should find a mate," he said, nodding. "I don't suppose I can spend the rest of my life in a cave with a dragon."

"A village girl, I suppose."

"I don't know. What about one of your fierce nomad women? Is there one you'd like to recommend?"

Her voice fell to a whisper. "Do you like fierce women?"

"I like you, and you're pretty ferocious." Nianki looked away. "When I wonder about a mate, I find myself thinking about women like our mother. She was a good companion to Oto and a good mother to us, don't you think?"

Silence. Nianki was staring into the flames and Amero put her lack of response down to weariness. He was certainly tired.

He yawned. "I'm done! You're welcome to stay here tonight. Sleep well, Nianki."

The fire shrank to a bed of glowing coals. Amero crawled into the hollowed-out bowl in the rock floor that was his bed. He was asleep in moments.

He dreamed he felt his mother's hand caress his face, like she did when he was a child. Though part of him knew it had to be a dream, it was a profoundly comforting one. He slept on in blissful peace.

# Chapter 19

～

After a stormy month, the valley grew quiet again. Fighting between nomads and villagers declined. Nianki seemed recovered and ceased her aimless wandering, muttering, and weeping. The rumor spread she cured herself by cutting her hair so severely, and later it became a common sight in Yalatene to see men and women with closely shorn hair after bouts of sickness or bad temper.

The last big harvest from the summer gardens was due, and Amero asked Nianki to organize the nomads to help gather in the vegetables. She convinced nearly all of the three hundred nomads to work the harvest, realizing the hard work would be a good outlet for her people. The only ones who did not work were the very old, the very young, the ill, and one other: Pa'alu. He had disappeared again.

Duranix continued to wear the harness on his broken wing. Fine weather made him yearn to fly, and frustration at his inability to do so led to dangerous displays of lightning in the valley. Finally, Amero suggested the dragon leave the village for a while.

"Take a journey," Amero said. "Explore."

"How am I supposed to do that?" asked the dragon, waving his one good wing. "I cannot fly, and being human hurts too much." Whatever human form he might take, he would still have a broken arm until his wing healed, and the more he shapeshifted, the longer the healing would take.

"Go as you are," Amero told him. "You have four good feet. Use them."

Duranix lifted one foreclaw and studied it. He frowned, considering his friend's words. "Walking is so undignified," he muttered.

"So is whining."

The voice belonged to Nianki. Amero and the dragon turned to watch as she approached.

Her face was scrubbed clean, and she wore a new buckskin shirt and divided kilt, bare of any beadwork. Her hair had grown back just enough to cover her nearly bald spots, and she did not wear her chieftain's headband. Aside from being thinner than before and having hair shorter than her brother's, she looked well. She carried a large basket in one hand.

"I'm going to pick apples," she said. "What about you?"

"I'll be there soon," Amero replied.

"I won't be," Duranix announced. He eyed Amero. "I'm going for a walk."

Nianki nodded, bid the dragon good-bye, and departed to join the column of plainsfolk heading for the rope bridge. Her brother watched her thoughtfully.

"She's come through it, whatever it was," he said. "I don't mind telling you, I was afraid for a while. I thought she'd lost her wits forever."

"She's a strong woman, but I don't think she's over her trouble, just coping with it more effectively."

"Oh? What do you know about her trouble?"

The dragon bent his long neck, bringing his horned, bronze-scaled face down to Amero's level. "She's human and your sister. That's trouble enough."

They walked side by side through the maze of tents and lean-tos that was the nomad camp. Eventually the shelters became too dense for Duranix, and he detoured to the shoreline of the lake. He waded out until his claws were submerged. The buoyancy of the water made it easier for him to move.

"Where will you go?" Amero asked, following along the shore.

"West, I think. I've spent a lot of time in the east and south this year. I should have a wider look around. Sthenn's been quiet since the Greengall incident, but it wouldn't hurt to reconnoiter the western plains."

They reached the foot of the bridge. To the right, the cattle and horses got wind of the dragon and began to mill about in anxiety. Duranix stretched low and slipped under the bridge. Once under, he climbed the west bank and stood erect, sunlight glistening on his wet scales.

"Have a good walk, and come back soon," Amero said.

"I don't know how far I'll go, but I should return in two or three days."

Duranix trundled away. Amero had never seen the dragon walk more than a few steps at a time. His rear legs had a wobble in them that Amero had never noticed before.

As he fondly watched the dragon depart, Amero suddenly realized he'd forgotten his reed hat. If he was going to work all day outside, he'd need the hat to keep the low autumn sun out of his eyes.

He walked briskly back to the foot of the waterfall. Soon he was descending in the hoist with the brown reed hat on his head. The scene beneath him was as still as a forest glade. The nomad camp was empty. A slight haze from burned-out campfires hung over the patched, irregular tents. Beyond the camp, a few solitary craftsmen stirred in the alleys of Yalatene, but the village too was unnaturally calm. As he surveyed the scene, only one thing stood out—a lone figure leaning against the dragon's offering cairn. Whoever it was, he took care to lurk on the shaded side, so it was impossible for Amero to see who it was.

The basket bumped into solid ground and stopped. Amero stepped out and tied off the counterweight. He detoured away from the lake, curious to see who was lingering by the cairn.

The tall, well-made person had his back to Amero. He was dressed in the skimpy clothes of a nomad and had waist-length chestnut-colored hair, drawn back in thick hank and held with a carved bone clip.

Amero's footsteps echoed dully off the stone sides of the cairn. The man turned suddenly, revealing his face.

"Pa'alu!"

"Greetings, Arkuden."

There was something in his manner—his voice, his posture—that reeked of menace. Backing up a step, Amero reminded himself of all the good services Pa'alu had rendered to the village and to Karada's band.

"Where've you been?" he asked lightly.

"Here and there. Hunting. Watching."

Amero had the distinct feeling he'd found a viper sunning on a rock, and his questions were as welcome as poking the serpent with a stick.

"We've missed you," he said, choosing his wording carefully.

"Who? You? Karada?"

"All of us, I'd say."

Pa'alu picked at the moss growing in the chinks between the stones. "Where is the dragon?" he asked.

Amero's eyes darted around, searching for a convenient way out of this conversation. "Gone for a day, looking around. He does that."

"And Karada?"

"She's at the harvest."

Amero heard movement behind him, but before he could react, he was thrown facedown to the ground. A knee pressed hard into the small of his back, and his wrists were secured by a long strip of rawhide. His captors rolled him over on his back. Glare blinded him until Pa'alu stepped over him, blocking out the sun.

"What's this? Let me go, Pa'alu!"

"I thought you were clever," Pa'alu replied coldly. "This place, this village of yours is full of clever things. But you're stupid and blind." He knelt and cupped his hands together. "I put her in your hands, and you never even realized it."

"What are you talking about?" Amero demanded.

At a nod from Pa'alu, his companions hauled Amero to his feet. They were Hatu and Nacris. He was stunned to see these three working together. There were footholds on the backside of the rock pile, and using them, Hatu swiftly climbed atop the cairn. Pa'alu and Nacris boosted Amero up, and Hatu dragged him onto the stone platform. The depression in the center of the cairn, where Duranix's oxen or elk usually lay, was filled with dry kindling and windfall wood. The sight filled Amero with horror. They wouldn't—

Pa'alu climbed onto the cairn and stood over the helpless Amero. "It's my turn to make an offering," he said. "Too bad the dragon isn't here to appreciate it."

"You waited for Duranix to leave!"

"Yearling bucks can do little when the bull is with the herd."

He strained against the rawhide restraints and tried to get to his feet. Pa'alu calmly kicked him in the ribs. Gasping, Amero lay still.

To the others Pa'alu said, "It's done. Tell the rest."

Hatu climbed down and ran toward the bridge, the only

way to the gardens across the lake. Nacris ran away too, but doubled back among the houses until she was within a few paces of the cairn. She hid in the shadows and kept her eye on the erect figure of Pa'alu, standing atop the dragon's altar.

Slowly, his agony faded, and Amero was able to breathe again. He avoided moving too much, lest he provoke more punishment from his captor.

"Pa'alu, may I speak?" he said.

"Say what you will."

"Let me go, Pa'alu. I don't know what ill you think I've done you, but you're wrong. I've done nothing knowingly to injure you. You must believe me!"

The plainsman's face was as hard and empty as the high peaks around them. "I don't do this on a whim, Arkuden. I've had many days and nights to think about it. I've been kicked about by chiefs and great ones with no more thought than if I were a pine cone—Karada, Duranix, Greengall, the elf priest, you. You've all made me do things I never wanted to do, but that's over now."

He's mad, Amero thought in horror. Nianki's insanity had passed from her to him.

Striving for a calm, reasoned tone, Amero said, "What did I do, Pa'alu? How did I hurt you?"

"You were given a great gift, and you scorned it. It's true I didn't mean for you to have it, but have it you did, and you turned your back on it."

"Please," said Amero. "I don't understand. Tell me what this gift is."

"Karada's love."

Amero heard the words, but couldn't fathom them. Of course he had his sister's love—why wouldn't he? He didn't want to challenge a madman in his delusions, but he didn't understand at all. He was afraid there wasn't anything to understand, that Pa'alu was simply crazed, and no amount of reasoning could bring light to the dark pit of his mind.

"I love my sister," he said. "I know you care for her too, and she won't have you."

"Karada's an idiot," Pa'alu replied. "She thought love made a person weak. Then the amulet showed her how love felt, and you didn't even notice!"

"Amulet?"

Before Amero could explore the puzzle of the unfamiliar word, the noise of an approaching crowd came to their ears. Pa'alu pulled a resinous pine branch out of the pile of wood and set to work lighting it with a flint. Horror washed over Amero.

"Pa'alu!" he said desperately. "What do you mean? What's an amulet?"

Once the pine branch was flaming, Pa'alu sat down on the edge of the platform, letting his legs dangle over the side. He looked down at Amero.

"Not so clever, are you? An amulet's a piece of metal, round, flat, with spirit markings on it. The elf priest made it for me when I gave him the yellow stone."

Amero grimaced. Vedvedsica had gained the spirit stone after all.

"What was the amulet for?" he asked.

"To make Karada love. She was supposed to love *me*, but you picked up the amulet that night instead of me, and she was stricken with love for you."

All at once the strange events since the feast came into focus. Nianki's behavior, her odd, disturbing questions, all of it made sense now—terrible, frightening sense. The amulet caused her to love the one man in the world she shouldn't desire. No wonder she nearly went mad!

Pa'alu stood up, the flaming torch in his hand. The sound of the crowd had grown much louder, though from his position lying atop the cairn, Amero couldn't see them. Pa'alu faced the village houses, the direction people would come from the orchard. By listening and watching his captor's face, Amero could tell when the villagers and nomads were close at hand.

There were shouts, and Pa'alu held the torch high above his head. Amero expected him to plunge the brand into the kindling with his next breath, but the crowd noise subsided, and he lowered the torch safely to one side.

"Pa'alu! Come down from there!" It was Nianki's voice. "Throw the torch on the ground and free Amero!"

"I'm not taking your commands any more, Karada. This may be the day I die, but if I do, I'll take Arkuden to the spirit world with me."

There were shouts of "No!" and "Let him go!" and Amero hoped his people or Nianki's would storm the cairn and save him, but he quickly realized that the torch was so near the dry kindling that no one dared move.

*Duranix! Duranix, if you can hear me, I need your help!* he thought frantically. How far away could the dragon hear him? A league? Two leagues? Ten? How far had the dragon walked in half a morning?

"Why are you doing this?" Nianki called out. "Amero's done you no harm."

"I'm doing this because you betrayed me—betrayed *us!* You promised us greatness, Karada. You said that under your leadership we would rule the plains! Yet we live in this tiny valley, relying on the favors of strangers, laboring for them in exchange for a little meat and a place to pitch our tents. Is this the greatness you promised, Karada?"

Her response was to throw herself at the cairn. She ran and leaped, landing halfway up the sloping stone sides. Without ready footholds, she had to climb, and that slowed her down. Pa'alu calmly shoved the torch into the pile of wood. Smoke curled from the broken branches, followed by a puff of red flame.

Nianki hauled herself up as far as the upper edge of the altar before she misplaced her foot and slid back to the ground. Pa'alu came to the edge and looked down at her.

"Amero!" she cried. Villagers surged around her, trying to reach the cairn before the fire claimed their chief.

While everyone was yelling and struggling, Nacris saw her moment and acted. She stepped away from the shadow of the house in which she'd been hiding. The crowd was between her and the cairn, and no one was looking at her. She picked up a loose stone.

"Free Arkuden! Death to the nomads!" she cried, and threw the stone.

The distance was short and her aim was good. The rock hit Pa'alu hard on the jaw. He reeled with the blow and toppled off the cairn. Flames erupted from the pile. More villagers surged forward, some of them echoing Nacris's cry, "Death to the nomads!"

Nianki got to her feet in time to avoid being trampled. She

shouted for order, but the crowd was too loud, too far gone in pent-up anger to hear her.

Makeshift weapons appeared: pruning forks, wooden hoes, rakes, stone hammers, and axes. Blows were exchanged. The press of the crowd drove Nianki straight into the stone side of the cairn. She was unarmed save for her flint knife, which she could not reach because of the weight of the throng at her back.

She struggled and cursed, her blood boiling as she watched her outnumbered people being clubbed senseless by outraged farmers, potters, and herdsmen. Nianki yearned to plunge into the fray and teach the villagers a lesson, but her first duty was to Amero, still bound atop the cairn.

Suddenly, the mob pinning her helplessly in place dissolved as the unarmed scurried to get away from the armed. She started climbing again, and this time desperation put new strength in her hands. By the time she made it to the stone platform, Amero was squirming frantically, trying to put some distance between himself and the flames. With only bark sandals on his feet, he kicked at blazing tree limbs.

"Amero!" She grabbed him by his shirt when he wormed his way close enough. Dragging him away from the fire, Nianki next climbed over him and sat astride his back, sawing at his bonds with her knife.

Rocks and thrown clubs whizzed by Nianki. She dodged them with uncanny flicks of her head and shoulders, never once looking up from her task. When the thong was finally cut, she slid aside. Amero dragged her down so she would be less likely to be hit by random missiles.

"What happened?" she said in his ear.

"Pa'alu's gone mad! He meant to kill me, and Hatu and Nacris helped him!"

She stared, disbelieving. "Hatu?"

He nodded furiously. A hammer hit the rim of the platform and exploded in a shower of rock fragments.

"We've got to stop this!" Amero said.

"Any idea how?"

"I'll try to calm my people! You'll have to see to yours!"

Below, those nomads not knocked out in the first minutes of the riot fell back to the animal pens. There, they began bridling their horses and mounting amidst a hail of stones and other makeshift missiles. Once on horseback, the nomads closed ranks and charged, relying on their speed and weight to knock the villagers out of the way. They quickly cleared the pathways between the houses and trampled the best-armed group of villagers, a band made up of the sons and daughters of the village elders. Yelling war cries, the mounted nomads galloped to their camp. While the villagers retreated to their houses, the nomads pulled down their tents and lashed their gear to their horses.

Nianki came upon Pa'alu, painfully crawling away from the cairn. He'd broken a leg and several ribs in his fall. She easily overtook him and pinned him to the ground by planting her foot in his back.

"Now you must kill me," he gasped, his face in the dirt.

"Kill you? I should roast you alive on the pyre you made for my brother! Were Nacris and Hatu involved in this?" she said.

"No."

"Liar!" She put more weight on her leg and his broken ribs scraped together. He writhed in agony. "They put you up to this!" she hissed.

"No! I did this myself! So kill me!"

Nianki removed her foot and grasped Pa'alu by the hair, turning him over on his back. She said, "You're going to live just long enough to tell the entire band this was a plot by Nacris to overthrow me!"

Pa'alu looked past the angry eyes of the woman he loved and into the face of death. A figure had appeared atop the cairn behind Nianki. She didn't see him, had no chance to block or dodge the spear he threw; however, the weapon wasn't aimed at her. It took Pa'alu low in the gut.

Nianki rolled to the side and jumped up, knife ready. She caught only a glimpse of the spear thrower as he leaped down from the other side of the platform. By the time she ran around the end of the cairn, Pa'alu's attacker had escaped into the maze of village houses.

She cursed heartily and returned to Pa'alu. His eyes were still open, but his breath was shallow.

"Karada," he whispered.

She bent low over him to catch his dying words. "Who else?" she hissed. "Who else is with Nacris and Hatu?"

"All of them." He tried to laugh, but it came out as a rasping, rattling wheeze. "Finish me."

Knowing he'd betrayed her, yet feeling some pity at last, Nianki found it in her heart to fulfill this last request.

She pulled the spear out of his belly. It was a boar spear, with a broad flint head and an oak peg lashed to the shaft to keep the spear from going in too far to be recovered. She positioned the tip over his heart.

"Peace . . . to you . . . Nianki," he rasped.

"There is no peace," she replied. "Not while I live." She leaned hard on the shaft. Pa'alu, so near death already, felt nothing, and his last breath escaped soundlessly.

She slumped against the stone side of the cairn, the bloody spear across her lap. Out of the swirl of dust and smoke appeared a towering figure, coming toward her.

Pakito.

Nianki straightened her back and wrapped her hands more tightly around the spear shaft. The last thing she wanted was a fight with Pakito, her most loyal friend and a formidable foe, but Pakito's brother was dead, and by her hand—how would the mighty warrior take that?

Pakito dropped to his knees beside his brother. He closed Pa'alu's eyes and, scooping up a handful of loose dirt, gave him a nomad's benediction—he poured the handful of dirt on Pa'alu's forehead.

"Pakito."

"Yes, Karada?"

"I killed him."

"I saw. Thank you."

She sat up. "You're grateful I slew your brother?"

"He was suffering. He'd been suffering in his mind for a long time. This was his cure, Karada."

She rose and laid the boar spear on her shoulder. "I see the band is breaking camp."

Pakito looked up at her. Tears streaked his broad, bearded cheeks. "I have your horse. Samtu, Targun, and a few others are guarding our mounts back at the corral."

"I knew you couldn't be with that viper Nacris."

His anguished gaze never wavered. "I follow you, Karada."

Nianki peered through the dust at the chaos of the collapsing nomad camp. "There's more blood to be shed before this is done," she said grimly. "Our blood I fear. I should have cleaned up all the traitors when Sessan was slain. You see the price for my generosity."

Amero appeared. He had minor burns on his arms and legs, and a few cuts and bruises, but he was all right. He was alone—not a single villager dared leave the safety of their stone houses to stand with him.

He saw Pa'alu's body and silently wished peace to the departed hunter. Then he turned to his sister and Pakito.

"The villagers will not come out," he said. "Eight are dead, and many more are hurt. How could this happen?"

"Envy," said Nianki. "Envy, jealousy, and spite. Nacris spread her lies in the band and turned more of them against me." She nodded at Pa'alu's corpse. "I see now she enlisted this mad fool to hurt me through you."

Pakito's broad shoulders shook with grief. Amero put a hand on his back and offered a few words of comfort.

The rumble of approaching horses grew louder. A column of mounted nomads appeared through the dust. Leading the column were three riders: Tarkwa on the left, Hatu on the right, and Nacris in the center. Three-quarters of the nomads had chosen to follow their new leaders. At the sight of her nemesis, Nianki drew back the boar spear, ready to cast.

"Stay your hand, Karada!" Tarkwa cried.

Nianki neither relaxed nor lowered her weapon. Pakito and Amero stood by on either side, ready to defend her.

"Get down off that horse, Nacris," Nianki said. "I'd hate to scratch a blameless animal when I kill you!"

"You're not going to kill anybody," Hatu replied. "We're done with you, Karada. Your cruel, mad ways have hurt the band long enough."

"I made this band!" she said. "You were nothing but lone scavengers, running scared on foot from elf hunting parties. I made you into a band of free men and women. We took horses from the elves and made the plains ours. Is this how you repay me?"

"No one is more important than the band," said Nacris. "You never understood that, Karada, and now you're out. We don't need you. We're taking what we want from this valley and going far away from you, the elves, and your dragon-master. Stay here if you like, live in unnatural love with your brother, and serve that beast!"

Nianki flung the boar spear, but Tarkwa and Hatu put up their own weapons and blocked it. Nianki snatched the flint knife from her belt, but before she could advance toward her foe, she found herself held back by Pakito and Amero.

"Let go of me!" she cried.

"No," said Amero. "I'm not ready to watch you die."

"Very wise," said Hatu, lowering his spear. "Continue your wisdom and give us what we want from your stores."

"My people will starve over the winter without stored food," he said.

"You're in no position to resist," Nacris retorted. "If you get in our way, we'll burn your gardens, drive off your oxen, and flatten this village to the ground!"

Amero's heartbeat pounded in his ears. Duranix was away and crippled. Though the villagers outnumbered the renegade nomads, Nacris's followers were seasoned fighters, and with their horses to give them mobility and force, how could Yala-tene withstand them?

He felt Nianki's taut muscles relax in his grip. Amero let go of her arm. Pakito did likewise.

"Here's my offer," Nianki said. "Leave, now. If I ever see any of you again, I'll hamstring the lot of you—all but you, Nacris. I promise I'll gut you like the yevi-spawn you are.

"You'll take nothing from Yala-tene. Ride out now, each with your horse, spear, and tent. You're nomads. I taught you how to survive on the plains and in the forests. Leave, and live. Take, and die. That's your choice."

Coming from anyone else in this situation—on foot, armed with a single knife, surrounded by enemies—such a declaration would have earned mocking laughter. However, the words, deadly calm and utterly serious, came from Karada. No one laughed.

Tarkwa, ever practical, broke ranks first. He rode past Amero without a word, heading out of the village. Slowly, others followed, guiding their horses in a wide, wary circle around Nianki. Nacris glared, but she didn't bother trying to stop them. She knew she did not command the respect—or the fear—that Karada did. When Hatu joined the stream of riders, Nacris could be silent no longer.

She said, "You too? I thought you had more spine than this!"

"I've walked away from many previous lives," Hatu said, urging his mount onward. "If I live, I can make another. Dead, I'm just carrion."

Nacris was alone. The odds had shifted so completely against her, Nianki felt bold enough to reclaim her thrown spear. Scowling fiercely, Nacris twisted her mount's head around and trotted after Hatu. She cast one glance backward as she rode. Nianki reversed her grip on the spear and jammed it forcefully into the sand, in the hoofprints of Nacris's horse.

Slapping the reins against her horse's neck, Nacris sped her departure.

* * * * *

It was nightfall before the villagers felt it was safe to leave their houses. The wounded were brought out for treatment, and the dead, who included Amero's old friend and counselor Valka, were laid upon the cairn for cremation. Pakito gently added Pa'alu to the line atop the platform. Some of the villagers grumbled at a nomad being honored along with their dead, but Amero silenced them and applied the first torch to the pyre.

Standing side by side, watching the flames leap skyward, Amero said to Nianki, "Pa'alu told me about the amulet."

She said nothing, only stared at the flames.

"I'm sorry," he added.

"Why?" she replied. "Nothing has happened, and nothing will."

"I'm sorry you had to suffer the way you did."

She shrugged. "It's nothing. Another scar. I have many."

He wanted to comfort her, put his arm around her shoulder or take her hand in his, but he didn't. Nianki had climbed a mountain to escape her feelings, and the last thing she'd want would be for him to climb up beside her and be within reach again.

Amero clasped his hands behind his back and moved away from his sister.

* * * * *

The glow of the funeral fire could be seen in the next valley, where the rebel nomads gathered to chew hard jerky and swig water from gourd jugs. At Hatu's order, they were allowed only one small campfire to keep off the worst of the chill night air. It was a quiet and subdued band of plainsmen that camped around this small fire.

Nacris lay on her back at a distance from the campfire. Though she appeared to be staring at the starry sky, her mind was not on the jeweled heavens. Nacris was furious. She was so angry she couldn't stop her hands from trembling.

Nacris's eyes flickered over to where Hatu walked among their comrades. He seemed completely unconcerned by their shameful defeat. She couldn't hear his words, but whatever he was saying caused low ripples of laughter among the nomads gathered in this small valley.

Tears of fury welled up in Nacris's eyes, and she dashed them away with one hand. She turned her face away from Hatu.

A line of red fire across the night sky made her blink, and she rubbed her eyes.

Another streak of light traced a path across the stars. And a third. And a fourth.

Several of her nearby neighbors noticed the display. A wave of exclamations worked its way across the band, until all eyes were turned upward.

The plainsmen were a superstitious lot and they fell silent as they watched. Even Hatu's talk was stilled. The lights continued their frantic display for several long minutes, then began to decrease in number.

The plainsmen began to mutter fearfully. Many voiced the thought that the dragon had somehow caused this, that he was angered by their rebellion against his son and would wreak his vengeance on them.

Nacris wasn't fearful. In fact, the sight of the racing lights brought an upwelling of joy to her leaden heart. She leaped to her feet, her eyes shining as brightly as the stars above.

"Don't be stupid!" she said. "The dragon doesn't control the stars! Such signs in the sky are omens. Don't you see? The stars fell directly over our camp! It was a sign meant for *us*!"

The plainsmen looked unconvinced. Hatu stepped close to the fire, so its light illuminated him for all to see.

"Nacris is right," he told them. "The mudtoes are feeling good right now. They think they're rid of us, but they're not. We needed this first fight to separate our people from Karada's and to get rid of that fool Pa'alu." Raising his voice, he added, "Now we know who's with us, and who's not!"

There were nods and grins around the campfire now, and Hatu's words were passed along to those camped farther from the center.

Nacris hurried to him. "You mean to go back!" she exclaimed. "You always meant to!"

"Yes, we're going back!" His face was hard, lines of anger etched in its surface. "I want my horse groaning under the weight of all the beef he can carry! I want my waterskins so full of wine they leak red on the trail behind us! I want that dragon's head, but if he's not around for killing, I'll have the head of the Arkuden!"

"What about Karada?" asked Tarkwa.

"What about her?" Hatu demanded. "She's no spirit-warrior, despite what some of you think. She bleeds the same as any of us. Are we going to slink away from her like a pack of whipped dogs, or will we be warriors and take what our might can get for us?"

The rebel nomads roared their approval. Even Tarkwa seemed fired with the fervor of revenge. "When do we strike?" he asked.

"Now! Tonight!" insisted Nacris.

Hatu shook his head. "Tomorrow. Let them sleep and think they're rid of us. When the sun rises over Vulture Gap, we'll hit Arku-peli like an avalanche!"

# Chapter 20

Amero didn't sleep that night. So many things crowded his
mind—the riot, Pa'alu's death, the final revelation of the
cause of Nianki's distress—he found no peace in the quiet
solitude of the great cave. After a fruitless session of open-
eyed brooding, he chose to pass the night in lonesome toil,
trying to figure out how to melt bronze.

Copper melted at a certain intensity in the fire. He reasoned that since bronze was harder than copper, it would
require more fire to soften it. He built a hardwood fire on the
hearth and, lacking a gang of children to fan for him, made
his own "gang" of fans by boring holes in a long, straight
plank and inserting eight reed fans in them. He hung the
plank by thongs from a tripod of poles. By pushing it back
and forth, he created a significant wind.

He set a clay pot on the fire and filled it with strips of
bright copper from his last experiment. In short order the
strips collapsed into reddish metallic beads, which in turn
coalesced into a fist-sized ball of molten copper. Amero
scratched out a long, thin trench in the damp sand at the
other end of the hearth, then, lifting the hot pot with a convenient pole, poured the molten copper into the trench. The
wet sand hissed, and gouts of steam arose.

The cavern slowly brightened to the pale hue of predawn.
Weary, Amero went to the pool and dipped his sooty hands
into the chill water drawn off the falls. Now to try his fire on
a few of Duranix's bronze scales.

A clinking sound from overhead caught his ear. The apex
of the cave was lost in shadow, but a sprinkle of dirt floated
down, easily visible by firelight. Darker, larger bits came
down with the dust. Amero went to where the debris fell
and pressed a damp finger to it. It was moss—green moss,
such as grew on the banks of the river above the cave.

He was still trying to fathom this puzzle when the sound
of horns, muffled by cave walls and the rumble of the

falls, penetrated to him. An alarm! Amero rushed to the opening.

The sky outside was barely light, but he could see some disturbance at the upper end of the valley near the cattle pens. A panther after a young calf, perhaps? Dust rose, and he saw people moving.

There was another noise behind him. Amero turned. Something was sweeping the floor halfway between the hearth and Duranix's sleeping platform. He frowned, trying to understand what he was seeing. It was a pair of rawhide ropes, braided and knotted. His eyes lifted, following the ropes upward. Descending the ropes in rapid hand-over-hand fashion were two men, nomads, with spears strapped to their backs.

Amero was so astonished by this sudden intrusion he froze for the two or three heartbeats of time that it took for the men to finish their descent and drop to the floor.

"What do you want?" he asked.

They whipped the flint-headed spears off their shoulders. "Your life!" said one of the men.

His first impulse was to jump into the hoist and flee, but that would simply make his attackers' job easier. They would certainly cut the rope, leaving him to plummet conveniently to his death. He was unarmed, and there were no weapons in the cave. He never imagined he'd need them here.

Amero ran to his hastily-made tripod of poles, thinking he could pull one of them free to use as a quarterstaff. By the time he got there, the two nomads were already upon him, thrusting with their spears. Amero grasped the suspended plank in the center and shoved it first at one man, then the other. The second nomad was a little slow, and the stout plank caught him on the chin, sending him reeling. Amero had no time to celebrate, as the first nomad's flint spear point tore through the reed fans and buried itself in the plank by Amero's hand. With a yell, the nomad pushed the tripod over, and Amero had to scramble not to be trapped under the contraption.

Now he was empty handed, facing a wary foe. The nomad—a dark-eyed fellow about his own age—held his spear in both hands and made short, vicious lunges toward Amero's belly. The floor, as usual, was littered here and there with Duranix's shed scales, and Amero fervently wished he at least had a sharpened scale to fight with.

He backed up a few steps, keeping just ahead of the nomad's jabs. Outside, the sounds of conflict grew louder.

"Nacris!" Amero exclaimed, understanding dawning. "She led you back here to raid the village!"

"I am Hatu's man," the nomad spat. "We've come to take what we can!"

"Then take what you want and be gone! Why kill me?"

"Hatu commands it. He wishes to injure the dragon as the dragon once injured him."

Amero backed up to the wall. The nomad grinned and set himself to run the village headman through. Amero carefully braced himself to dodge. This would require fine timing on his part. The nomad raised his spear to shoulder height and, with a yell, attacked.

Amero twisted aside and grabbed the shaft in both hands. He wasn't strong enough to wrestle the weapon away from the nomad, but that wasn't his plan. He pulled the warrior in the direction he was already moving, straight at the cave wall. Unable to stop in time, the nomad slammed into the hard sandstone. His spearhead snapped off, and the man slid to the floor, stunned.

Amero turned toward the second warrior. If he was still unconscious, Amero could tie him up before—

· Lip swollen and bleeding, the second nomad got up on one knee. He spied Amero, and met his shocked look with a glare of pure hatred.

"I'll have your head, Arkuden!" He spat the name like a curse.

Lying on the hearth a few steps away was the copper bar Amero had made during the night. It was only a trifle longer than his arm and not edged like a sword, but it was better than nothing. Amero sidled around, drawing the angry nomad away from the hearth.

"I've no quarrel with you," he said with as much calm as he could muster. "None at all. We welcomed you, shared our food with you—"

"Shut up! You're as bad as the elves! You would make us into cattle! Men aren't meant to grub the earth or squat under a pile of stones. A plainsman must be free, must roam!"

He held his spear loosely in his right hand, and without any warning, he swung it in a wide, flat arc. Amero felt something catch and rip on his chest. His goatskin vest hung in tatters, and red blood welled up from a long cut across his breastbone.

Though he was shocked by the suddenness of the injury, Amero retained enough presence of mind to use it to his advantage. Feigning greater harm than he'd actually suffered, he groaned and staggered to the hearth. With a dramatic gasp, he draped himself across the cold end of the fireplace and dug his fingers into the sand, closing them around the copper bar, now cool and hard.

The nomad approached and put down his spear in favor of a wide stone axe hanging from his belt. He raised the axe high.

Amero tore the copper bar out of the sand and presented the tip to his oncoming opponent. He meant only to use the bar to ward the fellow off. However, the shallow end of the trench had formed a narrow tip on the end of the bar, flat but sharp. The ax-wielding nomad ran right onto it, and it penetrated his chest, to their mutual astonishment.

The axe fell to the floor. Clutching the copper bar, the nomad tried to wrench it from his body. Amero released his end of the bar as though it had scorched him. As the color drained from the nomad's face, so too did horror whiten Amero's features. The nomad's knees buckled, and he fell facedown, driving the bar through his chest and out his back.

Amero's mouth hung open as stared at the fallen man and the widening pool of blood around him. Though he'd seen men die many times before, he'd never killed anyone in his life.

He continued to stare at the dead man. He tried to bring a hand up to wipe sweat from his brow, but the hand was shaking so badly he couldn't control its motion. Amero slumped on the edge of the fireplace and clasped his hands together tightly to stop their violent trembling. A bitter taste filled the back of his throat. He swallowed hard.

His paralysis was ended by the other nomad. The man grunted and began to stir against the wall. Amero jumped upright as though pulled by a string. He cursed himself as a fool—sitting here trembling like a child when the lives of his people were at stake.

Amero kept his eyes away from the dead man and concentrated on the living warrior, who could still pose a threat to him. Taking up a length of cord from his fallen apparatus, he went over and bound the semiconscious man's hands behind his back. He then dragged him to the hoist and looked out.

Smoke was rising from the village—more smoke than from ordinary campfires. Though close to the deafening waterfall, Amero's experienced ear caught other sounds: screams, shouts, the sound of animals and people in distress. He shoved the inert nomad into the basket and climbed in beside him. Once the counterweight was free, he sank quickly to the brewing battle.

At the foot of the hoist, a terrified group of children and mothers had gathered. They greeted Amero's descent with frantic cries, which faded when they saw his grim face and bleeding chest wound.

"Arkuden, save us!" some cried.

He said nothing, but pushed the nomad out of the basket and proceeded to shake him awake.

"You!" Amero said. "You want to live, yes? Tell me, are all your comrades attacking through Cedarsplit Gap?"

"I'll tell you nothing," answered the bloody-faced man blearily.

There was no time for lengthy interrogation. Amero gave the nomad over to the older boys and girls and bade them guard him.

"Where's the dragon?" asked one of the women, clutching two babes in her arms. "He's supposed to protect us!"

"He's not here," Amero said bluntly. "We'll have to defend ourselves."

He had the spear left behind by the nomad he'd killed. Shouldering it, Amero hurried down the hill to join the fray.

*　*　*　*　*

Nianki slept like a child that night. Despite the sundering of the band and the strange death Pa'alu had chosen for himself, she felt oddly at peace when the time came for rest. It reminded her of the aftermath of a storm. Once the lightning, thunder, and rain disperse, the land lies supine, washed clean by the torrent.

The only thing that still disturbed her was that Amero had learned her secret. Just when she had won a measure of control over her passions, his knowledge threatened to upset her fragile equilibrium. She couldn't look at him without having to fight down the horrible urge to blush, stammer, and run away.

She abandoned her stuffy tent and took her bedroll to the ledge overlooking the lake. She spread the ram's skin, wool side up, and lay down in such a way that she could see the lake between her feet. The dark glimmer of the water, coupled with the steady drone of the falls, soon lulled her to sleep.

Her rest was peaceful until near dawn. She dreamed a shadow fell across her face. Opening her eyes, she saw someone bending over her. His face was in darkness. She wanted to turn away, but she was paralyzed. She couldn't even close her eyes. She could only lie there helplessly as he came closer and closer, wafting an icy cold breeze before himself. Just before the man's lips touched hers, she saw a metal pendant glittering at his throat. Who was he? Why was he so cold? A single name formed in her mind: Pa'alu.

She woke, flailing her arms in horror.

There was no one there. Nianki hunched over, breathing hard. She uttered a curse and wiped the sweat from her cheek and brow.

The rocky ledge beneath her vibrated. Her imaginary battle with the unknown man had rolled her off the ram's skin. Now her feet and hips rested on bare rock. A rhythmic vibration ran from the rock and into her body. Curious, Nianki pressed her ear to the ledge and listened.

Vibrations that strong and regular could only be hoofbeats!

She was up in a flash, striding toward the remains of the nomad camp. It was easy to find Pakito's tent. His feet stuck out the end, and intertwined with them were Samtu's smaller, paler feet. Nianki kicked Pakito's soles. He rumbled threateningly and flung back the flap of his tent.

"What? Who's there?"

"On your feet, Pakito! There's trouble!"

"Karada?" He slid Samtu aside. She whimpered a little and tried to cling to his broad chest. "What trouble, Karada?"

"Nacris has come back!"

That sank in, and the big warrior was on his feet in short order.

Nianki went from tent to tent waking her greatly diminished band. In moments, eighty-six sleepy nomads assembled by the dragon's cairn. All were armed, but few were more than half-dressed.

"We haven't got much time!" Nianki declared. "The first sixty, follow me. Targun, take the others and pound on every door in Arku-peli. It's time the mudtoes fought for their own valley."

Karada and sixty warriors stumbled through the dark village toward the cattle pens. It was plain that if the rebel nomads were coming back, they'd have to use one of the passes at the northern end of the valley, of which Cedar-split Gap was the closest. At the top of the sandy hill that stood between the pens and the village, Karada halted her comrades.

"What is it?" asked Pakito, too loudly.

"Shh! Listen!"

The gap, lined with stone on all sides, focused the sound of massed horses into the valley. They all strained to hear, poised on the crest of the hill. The rumble was unmistakable.

"What'll we do?" whispered Pakito.

"They think they'll surprise us, catch us asleep," Nianki said. "Instead, we'll catch *them*."

She spread her meager force out along the hill, just below the crest and out of sight from the other side. The warriors went down on one knee and leaned their spears forward, bracing the butt against their feet. If the renegades came galloping over the hill, they'd run smack into a hedge of waiting spear points.

Behind them, Targun, Samtu, and the rest rattled every door in the village. Some of the villagers came out to see what the commotion was, but most bolted their doors and tried to get a glimpse of the situation from their upper windows. They were the first to catch sight of the oncoming attack.

The cry went up. "Riders! Riders!"

"Brace yourselves!" Nianki told her warriors.

Waving torches, the first wave of horsemen swept down on the unguarded cattle pens, their agile ponies jumping over the low stone wall. They threw ropes over the gate and tore it down, then screaming nomads got behind the herd and started driving them out of the pen.

"They're stealing our oxen!" wailed a villager.

Pakito eyed his chief. Karada shook her head. The warriors held their positions.

To her consternation, a sizable body of riders simply rode around the hill, along the pebbled shoreline. There was nothing between them and the village. Nianki was about to order her line to fall back when a second wave of mounted renegades, some eighty strong, came cantering over the hill. It wasn't quite the headlong charge she wanted, but several of the riders did run into the thorny line of spears. The renegades recoiled, and showered the nomads on foot with stones and thrown spears.

"Hold your place," Nianki said. "If something comes your way, knock it down before it reaches you."

Following her own order, she batted down a pair of light javelins hurled at her. The predawn darkness made it difficult to see every missile, and two of her warriors went down, scalps laid open by large stones.

"All right, on your feet!" she said. Nianki herself went to one of her fallen comrades and helped the injured woman stand. "Back to the houses—but slowly! Slowly!"

Under jeers and missiles, the slender line withdrew to the outermost ring of houses. Nianki gave the nomad she'd rescued to some householders, who took her inside. A few of the older villagers, who remembered fighting like this from their younger days, joined Nianki's defenders. They were armed with whatever came to hand—wooden rakes, shovels, staffs. Not one in ten had a stone-headed weapon. With no other options to hand, Nianki put them quickly into the line.

The renegades who'd ridden down the shore of the lake turned in to the village and began throwing torches at the housetops. One by one, the roofs caught fire, the families running outside to escape the flames. Hatu's riders let them go, racing inside to plunder the burning house before the roof fell in on everything. The terrified villagers ran to the foot of the falls, under the very mouth of the dragon's cave, and prayed for the aid of their great protector.

Into this scene of terror came Amero. He directed those fleeing to take shelter by the falls and moved on against the screaming tide. A few horsemen were harassing the fleeing villagers, tripping them with their spear shafts or knocking them around with their horses. Furious, Amero stormed at the nearest bully. The laughing nomad was chivvying an old man and teenage girl, pushing them this way and that, not letting them get clear to run. Amero rushed the nomad from his blind side and thrust his spear into the man's armpit. The horseman's head snapped around, totally astonished. He fell from his horse. Freed of its rider, the animal galloped away from the battle.

Villagers surrounded Amero and praised him for his prowess and courage. Impatiently he said, "All I did was stab a man when he wasn't looking! Go!"

A pair of riders bore down on Amero. He flattened himself against the side of the cairn just in time to dodge simultaneously thrown javelins. One came close enough to cut the waist of his trews.

For the second time in as many days, Amero found himself going up the side of the cairn. At least the horsemen couldn't reach him up there. Rocks and axes flew thick and fast as he scaled the sloping stone side. A few thumped him with glancing blows. Wincing, he kept his grip and made it to the top.

The dark sky was lightening to blue. Keeping low to avoid missiles, Amero crept to the other edge of the cairn and saw the battle raging among the houses.

Nianki's line had become a circle, bounded on all sides by stoutly defended houses. In the gaps between, her warriors and the armed villagers who remained fought tenaciously. The narrow lanes between the houses reduced the mobility of the renegades' horses, and many dismounted to fight on foot.

From his perch, Amero spotted Nianki. Her closely cropped hair made her easy to pick out as she stood in the center of the besieged circle. She directed the defense with cool words or fierce cries, as needed. Amero was deeply struck by this image of his sister. He'd seen her duel with Sessan, but he'd never before witnessed her commanding in battle.

A head bobbed up over the edge of the cairn, a long-haired nomad. With surprisingly little remorse, Amero put his foot in the man's face and sent him tumbling to the ground. Two others tried to scale the platform and reach him, but he fended them off with his spear. Amero felt a growing confidence in his fighting abilities. Another quick glance over at his sister and he thought proudly that warrior blood did run in the family.

A heavy pall of smoke wafted between the cairn and Nianki's position. Renegades on the outer edges of the battle were setting more and more roofs afire. When the flames reached the houses making up Nianki's defenses, her line would fragment, and the defenders would be cut up and defeated piecemeal.

Scooting back to the center of the platform, Amero knelt and bowed his head. Concentrating as hard as he could, he formed a single thought.

*Duranix! Help us, or we are lost!*

The blazing roof on the house nearest the cairn—Konza's home—collapsed. Inside, the wooden posts and flooring burned ferociously, tongues of flame spurting from the second-story windows. The heat was so powerful it drove Amero to the opposite end of the cairn. He fervently hoped no one was left inside the tanner's house.

Pakito, fighting with the long-handled axe so dreaded by his foes, cleared a swath in front of him. Through the smoke he saw Amero crouching atop the dragon's cairn.

"Karada!" he bellowed. "Isn't that Arkuden?"

Nianki spared a glance in the direction he indicated. She saw Amero, wreathed in smoke and flames. Her heart seemed to stop; her instinct was to fly to his defense. Instead, she said, "We can't reach him—there's too many on us!"

"I can reach him," Pakito said, planting his fists on his hips.

291

A fierce smile briefly lit her dirty face. "Do that, and you can name your own reward!"

The towering warrior jabbed a thick finger at his chief. "Remember those words, Karada!"

Gripping his axe, he strode past the line of smaller warriors—though all warriors were smaller than Pakito—into the lane between the rings of houses. At once he was set upon by a mounted renegade wearing a wood-and-leather breastplate: Tarkwa.

Tarkwa tried to ride Pakito down, but the big man was not about to be trampled under. He threw his left arm around the horse's neck and brought his axe up in a wide swing. Tarkwa tried to parry with his spear, but the heavy axehead shattered the shaft and Tarkwa's forearm as well. Howling in agony, Tarkwa tried to wrench his horse's head loose from Pakito's grip. The three of them—man, horse, and rider—skidded in a tight circle, slamming into the wall of a burning house.

Pakito found himself between the horse and the wall, for anyone else a bad spot. The giant warrior, however, drew his legs under himself, used the house for leverage, and threw the horse to the ground. Tarkwa rolled over and over in the sand, coming to a stop in the open doorway of a blazing house. Groggily, he sat up, just as the whole wooden interior of the house come crashing down on top of him.

Pakito moved on, swatting aside his former comrades as they tried to intercept him. After a few deadly swipes, they gave him wide berth, and he arrived at the cairn.

Coughing from the heavy smoke, Pakito called to Amero. The young headman's sooty, blood-streaked face appeared. "Pakito!"

"I've come to take you to Karada."

Such a declaration should have sounded ludicrous—battle and fire raged on all sides—but coming from Pakito, it was simply a statement of fact.

Amero half-slid, half-fell to the ground beside the giant. Pakito hauled him to his feet and propelled him forward.

Two of the six houses that formed Nianki's defense line were on fire. The villagers inside had to climb out the rear windows to drop down among their neighbors and Nianki's followers. By the time Pakito and Amero rejoined them, there were almost a hundred people in the shrinking circle.

Stumbling forward, Amero felt strong arms stop him. He looked up into Nianki's smoke-streaked face.

"Bad day," he said, taking her gently by the hand.

"Going to get worse," she replied. "There's a lot of people to kill."

Even as she said so, a lull struck. The renegades backed out of spear-thrust range. Nianki's defenders accepted the respite, some of them falling to their knees out of sheer exhaustion.

Hatu and Nacris rode forward into view.

"Karada! Arkuden! Can you hear me?" Hatu yelled.

"I hear only the screech of a vulture!" Nianki yelled back.

"What do you want?" Amero shouted.

"Lay down your weapons, and we'll spare you."

Nianki laughed derisively.

Hatu pointed over his shoulder at the falls. "There are a lot of helpless people over there," he said. "It would be a shame to slaughter them all just to persuade you not to be stubborn."

"Would he do that?" asked Amero, horrified.

"What do you think?" Nianki replied.

Amero started toward the mounted pair. "Then we must give up."

Nianki gripped his arm in her hard hand. "If we stop fighting he'll kill us all. He'll not spare your villagers."

"I can't let my people die to prolong my own life!" he said, pulling free. He started for Hatu once more. Pakito blocked his way until a shake of Nianki's head convinced the big nomad to stand aside. She turned away, unable to watch.

Amero walked slowly up to Hatu. "You tried to kill me once before," he said. "Ten, eleven seasons ago. You and your brothers caught me here in this valley. You thought I was the dragon in disguise."

"Sorry to keep you waiting so long."

"It's no good," Nacris said anxiously. "It's no good unless Karada comes out, too!"

"She won't," Amero said.

"Stubborn wench. Well, at least you'll be out of the way."

Hatu laid the flat side of his spearhead on Amero's shoulder. The point was just a finger's breadth from his throat. Amero closed his eyes.

Cries of alarm rose from the renegades on the shore. Nacris turned her horse around and met a pair of riders galloping up the hill.

"What is it?" she said.

"Something coming up the lake, coming this way!" gasped one of the men.

"It's big!" his companion added. "Very big!"

Big? Amero thought. Hah! At last!

He knocked Hatu's spear point off his shoulder and dropped to the ground. Hatu cursed and raked down Amero's back with his weapon. Amero felt the sting, but he kept scrambling. He scuttled under some other horses before rising to his feet and sprinting for Nianki.

The renegades milled about in confusion. Some charged Nianki and her warriors, while others formed a rough line on the shore and waited for whatever was coming down the lake. Hatu and Nacris rode to the water's edge to see for themselves.

The normally chill water of the lake was boiling. Waves propelled by some submerged object were surging down the lake toward the falls. As the astonished nomads looked on, trout, bream, and pike churned the water ahead of the object, some so frantic they flung themselves out of the water to escape. But to escape what?

The fast-moving mound of water drew abreast of the nomads on shore and slowed. Some of the renegades backed their horses away until drawn back in line by sharp words from Nacris. Twenty paces from shore the water split apart as a long greenish-gold neck rose from the depths.

"Duranix! It's Duranix!" Amero's cry was taken up by all the villagers until it became a roaring chant.

Fully half the renegades quit the fight there and then. The ones facing Nianki's line simply melted away. Laden with looted food and other goods, they mounted their horses and galloped for safety. Nianki and Amero led their singed, tired defenders away from the burning houses, drawing up in circle on open ground beyond the cairn.

Duranix opened his mouth wide and let loose a full-throated roar that loosened stones from the cliff tops. Taking in the scene with one sweep of his head, he swam past Hatu's position and climbed ashore between the renegades and the unprotected mass of children and old people cowering beneath his cave. Water rolled off the burnished scales of his back in silver sheets. He still wore the leather brace on his injured wing.

"Amero, are you alive?" he roared over the heads of the closely packed renegades. Pakito and another man hoisted the headmen onto their shoulders. Amero waved his arms.

"I am!" he shouted, grinning madly.

"Good. Stay where you are."

Duranix reared up on his hind legs and lumbered forward. Spears and javelins bounced off his scaly hide. Bronze-headed elven weapons pricked him, but he ignored them and darted his long neck into the mounted mass, knocking men and horses down with every sweep of his horned head.

The renegades disintegrated like snow on a hot rock. Duranix moved among them, hurling them this way and that with swipes of his claws. The ground was soon thick with the fallen, a few dead, most of the rest senseless. In the center of this tumult sat Hatu, calmly waiting. Beside him, a nervous Nacris fidgeted with her mount's reins and obviously wished she were someplace else.

Duranix dropped down to all fours and extended his head toward Hatu. The nomad's horse shied, but the one-eyed warrior controlled his animal skillfully.

"Why don't you ride away?" Duranix asked.

"I don't care to be struck down from behind," said Hatu.

"That's human thinking for you—as if it matters from what direction a blow falls!"

"An honorable man fights facing his enemy."

The dragon grinned, and Hatu's horse shied again as the nomad squeezed its sides convulsively with his legs. "Ah, you expect me to fight like a man?" Duranix hissed.

"I expect you'll fight like the evil beast you are!"

In a motion faster than a snake striking, Duranix seized Nacris in his mouth. She screamed and struggled, but he raised her high in the air and with a single sideways shake of his head, tossed her into the center of the lake. She screamed all the way until she hit the water.

Hatu swallowed hard. "Nacris is a good swimmer," he said, but his voice was unsteady.

"How unfortunate," Duranix replied.

Few were the men who could look up into an angry dragon's face and not give way to panic, yet Hatu stood his ground. For all his treachery, the one-eyed plainsman's courage inspired in Amero grudging respect.

"Come on," said Hatu, drawing an elven sword from his belt. "Let us fight."

"Absurd," Duranix replied. "If fighting a bull, should I lower my head and bang horns with him?" He advanced a step.

In his free hand Hatu held a ram's horn. He raised it to his lips.

Amero had a sudden, shocking insight. Two nomads had entered the cave to kill him at the beginning of the fight. There could be others—

"Duranix!" he shouted. "Beware! There are men on the cliffs above you!"

Hatu blew a single bleating note on the horn. Duranix reached out a claw to snatch Hatu off his horse, but the plainsman evaded his grasp. Just then, a boulder the size of a full-grown ox slammed into the sand steps away from the dragon. Villagers and nomads alike shouted in surprise.

High up, Hatu's men labored to lever another boulder off the cliff. Amero shaded his eyes, but the morning sun was behind the men, and he couldn't make out how many there were. Another huge slab of sandstone smashed to the ground. It shattered into many pieces, pelting Duranix. He ducked his head under the barrage. While he was distracted, Hatu galloped away with the last of his followers.

Instead of following them, Duranix did a bold thing. He slithered with serpentine grace to the foot of the cliff, dodging a third boulder. Fixing his foreclaws in the relatively soft sandstone of the cliff face, he began to climb.

Heedless of the danger from falling rocks, Amero ran to where Duranix was picking his way up.

"Come back!" he shouted. "You can't dodge them if you're clinging to the cliff!"

"How many boulders can they have?" replied the dragon coolly. A fourth missile, this time a smaller, harder slab of slate, whistled down. It struck Duranix a glancing blow to the right shoulder. Scales curled up under the impact, and bluish-green blood oozed from the wound.

Furious at the rebels and afraid for his friend, Amero grabbed Duranix's barbed tail just as it left the ground. The dragon paused and looked down at him.

"Let go, Amero. This is no place for pets."

"I'm not a pet!" was the young man's angry reply as he clung to the muscular tail.

"It's no place for a friend, either."

"I can watch out for falling rocks! Shut up and climb!"

Without another word or backward glance, Duranix started up the cliff. He didn't have to hunt for handholds or toeholds; his powerful claws gouged their own as he went. Faster and faster he ascended, until he was racing upward like a lizard on a canyon wall. Yet he was careful to keep his long tail as motionless as possible, to avoid injuring the foolish human clinging to it.

Amero held on for dear life. In spite of his brave words to the dragon, he wasn't able to keep watch for falling rock—his eyes were tightly shut. He did feel the powerful surge of the dragon's muscles as Duranix scrambled sideways to avoid being hit. At last Duranix's vertical tail lifted to horizontal, and Amero knew they'd made it to the top.

By the time he'd let go of the dragon's tail, Amero saw that Duranix had slain three of Hatu's men. The dragon sprang forward a full ten paces and caught one man as he was running away. With a sideways flick of his claw, Duranix hurled the luckless nomad over the cliff.

"Stop!" Amero cried. "Don't kill any more, please!"

"They're vermin. They'll make trouble if you let them go."

"They're men! They can learn from their mistakes!"

Duranix gave a disgusted snort, but he stopped. The remaining four renegades took the opportunity to race for their horses. They galloped away.

"You're too forgiving," said the dragon, resting on his haunches. He growled a bit as he bent his neck to examine his bruised shoulder.

The battle was over. Amero found himself shaking uncontrollably. He slumped heavily to the ground and toppled over on his side. The wounds on his chest and back were shallow, but very painful. As his eyes closed, he felt the dragon's cool metallic claws close gently around him.

"Lie still," rumbled Duranix. "I will take you home."

# Chapter 21

～

A day passed, then another, then five, and the renegades did not return. Nianki posted lookouts on the clifftops and across the lake to watch for trouble, but it seemed that Nacris, Hatu, and their followers had been defeated.

Though his wounds were not deep, Amero contracted a fever, and for many days his survival was in question. To provide the best care for him, a large open shelter was raised near the burned houses, and the people of Yala-tene took turns nursing him. While Amero was ill, his authority fell quite naturally to Nianki. No one disputed her orders now. The villagers, who'd seen her fight for them, obeyed her without question.

For Amero, the days passed like a single bad night's sleep. At intervals he would open his eyes—it was daylight and someone was feeding him broth; it was night and someone else was smearing larchit on his wounds. After these brief moments of wakefulness, he would lapse back into a deep slumber.

Once, he heard people around him talking, and he recognized Nianki's voice.

"Where did you try today?"

"South, in the lower valleys," answered a different voice. "There was no sign."

"If I know him, he'll go back to familiar territory, the land of his ancestors."

"And where would that be?"

"North," Nianki replied. "The north plain, close to the mountains."

"Then that's where I'll look."

The voices ceased. After what seemed like only a moment, he heard some scraping noises, and the sound of water being poured. Cool dampness caressed his lips, chin, and forehead. He opened his eyes.

"Nianki." His voice was a croak.

She dipped a scrap of chamois in the clay basin and squeezed out the excess. "How do you feel?" she asked.

"Dry. Water?"

She lifted a hollowed gourd to his lips, using her other hand to support his head. The small sip of water he managed to swallow tasted wonderful.

"Who was just here?" he asked once he was resting again.

"No one."

"I thought I heard you talking to someone."

She smiled. "You were dreaming again. You've been doing that a lot. You talk when you're asleep, did you know that?"

"No."

She gently wiped his neck and shoulders and rinsed the chamois again. He looked past her. His bleary gaze picked out movement—villagers moving to and fro, rebuilding their burned houses.

"How many people did we lose?" he asked.

"Twenty-three of the village, eighteen of my people."

So many. He closed his burning eyes. "How is Duranix?"

"Arrogant as ever. He and Pakito and that old man Konza took off after the oxen Hatu's riders chased away. Your dragon still can't fly, but his senses are keener than a falcon's, so I guess he'll be helpful tracking the wayward beasts."

He smelled the sourness of larchit paste. Nianki had peeled off the dressing of damp jenja leaves to apply a fresh layer of soothing paste to his chest wound. His eyelids felt weighed down by exhaustion. Fighting against the darkness that pulled at him, Amero yawned and said, "And how do you feel, Nianki?"

"I wasn't injured."

"That's not what I meant."

She continued her ministrations, loading a twig with a gob of larchit paste. "I don't want to talk about it," she told him calmly. "Ever. Stop asking questions and get well."

"Yes, Karada." He sighed and allowed sleep to claim him once more.

*   *   *   *   *

Amero's fever waxed and waned. On one of his good days, he was visited by Pakito. The giant warrior lifted Amero as though he were a small child and carried him outside.

The villagers and Nianki's loyal nomads had formed a

long human chain from the cliffs to the dragon's cairn. Stones came down the line, passing from one pair of hands to the next until they reached the ceremonial rock pile. With a final heave, some of the sturdier nomads added the new stones to the pile. They must have been laboring for quite a while, Amero realized, for the cairn had almost doubled in length and width.

Reclining rather stiffly in Pakito's mighty arms, Amero asked what was going on. Nianki, who had joined them, explained how the villagers needed some place to put the rubble from their ruined houses. At first they hauled the burned and broken rocks to the lake, then someone—no one could recall exactly who—suggested adding the rubble to the dragon's altar. The idea took hold, and everyone joined in to complete the task.

"The dragon saved us, at peril to his own life," explained Pakito. "We're doing this to honor him, and you."

"Where is Duranix?" asked Amero. It felt as though he hadn't seen his friend in weeks.

"Sleeping off dinner," Nianki said.

They watched the work in silence for a while. The cairn grew ever larger.

"The way they feel now," Nianki said. "They'd pull down the mountain and throw it all on the pile, if it pleased the dragon."

* * * * *

A chill mist filled the valley one night, and the next morning every stone and tree limb in the valley was coated with frost. The highest crags of the mountains turned white, and when the wind blew down from the heights, it brought the bite of winter with it.

The day Amero walked without a staff was the same day Duranix discarded his wing brace. Man and dragon faced each other on the sandy spit below the falls.

"Are you sure you don't want your stick?" teased Duranix.

Amero raised his thin arms over his head and flapped them up and down. "Are you sure you don't want your brace?"

The dragon spread his long, leathery wings and mirrored his friend's movement, raising a cloud of grit. "No more braces for me," he declared. "Today I fly!"

He launched himself into the air, wings flapping slowly.
He drifted back to the sand. Launching himself again, and
working harder this time, he gained height. His long neck
stood straight out from the strain, but he climbed upward in
a wide spiral, testing his newly healed wing. It was exactly
ninety days since he'd broken it.

Nianki appeared, draped in a mantle of white wolf fur. She
watched Duranix disappear into the low clouds that roofed
the valley. He roared with delight, and the eerie sound reverberated down the lake, causing people on both shores to look
up from their work.

"Someone's happy," said Nianki dryly.

"Yes, me!" Amero turned in a little circle, showing her he
wasn't supported by anything. "See? I'm walking on my own."

"It's about time," she replied tartly. "I was about to take
Targun's advice and shorten your walking stick a little bit
each day. He figured you'd give it up when you discovered
you were bent double."

"Ha, thanks!"

Nianki turned away, and he followed her. They strolled
down the water's edge together.

"How goes the planting?" he asked. It was past time for
the winter crops to go in, but so much work had been needed
to repair houses and pens in the village, the second planting
was late.

"It goes. The ground seems too cold and hard for anything to grow."

"That's all right. If anyone can grow vegetables through
ice, it's Jenla."

Nianki nodded. "Smart woman. She should've been a
nomad."

They reached the southern end of the village. Piles of loose
stones filled the circular holes where houses had once stood.
These houses on the periphery had been demolished and their
undamaged materials salvaged to repair the other homes. Most
of the people who lived in them had perished in the fight.

"I've been thinking—" Amero began.

"Oh, not again."

He gave her a mock glare, then continued. "We've relied
too much on Duranix to protect us. He is, as he will tell you

himself, only one dragon. Yala-tene needs to be a safe haven, a stronghold that can survive even if Duranix is away for ten days or more. What we need is not a series of strong, individual houses, but a way to defend all the houses at once."

The chill wind had strengthened. It whistled around her ears, as Nianki raised the white fur hood of her cloak. "How would you do that?" she asked, not really interested.

"As we do the cattle: put all the little houses into one big house!"

That caught her attention. She stopped and regarded him skeptically. "You want to build a house large enough to hold every family in Arku-peli? That's mad! Even if you could, all those people living together wouldn't last. They'd kill each other!"

Amero went to the stump of a wall, carefully lowering himself onto it. Many weeks of illness had left him with little stamina.

"I'm not talking about building a whole house to cover all the others, though that would be quite a feat." He looked up at the overcast sky, a far-off expression on his face.

She sighed impatiently. "Get to the point, will you?"

"Sorry," he said, looking at her again. He gestured with his hands, making a circle around himself and continued. "A wall, Nianki. We can build a wall around the village. That would keep any marauders out."

She folded her arms. "You want to build a wall around the entire village?" He nodded. "Sounds like a waste of sweat and stone to me. All you really need is a hundred stout fighters to defend the place."

"Every man and woman in Yala-tene could be trained to fight," he countered. "Spears would be provided to every family, to be kept at home for use when there's trouble."

"All very well, but pairing off your mudtoes and having them whack each other a few times doesn't make them warriors."

"That's where you come in."

Nianki scoffing expression froze. "Me?"

"I want you to train them—teach them to fight like your best warriors. With you to train and lead them, Yala-tene will never have anything to fear."

She leaned against the wall of the fallen house, feeling the cold stones press against her knees.

"Well?" he said.

A tiny flake of white floated down and came to rest on the back of Nianki's hand. For an instant, the perfect miniature net of feathery ice crystals stood out clearly against her deeply tanned skin. Then, warmed by her body, the flake vanished.

"Snow," she said. Nianki lifted her hooded face to the sky. More snowflakes were coming down now, but only a few.

"Nianki, will you stay and teach the people of Yala-tene how to defend themselves?" asked Amero insistently.

"No."

He was taken aback. "No?"

"I've stayed too long as it is. It's time for Karada's band to depart."

So saying, she stepped over the broken length of wall and strode quickly away. Amero opened his mouth to call to her, but she was out of sight before he thought what to say.

There was a rush of wind, and Duranix alighted on a patch of nearby open ground. He shook his head from side to side, sending a tinkling cascade of ice crystals to the ground. He flapped his wings before furling them, shedding more ice and snow in the process.

"I hate winter," he declared, "but I love it that I can fly again."

Amero said nothing. He was still looking off toward where Nianki had vanished.

Duranix used his foreclaws to preen slush and water from his horns and face. "Why so morose, Amero?" he said. "You're walking, aren't you? Or have your legs failed you? Is that why you're sitting out here in the cold by yourself?"

Amero stood—a bit wobbly, but upright—and said, "Nianki won't stay. I asked her to train the villagers to fight, but she won't do it. In fact, I think she may be leaving today!"

Duranix leaned down to his far smaller friend. The brazen nail of one clawed digit tapped the crown of Amero's head.

"Is there anything in there but bone?" he asked. Angrily, Amero brushed the claw away. Duranix added, "You aston-ish me, human. You asked her to do the one thing she can't do and still respect herself. Don't you realize that?"

"Well, no. I thought she was over the effect of the amulet."

Duranix rolled his huge eyes. He forced himself to adopt a patient tone. "I don't know if she'll ever be 'over it.' Someone else will have to come along and win her heart." He drew himself upright. "Not an easy prize."

Together they walked to the enlarged altar. The villagers, with the help of Nianki's band, had nearly tripled its size. Where once it had been a rectangular pile, it was now square, and over twenty paces to a side. When the rocks had kept tumbling down the sides, someone had thought to use the gray mud from the lake bed to hold the rocks in place. Soon the all the outer layer of rocks were stuck together with mud, which coupled with the yellowish sandstone, lent the altar a distinctly speckled appearance.

Konza and his eldest son, Tiphan, hailed Amero and the dragon as they neared the altar. They were an odd-looking pair. Tiphan had fashioned coats for his father and himself from cast-off bronze dragon scales. He had punched holes in the upper edge of the scales and, using hide strips, attached them in overlapping layers to two long cloaks. Though their demeanors were grave, both men clanked as they walked, and Duranix found the effect comical.

"They look like a pair of beetles," Duranix observed in a low voice. Amero had to stifle a laugh; the description was apt.

"You're walking again, Arkuden? That's excellent," Konza said. Tiphan, only sixteen, stood to one side looking grave. It was an expression difficult to maintain since Duranix kept exhaling gently on him, just to make his coat of scales clatter in the resulting breeze.

"Thank you, Konza," Amero said, studiously ignoring the dragon's actions. "I want to get back to work as soon as possible. I have many plans to discuss with you and the other elders—"

"There are no other elders," Tiphan said.

"What?"

"What my son means is, while you were ill, the surviving fathers and mothers of the village met and chose me to be their representative to you and our great protector." Konza smiled widely. "We all felt the old way of council meetings and arguments was too slow and awkward to deal with the dangers of this new life of ours. From now on, you can tell me what you want done, and I will tell the villagers."

Amero was astonished. "Tell you? But I don't want to—"

305

Duranix unfolded one wing just enough so that it came between Amero and Konza. "Arkuden shouldn't be out in this weather," Duranix announced grandly. "He's still recovering. He'll return shortly."

Amero couldn't reply with a mass of wing pressed against his face, but before he could free himself, Duranix whisked him into one claw and spread his wings to their fullest extent.

Without further warning, the dragon launched himself into the air, leaving Konza and Tiphan staring upward in awe and not a little confusion.

When they were aloft and heading for the cavern, Amero demanded, "What was that? And since when do you call me 'Arkuden?' "

Duranix ducked through the waterfall and landed on the cave floor. He used his wings skillfully to shield Amero, so not a drop got on him. The dragon threw several logs on the hearth and fanned the faint coals with his breath. Watching Duranix's cheeks bulge as he blew stirred an idea in Amero's agile mind—but he shook his head to clear his thoughts and returned to the issue at hand.

"What do they mean, I'll tell them what to do? I wouldn't feel right telling people twice my age what to do."

"You're so conservative," chided Duranix, basking in the warmth of the blazing fire. "When this settlement began, you were just thirteen years old. None of the elders wanted to listen to you then, but they did, mostly because they feared me. Now you're twenty-four. Many of the fathers and mothers who originally followed you here from the plains are gone. The younger ones have only known Yala-tene and you, and now they want you to lead them." Duranix brought his tail around closer to the fire to warm it. "I think you should."

"How can I? What if I make mistakes? People's lives are at stake!"

"When Hatu came back to destroy the village, you fought back, even killed people. Why?"

"To save those I care about," he replied.

"So!"

The fire crackled loudly. The hot yellow flames highlighted Amero's drawn face, making the lines of worry etched in his countenance seem even deeper. The silence

306

between them stretched on. Amero kicked at some pebbles.

"I guess I can try it Konza's way. I'll work hard, and find others to guide and counsel me," he said finally.

"Your dedication is almost dragonlike," Duranix replied.

Amero sat down on the hard stone floor and stretched out his tired legs. Despite the burden being placed on his shoulders, and the imminent departure of his sister, he couldn't stop smiling. He knew the dragon had just paid him the ultimate compliment.

*  *  *  *  *

It took two days for Nianki's band to pack their gear. Every inhabitant of Yala-tene insisted on providing the nomads with enough provisions to get them to the northern plains, where there would still be abundant game to hunt. In addition to their remaining fifty-three horses, Nianki's band was given six tamed wolves, ten oxen, and nineteen goats. The oxen were harnessed to five large travois laden with dried fruit, vegetables, and clay jugs of Hulami's best wine.

More surprising was the fact that ten villagers chose to go with Nianki. They were all young men and women whose families had perished in the battle. Starting anew in the valley of the falls was too painful for them, and they had asked to be taken into Karada's band.

"You are welcome," she told them, "though we have no horses for you."

Young Valka, grandson of Amero's old friend of the same name, said, "It's as well. We don't know how to ride your animals." He grinned and added, "Yet!"

It was on a clear, cold day that Nianki formed her people at the foot of Amero's bridge. The snow of two days past was only a light dusting, a harbinger of heavier falls to come. The trees and houses were covered with silver frost, and a blanket of mist rose from the lake.

Duranix joined the crowd of villagers who gathered to see the nomads off. He was in human shape, the first time he'd taken the form since breaking his wing. Konza and Tiphan were there in their coats of scales, though beneath them they wore furs to keep out the chill.

307

"Do you have enough food to get you past the Plains River?" asked Amero, looking over the heavily loaded travois.

"If we had any more, the oxen couldn't drag it," Nianki said. "Be at ease, brother. You've done right by us. More than right."

Pakito was to lead the nomads who traveled on foot. With much genial shouting, the amiable giant stirred his small band into motion. There were many farewells as the villagers who had joined Karada's band marched away, their tidy clothes and short hair marking them as different from their long-haired nomad cousins.

Samtu rode up in answer to Nianki's call. Her belly was beginning to swell with Pakito's child. She had been the object of much teasing, as nomads and villagers alike warned her that if the baby took after its father, she had a lot more swelling yet to do.

"Take the riders out," Nianki told her. "Once across the river, split into two columns. I want one to ride on each side of the walkers, to shield them."

Samtu nodded. "What track shall we follow, Karada?" she asked.

"Follow the river. It will lead us where we want to go."

Samtu whistled through her teeth, and the riders mounted their horses. Only Targun remained behind with Nianki.

"Well, dragon, you'll have more peace in your valley from now on," she said, leaning down from horseback to offer her hand to Duranix.

He clasped her hand. "I doubt it, Karada. Many people know about the valley of the lake now, including all the nomads who fled the fight Nacris lost. And there's Vedvedsica. He was here the night of the Moonmeet feast, prowling around for some reason."

Duranix had finally told Nianki that Vedvedsica was the one who'd fashioned the amulet for Pa'alu. Now, at his mention of the cleric's name, she frowned, recalling flashes of her bizarre dream about the city of elves. Then Targun, sitting on a horse by his chief, spoke, and she banished the images with a shake of her head.

"Do you think Silvanos will move against you?" Targun asked.

"I don't think so. There's little for him to gain here,"

Duranix said. "The elves will keep an eye on us though, I'm certain."

"I wish we knew happened to Nacris and that one-eyed wolf, Hatu," Amero said. "They worry me more than the elves."

Duranix arched one eyebrow and touched a finger to his forehead. From behind his back, he produced a small bundle, wrapped in a scrap of leather, and gave it to Nianki. She queried him with a look.

"A gift," he said. "To be opened once you're away from Yala-tene."

With that, his human face actually reddened slightly. He bade them good-bye and walked away. The rest of the villagers drifted away as well, until only Targun, Nianki, and Amero were left by the foot of the bridge.

"Go ahead, Targun," she said. "Watch after Samtu, will you? She looked like she might lose her breakfast at any moment."

"Aye, Karada." The elder plainsman gave Amero a silent, smiling nod and rode away.

Finally, it was just the two of them: Nianki on horseback, her white wolf's fur robe rippling in the breeze, and Amero, his leggings and sleeves stained with the soot of his hearth.

"Will you ever return?" he asked quietly.

"The world is a big place," she told him. "When I've ridden all the way round it, I may get back here."

"Might take a long time."

"I think it will." Nianki leaned down with her hand out, as she had done to Duranix. "You're a good brother, Amero. Oto and Kinar would be pleased."

He took her cold, callused hand. The mention of their parents brought a lump to his throat. He swallowed hard, and said hoarsely, "There is always a place at my fire for you, Nianki."

She abruptly pulled free and slapped her horse's neck with the reins. She cantered across the bridge, which swayed from side to side as they went. Nianki soon caught up to Targun and took her place beside him. Amero leaned against the last tall piling of the bridge and watched the nomads until they disappeared around the bend of the river.

Though he watched until she was lost from sight, Nianki never looked back.

\* \* \* \* \*

Duranix, still in human form, found Amero hunched over the hearth that evening. He seemed to be shaking gently, rocking back and forth.

The disguised dragon put an awkward hand on Amero's shoulder. "It will be all right."

His friend raised his head. He hadn't been shaking with grief as Duranix had thought, he'd been busy blowing on a bed of glowing coals.

Accustomed as he was to Amero's strange ways, Duranix still had to ask, "Why are you doing that?"

"It makes them hotter," he announced triumphantly. "I think I've found a way to melt bronze at last!"

Amero, Duranix decided, would be fine.

\* \* \* \* \*

The nomads camped ten leagues from Yala-tene that night, not quite on the open plain but sheltered from the icy night wind by a pair of low hills. Tents were pitched, and the old rhythm of the wandering life slowly resumed. They could feel it inside, like the pulse of a second heart.

The stars were out, so numerous and so bright Nianki could see all the way back to the snow-clad mountains, or ahead to the flat, endless savanna. The Winged Serpent, the sign of Pala, was in his place in the heavens, as was Matat, the stormbird.

Dragon, Nianki corrected herself. Matat was a dragon. Like Duranix.

Alone by a campfire, she opened the leather-wrapped gift Duranix had given her. When she saw what was in it, she smiled briefly and tossed the whole bundle onto the burning wood.

Flames slowly ate into the square of oiled leather, curling around the traitor Hatu's black eyepatch. Duranix's parting gift to her was a little peace of mind about the safety of her brother and his people.

In a flicker of silent orange flame, the gift turned to ash.

## Classics Series

Classic tales from the heart of the DRAGONLANCE saga.

# Dalamar the Dark
### Nancy Varian Berberick

As war simmers on the borders of Silvanesti, Dalamar will find a way to become a wizard. His quest will take him along dark paths toward an awesome destiny.

Available January 2000

# The Citadel
### Richard A. Knaak

Against a darkened cloud it comes, framed by thunder and lightning, soaring over the ravaged land: the flying citadel, mightiest power in the arsenal of the dragon highlords.

An evil wizard learns the secret of creating these castles in the air and seeks to use them to gain power over all Krynn. Against him are a red-robed magic-user, a cleric, an ancient warrior, and—naturally—a kender.

Their battle shakes the skies of Krynn.

Available August 2000

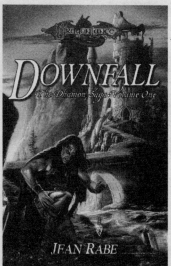

## Downfall
### The Dhamon Saga
### Volume One
#### Jean Rabe

How far can a hero fall?

Far enough to lose his soul?

Dhamon Grimwulf, once a Hero of the Heart, has sunk into a bitter life of crime and squalor. Now, as the great dragon overlords of the Fifth Age coldly plot to strengthen their rule and to destroy their enemies, he must somehow find the will to redeem himself.

But perhaps it is too late.

Don't miss the beginning of Dhamon's story from Jean Rabe!

Available May 2000

# Dragons of a New Age

## The Dawning of a New Age
Great dragons invade Ansalon, devastating the land and dividing it among themselves.

## The Day of the Tempest
The Heroes of the Heart seek the long-lost dragonlance in the snow-covered tomb of Huma.

## The Eve of the Maelstrom
Dragons and humans battle for the future of Krynn at the Window to the Stars.

From the best-selling writing team of Weis and Hickman

# Dragons of a Fallen Sun

The War of Souls • Volume One

Margaret Weis and Tracy Hickman

Change—for good or for ill—comes to the world of Krynn. A violent magical storm sweeps over Ansalon, bringing flood and fire, death and destruction. Out of the tumult rises a strange, mystical young woman. Her destiny is bound up with that of Krynn. For she alone knows the truth about the future, a future strangely and inextricably tied to the terrifying mystery in Krynn's past.

Sequel to
the best-selling *Dragons of Summer Flame*,
this is the first volume in a magnificent new epic trilogy
by the creators of the DRAGONLANCE saga,
Margaret Weis and Tracy Hickman.

Available March 2000

## Crossroads Series

Across the land of
Ansalon, these are stories
of places where fates cross
and legends are mad

# The Clandestine Circle

Mary H. Herbert

A knight working
undercover in the city of
Sanction earns a place on the
elite bodyguards of the
mysterious Lord Governor. She quickly learns the governor is
not the only one who needs protection. But who will protect
her from her own heart?

# The Thieves' Guild

### Jeff Crook

Available July 2000

Palanthas. Jewel of Ansalon, City of Seven Circles, heart of the old
Solamnic empire. For three thousand years she has shone as a
beacon to the world  Yet at the core of the gleaming city lies
a dark center: the Thieves' Guild.

### Available December 2000